THE TUDORS

King Takes
Queen

Also Available

The Tudors: It's Good to Be King
Final Shooting Scripts 1–5 of the Showtime Series

The Tudors: The King, the Queen, and the Mistress
A Novelization of Season One of The Tudors

THE TUDORS

King Takes
Queen

A NOVELIZATION OF SEASON TWO OF
The Tudors FROM SHOWTIME NETWORKS INC.

CREATED BY *M*ICHAEL *H*IRST
WRITTEN BY *E*LIZABETH *M*ASSIE

SIMON SPOTLIGHT ENTERTAINMENT

NEW YORK   LONDON   TORONTO   SYDNEY

Simon Spotlight Entertainment
A Division of Simon & Schuster, Inc.
1230 Avenue of the Americas
New York, NY 10020

First Simon Spotlight Entertainment trade paperback edition April 2008

SIMON SPOTLIGHT ENTERTAINMENT and colophon are
trademarks of Simon & Schuster, Inc.

For information about special discounts for bulk purchases,
please contact Simon & Schuster Special Sales at
1-800-456-6798 or business@simonandschuster.com.

Manufactured in the United States of America

10 9 8 7 6 5 4 3 2 1

Library of Congress Cataloging-in-Publication Data

Massie, Elizabeth.
King takes queen / written by Elizabeth Massie.—1st ed.
        p.   cm.
"A novelization of season two of The Tudors from Showtime Networks Inc. Created by Michael
Hirst." 1. Henry VIII, King of England, 1491-1547—Fiction. 2. Great Britain—History—Henry
VIII, 1509-1547—Fiction. 3. Anne Boleyn, Queen, consort of Henry VIII, King of England,
1507-1536—Fiction. 4. Great Britain—History—Tudors, 1485-1603—Fiction. 5. Queens—
Great Britain—Fiction. I. Hirst, Michael. II. Tudors (Television program) III. Title.

PS3563.A79973K56 2008
813'.54—dc22   2008000654

ISBN-13: 978-1-4169-4887-2
ISBN-10:   1-4169-4887-2

For my mother, Patricia Elaine Black Spilman, with love.

ACKNOWLEDGMENTS

Thanks to the exceptionally talented Michael Hirst for making King Henry VIII, Anne Boleyn, Thomas More, Katherine of Aragon, and many others of that time and place into more than distant, unfathomable figures in a textbook. These people lived and breathed, and with Hirst's research, imagination, and finely crafted scripts, they live and breathe once more.

Thanks also to Christopher Golden and Cortney Skinner for their support, and to Cara Bedick of Simon & Schuster for all her help.

Chapter One

A lone falcon circled the colorless sky above the River Thames, high at first, then dropping lower to gaze at the waterfowl bobbing amid anchored shallops and ships on the murky water. White swans arched their necks, posing for the other, lesser birds. Ducks and geese wagged their wings but did not make to fly. Perhaps they didn't care to, or perhaps they didn't know they could. Regardless, they seemed dully content to probe the filthy river for fish and insects to fill their bellies yet another day. It was the falcon alone that could see them for what they were and what they were not. It tilted its head haughtily and rose up again.

The regal bird passed over the grand Whitehall Palace beside the river and turned down by one of the many arched windows of the palace's chapel, where King Henry VIII and his mistress, Anne Boleyn, knelt upon cushions before an elegantly carved, marble altar topped with golden chalices and crosses to receive Mass from the king's chaplain. Up the falcon flew again, beyond the palace, over cottages, stables, and taverns, to an area much poorer, much less tended than the king's palace.

A simple church stood on a muddy knoll, flanked by a stone wall and a cemetery filled with cracked and tipping gravestones. The falcon landed on the church's windowsill. Inside, Mass was being performed to a congregation that was plainly dressed and poorly groomed.

At the wooden altar, separated from the worshippers by a rood screen, priests and altar boys went about the sacred ceremony. Nooks in the walls held statues and images of the saints, illuminated with the glow of burning tapers.

The congregation kneeled on the floor, for there were no seats. One at a time, the worshippers crept forward to receive the sacraments from the chanting priests.

"*Suscipe, sancte Pater, omnipotens aeterne Deus . . .*"

As the falcon watched, the door to the church blew open, and a cluster of young men, laughing and cuffing each other on the shoulder, poured into the chapel.

"*Deo meo vivo et vero . . . ,*" the priests continued in monotonic voices, ignoring the young men.

The congregation scowled at the intruders but returned their attention to the service.

"*In spiritu humilitatis, et in animo contrito . . .*"

The apparent leader of the gang shoved his hands against his hips and crowed, "Fuck the pope!"

There were gasps about the chapel, but the men only seemed encouraged by the shock and disapproval. They stomped about, pushing the kneeling supplicants out of the way, blowing out the tapers, and knocking the painted statues from their nooks.

An ashen-faced priest shook his finger at the ruffians. "For the love of God! Good people, I beg you to stop. This is a sacred ceremony."

The apprentices laughed more loudly, and the ringleader strode through the open door of the rood screen, sending altar boys scattering.

"Fuck off, you fat overfed priest!" the ringleader shouted. His entourage cheered. One of the others picked up a small statue and jabbed it with a sharp pin.

"Look at that! You see? They don't bleed! They're just fucking wood!"

The ringleader grabbed the bowl holding the Body of Christ from the priest and declared, "What is *this*?" He turned the bowl over, scattering the bits of unleavened bread.

Women and children hugged each other, pulling tightly together and away from the intruders. Men held their wives and glared at the apprentices.

"Please," said the priest, "go away! Leave us alone."

Several angry men stood and moved in unison toward the ruffians. Seeing they might soon be outnumbered, the apprentices backed toward the door. The ringleader bounded over the railing of the screen with a howl, and joined his friends.

"You should be ashamed!" declared the priest. "This is sacrilege!"

"No," shouted the ringleader. "It's the future!"

With a final, echoing roar, the apprentices ran from the church.

The falcon blinked, stretched its wings, and rose above the din.

"Tell me, Mr. Cromwell," said the king. "How are the improvements to Hampton Court proceeding?"

Thomas Cromwell, King Henry VIII's secretary, stood to the side as Henry considered himself in the large looking glass. Two grooms, dressed in black with the red Tudor rose embroidered on the breast of their jerkins, sprayed the king from head to toe with bottles of lavender flower water. The drapes in the king's bedchamber were pulled back, allowing an intense stream of sunlight into the room. The light danced on the floor, the mirror's surface, and the king's dark hair, surrounding his head with a crown of light.

"Well, Your Majesty," Cromwell said, "work has already begun on the new great hall."

"And the new palace at St. James?"

"It already boasts some fine lodgings for Your Majesty. And sixty acres of nearby marshland have been drained, to make a park stocked with deer for your greater commodity and pleasure."

Henry held up his hand to stop the grooms from spraying the waters. He stared silently at the mirror, taking in his appearance. He was a handsome man; none could deny it. A handsome man with incredible power. A man to whom all men of England, in their most secret of hearts, compared themselves, and with whom all women, regardless of station or age, imagined themselves abed.

"When the royal manor house at Hanworth is refurbished," Henry said, "it is to be presented to the Lady Anne Boleyn."

Cromwell nodded. Henry dismissed the grooms, and turned from the mirror. His head tilted slightly. "Are you married, Mr. Cromwell?"

"Yes. I have a wife and son."

"You must present them to me one day."

Cromwell nodded.

Henry walked to Cromwell and put his hand on the man's shoulder. His expression was hard, but then it softened. "I have made a decision to admit you to the Privy Council," he said, "as our legal advisor."

Cromwell's breath caught at the announcement, but he did not let the surprise register on his face. He was never a man to let his emotions show. Such was weakness.

Sir Thomas More, King Henry's chancellor, strolled through the corridors of the court in his black robes, moving purposefully as courtiers bowed and stepped out of his way. He glanced at some of them briefly, acknowledging their deference.

A face in the crowd caught his attention. It was the Imperial ambassador to England, Eustace Chapuys. Chapuys was a tall man, with a cap of curly hair and a prominent nose, dressed in brown brocade trimmed in pearls. More hesitated as Chapuys bowed, but he continued walking. Chapuys fell in step beside the chancellor.

"Ambassador Chapuys," said More without looking at the man. "I thought you had abandoned us."

"I did. Or tried to." Chapuys took a breath and his voice lowered. "But, in all conscience, how could I ever abandon Her Majesty? She is the most gracious and wonderful woman in the world. And the saddest."

"I agree with you."

The ambassador's voice dropped even more. "So does the emperor.

He has written this letter of encouragement and support for your efforts on her behalf." He held out a folded paper. More, shocked, glanced about and pulled Chapuys into an alcove.

"I beg of you not to deliver it to me!" More whispered through clenched teeth. "Although I have given more than sufficient proof of my loyalty to the king, I must do nothing to provoke suspicion . . . considering the times we live in."

Chapuys quickly tucked the letter back into the folds of his jacket.

"I don't want to be deprived of the liberty which allows me to speak boldly," continued More, "in private, about those matters which concern your master. And the queen."

"I understand. You need say no more," Chapuys replied.

"Remember I have already offered my affectionate service to the emperor."

Chapuys nodded. He remembered. More strode away toward the king's quarters, fresh sweat caught beneath his arms and at the brim of his cap.

As More entered the king's private chambers, Thomas Cromwell was on his way out. Each bowed to the other. More approached the king, who stood with his arms crossed in the center of the room, and stooped low. He was not looking forward to this conversation, for it would be painful for them both.

"Sir Thomas," said Henry evenly.

"Majesty." More stood, his gaze meeting the king's.

"I must tell you," said the king. "I have received a petition from the members of the House of Commons, complaining about the cruel behavior and abuses of the prelates and the clergy, touching both their bodies and their goods." His lips pursed. "Thomas, people are asking for freedom from clerical rule. The members implore me to establish my jurisdiction over the church. In that way, I can bring *all* my subjects, both clerical and lay, into perpetual unity."

"Your Majesty knows very well that I have always condemned the abuses of the clergy, when they have been brought to light. As your chancellor, I've worked hard to eliminate them, and purify our Holy Church . . ."

"But . . . ?"

"You know where I stand," More said. "You have always known. I'm fully acquainted with the frailty of we poor worldly men. That is why I cannot condone the newfangled version of private belief and personal grace." The rhythm of his speech picked up; he could not help himself. "For me, the Church *is* and always *will be* the permanent and living sign of God's presence, sustained by inherited custom and maintained by tradition. It is a visible, palpable community, not just a few 'brethren' gathered in secret rooms."

Clearly the king heard the fervor in More's voice. Henry strode away across the floor, hands drawing into fists. He turned back, his face darkened. "Then you will speak out against me?"

More shook his head. "My loyalty and love for Your Majesty is so great that I will never say a word against you in public, so help me God."

The king did not challenge this declaration of devotion, but his expression told More that His Majesty was not quite convinced.

The dining room of Thomas Cromwell's home was filled with laughter and convivial conversation. Though not as elegant as the royal dining chambers, the room was nonetheless impressive, with oak paneling, a marble fireplace, and a massive wrought-iron chandelier bearing countless white candles.

Seated before a spread of roast duck, vegetables, and freshly baked breads, Cromwell and his guests, George Boleyn, son of Thomas Boleyn, and the poet Thomas Wyatt—young, ambitious men both—drank fine wine from pewter tankards. Servants moved in and out a rear door, bringing even more food on broad silver trays—meat pies, roast tongue, broiled fish.

The dining room's main door opened, and another young man entered the room. He was dressed modestly in gray and black.

"Mr. Cranmer," announced Cromwell, standing and motioning the visitor to the table while flicking his fingers to send the servants out.

"I'm sorry to be late, Mr. Cromwell," said Cranmer, removing his hat and bowing respectfully. "It's unforgivable."

"Nonsense," said Cromwell as he shook his visitor's hand. In turn, Cranmer nodded at the other two men. "We haven't begun to dine. It's very good to see you."

"Mr. Cranmer," said Wyatt, his cup poised at his lips. "You're a man of the cloth, I believe?"

"Yes, sir. And are you not a poet, Mr. Wyatt?"

Wyatt grinned. "That's the least of my sins, Mr. Cranmer. You may take my confession after supper."

"I wouldn't," joked Cromwell. "It would certainly turn your hair white!"

The men laughed, and Cranmer took a seat beside Wyatt. Cromwell held up the flagon of wine, and Cranmer nodded appreciatively. Cromwell poured a tankard for his newest guest.

As Cranmer tasted the wine, Cromwell leaned forward on his elbows and rubbed his chin with his thumb. "Before you arrived," he said, "we were discussing the progress of the Convocation of Bishops, which, as you know, is now sitting at Westminster to decide whether the king is to be made head of the Church."

Wyatt and George sat back in their chairs. Wyatt crossed his arms.

"In the absence of the Duke of Norfolk," continued Cromwell, "His Majesty has wisely appointed George Boleyn here to negotiate with Their Graces."

George nodded. "I find most of the bishops accommodating. Of course, there are a few stubborn exceptions."

Cranmer put his cup down. "Bishop Fisher, I assume?"

"Naturally."

"May I ask who else?"

"The archbishop himself, Warham, after years of being perfectly pliable, has suddenly become rather intransigent."

"That's because Warham's old," explained Wyatt. "And consequently closer to his Maker, to whom in due course he must explain himself."

Cromwell tapped the tabletop. "It should be a simple matter to explain that he helped liberate his Church from superstition, religious falsehoods, and clerical greed."

Wyatt raised his cup. "Touché."

The men smiled in unison. Cromwell passed the flagon for all to refill their tankards.

"By the way," George asked Cromwell, "how *is* our friend the Duke of Norfolk?"

"The king has sent him away, to York. He hates it." Cromwell took a long sip of wine. It was the best his household had had in years, warming his throat and his belly. "He invited me to stay with him. He wrote me a rather teasing letter, saying that if I didn't, quote, 'lust after his wife,' then he could easily supply me with 'a young woman with pretty proper breasts.'"

The men laughed again, and Cromwell shouted for the servants. The rest of the food was delivered to the table, and the men changed the subject of their conversation.

The blare of horns and roll of tabor drums cut the air of the magnificent Great Hall at Westminster, and all in attendance craned their heads and shifted about to see the monarch's arrival.

"All arise for the king!" called the chamberlain. He banged his staff and those who were not already up, stood, and bowed deeply.

King Henry entered the room dressed in blue doublet and silver-threaded coat trimmed in ermine, his crowned head cocked back. To the king's right walked Charles Brandon, the Duke of Suffolk and Henry's friend and companion since childhood. To the king's left was Thomas Boleyn, the new Earl of Wiltshire. Several paces behind the king, moving with the nobles of second rank, walked George Boleyn, and following up the procession, in official scarlet robes, was Thomas More, his face stoic save for the slight pinching at the corners of his eyes.

The king took the dais in a broad stride and sat upon his throne to gaze out at the gathering. Archbishop Warham, an elderly man of bent body and spotted cheeks, stood at the front of the crowd. Beside him was Bishop Fisher, arms steady at his side, his mouth a tight line across his face.

Drumming his fingers on the arms of his throne, Henry studied his subjects. "My lords," he said at last, "and Your Graces. We have come here among you to hear your response to the charges and responsibilities laid against you. You are generally charged with supporting the authority of the late Cardinal Wolsey and the Bishop of Rome, against those of your own king and country."

Bishop Fisher, clearly disgusted, shook his head at the remark. Though many in the room had been dabbed with sweet waters prior to coming before the king, More could smell sour tension in the air.

The king linked his fingers together. "Some among you may suppose that I am here to seek personal advantage. It is not so. As your king, I am commissioned to restore a right order on earth and assert the immunities and princely liberties of our realm and crown. This is my sacred duty, sealed before God by solemn oath at my coronation."

No one spoke. No one nodded.

Henry trained his eyes on the old archbishop next to Fisher. "What is your conclusion, Archbishop Warham?"

"Your Majesty," Warham replied in a rasping voice. "Before I deliver it, I give way to His Grace the Bishop of Rochester."

Henry's eyes narrowed, but he nodded.

"My lords," Fisher said, stepping forward and turning to address his fellows. "We have been asked to admit His Majesty as supreme head of the Church in England. Unfortunately we cannot grant this to the king without abandoning our unity with the Holy See of Rome. If we are to renounce the unity of the Christian world and leap out of Peter's ship, then we shall be drowned in the waves of all heresies, sects, schisms, and divisions."

Thomas More noticed dissent in the crowd, whispered complaints by those who felt it best to agree with the king's position. The murmurings grew louder as Fisher continued to speak.

"I say to you, the acceptance of regal supremacy over our church would represent a tearing of the seamless coat of Christ asunder!"

Many of the clergy nodded at this, and their voices rose to tangle with those who disagreed with Fisher. The king leaned forward on his throne, his eyes widening in furor.

"Your Grace!" cried the chamberlain, pounding his staff on the floor. "We will have your judgment!"

The bishop grew silent. More let out a breath and gave the circumstance up to God.

All eyes fell upon Warham.

"I will put this proposal to Convocation," Warham said carefully, "that Your Majesty has a new title, which is Supreme Head of the Church and Clergy of England . . ."

The king stared at the old archbishop, waiting for the rest of the proposal.

"But I add the caveat, 'so far as the law of Christ allow.'"

The king did not move, but his gaze traveled the room, taking in each of the clergy. More felt the appraisal on him, searing like a brand, and then felt it move on.

"Those in favor?" asked Warham.

No one in the room spoke. Henry frowned.

Warham cleared his throat. "Very well," he said. "*Qui tacet consentire videtur.* Whoever remains silent can be assumed to agree."

Still, no one spoke. Some of them looked at Fisher as if for direction, but he merely crossed himself and lowered his head.

The bishops had given assent, though unwillingly.

Henry sat back in his throne. More could see the king was not pleased, though he had gotten what he had wanted. Well, almost all.

*   *   *   *

But ever the nearer he was,
The more he burned—
The nearer the fire, the hotter, as all this company knows . . .

Anne Boleyn placed her hand upon the page, upon Chaucer's epic, and wondered about poets and their understanding of the human heart and desires. She thought for a moment that should she have been born a man, she would have liked to have penned such thoughtful words.

But, she thought, *should I have been born a man, I would not have found my heart's desire, Henry!*

She reclined on her window seat, book against her knees, one finger twisting a strand of hair. Warm sunlight blanketed her lap.

Not an hour of the day passed
that he said not to himself a thousand times,
"Goodly one whom I labor to serve as best I can,
Now would to God,
Criseyde, you would pity me before I die!" . . .

Movement in the room brought her from her reverie, and she sat up, startled. It was Henry, smiling down at her. She put the book aside and began to rise.

"No. Stay like that," said Henry. He knelt and kissed her bare shoulders. "You're so beautiful. So very . . . desirable." He lifted her face to his and kissed her fully. "I need to possess you utterly."

Anne felt his heart, his soul, his desire burning in his hands, in his lips. She returned the kiss, hungrily, then threw back her head and moaned softly. A fire erupted in her belly and her private place, a dreadful, delicious ache that demanded to be acknowledged, to be tended. She drew her legs around the king's waist, and he threw up her skirts.

The king groaned loudly, his teasing, insistent hand traveling up her leg toward the center of her longing. "I can't wait!" he whispered through his teeth.

But then Anne drew his face up to hers with one hand, and his probing fingers down and away with the other. She closed her legs and brushed down her skirts. "Oh, my love," she panted. "Just a little longer, and then . . ."

Henry snarled and raised his eyes Heavenward as if in divine surrender, but then laughed. He gathered his lady in his arms and tucked his cheek against hers.

After a long, tender moment, he said, "I am made Head of the Church."

"So it has happened!" Anne exclaimed. "Now you can do as you will!"

Henry nodded, kissed Anne's cheek, and stood to leave. "I'm going to tell Cromwell to have some apartments in the Tower refurbished. Every queen of England stays there before her coronation."

Anne blew her king a kiss and, with a dramatic bow, he left the room. Wrapping her arms about her waist, she imagined they were her lover's arms, there forever, never to leave her.

There was a cough. Anne turned to see her father standing in the rear doorway, looking very unhappy.

"Papa! What's wrong?" she asked. "Don't you want to celebrate?"

Thomas Boleyn scowled. "It's far too early for that. The bishops were not really defeated. By default, they voted to make the king head of the Church, but only 'as far as the law of Christ allows.' You don't have to be a clever lawyer to know that 'the law of Christ' may be used to invalidate the vote itself."

Anne's breath caught. "It was all for nothing?"

"No, not for nothing. The principle has now been effectively conceded by most of them. As George told me, their resistance and recalcitrance really stem from only one man, that bloody Bishop Fisher."

Anne picked up her book, stared at it, but then tossed it aside in frustration. Her father walked over and touched her hair. "So," he said, "if he can be . . . persuaded . . . to act properly, then I trust our quarrels will soon be over. And we shall indeed have cause to celebrate."

CHAPTER TWO

"Your Majesty," said Thomas Cromwell with a bow as he ushered a young man into Henry's presence chamber. "This is Mr. Thomas Cranmer, of whom I have often spoken."

Henry's energy, which had been drained from a long day dealing with piddling issues that had no importance to his unresolved situation with Anne, picked up on seeing Cranmer. The young man appeared hesitant and awkward in the king's presence, wearing only a simple gray shirt, trousers, and shoes that appeared ill fitting.

Cromwell continued. "It was Mr. Cranmer who first spoke to the fact that Your Majesty's Great Matter was a theological issue, not a legal one."

Beaming, Henry stepped from his throne and gathered Cranmer in an enthusiastic embrace. Then he held the young man at arms' length and almost laughed at the surprise on Cranmer's face.

"Majesty," said Cranmer. "I—I—"

Henry clapped Cranmer affectionately on the arm. "It's funny," he said. "Some of the greatest, most celebrated minds of my kingdom struggled and sweated upon an issue which you, an obscure cleric—if you will forgive me—were able to resolve with perfect simplicity and a clarity of mind which put them all to shame."

Cranmer was clearly embarrassed with the praise. "Majesty, I—am not worthy."

"His Majesty has agreed to your appointment as his chaplain," explained Cromwell.

Cranmer looked from secretary to king, unable to utter even a word.

"Mr. Cranmer," said Cromwell. "You must thank His Majesty."

Cranmer took a breath to gather himself, and another, and fell to his knees before the king.

The Church of St. Peter in Rome was the center of religious purpose for devout citizens and pilgrims, an enormous structure of both decay and glorious rebirth, of rot and marble, of mold and gild, of rats and statues. It was a grand cathedral in the throes of experimental renovations intended to, when at last completed, reveal an utmost reverence for God and His Church. The grounds, chapels, annexes, and hallways were constantly filled with the faithful, hoping to catch a glimpse of the Holy Father and to receive a blessing.

Pope Paul III entered his private study in St. Peter's, his hands still smelling of those who had clutched and cried over them on his arrival at the church. Waiting for him was Cardinal Campeggio, a somber man of many years who required a cane to move about.

The Cardinal kissed the pontiff's ring. "Holy Father," he said.

"Sit down, Cardinal Campeggio. I know you are a martyr to gout." The pope motioned toward a cushioned chair at the table. "And my feet are killing me, too."

Both seated, Pope Paul folded his hands atop the table. "What do you want to see me about?"

"We have received two new letters regarding the king of England's— Great Matter."

"Ah," said the pope wearily. "That again. What do they say?"

Campeggio opened a leather satchel and removed the letters. "The first is from the king himself, urging the Curia to make a final, and unfavorable, decision on the annulment of his marriage, for the sake of peace in England. He . . . uses some intemperate language, Holiness, complaining that 'Never was there any prince handled by a pope as Your Holiness has treated us.'"

Pope Paul nodded solemnly, disheartened but not surprised. "He meant my predecessor. And, frankly, he has a point. Clement was a terrible procrastinator."

The cardinal nodded and sighed.

"Although it was very wrong for some people to dig up his body after he was dead and stab it in the street, I could well understand their feelings. He was never popular." The pope crossed himself and spoke a short, whispered prayer for the peace of Clement's soul. "And the second letter?"

"From the emperor. On behalf of his aunt, Katherine, the 'unhappy queen,' he urges you to prevent the marriage annulment and excommunicate the king."

"It's true we must come to a judgment. On the other hand, to protect the interests of the Church, we should try not to antagonize one power above the other. After all, they have guns and soldiers, whereas we must make do with beauty and truth." It was a sour joke, one Campeggio did not pick up on or did not care for. "What of this girl, this *putaine*, the king's whore?"

"Anne Boleyn." Campeggio looked down, gingerly touched his gouty leg, and winced.

"Yes," said the pope. "Why doesn't someone just get rid of her?"

Campeggio looked up again, shocked at the comment, yet realizing the pope was probably right.

Whitehall Palace's private garden was alive with the soft, sweet songs of garden warblers and wrens as they fluttered amid the hedges and perched upon the branches of the ancient oaks and willows. Blankets of water lilies floated upon the fish ponds, topped with white flowers and frogs taking in the morning's warmth. Dragonflies held in the air, tiny, jeweled creatures on the gown of morning.

Henry strolled with his friend, Charles Brandon, amid the hedges and trees, enjoying the youth of the day and the smell of fresh air.

"So," Henry said cheerfully. "You married your ward. What was her name?"

"Catherine Brook."

"Catherine," said Henry. "Why her?"

"I love and admire Miss Brook," said Brandon with a shrug. "And my young son needs a mother."

Henry eyed his companion with a conspiratorial grin. "How old is Miss Brook?"

"Seventeen."

Henry laughed aloud and shoved Brandon playfully. "Some mother!"

They continued their walk, circling the largest pond, staring down at the orange and silver fish that darted beneath the surface.

"Poor Catherine," said Henry. "You're incapable of fidelity, Charles. You always have been."

Brandon stopped, his voice suddenly serious. "This one is different."

"How different?"

"I don't know. I just feel it. It's not just that she's beautiful. It's . . . it's a marriage of true souls. Surely you can understand that?"

Henry watched his friend's face, and felt a new and deeper kinship there. Yes, he understood. He understood completely.

Thomas Boleyn sat in a small, darkly lit chamber in the bowels of the palace. A single candle was set upon the floor, casting a sickly yellow glow, though the light was not strong enough to define Boleyn's features, nor those of the two men with him. It was as Boleyn wanted it. This was a dreadful and secretive meeting. Anonymity was crucial.

On the other side of the desk, his fingers fighting themselves in his lap, was a bald man named Roose. Roose had just arrived, having been escorted clandestinely through a back passageway. He looked at his hands, awaiting further instructions.

"Mr. Roose?" said Boleyn.

"Yes, sir."

"A cook, by trade?"

"Yes, sir."

"You understand what's expected of you?"

"I do. Yes."

Boleyn nodded, though he knew the man could not see him nod. It was more for himself, for his own assurance. "This is for your trouble." He slid several gold coins across the desk toward the cook. But before Roose could snatch the coins, Boleyn's hand darted out and covered them.

"If you betray us," Boleyn said coolly, "I will destroy your entire family."

Roose swallowed with an audible click, and then scooped up the coins and dropped them into his pocket. Someone else moved in the darkness, placing a small leather pouch on the desk and sliding it forward toward Roose. Roose stared at the pouch as if it were a scorpion, but took that, as well.

As Roose stood to leave, the candle flared and he caught a brief glimpse of the man at the desk. He and Boleyn exchanged a chilling glance before Boleyn drew back into the darkness.

Anne's apartments at the palace were crowded and busy, filled with courtiers—old and young, important and less-than-important—all anxious to pay their respects to the young woman who, most now acknowledged, would be the next queen of England. Her ladies ushered the visitors in and out with great composure.

Anne stood in the midst of it all, doing her part to be both accommodating and regal while savoring the attention and excitement. Thomas Cromwell, standing beside her, watched silently and appreciatively at the parade of adoration. He gave Anne a knowing look then bowed and left the room.

"Lady Anne," said the next visitor in line, the Earl of Oxford, a gaunt man with a slightly crooked nose. He stooped low and kissed Anne's hand. "I come to pay my humble respects to you."

"Thank you, Lord Oxford. I'm grateful. If I can further your cause in any way, or that of your family, you need only ask."

Oxford tipped his head and backed away.

Next in line was the poet Thomas Wyatt, who bowed most dramatically, sweeping his hat out with an almost dancelike movement. "Lady Anne, you are to be congratulated, for reaching so high."

"Thank you, Thomas," said Anne with a smile. Then she lowered her voice and leaned forward. "I shall never forget that we were once true friends."

"Oh," whispered Wyatt. "I wish I could forget."

"But I see you are raised, too?"

"Only to a sometimes diplomat, thanks to the patronage of Mr. Cromwell. We poets and painters sometimes have our uses!" He kissed her hand then stood straight. "There is someone here I should like you to meet."

Wyatt gestured toward a young man who had been standing behind him. The man was well built and handsome, with curly hair and a gleam in his eye that caused Anne's pulse to quicken. He carried a violin beneath his arm.

"Lady Anne Boleyn," said Wyatt, "this is Mark Smeaton, dancing master, musician, singer, general all-around genius."

Anne laughed and held out her hand. "Mr. Smeaton."

"He likes to be called plain Mark," said Wyatt.

Anne tipped her head coquettishly. "How could he *possibly* be called plain?"

"My lady," said Smeaton. "It's a great pleasure and an honor."

"You play the violin?" asked Anne, gesturing toward the instrument. Smeaton nodded.

"Play something for me."

Smeaton tucked the violin beneath his chin, lifted the bow to the strings, and smiled at Lady Anne. He drew the bow across the strings, releasing a clear note of ethereal beauty, then bent into the violin and began to play. With movements both delicate and powerful, Smeaton filled the chamber with a beautiful song that caused all within to listen and marvel.

When he was done, Anne said, "Will you show me?"

Smeaton handed the violin to Anne. She put it to her chin but was unable to position her fingers properly on the frets. With a sympathetic grin, Smeaton reached for her hand. She looked up at him as he gently guided her fingers upon the neck of the instrument, her face so close she could see the length of his lashes and the passion in his large eyes.

When the serving boys had left the kitchen to set the dining room for Bishop Fisher and his guests, Roose, the bishop's cook, turned his attention back to the vegetable broth he was preparing in a large copper pot upon the hearth coals. Alone now, his heart thundering, he opened the leather pouch he'd been given earlier and sprinkled a little of the powder into the soup. *No, that won't do,* he thought. *I cannot fail at this.* He emptied the entire pouch into the soup and stirred it in.

Several hours later, the bishop and his fellow clergymen were gathered for the meal in the dining room. The table was laden with baked lamb, eggs, cheeses, and a large bowl of nuts. A serving boy carried a soup tureen from the kitchen and placed it upon the sideboard, where another boy served it into bowls.

Bishop Fisher addressed the men. "I do believe that the caveat 'so far as the law of Christ allows' does indeed invalidate the whole bill. Since how can the law of Christ permit a layman, even a king, to be head of a Church?"

Thomas More, at the far end of the table from Fisher, nodded.

The bishop, seeing the meal was ready, folded his hands and blessed the food. The men responded, "Amen."

The soup bowls were served. Fisher, who did not have much of an appetite, selected a bowl less full than the others. More shook his head when the soup was offered, but the other men accepted the broth and spooned it up with relish.

"I must ask you, Sir Thomas," Fisher said, "if you still have a mind to resign from your office?"

More sighed. "After the vote, Your Grace, I confess I was sorely tempted. But, on reflection, I am content to stay and fight for Christendom."

"That is an excellent move." Fisher sipped his broth. It had an odd taste, or perhaps it was his tongue, growing old and unreliable. "As, indeed, is the turning again of the archbishop."

Down the table, one of the clergy had stopped eating his soup and was smelling it. He made a sour face.

Fisher ignored it. "I thank God that his conscience has finally moved the archbishop to condemn the king's nullity suit, and he has stated his intention to oppose any legislation that could be injurious to the Church. I—" He stopped suddenly as a sharp pain cut his stomach. "Ah!" Fisher held his abdomen as the pain spread.

"Your Grace?" cried More.

Another man groaned and clutched his gut. Then another. In only a moment, all who had eaten the soup were dropped across the table and onto the floor, grunting, vomiting. Fisher watched in pain and horror as his guests writhed and wailed as if they would die.

More raced to Fisher's aid. "Boy!" he shouted to a servant. "Fetch a doctor! A doctor, for the love of God!"

King Henry sat in the mahogany chair in his private chamber, arms crossed over his chest, as More told him the news.

"Four men died of their pains," More said. "Bishop Fisher survived only because he ate very little of the soup."

The king shook his head. "It's very unfortunate, Sir Thomas."

"It's more than unfortunate, Your Majesty! Fisher's cook has been arrested. But I must tell you that rumors abound as to the identity of those who plotted against him."

"Who . . . ?"

"Wiltshire has been named."

Henry drew back in surprise. "Boleyn?"

"Yes! And . . ." It was clear More did not want to speak the name, but he did. "Some even blame Lady Anne."

Shocked, Henry jumped to his feet and pointed a finger at More. "Some people will blame her for *everything*! They will blame her if it rains or if the rains fail! They blame her for the barrenness of the queen, for the fact that I love her! They blame her for winds that destroy crops and storms that sink our ships! It's *all* the fault of Lady Anne! Do *you* think she tried to poison the bishop, Thomas?"

More said nothing. Henry turned away, disgusted.

More began, "Harry, I . . ."

The king spun about. "*Now* is not the time for Harry! Those days are gone."

The two men stood staring at each other. The gulf between once close friends was growing, widening.

"Whoever was to blame," said More, his voice controlled, "the cook Roose tried blatantly and almost successfully to poison one of Your Majesty's great public servants, a bishop of our Holy Church, as well as me! If Your Majesty was to turn a blind eye to the offense, then everyone would be forced to assume that the attempted murders were . . . were done with your blessing."

Henry snarled, threw out his hands, and stormed off.

The passageway through the Tower of London was dark and oppressive, stinking of mildew, excrement, and terror. Thomas Boleyn joined his son outside a locked cell beside which an impassive guard stood watch.

"Has it started?" Boleyn asked, dabbing his nose with a scented cloth.

George nodded. "Can't you hear the screams?"

Boleyn could. The sound drew his muscles into knots. "He blundered," he whispered angrily to his son. "He deserves everything that's coming to him."

Boleyn nodded at the guard, who opened the door to let him and his son enter.

The cell was dark as night, with only ambient light from the small barred window in the door. It took Boleyn a full minute for his eyes to adjust, though he could hear panting and a clinking from the center of the cell.

And then he saw the man. Roose stood, shoulders stooped, weighted down with chains at his neck, wrists, and ankles. He was breathing heavily, and staring at the far corner, as if seeing something they could not see.

Pacing about Roose was Cromwell. He noted the Boleyns' arrival with a curt nod. Then he spoke to Roose gently, almost sympathetically. "One more time. Who gave you the poison?"

Roose looked at Boleyn. His face was swollen and bruised, with several deep gashes across his cheeks.

"Mr. Roose," said Cromwell, "it's inconceivable that you should suddenly take it upon yourself to murder your master and his household. You had served so diligently these past four years." A breath. "Who gave you the poison?"

Boleyn felt his entire body stiffen. Roose would not tell. *He could not tell!*

Roose spoke through battered lips. "Sir, I have three daughters."

"What is that to me?"

"It is nothing to you, sir." Roose coughed and spit out blood. "Yet to me it is everything. Their mother died. I have brought them up myself. Beautiful girls, and so gentle. I want them to find good husbands . . . but that takes money."

Cromwell moved closer to the chained man. "Perhaps we will pay you for your information."

"No, sir. The payment is already made, the account settled."

Cromwell swore silently, and shook his head. "You're a fool!"

"Yes sir, indeed. Anyone who loves their children is a fool."

Yes, thought Boleyn, smiling to himself. *Wise answer, Roose.*

Bishop Fisher lay abed, propped up on pillows, his fingers drawn up upon his blanket. Several candles burned on the mantle beneath a wooden crucifix. For a moment, More thought the man had died, and crossed himself reflexively. But then Fisher stirred.

More stood by the bed, leaning over so his friend could hear him.

"The king has agreed to a new and harsh treatment of poisoners," More said. "They are to be boiled alive."

Fisher's lids fluttered, but his eyes remained closed.

"He is wise to have dealt so severely in this case. But he cannot avoid some suspicion, at least against the lady and her father."

Fisher's lips parted, closed, and opened again. "We are all in the hands of God," he said faintly. "But I worry that, while I lie here uselessly, the king may proceed with his divorce, since he has given himself the power."

"I doubt it. It's not so simple. He must know the depth of feeling toward the queen, and against the lady." More put his hand on the bishop's arm, gently. "I was told that at the last council, the king became angry and demanded to know what would happen if he went ahead and married Anne without the pope's permission."

"What did they say?"

"Only Boleyn supported him. Not even his friend Brandon. And one noble actually said that it would provoke civil unrest, and he begged His Majesty not even to consider it."

Fisher sighed with relief. "Thank God. More, let us pray for the king, and for the salvation of his soul."

"Gladly," said More. *Gladly*, he thought. He knelt beside the bishop's bed, crossed himself, and began to pray.

"*In nomine Patris, et Filii, et Spiritus Sancti . . .*"

The orange glow and the heat in the Tower's dungeon were intense. Roose shuffled into the room, a guard to either side. The cook wore a simple shift, and his beard had grown long and matted over the past weeks. His head was down; his arms, covered in a sheen of sweat and blood, were chained to his waist. Before he looked up, he tried to prepare himself for what he was going to see.

God have mercy.

He looked. The scene was one from hell.

Torches burned in brackets on the tall, wet walls, illuminating the ghastly vision before him. A scaffold of planks surrounded and supported an enormous pot in which steaming oil bubbled. Bare-chested men stoked the fire beneath the cauldron to keep it roaring. At the top of the scaffold beside the pot was the master torturer, checking the straps of a leather harness that was attached to a wooden crane and pulley. The torturer looked down at Roose with a smile of hideous delight. To the right stood Thomas Boleyn, George Boleyn, and Thomas Cromwell. Boleyn and George seemed eager to watch. Cromwell, on the other hand, appeared tense and shaken.

Christ have mercy!

Roose licked his dried lips and looked directly at Cromwell. "If you can spare the time, sir, tell my girls I died easily and with no pain, and they must live with only good thoughts about their loving father."

Cromwell was clearly moved. His voice was tremulous. "I swear to you I shall tell them."

Roose closed his eyes, thinking for a moment of his sweet children and the fact that they would not know the truth of what he suffered. "Then I consign myself to God's mercy," he murmured. "Bless you, sir."

A guard knocked Roose forward, and his eyes flew open. The leather harness had been lowered to the floor. With quick, rough movements, the guards lashed the straps about Roose's body and another pulled the rope. Roose, in a prone position, was raised up until he was five feet higher than the cauldron. The edge of his gown had been caught up in the straps, exposing him, stripping away any dignity he might have had.

The torturer reached up for the harness and pulled it around so he was face to face with Roose. Roose did not focus on the torturer, however, but on the steaming, bubbling oil in the cauldron below. His heart pounded a painful pace, and his breaths came in rapid gasps.

Jesus my Lord my Christ my Savior!

The torturer considered the moment. "Head first?" he asked Roose. "Or however it comes?" He signaled to the operator of the crane, and the harness swung out and over the lip of the cauldron, bringing Roose directly over the oil.

Roose shut his eyes and lifted his head to the heavens. He felt the harness tremble, and begin to lower.

Bless me Father, help me Father, have mercy on me Father!

The heat intensified, blistering his arms, his face, his bare feet. The harness shifted so that his legs would reach the oil first. He prepared himself as best he could for that which he could not imagine.

Hold me Father, forgive me, take me home!

Roose's feet went into the boiling liquid. He threw back his head, biting through his tongue against the supreme agony, no longer able to pray to God but holding out so as not to cry.

He did, for a long moment.

And then he began to scream.

Chapter Three

Katherine appeared in Henry's chamber dressed in a blue silk gown studded with pearls and sapphires, a gift he had given her several years earlier. She was followed by three of her ladies, who held back near the door to allow their mistress privacy.

It was all Henry could do not to command her to leave immediately, as she had not been summoned, and this was a brazen breach of protocol. Instead, he stood from his chair and walked across the floor to her, his fists clenching. Katherine appeared to have aged a great deal recently, though the poise she retained was formidable, and this angered Henry even more.

"Husband," said Katherine with a curtsy and a smile. "How are you feeling?"

Henry bristled. "What?"

"They told me you have been suffering from a toothache. Someone even told me you had a touch of gout."

"Of course I don't have gout! Why do you listen to stupid rumors?"

"Because I care for you."

Henry snorted. Could not the damnable woman stop caring for him?

"Henry," Katherine said.

"What?"

"Will you not dismiss that shameless creature, Anne Boleyn, from your court? I beseech you—"

Henry raised his hand as if to slap her, but stopped short. "No! Don't even speak of her! I forbid it!"

Katherine did not flinch, nor step back. Her voice, however, softened. "Our daughter Mary has been ill. She has not kept any food down for eight days. Don't you think we should go visit her?"

"You can go," said Henry. "Visit the princess if you want. And you can also stay there."

Katherine clearly saw what he was implying. "Henry," she said evenly. "Neither for my daughter nor anyone in the world would I dream of leaving *you*. You know that my proper place is at your side."

With a roar of rage, Henry thrust his hand in the direction of the door. Katherine curtsyed slowly, turned, and left the chamber, her silent ladies falling in behind her.

Cromwell did not want to be there, but he had made a promise. He bowed to the three girls, who clutched one another and stared at him with anguished eyes. They were Roose's daughters, the oldest no more than fourteen, the youngest about ten. All were pretty girls, though dressed in plain, commoners' gowns. The parlor of the Roose house was simple, dirt-floored and bare-windowed.

"You father . . ." began Cromwell.

The eldest girl, tall and brown haired, held her sisters more tightly. "We know how my father died. You don't need to speak of it."

The younger two girls, who had been silent on Cromwell's arrival, began to weep.

Cromwell continued, the words tumbling from his mouth. "He wanted you—he loved you so much. He wanted you to admire him. He—"

The girls crumpled to the floor, wailing and rocking, crushed by his words and by the truth of their father's death. Cromwell rushed ahead, hardly able to bear the moment.

"He told me how good you were, and how beautiful. He wanted you to marry well. He said he had already received some money to—to put toward your dowries. But to marry well is very expensive."

The girls were beyond listening. Cromwell pulled a large purse from his coat and put it on a small table. Then he took out a second, and a third.

"God bless you," he whispered, and then hurried from the cottage and into the sunlight.

The king's select musicians, dressed in feathered caps, played lutes, pipes, and drums in the balcony for the entertainment of the merrymakers below. The Great Hall of Whitehall Palace was adorned with flowers and fruits, ribbons and candles. The air was heavy with odors of spiced foods and good, fatty meats, and the servants, dressed properly in red and black, went quickly about their business bearing food-laden chargers and platters. Dancers moved about in the proscribed movements, weaving beautiful, shifting portraits upon the floor as the audience along the walls sipped from goblets and nodded in approval. Lady Anne was clearly enjoying the festivities, dancing with both her brother, George, and the musician Mark Smeaton.

King Henry watched the dancing from his chair on the dais, tapping one finger, though not to the music, but to some other, more serious rhythm within him.

Charles Brandon sat beside the king, waiting to find out why Henry had called him away from dancing with his wife, Catherine.

At last the king spoke, though he did not look at Brandon. He watched Anne instead, as Smeaton passed her in the dance, whispered to her, and made her laugh.

"Your Catherine is very beautiful," he said flatly. "You seem very happy together."

"We are, Your Majesty."

"A happy marriage is something devoutly to be wished for." The king winced and touched his jaw. Brandon waited. "Talking of which, I want you to do something for me."

He gestured for Brandon to lean close and he whispered the order in his ear.

Brandon did not relish the task. He took the corridors to the queen's chambers as quickly as he could, uncertain of the reception he would receive.

A lady-in-waiting announced his arrival, and he entered the outer room. Unlike the jovial mood of the Great Hall that evening, Katherine's chambers held an aura of long-suffering duty and patience.

Brandon bowed to the queen. "Your Majesty," he said. "I need to speak to you alone."

Katherine gestured for her ladies to leave. Then she looked at Brandon as if expecting a blow. "The king has sent you? At this hour? Why?"

Brandon took a deep breath and raised his hand in a gesture of appeal. "His Majesty just asks you to be sensible. Withdraw your appeal to Rome. Entrust your affairs to his hands. He promises to be more than generous."

The corners of Katherine's eyes tightened, but she said nothing.

"As you know," Brandon continued, "Parliament has now voted to make him supreme in spiritual matters as well as temporal ones."

"No. Only the pope has the power of God on earth and is the image of eternal truth."

"Yes, but the king—"

"Your Grace, I love and have loved my lord the king as much as any woman can love a man, but I would not have borne him company as his wife one moment against the voice of my conscience. I *am* his true wife. Go to Rome, if you want, and argue about it with lots of important men, not just here with one poor woman!"

The honesty, the piety in the queen's voice touched Brandon, though he struggled not to let it show. However, Katherine could see it, the melting of an old enemy.

Back in the Great Hall, Brandon was summoned impatiently by the king.

"What did she say?" Henry urged as Brandon sat next to him.

"She—she told me she was ready to obey Your Majesty in everything. Everything save for the obedience she owes two higher powers."

Henry's face contorted with sarcasm. "Which two 'higher powers'? The pope and the emperor?"

"No. God and her conscience."

Henry jumped to his feet and moved off, courtiers and nobles bowing quickly in his wake.

Damn it all! Henry thought. Had he truly believed Brandon would succeed in convincing Katherine to let it go, once and for all? Well, what he *did* expect was that the queen, his subject and subordinate, would obey his commands!

Henry ignored the bows from the partyers as he pushed past, but when he saw Chapuys's face among them, he stalked over.

"Chapuys!" Henry called, savoring the bitter taste of menace on his tongue.

Chapuys bowed low. "Majesty."

"You will tell your master and anyone you like, I will never agree to be judged by the pope in this matter. I don't care a fig for his threat to excommunicate me. He can do what he likes in Rome. I shall do what I like here!"

Chapuys, for the barest moment, looked shocked. It was the reaction Henry wanted.

"Majesty," said Chapuys, bowing again.

Henry, content, strolled to the Great Hall door to leave, then turned back and called out, "And by the way, welcome back to court."

The fire on the hearth in Thomas Cromwell's study crackled and spit, warming the room and offering a sense of peace to the two men who sat before it, legs stretched out, enjoying wine after a long day.

Cromwell savored the quiet for a long moment and then spoke to his guest. "How do you find the king, Mr. Cranmer?"

Cranmer, quite relaxed from the wine he'd already consumed, said, "I swear to you, Mr. Cromwell, that he is the kindest of princes."

Cromwell smiled. "I can tell you that His Majesty has already formed for you a strong respect and affection. I think you were born in a happy hour, for it seems, do or say what you like, the king will always take it at your hand."

Cranmer put down his wine and stared into the fire. "I am not so conceited as to suppose I am anything more to His Majesty than a diligent servant."

"Your modesty does you honor." Cromwell took another sip. "But His Majesty clearly thinks you are meant for higher things."

Cranmer looked up quickly. He lifted his goblet and took a drink without taking his eyes from Cromwell.

"Which," Cromwell continued, "is why he is appointing you a special envoy to the court of the emperor."

Cranmer gasped, spraying the mouthful of wine back into his cup. Cromwell chuckled.

"He can't do that!" complained Cranmer. "I mean, why me? I am nothing!"

Cromwell leaned forward. "His Majesty trusts you absolutely. He knows that you understand his Great Matter, better than anyone else, and that you take his part. You are in a better position than most to represent him at the Imperial court."

Cranmer put his hand to his mouth. The glow of the fire danced on his cheeks. Cromwell poured him some fresh wine.

"You will be a great success," Cromwell said. "I am sure. And on your journey there, you will have a chance to visit the city of Nürnberg."

"Why is that so special?"

Cromwell sat back in his chair. "It is one of the first cities wholly run by Lutherans and reformers. It is a free city, free of ancient superstitions and idolatry. Free of popery and the abuses of the clergy." He looked at Cranmer fully. "I shall look forward to your report."

Sometimes, taking in his lover's scents was as comforting as exploring her with his fingers. Brandon shut his eyes, pressed his face to his wife's pillow, and drew in the essence that lingered from the previous night.

Then he looked out through the bed curtains as his wife slipped on her nightdress, parted the curtains, and climbed into bed next to him.

Brandon put his nose to her neck and inhaled.

Catherine giggled and pushed him off. "How was the queen?" she asked.

"She was beautiful," replied Brandon, his thoughts suddenly back in Katherine's chamber. "It's like a thing of the other world to watch her courage." He scooped his arm beneath his wife, brought her close, and kissed her gently. He kissed her again, urgently.

Catherine looked at her husband, noting his serious demeanor. Her lips pursed. "I remember . . . I remember you once told me that you might sometimes have to make me feel sad. Even if you didn't mean to. Are you *really* going to make me sad?"

"No," said Brandon, touching her face gently. "I swear to you by all that is holy, worthy, and good, that to you I shall be true, and never changing."

She smiled a small, hopeful smile.

"Yet I wouldn't blame you if you didn't believe me. Do you believe me?"

There was a long moment of silence, disturbed only by the distant call of an owl in a tree beyond their home.

Catherine whispered, "Yes." She moved to him and shrugged from her nightdress. Relieved for the moment, Brandon abandoned the worries of the soul for the bliss of the heart and flesh.

That same evening, Henry was alone, pacing the floor of his outer chamber, past tall iron stands holding burning candles that threw long shadows before him. His skin prickled with excitement. He was on the verge of a momentous decision, one he needed to speak aloud, but not to just anyone. He would speak only to his love.

The door opened and Anne entered, curtsying low. The groom closed the door from the outside.

Henry could barely contain himself. "Sweetheart!"

It was clear from the way her brows rose and her mouth parted that she knew Henry had something important to say. Yet Anne, ever Anne, feigned innocence. "Majesty?" she said sweetly. "You sent for me?"

Henry took her hands in his. "How would you like to go hunting tomorrow?"

Anne blinked, confused. "If this is what Your Majesty desires . . ."

Henry continued, barely able to contain his joy. "We shall be away for a while. We may visit people. *Stay* with them."

Anne frowned. She knew he was teasing, but couldn't know why. "Majesty, what is this all—?"

"And when we come back, we shall be alone!"

"Alone?"

"You and I. Here. There will be no third person."

Then he saw she understood. Her eyes opened wide and her hand flew to her mouth. "Do you mean it?"

"I just gave instruction for Katherine to leave."

"Oh, my God!" Anne began to laugh, and then to cry. She threw her arms around Henry and buried her face in his shoulder.

"Are you 'the most happy'?" he whispered.

He could feel the grateful nod, and thanked God things would finally be made right.

The night had grown long, laden with the doubts, joys, and fears of mortals. Rain came and went, and stars found their way through the clouds above the English countryside.

At Chelsea, all was still in the house of Thomas and Alice More. The moon poured silvered light onto the floor of their bedchamber.

Suddenly, More sat up in bed, a strangled shout tearing from his throat. His heart pounded and his hair was plastered to his forehead with cold sweat.

Alice was instantly awake, her hand on his arm. "Husband, what is it?"

"I *saw* it," More gasped.

"What? What did you see, Thomas?"

"I've thought about it a long time. I've thought Luther and Tyndale to be his false prophets. There are so many signs!"

Alice clutched her chest and watched her husband with widening, terrified eyes.

More took a rasping breath. He did not want to tell his wife but he had to speak it aloud, for it had not been a dream, but a vision, a vision from God. "I have seen the Beast! The Antichrist. He is near at hand. Alice, the Apocalypse is almost upon us!"

Katherine stood at the patterned glass window, one hand on the pane, the other to her breast. In the courtyard below, her husband was preparing to leave for a hunting party, one that would keep him away for a long time, given the number of wagons, grooms, and servants accompanying him. The morning was fresh from a night rain, and the world was alive with autumn colors—orange and bronze, scarlet and gold. But Katherine's heart was dark with dismay.

In a moment, Anne Boleyn appeared with her ladies-in-waiting. Anne was dressed in cream-colored riding attire, her brocade hat adorned with bouncing peacock feathers and mesh veil. She practically skipped to Henry, who kissed her openly and helped her onto her sorrel mare. Henry mounted his horse and with a cheerful shout of "Let's go!" he was off, with Anne trotting at his side and the wagons and other riders falling in line.

Katherine withdrew from the window, pulled the draperies, then sat at her desk and picked up her needlework. Not a shirt for Henry, no. He would have no more of those. Today, she was mending stockings.

Footsteps echoed outside the door. Katherine's heart clenched. She knew who it was and what he would tell her. She took a deep and painful breath. A lady-in-waiting opened the door and announced, "My lady, Mr. Secretary Cromwell is here."

Cromwell entered and bowed. "Madam," he said. "His Majesty commands that you be gone from the place within the month and settled at his house The More."

Katherine's fingers moved as if to continue sewing, though she could not look at her hands. She stared, instead, at the window with the drawn curtains. "He—he did not even say good-bye."

"You are free, of course, to take your attendants and servants."

She looked at him, knowing he had no sympathy, but wanting to let someone know of her heartache. "Go where I may," she said, "I remain his wife, and for him I will pray."

"There is . . . one further matter."

Katherine waited.

"His Majesty wishes you to return to him the official jewels of the queens of England."

This came as a shock, and Katherine glared at Cromwell. "No! I will *not* give up what is rightfully mine, to adorn a person who is the scandal of Christendom!" She stood, threw the stocking onto the chair, and turned away from him, waiting until she could hear his footsteps leaving.

The country estate was not particularly splendid—the abode of some noble or other—Henry could not even recall to whom the house belonged at that moment, not that it mattered. He and Anne had been away from court for several weeks, and when they returned, Katherine would be gone and his life would begin anew. He would have all he desired—complete power over all civil and spiritual matters, and a beautiful new queen whom he loved with all his heart.

Henry and Anne enjoyed a private dinner in a small room, feeding each other slices of pears and bits of baked coney. Henry missed Anne's lips with a dab of honey, and he leaned over to lick it off. Anne laughed and kissed his sticky mouth.

There was a knock on the door. Henry sighed impatiently and called, "Yes! Come in!"

A messenger entered the room. He bowed silently, his eyes twitching like nervous spiders.

"Well?" Henry demanded.

"Majesty, I am asked to pass on a message of farewell from the queen. She regrets that you did not wish her good-bye . . . and she inquires after Your Majesty's health."

Henry could not believe his ears. Katherine, yet again, had thrown her godforsaken, insufferable, feigned selflessness in his face. He jumped from his chair, knocking it over, and drove his fist into the messenger's face.

"Tell the queen I do not want her good-byes!" he cried, grabbing the messenger by the shirt and striking him again and again. "I have no wish to offer her consolation! I do not care if she asks after my health or not! Let her mind her own business! I want no more of her messages!" He let go of the messenger, who fell to the floor, blood drooling from the corners of his mouth.

"Do you understand?"

The messenger staggered to his feet, wiped at the blood, and said, "Yes, Your Majesty." He bowed and withdrew from the room quickly.

Henry stood, panting, for a long moment. Then he went to Anne, put his hands on her shoulders, and kissed the top of her hair. "I'm sorry."

"Don't apologize."

Henry considered her words. She was right. "No," he said. He sat beside Anne and gazed at her.

Anne touched his face. "How could it have been different? And yet, everything is beautiful." She smiled with confidence and sweetness. "Don't you think everything is beautiful?"

"Yes," said Henry, leaning down into her love and softness, knowing she spoke the truth. "It is."

The crowd in the courtyard of Whitehall Palace had gathered not to celebrate, but to mourn. Their lady, their queen, was leaving, banished by the king, to places far removed. Katherine stepped out into the gray daylight and walked toward her carriage, doing her best to keep her composure and dignity. Her ladies-in-waiting, who followed close behind, were unusually somber. Weeping well-wishers stepped forward to kiss Katherine's hand; others knelt on the rough ground to show their devotion. Among those gathered were Sir Thomas More and Charles Brandon. Though More did not make a scene, Katherine could see the anguish in his eyes.

A man in the crowd shouted, "God bless Your Majesty!"

Katherine stopped, offered a smile, and said, "Thank you. Thank you, all." Then she walked up to More, who bowed and kissed her hand. Brandon held at a distance, silent, brooding.

"Gracious lady," said More. "Queen of Hearts, there shall be even greater crowds than these to welcome you when you return to London."

Katherine smiled and climbed into the carriage. As it passed through the gates for the last time, the tears she had been holding back streamed down her cheeks.

Ambassador Chapuys did not care for the palace cellars. They were dark, wet, and filled with slimy, skittering creatures. Chapuys was there to speak privately to another, who stood unseen, obscured by shadow and pillar.

"And you will assassinate the Lady Anne?" Chapuys asked, his voice nearly a whisper.

The hidden man answered without emotion. "Yes, Excellency."

"Why?" pressed Chapuys.

"She has come between the king and his true wife. With her lust and witchcraft, she has seduced and bewitched him, even so he considers betraying his lawful wife, His Holiness the Pope, and our Holy Church. She is a goggle-eyed whore, a witch, and deserves no other fate than to be dispatched to Hell."

Chapuys weighed the words. They were heavy, indeed. Then he heard distant footsteps, moving through the cellars in his direction.

"You must not stay longer," he said. "But our prayers and hopes go with you."

There was a rustling, then silence. Chapuys glanced around the pillar, but the man to whom he was talking was gone.

Chapter Four

Atop a desk in a darkened room, a single candle cast its light upon the collection of items—a bowl of fruit, an ornate pistol, a carving knife, a string of rosary beads, and a single red rose. The items appeared to have been placed there with purpose, as if an artist had arranged them.

Beside the bowl was a sheet of parchment paper.

From the darkness emerged the hand of the artist, holding a quill dipped in ink. The pen poised above the paper and then quickly sketched three crude figures—a man on the left with two women to his right. Above the head of the man the artist inscribed the letter *H*. Above the woman on the far right, the artist inscribed a *K*. And above the woman in the center, the one who stood between the other two figures, the artist scratched an *A*.

The artist leaned back again in the darkness, observing the sketch, considering the next stroke of pen.

Whitehall Palace was finely decorated on Christmas Day, its corridors, alcoves, and vast rooms adorned with garlands of greenery, buntings of silver, and holly wreaths woven with gold ribbons. Yet in spite of the season, the mood of the court was subdued, unlike the grand and festive celebrations of years past. Courtiers stood about in small groups, talking quietly.

On entering the court, Mark Smeaton was struck instantly by the solemn atmosphere. He studied the crowd for a familiar face and found Thomas Wyatt. Smeaton approached his friend.

"What *is* this?" asked Smeaton, gesturing about. "It's Christmas! The season of goodwill. What's wrong with everyone?"

Wyatt shook his head. "There's no mirth because everything's different this year. If you hadn't noticed, the queen and her ladies aren't here."

"Why should we be sad about that?"

Wyatt grinned. "You know what the French say: A court without ladies is like a garden without flowers."

Though the presence chamber was gaily adorned for the season, it was nearly empty. On this joyous anniversary of the Christ child's birth there was only the king, Lady Anne, the chamberlain, Henry's grooms, and several courtiers in attendance for the royal giving of gifts. However, Henry would not let anything spoil his first Christmas with his darling. Anne, dressed in a forest green gown and ruby-covered cap, sat upon the chair next to Henry, the chair that had once belonged to Katherine.

The chamberlain announced, "Lady Anne, a Christmas gift from His Majesty."

Henry could see the expectation in Anne's eyes. It was quite delectable.

Two grooms stepped forward, bearing bolts of the finest gold and crimson satin. The cloth was run through with lavish embroidery.

Anne clasped her hands. "Thank you, Your Majesty, for such rich presents!"

"I'm also having a great bed made for you," Henry said with a wink. "It's almost ready."

Anne nodded at the chamberlain, who announced, "Your Majesty, a gift from Lady Anne."

Two more grooms came forward, holding long, richly ornamented spears.

Henry hopped from the dais, delighted. "Boar spears!" he declared. He took one and balanced it in his hand, testing the weight.

"Made after the Biscayan fashion," said Anne.

The king turned suddenly and made to throw the spear at one of the grooms. The groom closed his eyes and bared his teeth. Henry laughed and returned to his throne. "Thank you, sweetheart!"

The cloth and spears were laid out on the sideboard with the couple's other gifts. Then Henry caught sight of a plainly clothed man near the door. He glanced at the chamberlain inquisitively.

So prodded, the chamberlain announced, "This messenger has another gift for Your Majesty."

The messenger stepped forward. Henry could see the gift now, an elegant standing cup of silver set with jewels.

"Come closer," said Henry. "Let me see the cup!"

The messenger moved to the foot of the dais.

"It's very fine. Who sent it to me?"

"Her Majesty Queen Katherine, Your Majesty."

Henry felt heat rise on his neck. "I will not receive it!" he said. "Take it away!"

A groom escorted the messenger, who was shaken but silent, from the room. Henry stared after the closed door.

Anne took Henry's hand and whispered. "Don't let her spoil everything."

Henry steadied his breathing. Anne was right. He squeezed her fingers gently.

The doors opened again, and the chamberlain announced, "Your Majesty, the Chancellor Sir Thomas More."

More strode into the room, followed by a servant carrying a small item covered in cloth. More glanced at the couple on the thrones, at their clasped hands. Anne tried to pull her hand from Henry, but Henry held on tightly.

"Sir Thomas," said Henry.

"Majesty," said More with a bow. "I have a seasonal gift for you. With your permission?"

Henry nodded. More unrolled the cloth, revealing a small silver crucifix, crafted with beautiful detail. Even from the dais, Henry could see the features of the Lord Christ, agonized, nailed to the cross.

It was clear what More was trying to say.

"Thank you, Sir Thomas," said Henry, his expression unchanged. "I will treasure this. And I have a gift for you."

Henry nodded toward a groom, who brought a large golden bowl to More.

"A golden bowl," said More. "A perfect receptacle for trust and friendship. Your Majesty is more than generous, as always."

Henry and More looked at each other steadily. Henry stroked Anne's hand. "We must meet soon, Sir Thomas. There is a great deal of business to do in the management of this kingdom. There is still a great clamor against the privileges enjoyed by the clergy, and their abuse of it. Further measures will certainly have to be taken."

More's words were slow and certain. "I look forward to consulting with Your Majesty."

More bowed and turned to leave.

"Thomas," said the king.

More looked back.

"Happy Christmas."

Anne had retired to her chambers to rest from the morning's celebrations. Henry had willingly let her go, for he had much to do and was bristling with energy.

He searched the corridor outside the presence chamber, ignoring the courtiers who bowed to him on his passing. Then he spotted the chamberlain and took him aside.

"Tell me," said Henry. "Has the messenger from the queen left the palace?"

The chamberlain bowed. "Not to my knowledge, Your Majesty."

"Good. Then retrieve the queen's present and place it with the others. I don't want him trying to present it to me again in public. Do you understand?"

The chamberlain nodded, bowed, and moved away.

Henry let out the breath he'd been holding. He scanned the corridor and spotted Charles Brandon engaged in conversation with some lesser men. Henry gestured Brandon over with a smile.

"Majesty," said Brandon, bowing.

Henry directed Brandon to walk with him. "How about a game of tennis?"

"Good idea," said Brandon.

Henry grinned and slapped Brandon on the back. It was excellent, this moment. Henry felt as he had before, before all the trouble with Katherine and with the Church. He felt as a very young man, full of joy, preparing to spend time at sport with his best friend.

As they walked, Brandon lowered his voice. "Can I be honest with you?"

"I hope so!" Henry said gaily.

"Are you really going to marry the Mistress Boleyn? Whatever the consequences? Whatever her history?"

Curses! Cannot a single moment be free of interferences? Henry pulled Brandon aside, away from the prying ears of the others in the hallway.

"That's my affair," he said.

Brandon looked at the king and said nothing.

"Why did you ask? What do you know? What do you mean, 'whatever her history'?"

Brandon seemed unable to spill his thoughts now that Henry was angered.

"I asked you a question," Henry insisted.

"I—I have it on very good authority that she and Thomas Wyatt were lovers. Apparently she fornicated with him on many occasions, sometimes brazenly entering his chambers at night."

Henry spit air. "I've heard that rumor. She denies it."

"Well, she would, wouldn't she?"

Henry grabbed Brandon by the collar. "I said she denies it!" he shouted. His voice echoed up and down the corridor.

Brandon stared at the floor. Henry studied his old friend for a moment and then elbowed him roughly aside. "Go," he said, "and play with yourself!"

Archbishop Warham loved the music of God's house. He sat on the front bench of the chapel of Whitehall Palace, his gnarled and pained hands folded, head nodding in time with the sweet harmonies from the choir of boys in the loft. The music carried his spirit to the arched ceiling and beyond, bringing him peace amid a time of great personal and great public turmoil.

Someone slid onto the bench beside him. Warham opened his eyes. It was Thomas Cromwell. Warham was sad, for he had hoped for another minute of solitary communion with his Lord.

"Your Grace," said Cromwell. "May we speak?"

Warham nodded.

"I am here to inform Your Grace, as archbishop of Canterbury, that the king intends to put a bill before the new session of Parliament."

"What does it concern, Mr. Cromwell?"

"In the first place, it means to deny the pope much of the revenue he now receives from the English Church. It will also lay indictments against the privileges of leading clergy in this country."

Warham sighed and put his hands on his stiffened knees. "Mr. Cromwell, what must be the cause of this further attack upon our Holy Church?"

"Surely, Your Grace is aware of a large and growing sentiment in the House of Commons, and elsewhere, against spiritual abuses? People can see for themselves that the monasteries are already sitting on great wealth that could be better applied elsewhere, for the good of the whole commonwealth. For the good of ordinary, hardworking people."

"This does not strike me as an attack against abuses," Warham said, "but rather an open attack upon our faith, and the faith of our ancestors."

Cromwell rose from the bench, and inclined his head with a cool smile. "If that's your judgment, Your Grace, it is not mine. And neither is it the king's."

Warham watched Cromwell as he left the chapel, pausing for a moment to take in the music that had risen to a glorious crescendo. Bowing his head, Warham began to pray.

The gardens of Whitehall Palace in the winter bore a new kind of splendor, one of frost-covered hedges and ice-sheeted ponds. Dressed in a voluminous white fur cape, Anne strolled arm-in-arm with Henry, pressed close to him. Henry savored the solitude that came with braving the frigid weather while the rest of the household, save two grooms following twenty paces behind, stayed inside. They moved without talking for a long time, Anne's head against Henry's arm, meandering through the maze of boxwoods and around the sleeping flower gardens.

After a while, Henry broke the silence. "I thought you might like to know. I have asked the French ambassador to come and see me. I want to draw up a new treaty of alliance with France. To nullify the threat of the emperor."

"I'm glad," Anne said. "You know my sentiments toward France. But, forgive me, what is it to do with me?"

"There is another reason for wanting to see him. I intend to arrange a visit to France for both of us." He smiled. "I want to present you, formally, to King Francis, as my future wife, and the future queen of England."

Anne stared. "Oh, my God!"

She threw her arms around Henry and laughed. He drew in the cold air. That, and Anne's love, was a cleansing balm upon his heart.

They moved on, circling the largest fishpond, where Anne paused to toss a stone onto the ice to watch it crack.

"The Duke of Suffolk has taken it upon himself to repeat the gossip," said Henry. "About you and Mr. Wyatt."

Anne made an exasperated sound. "And do you believe any of it to be true?"

"If I did, would I be walking here with you?"

Anne gave a Henry pout, then a hug. She gazed back at the shattered ice on the pond. "I suppose you've banished the Duke from court?"

Henry didn't answer. Anne looked at him and he gave her a smile. It was all he could give her for the moment. He hoped it was enough.

"Nan!"

Anne entered her apartments, rubbing her elbows vigorously and calling for her servant. Though the wooden pattens she had strapped beneath her shoes had kept her feet from the puddles, she was still damp and chilled.

Nan Saville, a narrow-faced girl with pale curly hair, hurried from another room. "Yes, madam?" she asked as she curtsyed and took the cloak from Anne's shoulders.

"Draw me a bath. The walk has made me cold."

Nan curtsied again, then hung the cloak up by the hearth and stoked the fire beneath a pot of already steaming water.

"I've got such exciting news, Nan," said Anne as she brushed her hair back and moved to her desk. "We're going to Paris. I'm going to be presented to the king!" Then Anne looked down at the desk. Her eyes narrowed.

Amid her other items—her inkwell, books, and papers—was a crudely drawn picture, placed where it could be easily seen. The picture showed three figures. One was a man labeled *H.* A second figure was a woman labeled *K.* The third figure, drawn between the other two, was a woman labeled *A.*

The female figure labeled *A* was headless.

Anne stared, stunned into silence, her mouth open. Then she found her voice. "Nan!"

Nan hurried to her mistress' side, her cheeks pink from the fire.

"Who has visited this apartment today, Nan?"

Nan bit her lower lip. "Nobody, Madam. Not to my knowledge."

"Were you here the whole time?"

Nan looked at the floor. "No, Madam. I slept a little." Then she looked at her mistress. "Why?"

Anne lifted the drawing from her desk, holding it by the very edge, not wanting her fingers to be too close to the picture. "Here is a book of prophecy," she said slowly. "This is the king, this the queen, and this is myself, with my head cut off."

Nan looked at the floor, clearly disturbed. Her voice trembled. "If I thought it was true, even if he was an *emperor*, I would not marry him to end up like that!"

Nan's simpleminded simpering brought Anne a new, sudden resolve. She tossed her head back. "It's nothing! Only a bauble!" She shook the picture as if to prove it was only paper, nothing more. "In any case, I'm resolved to marry the king, so my issue will be royal, *whatever* happens to *me*."

Nan, put in her place, backed away and turned to the fireplace to draw the water. With Nan no longer looking on, Anne shuddered, then rolled the paper up and shoved it into a drawer where she would not have to see it.

Nürnberg was a bustling trade city, even during the cold months. Markets and trade fairs bustled with bundled shoppers and vendors selling poultry, goats, eggs, rugs, and fabrics. Spires of hillside churches poked at the base of heaven. Gathered around the churches like chicks around a hen were houses of timber frame and whitewashed plaster. Atop the tallest hill in the city was the Kaiserburg, the German king's grand, walled castle.

Thomas Cranmer stepped from the cobblestone street into the front hallway of a large house and was led by a stocky servant along the corridor to a well-lit room at the far side of the dwelling. Cranmer paused at the open doorway, gazing about at the adornments on the paneled walls. There were copper engravings and woodcuts featuring animals and plants, paintings representing the life of Christ, and prints of landscapes and cityscapes. The ceiling was crossed with wooden beams, a string of dead game birds and rabbits hanging from one.

At a large table in the center of the room stood two men and a young woman. They were engrossed in a dissection of a rabbit that lay, legs splayed, in a wooden pan.

". . . *Sie lugen, inneres, Adern*," said the elder man, who was unshaven and disheveled, with long hair and a dirty shirt. "*Und Sie sehen die Leber . . .*"

The younger man and the woman nodded in fascination.

Cranmer cleared his throat and the male spectator looked up. He was close in age to the other man, though a bit tidier.

"Mr. Cranmer!" he said. "You must forgive us. We were so preoccupied with Mr. Dürer's lesson."

Cranmer stepped forward to shake the man's hand. "I can well imagine it."

"I'm Andreas Osiander," the man said. "And this is Nürnberg's genius, Mr. Albrecht Dürer—"

Cranmer nodded.

"—and my niece, Katharina Prue."

Cranmer bowed. "Sir. Madam."

Katharina was a petite woman with large brown eyes, dressed in a green gown, apron, and white cap. She gazed directly at Cranmer with an expression that unnerved him. He glanced away toward the rabbit on the table.

"We are establishing here in Nürnberg, Mr. Cranmer, a Christian commonwealth," Andreas began. "You will find that many things are different. For example, there are no more private masses, only public services in German. We have been liberated from thousands of years of slavish adherence to the Roman Church. No longer do we have to worship images and false idols. Mr. Dürer's work exemplifies our beliefs."

Cranmer tilted his head, confused.

Dürer gestured at the animal in the pan. "He means this is a *rabbit*! Not a symbol of something more than itself. It doesn't represent anything, except itself. Its lungs, heart, and kidneys, its eyes and fur—they are all real. They are all rabbit."

Cranmer moved closer to the table, and Dürer took it as an invitation to continue.

"But the rabbit, humble as it is, is still, like all of us, one of God's creations. So the more and better we study it, the closer we arrive at God's great design. Frankly, I would rather have a rabbit than a painted statue of a saint any day. It reveals God's glory a great deal more."

"Indeed," said Andreas. "I only wish they did not eat all my lettuces!"

They all laughed.

"What a truly exciting intellectual ferment you have created here," said Cranmer.

Katharina nodded. "It's not just intellectual. As a cleric, Mr. Cranmer, no doubt you will be interested to know that, in Nürnberg, the clergy are allowed to marry. We think marriage is a more honorable and more fulfilling course for a priest." She touched her chin and raised a brow. "What do *you* think?"

Cranmer, for a moment, was unable to think at all. Katharina's direct gaze had stolen his thoughts.

"I tell you!" Bishop Fisher began his declaration to the noisy, packed chamber of Parliament. "We shall continue to insist upon the Church's immunity from secular interference; and we shall continue to insist upon it because that immunity is ordained by *God*."

In the vast gallery, tucked amid countless other nobles and onlookers, Thomas and George Boleyn listened on. George's arms were crossed. His father's teeth were set against each other.

Fisher continued. "And this immunity from secular interference should extend to the ordained priests and servants of our Holy Church, who should be free from the threat of murder and harm, by the use of poison or any other foul means, when their only crime has been to obey God's law and the sanctity of the Church!"

Many of the bishops in attendance applauded and called out words of approval, clearly moved by the potential danger to their brethren and the grievance of the circumstance. Cromwell stood silently and solemnly among them.

Boleyn drew his son close. He whispered, "The king can't allow this. The vote is crucial."

George nodded.

"One way or other," said Boleyn, "he must break the Church, once and for always."

Sir George Throckmorton, a member of Parliament, found Sir Thomas More in his private chamber of Parliament, chatting quietly with William Peto, a square shouldered, balding Franciscan friar. The room was small, lined with bookshelves bearing More's collection of massive volumes, crucifixes, and religious statuary. A single window shed light on More's desk, upon which sat even more volumes and stacks of papers. Upon noting the visitor, Peto shook More's hand, nodded at Throckmorton, and left the room.

"I am most glad to see you, Sir George," said More. "I know you are a good Catholic man, who has never been afraid to speak his conscience."

Throckmorton inclined his head. "So, in truth, should every man, Your Honor."

More smiled, though it was a smile that seemed to hide much pain. "Yet these days," he said, "it seems, many can be bullied into silence, or worse, into acting against their conscience." He clasped his hands behind his back and began to pace back and forth. "Make no mistake, these next few days will determine the future of our faith. Whatever words Mr. Cromwell uses, however he dresses his case up with honeyed words, it amounts to the same—he is demanding that the clergy submit themselves totally to the king's will, and to secular authority."

Throckmorton drew back at the intensity of More's words.

"God forbid he should ever succeed!" More said, his voice growing louder. "If he did, there will be no more church, no more religion, no more spiritual life in this kingdom! Mr. Cromwell might as well rape the Blessed Virgin!"

Shocked, Throckmorton crossed himself. "Your Honor!"

More stopped in the center of the room, steepled his hands beneath his chin, and bowed his head as if in momentary prayer. Then he looked up at Throckmorton. "That is why I ask you, and others like you, to stay true and strong. If you do, then you will deserve God's great reward, and much worship will come to you personally. And in time, believe me, the king himself will thank you."

Throckmorton nodded, feeling pinned by More's unblinking stare.

Cromwell leaned over papers on his desk, gazing at the hearth upon which a healthy fire crackled. He coughed and rubbed his mouth. The room held a filmy layer of smoke; it was well past time a servant cleaned out the flue. Cromwell dipped his pen back into the inkwell.

The office door opened and a servant announced, "His Grace, the Duke of Suffolk."

Let's have this over with, thought Cromwell, putting his pen aside.

Brandon walked into the office, bowed, and waited for Cromwell to speak.

"Your Grace," said Cromwell. "I have His Majesty's order to banish you from court. You have displeased him, it seems."

Brandon, as expected, looked stunned. Then he found his voice. "Who *are* you, Mr. Cromwell? I feel I should know, but somehow I don't."

"I am exactly as Your Grace finds me. I serve His Majesty to the best of my ability."

Brandon's face darkened. "Someone told me you were once a mercenary soldier."

"I saw some action in my youth. As did Your Grace, I believe."

"But I was never a soldier of fortune." Brandon stepped forward and leaned on the desk, a clear attempt to intimidate. "If I displeased the king it was in a good cause."

"I'm sure. Although some would argue otherwise."

"Like you?"

"I would never have the temerity to argue with Your Grace."

Brandon let out a single, bitter chuckle. "Not to my face anyway."

Cromwell drew a paper from a stack to his right, and showed it to Brandon. It carried Henry's bold signature. "Here is the order," he said. "You are to leave court at once."

Brandon snatched the paper and stormed from the office.

"We give thanks for the reign of the King's Grace," Friar Peto addressed the Sunday congregation from the marble lectern of the Chapel Royal of Whitehall Palace. "And we ask God's blessing on him, and on his people."

On the front pew, side by side in their most regal clothing, sat King Henry and Lady Anne. Their hands were folded and still, giving an appearance of humility and piety. Beside the couple was Thomas More, his head inclined to the friar's words. The interior of the chapel glowed, the tiled floors freshly cleaned, the railing and lectern polished, and the altar topped with gold and silver chalices and crosses.

Friar Peto cut a glance at More, but More did not react. It did not matter. The friar knew More agreed with what he was about to say, and more importantly, that God agreed.

"But on this holy day," Peto continued, leaning forward, his hands clutching the sides of the lectern, "we are obliged to say that some of Your Highness's preachers are too much like those of Ahab's days, in whose mouths was found a false and lying spirit. Theirs is the gospel of *untruth*, not afraid to tell of license and liberty for monarchs, which no Christian king should dare even to contemplate."

Murmurs of unease began among the worshippers, a low rumbling that sounded much like a coming quake. Henry's eyes narrowed. Anne put her hand atop his as if to calm him.

Peto's voice rose with the glory and truth of his words. "I beseech Your Grace to take heed, not to pursue the course you seem to be taking, or else you will follow Ahab, who married the whore Jezebel, and surely incur his unhappy end, *that dogs will lick your blood* as they licked Ahab's, which God avert and forbid!"

Courtiers and some of the clergy leapt angrily to their feet to shout the friar down. Henry turned abruptly to stare at More, as if suspecting he was involved. But More gave the king a passionless gaze and said nothing. In an instant, several courtiers rushed forward to grab Peto's arms and hustle him out of the chapel and into the adjoining corridor, where Cromwell stood, snarling.

"You shameless friar!" Cromwell cried. "You will be sewn into a sack and thrown into the Thames if you don't speedily hold your tongue!"

Peto gathered himself and stood boldly before Cromwell. "Make those threats to your fellow courtiers," he said. "As for us friars, we take no account of them at all, since we know very well that the way to Heaven is just as good by water as by land."

With a small yet defiant smile, he shoved past Cromwell and walked quickly away.

Henry sat upon his throne in his presence chamber, flanked by Cromwell and Thomas Boleyn. He leaned forward, his fingers clutching a rolled paper, his mouth full of words he wanted to shout but keeping them at bay for the moment. He would let his secretary begin this meeting.

On the floor had been gathered bishops and prelates of the church. They were clustered in several groups like beetles before a predatory bird. Bold, brash beetles adorned in red satin, but insects all the same.

"My lords," said Cromwell, raising his hand slightly. "In your supplication, you have asked the King's Majesty to defend what you are pleased to call the ancient rights of the Church. I'm afraid his answer will not please you. It is that, in return for royal favor and protection, the Church must agree to hand all legislative power over to His Majesty."

The beetles muttered among themselves, their tongues clicking.

Cromwell's voice rose. "The king also wishes bishops not to have the power to arrest persons accused of heresy."

The beetles grew louder. Henry had had enough. He banged his arm on his chair then stood, bringing on silence.

"I have here, in my hand," he declared, lifting the paper high, "the oath which all members of the clergy make to the pope at the time of their consecration! It is clean contrary to the oath they swear to *us*! My beloved subjects, we thought the clergy were also, *wholly*, our subjects. But now we see that they are only *half* our subjects . . . if they are subjects at all!"

Henry rose and stepped from the dais, his face hot, his arms shaking. "My lords," he said. "I demand to know! Whose subjects *are* you? Mine . . . or the pope's?"

The beetles looked at the king. They did not answer.

Elizabeth Darrell, Queen Katherine's lady-in-waiting, opened the door and stepped back to allow Thomas Wyatt to enter. The More, a cold, bleak house in the forested countryside days away from London, was Katherine's residence. It had once belonged to the former Cardinal Wolsey, a favored and well-tended manor, but now it was forgotten, untended, and decaying. The front room was decorated with bits and pieces of what was now the queen's former life—several carved chairs, an oaken trunk, a shelf bearing numerous volumes, and a large portrait of the queen, herself, on the wall.

"Mr. Wyatt," said Elizabeth with a quick curtsy, uncomfortable to be alone in his company.

"Lady Darrell," he said. "I have come on the king's business. Where is the Lady Katherine?"

"Her *Majesty* is at prayer. She cannot be disturbed."

Wyatt nodded, and pulled a letter from the pouch at his waist. The missive bore the great seal. "I am charged to deliver this."

"What is it?"

"A command that Lady Katherine return her official jewels."

Elizabeth looked at the letter but did not take it. Wyatt kept his eyes on Elizabeth as he stepped past her to put the paper on a small table.

"Lady Elizabeth . . ." he began.

Elizabeth still would not meet his gaze. "What do you want?"

"You know what I want," he said teasingly.

Elizabeth touched the crucifix at her neck and felt her cheeks grow warm. She stepped close to Wyatt and whispered, "Mr. Wyatt, I have no intention of becoming your mistress or anyone else's. I shall be a virgin when I marry, but I doubt I shall marry at all. I would rather be a bride of Christ!"

Wyatt tilted his head, clearly doubting her words. "A nun? I don't think so!" He bowed. "Check your pocket." With that he turned and let himself out.

Elizabeth felt inside her skirt pocket. Wyatt had slipped a small folded piece of paper into it. Opening it, she could read the perfectly penned heading: "Poem Dropped Into a Lady's Pocket."

She quickly returned the poem to her skirt and hurried to her own small room, where she settled upon her mattress and read the poem by moonlight.

> *Would God thou knewest the depth of my desire,*
> *Then might I hope, though nought I can deserve,*
> *Some drops of grace would quench my scorching fire . . .*

Parliament's chamber was packed with prelates and members, shoulder against shoulder, standing as the trumpets sounded, and bowing low as King Henry strode in. The king was dressed in his finest clothing—breeches of purple and silver brocade, jeweled shoes, and mantle so encrusted with diamonds, rubies, and pearls as to make the fabric almost invisible. His crown glistened. Cromwell and three councilors flanked the king.

Henry took his chair and surveyed the assembly. His gaze fell upon Sir Thomas More, dressed in his scarlet robes. From More's position beside the bishop, it was clear which side the chancellor had chosen. Thomas Boleyn stood apart from More and Fisher, arms crossed, his neck tight and hands cold, awaiting the outcome of the meeting.

"My lords, Your Graces," began the king. "What is your decision? Do you still deny me, or do you accept the authority of your king?"

There was no answer, but the crowd slowly parted to let a frail and tottering figure pass through to the dais. It was Archbishop Warham, carrying a velvet cushion upon which was a scroll of paper.

"Your Majesty," said Warham as he knelt unsteadily before the dais and held out the cushion. "Here is the Submission of the Clergy, to Your Majesty's will." He lowered his head and placed the cushion on the step.

Ah, thought Boleyn. *They have surrendered. The Church is broken.* He could clearly see the triumph on the king's face.

The crowd shifted about uneasily. Boleyn walked closer to Fisher and More, both of whom looked grim.

"I have never thought I would live to see this day in England," Boleyn said to More.

More glanced at Boleyn yet addressed Fisher. "Now, by act of Parliament, heretics will be free to swan around the streets of London without check."

Fisher bowed his head. "If I could weep, Sir Thomas, I would weep tears of blood."

CHAPTER FIVE

Henry stood alone in his private chambers, arms behind his back, waiting. The door opened and Cromwell entered, announcing, "Your Majesty, Sir Thomas More."

More stepped into the room, dressed once more in his black robes, a white leather pouch in his hand. He kneeled before the king without word.

"Sir Thomas," said Henry.

"Your Majesty," said More.

Henry took More by the arm and raised him to his feet. There was a great agony in his old friend's eyes, and at that moment, it hurt Henry's heart.

"Majesty," said More. "I have come to offer my resignation from my office as chancellor. I ask Your Highness to allow me to withdraw from public life, so I might spend what remains of my life provisioning my soul and in the service of God." He held out the pouch. "In this bag is the great seal of my office, which I now find too heavy to hold."

Henry gestured for Cromwell, who took the pouch. More seemed relieved to have it gone from his hands.

"I discharge you most unwillingly," said Henry, considering the humble man before him. "In all the services you have done for me, Sir Thomas, I have found you always to be most good and gracious, in private and in public affairs."

More bowed. "Majesty, I . . ."

"Yes?"

More took a breath, then said, "I promise on my honor that I shall never speak publicly of Your Majesty's Great Matter. But in private now, I confess to you, as someone who once enjoyed Your Majesty's confidence and friendship, my deepest belief that, if Your Majesty saw fit to be reconciled to Queen Katherine, the divisions and hurts of your kingdom would at once be healed."

Henry stared at More, the small feeling of tenderness immediately knocked down with Sir Thomas's comment.

"There. I have said it. And now my lips are forever sealed." More bowed and turned to move away.

"Thomas!" called Henry. More looked around. "I shall hold you to that promise."

It was a grand and festive evening. The Great Hall was filled with cheerful laughter, music, and dancing. Henry was particularly happy, as the French ambassador had just informed him that his trip to France had been arranged, and that Lady Anne would be received with all due honor by French society and the queen of France, herself.

Anne left the dancing to approach Henry in his chair. With her was the young musician he'd seen about court.

"Sweetheart," said Henry playfully, nodding.

"Your Majesty," replied Anne with a curtsy, her tone equally lighthearted. "This is the gentleman I told you about, Mark Smeaton."

Henry considered the well-dressed young man. "Mr. Smeaton, you are welcome. Lady Anne has told me a lot about you. She says you play very well. Play something for us."

Smeaton nodded. A servant handed a violin to Smeaton, and Henry raised his hand, causing the other musicians to stop in the middle of their song. Smeaton pulled the violin close and with skilled fingers, bowed out a lovely tune. The court listened in awe. As the music played, Henry took Anne's hand and drew her close.

"I know the Duke of Suffolk was wrong to say what he did," he said in a whisper. "But, is it possible we can forgive him?"

Anne frowned. "If you forgave him so quickly, some people might think that there was some truth in what he said."

Henry chose his next words carefully. "Yes, but, to refute them—to answer the matter directly—to show how much I trust you, I will do a more important thing."

Anne looked at him doubtfully.

"I will invite Mr. Wyatt to come with us to France," said Henry. "Then no one can accuse me of jealousy, or the slightest suspicion."

Anne's lips parted in a smile. She kissed him. "My love. You have no reason to be suspicious. Nor ever will have."

"There is something else," said Henry, "something important to be done before we sail for France."

"What? Tell me?"

But Henry only shook his head and kissed her again.

Cromwell and Thomas Boleyn applauded politely as Smeaton finished his tune and began another. Then they picked up their private conversation.

"You will be interested," said Cromwell. "I've received a letter from Cranmer, who is still at Nürnberg."

Boleyn leaned close and asked urgently, "What does he say?"

"Firstly, he says that, contrary to what some people here think, the revolution in religion has not in the slightest affected the good order and prosperity of the people."

"I have no doubt that's true," Boleyn replied. "Indeed, I'm sure religious liberty will only increase the people's prosperity."

The conversation paused as two laughing courtiers passed the men. Once they were out of hearing range, Cromwell said, "However, Mr. Cranmer left his most eloquent testimony til last. It appears that in Nürnberg, the clergy are allowed to marry. And Mr. Cranmer has taken advantage of this."

Boleyn's mouth dropped opened in astonishment. "He got *married*?"

"Just last week, to Miss Katharina Prue, niece of Andreas Osiander, one of the country's leading theologians."

Boleyn shook his head, bemused. "It won't do his career much good here. Being illegal."

"It's illegal for the clergy to marry *now*, yes," said Cromwell.

Boleyn cocked his head, no longer smiling. "What are you saying? You want priests to be able to marry?"

Cromwell led Boleyn to an unoccupied alcove. "Perhaps I have never explained myself properly to you, Your Lordship," he said, his hand still tight around Boleyn's arm. "When, to you and others, I have attacked the practices of the Catholic Church, I have never really been interested in reforming them. On the contrary. My real and only interest is in *destroying* them."

Boleyn looked at Cromwell, at the purpose in his face and the lack of apology in his eyes. He felt a kinship he'd not felt before. "On the contrary, Mr. Secretary," he said. "I think we understand each other perfectly."

"Make way!" shouted the garter king of arms, the chief herald of England, dressed in gold and red and carrying his crown-topped scepter. "Make way there for Lady Anne! Make way!"

The morning was perfect for ceremony. Beyond the arched windows of the presence chamber flew the first spring birds, fluttering happily, seeking out nesting places in the palace eaves. The sun was kind and warm, spreading golden fingers upon the floor, creating a carpet for the elegant procession entering the room.

Lady Anne moved gracefully, preceded by two young pages who were taking their jobs so seriously that their faces were screwed into tight little scowls. Anne, herself, was stunning in a crimson velvet gown edged in soft fur and heavy with gems. Her black hair was tied about her shoulders with a string of pearls. Following Anne were noble ladies bearing a crimson velvet mantle and gold coronet. Henry, on his throne, caught his breath at the sight of his dearest, coming to him in such pomp and pageantry.

To the king's right off the dais stood Charles Brandon, the Duke of Suffolk, welcomed back to court, and the Earls of Oxford and Arundel, Thomas and George Boleyn. The room was otherwise filled with courtiers, nobles, and officers of arms in their embroidered, belted tabards. The French ambassador stood amid them, clearly enjoying the regal affair.

Anne knelt before the king, her eyes downcast.

Cromwell unrolled the patent and read in a clear, steady voice. "To all and singular as well nobles and gentills as others whom these presentes shall come. It is the king's pleasure, by this patent, to confer on the Lady Anne Boleyn, in her own right, and on her offspring, the noble title of Marquess of Pembroke. And also by this patent, to grant her lands worth one hundred thousand pounds a year, for the maintaining of her dignity."

Anne looked up, beaming. Henry stepped from the dais and lifted the lady to her feet. He held out his hand for the mantle and placed it upon her shoulders. Next was the crown, which he put gently upon her head.

"And now," he said, reaching toward Cromwell, who handed him the paper, "here is the patent of your nobility."

"Thank you, Your Majesty," said Anne, peering at her king from beneath lowered lids. Henry's heart swelled. Such beauty, obedience, adoration. If God Himself knew the ecstasy Henry knew at that moment with his lady, then the Almighty was a joyous creator, indeed!

Henry took Anne's hand and led her to the French ambassador.

"Majesty," said the ambassador, bowing to Henry. Then he bowed to Anne. "And *Madame la Marquises.*"

Anne replied in her most gracious tone. "Thank you, ambassador. You know how much I love France and its people."

She slipped her arm into Henry's and they left for the court with the horns sounding.

"Mistress Darrell!" Thomas Wyatt called up the rugged hill on the outskirts of The More. Elizabeth Darrell moved down the grassy slope toward the tree where he stood, her hands out before her so she would not tumble. Breezes caught her hem and tossed it about, wildflowers bowing as she passed. It was a lovely scene, her childish nature, her buxom and womanly bounties bouncing before her.

When Elizabeth reached the tree, she stopped and took a paper from her pocket. "I came to give you your poem back."

Wyatt moved close to Elizabeth and noticed her shiver. It made her all the more desirable.

"I am sorry you are unhappy," she continued, "burning, as you say. I am sure I have done nothing to cause it."

"Nothing?" Wyatt replied. "My lady, you are full of causes! Your hair, your eyes, your lips. All are causes of my desire." He put his index finger to her cheek, then drew it to her lips. She inhaled sharply, a mixture of desire and trepidation in her eyes. Holding her shoulders, he pressed his lips against hers.

Over the hill, a church bell began to ring, steady, insistent. Elizabeth gave in for a moment, but then pushed away. "Please don't. I must go to Mass."

Wyatt stroked her neck. "Yes, I know. You must. Just stay an instant." He drew her close again and kissed her softly, then slid his fingers to the ribbons at her shoulder, untying them, allowing him to pull the sleeve free. The white skin of her naked arm stood up against the chill of the air.

Elizabeth gasped as Wyatt removed the second sleeve. "What are you doing?"

"Giving you a chance to be penitent, my beautiful, pious lady."

She glanced in the direction of the tolling bell. "Please, don't . . . !"

Wyatt unlaced her bodice and opened it, revealing small, virginal breasts. He kissed them roughly, pushing her body against the scabby trunk of the tree. Elizabeth squeezed her eyes shut and began to recite bits of Mass in Latin, her words quivering with fear and Wyatt's increasingly powerful, rhythmic groping.

And the bell continued to toll.

Archbishop Warham's body lay upon a bier, countless candles encircling him, his hands, holding a silver crucifix, folded reverently over his chest.

Many had come to pay their respects—old and young, noble and commoner.

Bishop Fisher and Sir Thomas More watched the procession from a corner of the room.

"He is fortunate to be gathered now into Heaven," said More. "Before the final ruin of the church he loved and served."

Fisher frowned. "You are resigned then, to our ruin?"

"I don't know what else can be done. We fought and we failed. All I want now is to be left in peace, to write, to pray, in private."

"But surely we've another duty still to act in the interests of Christendom, whatever the cost!"

"I'm not afraid of the cost, Eminence. But I have abjured the public realm. It no longer interests me."

More moved silently to the bier and gazed down at the waxy face of the archbishop. "As it no longer interests His Grace."

"What do you think?" Anne spun about in her new gown, an elegant creation of gold cloth covered in diamonds over a silver kirtle. Across a large table lay several other new dresses, one of red velvet, several of brocade, yet more of silks, many trimmed in fur.

Hands on hips, Henry watched his lady, thrilled to see her joy at preparing for the trip to France.

"You gave me this damask," she said, lifting a green gown from the collection and holding it against her breasts. "Do you like them? I *so* much want you to be proud of me!"

Henry picked up a black satin nightdress. "Oh, I shall be." He gestured toward a groom, who stood beside the door. The groom opened the door, allowing in a servant carrying a large casket inlaid with mother-of-pearl. "And these will also help."

The servant bowed and passed the casket off to Henry, who opened it for Anne to see. "The jewels of the queens of England. They will be reset for you."

Anne looked between the king and the jewels, unable to speak. She reached for one of the bracelets and held it out before the window, staring, unblinking, at the perfection of cut, the dazzling brilliance of the priceless stones. "I—I don't know what to say."

"Yes, you do."

Anne put the bracelet back. "I love you," she said. "I love you with my every breath. With every fiber of my being. I love you and I am yours."

Henry drew his lady close, kissing first her lips, then his mouth hungrily taking in her cheeks, chin, and slender neck.

"Wait!" said Anne. "You have been so kind to me. Let me be kind to you."

Henry drew his head back slightly to see what she meant. But he did not have to see, he could feel her hand traveling down his chest, where her fingers deftly opened his trousers. Anne kissed him again, then wriggled her fingers into his braes and slipped his member from within the linen. She began a steady stroking that caused the king to groan with pleasure and arch his body into her firm grip.

"Oh, my love," she said softly. "My love . . ."

The darkness of the cellars pressed heavily upon Ambassador Chapuys as he hurried toward the spiraling stairs that would take him up to a rear corridor of the palace. The secret conversation he'd just held echoed in his mind.

The man with whom he spoke would be traveling to France with the king. He had agreed to carry out his mission if there was a good opportunity.

"I tell you this," Chapuys had told the man in an urgent whisper. "Should you succeed in killing the king's whore, you would be the beloved of God, of His Holiness, and of the emperor, and truly of all the faithful people of England."

"And if I die in the attempt?" the man asked from the shadows behind the pillar.

"Then the emperor would look after your family here on earth. And you would be welcomed into Heaven by a fanfare of angels."

Chapuys knew this to be true. The Lord would bless this glorious goal and the soul who dared all to save the Church. God would also bless the one who made the arrangements.

Though for some reason, at that moment, it felt as if there were a demon in the cellar's darkness, nipping at his heels as he quickly took the staircase.

Calais, in northern France, was a beautiful region, lush and English occupied. The grand mansion at Exchequer was the ideal residence for Henry and Anne during their extended stay. It was there they would entertain and be entertained by the French king, Francis. Though Henry and Francis had met in Calais years earlier to seal an alliance against the Spanish, the alliance had been a failure. This time, however, English hopes were high that the wounds were mended and all would be well between the heads of the two countries.

The feast laid out in the Grand Hall was exquisite, a bounty boasting porpoise, carp, and venison pastries. King Henry was dressed in a burgundy velvet doublet and coat. His guest, King Francis, wore a cloak of red silk studded with jewels. The young French king had striking features—a sharp chin, long nose, and a prominent brow, and he sported a heavy yet well-groomed beard. His lids were often lowered, as if he savored the fact that most things and most people were beneath his station. Side by side at the table, the men looked to be the best of friends, even brothers, as they celebrated over the rich foods. Musicians entertained from the gallery above the kings, offering delicate love songs and lively tunes on harp, lute, and shawm. Among them was Mark Smeaton, who presented several of his compositions on the violin.

Thomas Boleyn sat at a table not far from the royal pair, watching closely, listening carefully, chewing on a pastry. He had been commanded to attend Henry on this trip, as had his son George, along with Charles Brandon and Thomas Wyatt.

"This is a wonderful feast!" exclaimed Francis as he dug into a bone with a marrow spoon. "But where is she? Where is the Lady Anne?"

Henry offered an enigmatic smile. "She will be here."

Francis licked the marrow from the spoon, then tossed the hollowed bone into a bowl. "I'm sorry my wife and sister changed their minds about meeting her. But what do you expect? *Souvent femme varie. Et bien fol qui s'y fie!*"

Henry laughed. "Women are often variable. And only madmen believe them!"

Francis stroked his beard. "I have it in mind, brother, that you and I should make arrangements for a joint crusade. Such a crusade as our forefathers took upon themselves, for their own glory, and the glory of God Almighty. What do you say?"

"Like Richard Cœur de Lion!"

Francis, filled with wine and confidence, grinned broadly. "*Absolument!* Warriors of God!" He leaned in toward Henry. "And no one will be happier than His Holiness if we should commit ourselves to reconquer the Holy Land."

A servant brought two large, spouted flagons of fresh wine. Henry grabbed one before the servant could put it on the table and drank straight from the serving vessel. His expression changed a little and he looked at Francis full in the face.

"But still we would be *joint* leaders of the crusade, yes?"

Francis shrugged, smiled. "Of course, we would be equals. Why not?"

Boleyn turned his attention from the king to Charles Brandon, who was with his wife, Catherine, holding her hands and enjoying her company as if they were still newlyweds. Boleyn dabbed his mouth, stood from his chair, and strode over. On seeing Boleyn's approach, Brandon leaned forward as if protecting his wife from a poisonous snake.

"Your Grace," Boleyn said with a forced smile. "I am delighted to see you returned to His Majesty's good graces. It gives me pleasure to invite you and the Duchess to dine with us while we are in Calais."

"Not as much pleasure as it gives me to refuse your invitation . . . my lord."

Boleyn lowered his voice. "There are rumors that Your Grace secretly supports the queen and that you are against the king in this Great Matter. And yet, for so long, you took immense pride in being totally indifferent to the machinations and politics of this world."

Catherine looked from Brandon to Boleyn, the corners of her lips twitching.

"So, what happened to you?" asked Boleyn.

Brandon laughed sourly. "I grew up!"

Boleyn raised a brow, inclined his head, and went back to his seat, not at all surprised with the answer he'd been given.

Dining continued into the evening, with conversations and music flowing about the tables, mingling and rising cheerfully to the vaulted ceiling. Suddenly, the music stopped. The abrupt quiet caught the attention of everyone in the room.

A drummer began a steady, hypnotic beat. A door on the far side of the banquet room opened, and six ladies entered. They were dressed alike in loose dresses with sashes of crimson satin. All the ladies' faces were hidden behind sparkling masks.

There were sounds of approval and applause as the masked dancers stepped into the center of the room, their movements measured with the beat of the drum. One by one the masked ladies chose a Frenchman with whom to dance. The last lady selected King Francis, who cast a look of surprise and pleasure at Henry. Perhaps he guessed, and hoped, that the mysterious woman was Lady Anne. The dance began, the ladies moving in unison like flowers in a breeze, the men following along, some trying to catch glimpses behind the masks by tilting their heads.

Mark Smeaton had escaped the other musicians and joined the diners. This performance did not require a violin, and he was famished. He selected a succulent leg of duck and a tankard of wine, and settled himself behind a young woman he'd not seen in a long time.

"Lady Mary," said Smeaton.

Mary Boleyn spun about in her chair and smiled.

"You must feel excited to be back in France," said Smeaton, "after all your adventures here."

Lady Mary was still a beauty, her hair swept into a ribboned sculpture at the nape of her neck. "Tut, Mark," she said. "You ought to remember that I'm still in mourning for my poor husband."

"Well, I wouldn't have called him poor," said Smeaton. "But dull, certainly."

Mary laughed. "And impotent."

"Really?"

"The only time I ever saw him stiff," said Mary with an exasperated puff of air, "was when he was lying in his coffin." Then Mary looked at the French dancers in the center of the room. "I can't wait to ride some young French stallion while I'm here."

Smeaton grinned. "Between you and me, neither can I!"

The masked dancers took their curious partners through the paces. Francis was clearly anxious to discover the identity of the lady with whom he danced. The lady behind the mask tried her best not to laugh at his eagerness.

"Do I know you?" he whispered.

The lady turned, dipped, and circled Francis silently. Then, the music stopped. The ladies froze in position. Francis waited, his brows drawn, a smile lingering. Henry joined them on the floor and stood behind the lady. Slowly, Henry untied the mask and lifted it from her face.

"Ah!" said Francis. "*La Belle* Anne!" He kissed Anne's hand and looked at Henry. "With your permission?"

Henry smiled and nodded. Anne bowed to the French monarch, glad to be done with the masquerade. Francis took her hand and led her away to a small window seat in a private corner.

"I remember you so well," said Francis, still holding Anne's hand. "When you and your sister were here, as ladies to my wife."

"*Vous êtes aimable,*" said Anne. "But there are some things, perhaps, which Your Majesty knows about me which I would rather you kept secret and never mention to the king."

Francis smiled. "*Madame la Marquise*, I am a Frenchman. I would never betray the secrets of a beautiful woman, who must naturally have a great many."

Anne watched his face for a moment. "Do you really support my marriage to the king?"

Francis's fingers held Anne's gently. "*Bien sur.* For one thing, I hate the emperor, so that anything that discomforts him, like the divorce of his niece, pleases me immeasurably. But also I know you are a friend of France, so we can do business." Then he took his hand away and gazed for a moment out the window at a season-barren garden. His mood had changed. Anne felt her heart quicken.

"There is something else?" she asked.

"*Oui,*" said Francis, looking back at her. "It is not my place to say this, Madam, but perhaps we know each other well enough. The fact is, the station you will be asked to occupy is not an easy one, especially for those not born to it. I do not say this to patronize you. You are too intelligent for that. Rather I say it to warn you. It is much harder to have everything than to have nothing. If I had not been born to be king, I would not have wished that fate upon myself."

Anne nodded slowly. "I understand."

"I hope you do."

Their conversation over, Anne and Francis stood, and Anne kissed his cheek. Then she excused herself to find her sister.

Anne and Mary sat side by side, holding hands, watching the glittering people in the sparkling hall, much like they had years ago when they were but girls.

"When you remember how it was," Anne said at last, "when we were here before, could you ever have imagined this, Mary?"

Mary replied, "Not for all the world. "But then I am not so clever as you."

"I promise you," said Anne, her voice lowering, her cheek coming close to her sister's, "and I can tell only you, that the thing I have so longed for will be accomplished here."

The look Mary gave Anne told her she understood.

A gale rose up from the sea, tossing violent winds and rain over Calais. Trees of the forest bowed in the wake of the storm, trembling against its power, some losing branches and limbs to its power, others bending low and avoiding the worst of the blasts. The land sounded as if it were in great pain, wailing and groaning without relief into the night.

The banquet was done, the music ended, and the guests gone. The great house was quiet but for the winds that shook the stone and battered the windows.

Through the darkness, a man moved from room to room undetected, searching, a weapon clutched to his side. Patiently, steadily, he traveled the hallways and rooms until he found one with a candle burning. He took a silent breath and stepped toward the door, where he hid in the shadows.

Lady Anne Boleyn sat alone at a desk, writing. Several candles illuminated the desktop, the quill pen, and the face of the man's quarry.

He lifted the wheel-lock pistol and aimed.

A far door opened. Henry came into the room, walked to his lady, and kissed her hair.

The man hesitated. Should he kill them both?

No.

That was not God's will.

He lowered the pistol and backed away.

Lightning flashed against the window glass, bringing into clearer focus the murals on Henry's bedchamber walls. Henry, dressed only in his linen braes, stared at the paintings. They were colorful and brazen, depicting scenes from the book *Metamorphoses* by the Roman poet Ovid. In life-sized glory, plants were changing into animals, animals into humans, humans into gods.

Yet these were not gentle, pastoral depictions. The males bore bountiful and erect phalluses; the females round and ample breasts. The figures reached for each other boldly, clutched each other, unabashedly enjoying each others' sensual charms.

Henry opened the door that separated his room from Anne's. For a moment he could not see her, for she had blown out the candles. The only light in the room came from the glowing clinkers in the hearth. But then lightning erupted again, and he could see her there in the center of her bed. She was naked, willing and waiting.

Henry went to her, his heart pounding in his temples and his loins. She drew her arms about his neck and his body down to hers.

"Now, my love," she said. "Let me conceive. And we shall have a son!"

Chapter Six

Sir William Pennington, one of Charles Brandon's principle retainers, strode up a narrow London lane toward Whitehall Palace, stepping carefully around the mud and manure, accompanied by his short-legged servant. Pennington's cape was of a heavy, rich weave and did a fine job keeping the chill from its wearer's arms and back.

As the noble and his servant passed the door to a noisy tavern, four drunken men spilled out. One spit on the ground and called, "Pennington!"

Pennington looked back, disheartened to see that the four inebriates wore the Boleyn colors and crest. They were the Southwell brothers, a hotheaded lot with wagging tongues and hair-trigger tempers.

"The Southwells," said Pennington with a shake of his head. "How's your master, Boleyn?"

Richard Southwell, the eldest of the four, puffed up his chest. "That's Lord Rochford to you, Pennington!" he crowed.

"*Sir William* Pennington to *you*, Southwell."

The drunken quartet made disgusted sounds. As Pennington made to move on, two of the brothers ran forward to block his path.

Southwell leaned in toward Pennington, who held his position, his feet planted apart. "And how is your master, Master fucking Brandon? Does he still persist in using the foulest and most abusive language against my master's daughter, Lady Anne, who is soon to be queen?"

"The *Duke* can speak for himself."

"I'm asking *you*!"

The hair on Pennington's neck rose, and the muscles of his arms tightened. "His Grace wants nothing to do with the elevation of the king's *whore*."

"What's that?" demanded Southwell, looking at his brothers as if he were shocked. "Who's a whore?" In a moment, all four had unsheathed their swords.

"Let me pass," said Pennington.

"Not until you've paid for that!"

The brothers lunged forward. Pennington and his servant drew their swords and countered, knocking back the drunkards but with great effort, for it was two against four. Pennington, a skilled swordsman, drove his steel forward, the blade glancing off Richard Southwell's weapon. Southwell growled and leapt aside, only to bring his sword up and over again, cutting a vicious slash in Pennington's cape, close to the man's ribs. Pennington looked to his servant, who had been separated by two of the brothers and was struggling to keep the blows from slicing his neck.

"Fetch the Duke!" Pennington shouted to the servant. "Go!"

The servant struck right and left, panting and snarling, then managed to break free and stumble away. Pennington feared for a moment that one of the Southwells would chase the servant down, but they all turned their attention to Pennington. He had no choice now but to run.

Pennington warded off several more blows and then spun about and dashed toward a church up the narrow street, his boots scrambling for purchase on the cobblestones. He took the front steps two at a time and slammed through the door.

There was no one in sight, only the holy saints, carved in wood, watching from their nooks in the walls. Pennington hurried down the aisle and dropped to his knees before the altar. He crossed himself with his left hand, his heart pounding. His right hand clutched his sword.

The doors banged open and the Southwells burst into the church, swearing loudly. Pennington jumped to his feet, holding his sword out against the four.

A priest, huffing and puffing around a bulky girth, hastened from the back, drawn by the sounds of angry men.

"Father!" said Pennington, never taking his eyes off his enemies. "I seek sanctuary in this place."

The priest clasped his pudgy hands. "Of course, my child." Then he nodded at the Southwells. "Put up your swords, gentlemen. This is a place of God."

Richard Southwell bared his teeth. His brothers followed suit. With swords raised, they advanced on Pennington.

"Defend yourself!" Southwell snarled.

The priest held up his hands as if they would magically stop the assault, but when the brothers were within feet of Pennington, he crossed himself and stepped back.

Richard Southwell lunged forward, the tip of his blade grazing Pennington's cheek. Blood welled along the ragged line. Pennington drew his sword and held it out.

"You dishonor yourself," he said. "You dishonor your master. And you offend God, by offering violence here." He took a breath. "I'm sorry for how I spoke."

Southwell cried, "Not sorry enough!" He lunged again but Pennington deflected the blow. One of the brothers jumped forward with his sword, which he drove in toward Pennington. Pennington, panting, knocked this blow aside as well. A third brother came forward with his sword. Again, Pennington drove the blade down and away.

The blows came more quickly, brother after brother, air whistling against flailing steel, metal crashing against metal. Pennington countered left and right, high and low, backing up the steps to the altar, his arms aching now, knowing that he could not keep this up much longer, praying to God it would not end as he feared it would.

"Stop!" the priest shouted. His voice reverberated against the walls, the ceiling, and the figure of the Blessed Mother Mary on the altar. "For the love of God, enough is enough!"

This seemed to bring the Southwells to their senses. Three of them stopped in midthrust, hesitated, and lowered their weapons. They looked at each other, their breaths coming in noisy gasps.

Richard Southwell lowered his sword, as well, but he did not look at his brothers. His eyes were blood red, and it seemed as if all reason had drained from them. Suddenly, he lunged forward up the steps and buried his blade deep into Pennington's heart. Pennington grunted, dropped his sword, and collapsed.

"You fool, Richard!" cried one of the brothers. "You've killed him!" Richard stared at the dead man and threw his blood-streaked sword aside.

The church doors slammed open. Charles Brandon ran in, followed by Pennington's tight-faced servant.

Brandon stared at the ghastly scene. Then he shouted, "Murderers!" He grabbed his sword and raced up the aisle.

The three Southwell brothers stepped away, but Richard held his ground, staring at his sword across the room. Brandon reached the front of the church, his sword ominously slashing the air to his side.

The priest was beside himself. "My lord," he begged. "In the name of our Lord, one murder has been committed here already!"

Brandon took the steps to the altar and pointed his sword at Richard Southwell's chest. "You scum!" he said.

A Southwell brother stammered, "Your Grace, we—"

"Shut up!" said Brandon, not taking his eyes off Richard. "You're both dead men!"

"I beg you," said the priest, almost in tears. "Those who commit murder in church have committed sacrilege. They are damned in the eyes of God and doomed to suffer in purgatory for eternity." He gestured toward the Southwells. "So it is with these men. But I pray God, as you are a good Christian, do not follow them there!"

Brandon's fingers strained against his sword's grip, his eyes blazing, set on the man who had murdered his retainer. Richard stared back, taunting, silent. Brandon lowered his sword, sheathed it, and walked back down the aisle to the front door. Suddenly, in the corner of the church, he saw Thomas Boleyn. At some point the man had slipped in, unnoticed, to watch the struggle. Brandon and Boleyn glared at each other.

"Boleyn," said Brandon, the word foul on his tongue.

Then he walked out into the gray day.

Anne's chambers at Whitehall Palace were no longer those of a lady, but of the queen-to-be. Courtiers clambered mightily for an audience with Anne, spending hours milling about the corridors and her outer chamber for a chance to be noticed, spoken to, and hopefully, remembered. Anne's ladies had learned well how to protect their mistress, and Henry had sent additional male servants to guard against any unruly situation that might arise.

"Suddenly everyone is beating a passage to Lady Anne's door," said Mark Smeaton when he found Thomas Wyatt among the crowd in the outer chamber, standing next to a small table by a window. Wyatt had a quill in hand and paper on the table; his inkwell was set in the windowsill. "Why do you suppose that is, Mr. Wyatt?"

"Because people always prefer a rising to a setting sun, Mr. Smeaton."

Smeaton considered this, and then nodded at the paper. "What are you writing?"

"A satire."

Smeaton smiled. "Do you find all of this funny?"

Wyatt shrugged. "It has its funny side, like all serious things. For example . . ." Wyatt tapped the feather end of the quill to his cheek. "And this will make you laugh, Mark. Cromwell just told me I've been appointed to the Privy Council. I have no idea why. Why should poets and gamblers be made legislators? It's ridiculous."

"But everything in life is ridiculous, really," said Smeaton, clapping Wyatt on the shoulder. "Especially our coming into it, and our going out. Don't you think? To suppose otherwise is simply human vanity."

Wyatt tried to think of a witty answer, but the door to the inner chamber opened and Anne appeared, dressed royally with a tall, jeweled headpiece, followed by several ladies.

The buzz in the room was instantly focused as courtiers tried to get in front of each other to speak to the lady. Anne's attendants formed a circle around her, giving her time to prepare for the introductions. But instead, Anne made a straight line to Wyatt, pushing through the clot of visitors, her ladies trotting after her.

"Mr. Wyatt!" she said, taking his arm. Her face was flushed and her voice trilled with excitement.

"My lady," said Wyatt, bowing deeply. He could feel Smeaton's gaze on him, curious.

"You know what?" asked Anne.

"No," said Wyatt. He didn't know what to guess, or if he should guess. Once he was comfortable around Anne Boleyn, so comfortable that he would tell her his dreams and she would tell him hers. But now, everything was different.

"I have a furious hankering to eat apples," she said with a light giggle, "such as I've never had before. It started three days ago."

"Apples?"

Anne frowned and whispered a little too loudly, "Yes, apples!"

Wyatt turned his hand up to show he still didn't understand her point.

"The king told me it was a sign I was pregnant! But," she added with a toss of her head, "I don't think it's anything of the sort!" She laughed again, then, with her ladies parting the way, returned right away to her private chamber.

Wyatt watched after, as did several others nearby who had heard the declaration.

Smeaton stepped over to Wyatt and vocalized what the poet was thinking. "What was *that* all about?"

"What news from France?"

"None to give Your Majesty any satisfaction."

Henry shook his head and paced his private outer chamber. Outside, the world seemed unaware and unmoved by his nervous excitement. Tiny emerald vine leaves fluttered at the corners of the arched windows. A small flock of swallows flew past, chased by a raven.

Cromwell continued, "Although he promised to make representations to the pope on Your Majesty's behalf, King Francis did no such thing. He—"

Henry waved his hand. "It doesn't matter. What else should I have expected from the king of France? The fact is I now have a good reason, a very good reason, for not waiting for the pope's decision. The annulment of my marriage must be declared immediately."

"Well," said Cromwell, "since your Majesty is now head of the Church, you yourself could—"

Henry veered from his pacing and walked up to Cromwell, his finger pointing. "No. The annulment should still be declared by the church proper, which is to say, by the archbishop of Canterbury."

"As your Majesty knows, there remains a vacancy for that position."

Henry considered this, taking a breath, holding it, letting it out. He said, "I think I know exactly who will suit."

Thomas Cranmer ignored the sweat streaming down his forehead as he hammered a lever along a panel on the huge wooden crate and pushed down with all his might to loosen the seal. The crate, four feet wide by four feet tall, had been delivered by horse cart to his London home more than an hour ago, in broad daylight, his "belongings from Germany," the driver had called them. Twilight had come, and Cranmer was working in secret in his parlor.

Belongings, indeed! Cranmer thought anxiously as he moved the lever to another place along the seal, hammered it in, and pushed down. *Please be all right, my dearest belonging!*

At last the panel came free, and Cranmer shoved it aside. He stared into the darkness, one hand to his heart, one hand moving forward slowly. Then warm fingers reached out and grasped his own. Cranmer laughed aloud with relief. Carefully, he drew out his wife, Katharina, who was disheveled and exhausted and wrapped in a blanket. He held her gently, closely, thanking God she was safe. Then he offered her water from a stoneware mug. She drank noisily and desperately. When done, she returned the mug to her husband.

"Katharina," said Cranmer. "It's over now. You're here. Welcome to England."

"I'm very relieved to see it, Thomas," she said, her voice raspy. "Very relieved indeed. I thought I was going to die." She gave Cranmer a small smile. "It's not the nicest way to travel, even for an illegal wife!"

"I'm so sorry." Cranmer drew his wife close, carefully. Katharina touched his lips and pulled his face to hers, kissing him passionately.

Then she leaned back, looked about at the dark and tiny room and said with a touch of dismay, "So *this* is England?"

Chelsea was a large and comfortable estate, a stone mansion southwest of London along the Thames, surrounded by gardens and orchards, fields and forests, a place intended to be apart from the world of politics and intrigue. Now resigned from his office, Sir Thomas More had come home to Chelsea from Whitehall Palace looking for peace, to be with his family, and time to pray alone in his closet. None of it, however, had come to pass.

More, Chapuys, and Bishop Fisher sat at a table in More's library, the shadows of twilight beginning to fill the corners of the room. More's wife, Alice, stood apart from the men, waiting to see if they needed anything, wanting yet not wanting to hear their conversation.

"They want to make Cranmer archbishop!" declared Fisher.

Chapuys nodded. "I wonder if the pope knows of the reputation Cranmer has for being devoted heart and soul to the Lutheran movement?"

"He is the lady's servant," said Fisher. "He was once chaplain to the Boleyns! He ought to be required to take a special oath not to meddle with the divorce."

More rubbed his pounding forehead. "Of course he'll meddle! That's what they want! They don't care about the Holy Church anymore. They don't even care about the people!"

"The king, in his blindness, fears no one but God," said Chapuys.

"It's the queen I care about," said More. He pushed away from the table and went to the lead-patterned window to look out at the night. "What will happen to her? They say Anne Boleyn hates her openly, and her daughter, too. That she's made threats against the child!"

More glanced over at Alice by the door, and saw the dark expression on her face. He went to her, offering what he hoped was a smile of encouragement, but it was clear she would have none of it.

"Those are dangerous words," she whispered to her husband. "Think also of the lives of your own children!"

Pope Paul III leaned over his desk, his right sleeve pushed back and held with a black ribbon, dipping his pen into the inkwell and signing a steady flow of correspondences and papal bulls passed to him by a dutiful Cardinal Campeggio. Campeggio stood before the desk, leaning on his cane, taking care not to grunt with the effort each move required.

The pope scanned each paper briefly, almost absently, before adding his signature. One, however, caused him to stop and look up at the cardinal.

"What is this?" the pope asked.

"The king of England asks your approval to appoint a new archbishop of Canterbury, after the death of Archbishop Warham."

This caused the pope to smile. "Ah, and the people say he doesn't care! What's the name of the candidate?"

"Thomas Cranmer."

The pope thought for a moment, yet couldn't recall having heard the name before. "What do we know of this . . . Cranmer?"

Campeggio raised a brow. "Virtually nothing, an obscure cleric. A nobody." He cleared his throat. "There are strong rumors he is a secret Lutheran."

"Then we should not approve of his appointment!"

"Not in my opinion, Holiness."

But the pope hesitated, staring at the paper, tapping a curled, arthritic finger on the paper. Campeggio waited, silently.

"And yet," said the pope, "we want to give the English Church the opportunity to return to its first allegiance, and to our true faith. We want to please the king. We want to make him beholden to us. What better way to please him than to approve the appointment of a nobody? After all, what harm can a nobody inflict upon our Holy Church?"

The dark, clammy cellars of Whitehall Palace were a place without a sense of daytime or nighttime. The only light to enter this place came by the hand of man, not the hand of God.

On this January day, a small gathering stood in one of the wide, low-ceilinged rooms used for storing barrels of grain and beer. Candles and lanterns had been placed on stands and atop barrels, offering a forced sense of cheeriness to the place. Guards had been posted at each door to assure no uninvited persons would enter.

A lowly clergyman named Rowland Lee stood before King Henry and the Lady Anne, clutching a Bible, looking at once uneasy and uncomfortable. Henry didn't give a fig as to the man's ease or comfort; the man had been commanded to do a job and he would do it. Anne did not seem to be bothered by the lowly surroundings; she was radiant in her silvery dress, a gown that did not hide the small, rounded bulge of her abdomen.

Henry looked impatiently at the witnesses and then at one of his grooms, William Brereton. "Where is he? Where is Suffolk?"

Brereton blinked and said nothing. The young groom couldn't know that he, like Lee, was unhappy for reasons Henry couldn't fathom and, in truth, couldn't care less about. What was a groom's concerns compared to a king's?

There were hasty footsteps down a narrow corridor and the guards parted to allow Charles Brandon passage. Henry could see immediately that Brandon did not want to be there. He was attending only on command.

Henry turned back to Lee and gestured for him to get on with it. Lee opened his Bible and addressed the king, the lady, and the witnesses.

"We are gathered here together in the sight of God Almighty, to join in holy matrimony this man and this woman. And will you both answer that you will keep all these coming days rightful, with right-wiseness and discretion, with mercy and truth, so help you God?"

Anne reached for Henry's hand and squeezed it. Henry swallowed down his frustration, and focused his attention away from Brandon and onto the ceremony that would unite him with his beloved, forever.

"Your Grace," said Katherine as Charles Brandon entered her sparsely furnished room. She could not rise from her chair; her body was yet again drained from illness, and it took all the energy she possessed to accept a visitor. In times past she would have received the Duke of Suffolk reluctantly or not at all. Now, however, she knew his loyalty was genuine. As the Duke stepped forward and bowed, Katherine held out her hand.

"My lady . . ." said Brandon, carefully kissing the outstretched hand.

My lady? she thought sadly. *So it is no longer "Your Majesty."*

Brandon stood straight, clearly despondent over the reason for his visit. He spoke haltingly. "His Majesty has ordered me here. He asked me to tell you—His Majesty warns you not to try to return to him, since he is now married—to the Lady Anne."

Katherine's eyes narrowed.

"From henceforth," said Brandon, "you must abstain from using the title of queen. You will be referred to as . . . the Princess Dowager of Wales."

Katherine shook her head violently.

Brandon continued, speaking the words he had thought through in his mind, agonized at having to hear them on the air. "You will have to cut your household expenses. In his . . . generosity . . . the king will allow you to keep your property, but he will no longer pay your servants' wages or . . . your household expenses."

Katherine drew a sharp breath. "And my daughter? What about Mary? May I see her?"

Brandon looked at the lady, then bowed his head. He had no answer about young Mary. "Madam, forgive me."

Katherine closed her eyes and offered a quick prayer to God for strength. She looked at Brandon, tears blurring her vision. Her voice softened. "You know something, Mr. Brandon, if ever I had to choose between extreme happiness or extreme sorrow, I would always choose sorrow." Brandon's eyes met hers; he was confused. "For when you are happy you forget about spiritual matters. You forget about God. But in your sorrow, He is always with you."

Brandon's voice was raspy with emotion. "God bless you and keep you, my lady." He bowed, and walked out.

Elizabeth Darrell stepped into the room as Brandon stepped out. She glanced between Katherine and the window, where in a moment, Brandon could be seen trotting off on his bay mount, his shoulders stooped in despair.

"You heard?" asked Katherine.

"Yes, Madam," said Elizabeth.

Katherine sat as straight as she could, even against the pain and weariness in her body. "As long as I live, I will call myself the queen of England. And if there is no food for either me or you, then I shall go out and beg for it, for the love of God."

Elizabeth put her hands to her face and wept piteously.

Henry smiled broadly as Thomas Cranmer, dressed for the first time in his elegant and heavy ecclesiastical robes, joined Henry in the king's private chambers. The young man looked amusingly self-conscious, though Henry knew it wouldn't be long before he found himself too busy with his duties to even think of himself. Henry glanced at Cromwell, who stood beside the king's chair. Cromwell smiled back.

Cranmer crossed the floor silently, head up, peering from the corner of his eye at the royal portraits on the walls, the massive and colorful tapestries, the marble and silver figures upon the wall-side tables and sideboards, the massive and intricately carved desk. He was clearly struck to the core by his first visit to the king's most personal rooms. Cranmer reached the king's chair and knelt, the robes seeming to pull him down.

"Your Grace," said Henry. "Rise. We are most pleased to see you confirmed as archbishop."

Cranmer stood and spoke quietly. "Your Majesty, I must confess that I had some scruples about accepting the office, since I must receive it at the pope's hand. This I felt I neither would nor could do, since Your Highness is the only supreme governor of this Church of England."

"You are not beholden to Rome," said Henry. "Only to God, and to me. And now, as the principle minister of spiritual jurisdiction in our realm, I ask you to determine, once and for all, my Great Matter. Whether or not my first marriage was valid." He looked Cranmer straight on, making sure the archbishop knew exactly what he was to do.

"Majesty," said Cranmer, "I shall address the question with the greatest urgency, and presently pronounce my verdict." Henry nodded, giving Cranmer his leave. Cromwell turned to follow after him.

"Mr. Cromwell," said Henry.

Cromwell stopped and spun back. "Majesty?"

"Since the departure of Sir Thomas More, England has lacked a chancellor."

Cromwell waited.

"I am trusting you to fill that office."

Cromwell's normally unemotional countenance gave way, and it took a moment for him to find his voice. Then he bowed deeply. "Majesty!" he said.

Thomas Wyatt sat hunched over his desk late in the evening, his neck and shoulders tight from the hours spent composing a new poem. He didn't hear his servant open the door. When the servant spoke "Sir," Wyatt's hand flinched, causing a jagged scrawl where a word was to have gone.

But then Wyatt saw the visitor the servant had ushered into the room—Elizabeth Darrell. Quickly, Wyatt snapped shut a small silver medallion on his desk, rose, and walked over to her. The soreness in his shoulders gave way to an urgent stirring in his groin.

The servant withdrew quickly, and with that Wyatt leaned in to kiss his lovely lady. But Elizabeth turned away.

"No, not that," she said.

Wyatt was irritated at her reaction. "Then what?"

Elizabeth looked at the floor, then back at Wyatt. "I came on behalf of my lady, though not with her permission. Thomas, she is in a most wretched way, abandoned and betrayed. It seems so cruel of the king to humiliate her in every way, pretending to marry that harlot—"

"What?"

"Did you not know? The Duke of Suffolk came to tell her that the king has married—" But Elizabeth stopped, unable or unwilling to speak the name.

"Anne Boleyn?"

Elizabeth nodded. Wyatt touched her cheek. "But what can I do about any of that?"

"You are now a Privy Councilor," she said. "And a client of Mr. Cromwell. I thought you could speak up for my mistress."

Wyatt shook his head. He felt for Elizabeth's agony, but what she was asking was impossible. "You must know that Mr. Cromwell is the least likely man to sympathize with your mistress."

"But what about *you*? If you still have feelings for me, then you could speak out for her."

"I—" There was nothing he could say. He could do nothing to help her, for trying to do so would be to put himself and his position in jeopardy. "I'm sorry."

Elizabeth stared at him, dumbfounded, and walked out.

Wyatt stared at the empty space where she had stood, then slowly returned to his desk. He gazed at the poem on which he'd been working, over which he'd been agonizing. The paper was crossed through with countless corrections in his attempt to make the perfect verse.

Wyatt sat, clicked open the silver medallion, gazed at the tiny image of Anne Boleyn, and picked up his quill again.

Pope Paul stood solemnly as the chamber in St. Peter's Church was cleared of foreign ambassadors and papal officers. His soul was heavy with sadness and anger. The king of England had made his royal bed and would soon be forced to lie in it. As the spiritual father of the kings of Europe, Pope Paul had tried his best to ease the pathway back to the Church for Henry. But Henry had taken his own path, a path of destruction, and soon, if he did not turn back, he would be lost.

The meeting had been brief and to the point. The pope had told the ambassadors and officers that he condemned the marriage of Henry to Anne and he declared it null and void. He had also stated the validity of Henry's marriage to Katherine had not been decided, and that the king had until September to take Katherine back as his wife, on pain of excommunication.

Pope Paul lowered himself back into his cushioned chair beneath a large wall painting of Christ clearing the temple. He uttered an audible sigh and a silent prayer.

"Holy Father?"

The pope glanced up. Cardinal Campeggio was there, leaning on his cane. Beside him was a young man of average stature and large nose. "This is the English gentleman I told you about, Master William Brereton, King Henry's groom."

"My son," said the pope.

Brereton stepped forward, dropped to his knees, and kissed the pope's ring. The pope gently raised him to his feet, then stood and kissed the young man on both cheeks.

"We are grateful to you for bringing news of these terrible events, and for all you have tried to do to prevent them."

Brereton's voice was tight with despair. Worry lines made his young face appear older. "I tried, Holy Father, but I failed."

But the pope gave him a kind smile. "Who knows, my son? God works in mysterious ways. Cardinal Campeggio tells me you want to stay in Rome now, and not return to England."

Brereton nodded. "Yes, Holy Father. I would rather remain with the flock of the faithful than live with the wolves who daily devour us."

Pope Paul smiled again, and gestured for both men to sit in smaller chairs near his. When they were settled, he said, "Recently, Master Brereton, I have ordained a new and very special order of monks. They are the *Militantis Ecclesiae,* the soldiers of Jesus. These Jesuits, as they are called, these soldiers, will go where others fear, where often there will be great danger, in order to promote the Catholic faith and take the word of God to heathens and heretics."

Brereton's expression shifted from angst to curiosity, returning the natural smoothness of youth to his brow.

"I see already your passion for this cause," continued the pope. "I beg you, join the order, join the crusade against heresy, and return to England."

The pope heard the young man gasp, ever so softly, and it was a sound of utter joy and purpose.

"Will you do that, in my name, even though it is a great deal for a father to ask of a son? Yet still, I ask you."

Brereton fell from his chair and came on his knees to the feet of the pope. His eyes were already wet with tears. He buried his forehead against the pope's feet and covered his feet with grateful kisses.

"Benedictio Dei omnipotentis," said the pope, closing his eyes and blessing his young solider. *"Patris et Filii et Spiritus sancti descendat super vos et maneat semper. Amen."*

"Amen," said Brereton, so softly that only he, the pope, and God could hear.

"Madame la Marquise?"

Anne spun about on her toe, the gown she was holding against her flying out in a swirl of red and purple. She had been alone in her private chamber at Whitehall Palace, exploring her trunks and chests for the best outfit to wear at her coronation. Her bed drapes were tied back as tightly as they could be tied, and the mattress was weighed down beneath a rainbow array of fabrics and furs.

"No," said Anne with a smile. "Just sister."

They embraced, then Mary gently touched Anne's belly. "How are you? Both of you?"

"We are both very well." Then Anne's voice lowered, so her ladies in the next room would not chance hearing her. "Listen. The king and I have visited a famous astrologer. He confirmed what the physicians say, and what I know in my heart, that it is a boy."

"Oh, Anne!" She embraced her sister, her chin quivering with joy. "Darling Anne!"

"The king is overjoyed," Anne continued, her voice growing quivery with emotion. Mary noticed and touched her sister's arm gently. "He keeps wanting to tell people, but I tell him not to. Not yet, anyway."

Anne tossed her head, regaining her composure, and took Mary's hand and led her to a large table against the wall. Spread upon the table and tacked to the wall behind it were countless drawings of costumes, stages, arches, banners, and drapes—all decorated with the heraldic designs of the falcon and the crown. "The German painter Hans Holbein has been designing all kinds of things for the coronation procession," Anne said. She felt the emotion rise again in her throat, a hot, choking knot of anxiety.

"They're very beautiful," began Mary, gazing at the sketches, but then she saw Anne's face and stopped. "Are you scared?"

Anne said nothing, but turned away, her body shaking.

"Anne? What is it?"

Anne could hold it back no longer. She dropped to the floor, her gown billowing out around her as if to catch her fall. Mary gathered her sister in her arms and held her as she sobbed uncontrollably.

* * * *

As Bishop Fisher left the Chapel Royal following Mass, Thomas More met him in the corridor.

"Your Grace, I have some news," More said.

The two men found a quiet place near a small window. More pulled a piece of paper from inside his robe. It was clear from Fisher's tight expression that he knew the news could not be good.

"I have learned that Mr. Cromwell is to present another bill to Parliament," said More, "the Act of Restraint of Appeals, and so under its innocuous title does it conceal its most revolutionary intent."

"What does it say?"

More read, "'This realm of England is an empire, governed by one supreme head and king, and owing no allegiance except to God.'"

Fisher made a hissing sound.

"In the future, final appeals on spiritual matters will be heard, not in Rome, but in England," More said. "Where the king will now enjoy," he began reading again, "'plenary, whole and entire power, preeminence, authority, prerogative, and jurisdiction.'"

"Which means that the act prohibits the hearing of the king's nullity suit by the pope!" Fisher spat out, disgusted. "And, by the same token, bars the queen from appealing to the Vatican against any decision made here."

More nodded. "No English sovereign has *ever* been granted such absolute power."

"Poor Katherine!"

"It's worse." More could barely utter the bitter words. "There are rumors that the king has married 'that woman' in secret. And that she is already with child."

"No!"

"All the world is astonished at it. And even those who took part, so they say, know not whether to laugh or cry!"

In a small room at Dunstable Priory, a gathering of clerics—Henry's ecclesiastical court—sat about a wide table, hands folded in pious patience, waiting for the pronouncement. Thomas Cranmer, the king's appointed archbishop, stood at the head of the table in the robes and skullcap of his position, nodded solemnly to his fellows, and read the decision—the union of King Henry of England and Katherine of Aragon was null and void. The king's marriage to Anne Boleyn was valid and lawful in the eyes of God. Cranmer put the judgment on the table and affixed it with the great seal.

Chapter Seven

Cromwell's office at Whitehall Palace was well furnished and comfortable, with dark wood paneling, portraits and paintings of holy scenes, and windows overlooking one of the flowering orchards to the north of the palace. Cromwell took solace in this room, where he could think, plan, and savor the position to which he had risen over the years.

The office door flew open and King Henry stormed in, his face flushed. Cromwell, at his desk, immediately put down his quill. "Majesty?"

"How are the preparations for the coronation?"

"Well, Your Majesty."

Henry stepped closer and leaned on the desk. His fingers tapped the wood fretfully. "I want them to outrival in splendor those for *any* of her predecessors."

"I think I can assure Your Majesty that such will be the case."

Henry pushed away from the desk and went to the window. There was something he wanted to say but it was obviously very difficult for him to speak it. Cromwell waited. Then, at last, the king spoke. "I want the people to love their new queen as I love her. And if I love her, why shouldn't they?"

It was Cromwell's duty to allay the king's fears regardless of what might be true. "I assure Your Majesty," he said, "that they *will* love her, and will have every reason to do so."

Henry looked over his shoulder at Cromwell. It was clear he wanted to believe his words, though was having a difficult time doing just that.

"I hate the Boleyns!"

Catherine Brandon looked up from her needlework. Her husband was seated in his chair near the hearth of their palace apartment, his face taut and grim. Catherine could see the frustration roiling behind his eyes. It hurt her heart to have him suffer so.

"But I must attend on the king and that bitch of his tomorrow," Brandon continued. "What did Wolsey call her? The black crow!"

Catherine put her needlework down. "Can you not plead some indisposition?"

"I could, even though the king has appointed me high constable for the day." He spit air. "If I did His Majesty would remove my head, and then I should be genuinely indisposed."

Catherine got up, knelt beside her husband's chair, and stoked his face gently. "So keep your head. It's a pretty head, in any case. And I don't want to lose it, either." She kissed his cheek, his forehead. "But store up your knowledge and your anger. Don't act impulsively; it's always a mistake. But one day, with others so disposed, use them both. And if you can, bring her down and destroy her."

Brandon's eyes widened slightly as a newfound admiration registered on his face. "How old *are* you?"

Catherine smiled.

Come early May, preparations for Anne's coronation were in earnest throughout the palace, Westminster Abbey, and the City of London. The royal processional route, a full mile in length, which would begin at the Tower and end at Westminster, was strewn with fresh gravel to soften the journey. Following Holbein's detailed plans, workmen constructed numerous stands and performance stages along the route and decorated them with colorful, elaborate tapestries woven especially for the occasion.

Signs of Katherine's life as queen were quickly obliterated. The initials *H & K* were stripped from the side of the royal barge, and plaques along the city streets that bore the initials were defaced and promptly repainted with an intertwining *H&A*.

On a busy block along the coronation route, a worker stepped back from the plaque he had just finished decorating with the new royal initials. He stared at the letters, grinned, then read them aloud. "Ha!"

Two of his colleagues nearby, attaching a floral tapestry to the back frame of a newly constructed platform, stopped to look. "Ha! Ha!" said one.

All three burst out laughing, pointing to the initials. "Ha ha ha, ha ha ha ha!"

Thursday night, three days prior to her scheduled crowning on June 1, Lady Anne stood at the window of her bedchamber in the Tower of London, watching fireworks of silver and gold slash the black fabric of sky like the shimmering talons of some great and ethereal bird. She held her sister's hand so tightly that it hurt Mary, though Mary said nothing.

"Look, Mary!" she exclaimed, bouncing clumsily on her toes, as her condition was well along now, her belly swelled fully against the fall of her gown. "And it's all for *me*!"

And Anne began to laugh, a laugh so loud and violent that Mary feared her sister was nearing a state of hysteria. Was it joy? Or could it be fear?

The small London church was vacant Saturday morning save for a few priests who had collected at the open front doorway to watch the approaching procession. It gave William Brereton the perfect opportunity to steal in through the church's back gate with his heavy, wrapped parcel, and climb into the gray stone bell tower that overlooked the street and the river.

Brereton squatted in the shadow by an open archway, looking out and down. The royal procession was moving slowly through the early summer heat in the direction of the church. Knights in armor and ribbons preceded the pageant, their horses nodding and prancing. Nobles and ladies, lords and squires, peers of the realm, all, dressed in the finest capes, robes, and gowns, followed after, their presence heralding the arrival of the soon-to-be-queen. Anne appeared next, seated upon a silver-draped litter that resembled a Roman chariot, pulled by two matching palfreys in leather harness and plumed headdresses. She wore a kirtle of red velvet, a gown of purple trimmed in Baltic fur, and a satin caul beneath her coronet. Her hair was arranged over her shoulders, dark and shining. Four knights rode behind the litter, holding a canopy above the lady's head. Numerous servants kept pace alongside the litter. Charles Brandon, Thomas Cromwell, and George and Thomas Boleyn rode to Anne's left, while King Henry rode in splendor to her right.

It took no time for Brereton to see that although the procession was magnificent, the crowd lining the road to watch it was pitifully small and notably quiet. Anne smiled and waved at the people, though most only gawked. Then one lone voice called out unenthusiastically, "God save the queen."

Brereton untied the binding string from the parcel and tossed the string aside. Beyond his hiding place, from other bell towers nearby, there was an echoing and steady chorus of ringing. Brereton thanked God the priests of this church did not feel compelled to ring theirs. Unrolling the bundle, he removed a flintlock rifle, a pouch of powder, a wad and ball, and then bent over the weapon to prepare it to fire.

The cold expressions on the faces along the street wounded Anne to her soul. Her heart pounded beneath the bodice of her kirtle, and it felt as though her unborn child was equally upset as he tossed and turned beneath her ribs. Yet Anne smiled and waved, believing the only thing she could do in this moment was to act as the queen she would soon become.

Henry noticed the lack of respect, and he shouted at the men lining the street. "You must all have scurvy heads, since you don't want to uncover them!" He leaned from his saddle and struck one man across the head, sending the cap flying. Suddenly all the men within hearing distance had snatched their caps from their heads and were bowing, eyes downcast.

The king drew his horse closer to Anne's litter and smiled reassuringly. She returned his smile as if she were perfectly happy and content. Pretending could be a woman's finest skill.

Brereton, his flintlock ready, shouldered it and brought it around to aim through the archway. A fly buzzed close by his ear and he ignored it. He need only be steady for a few seconds, a few most crucial, critical seconds.

A wide stage had been constructed on the street below the bell tower, and it was filled with robed choristers and costumed musicians. As the first knights rode past, the trumpeters raised their instruments and the singers took a collective breath. And then, as the first of the nobles passed, the trumpeters sounded a triumphant note and the choristers broke into a jubilant song.

At that very moment, Brereton fired his rifle in the direction of Lady Anne's litter.

A servant walking near Anne's litter gasped, clutched his neck, and dropped to the dusty gravel. The servants near him shouted, and the procession drew up short, horse hooves churning the gravel. Guards raced over, circling the fallen man to prevent those along the street from seeing what had happened. Boleyn, George, and Brandon urged their horses through the tight knot of guards, forcing them to step out of the way.

"What the hell happened?" demanded Brandon. Boleyn nodded at the ground where the servant's body lay, sticky blood pooling through his now dead fingers.

The captain of the guard spoke quietly. "He's dead. Shot, it seems."

George Boleyn, the reins tight in his grasp, stood up in his stirrups and glanced nervously at the buildings and commoners lining the street. "My God, it could have been—"

But his father cast him a sharp look, and George went silent.

Up ahead, Henry and Anne had stopped and were looking back, unable to see what had happened but clearly not happy with the interruption. Some of the singers and musicians, confused by the interruption in the procession, stopped their music making, while several others kept on, creating a lackluster sound on the air.

"Your Grace," Thomas Boleyn said to Brandon. "We don't need a great fuss."

Brandon nodded, then waved his arm. "Keep the procession moving! Keep moving! Now! Go! Go!"

The order was passed along toward the front, and everyone started forward again. The hesitant musicians on the stage joined their fellows, filling the air again with a glorious chorus of praise and adoration for the king and new queen. Boleyn heeled his horse and trotted to Anne and Henry, smiling at the crowd and waving as if all was well.

"What was that?" asked Henry.

Boleyn shook his head and scoffed. "It was nothing. An accident." Then he gave Anne an especially warm and fatherly smile. "Nothing on earth is going to spoil this day!" He waited until Anne returned his smile to let out the breath he'd been holding.

Silently cursing himself, Brereton tried to reload the rifle with ball, wad, and powder, but by the time the weapon was ready, it was too late. The queen was gone, down the road and out of sight.

The bells of Westminster Abbey's tower ceased their pealing, though the echoes reverberated through the stone walls and vaulted ceiling of the cathedral for long afterward. The abbey was filled with bishops in their peaked mitres, gold-robed monks and abbots, witnesses and royal invitees in their most extravagant gowns and jackets, jewelry and capes. Tapers and incense filled the air with acrid, spicy smoke as countless marble saints, the Virgin Mary, and the mournful, crucified Christ watched over the proceedings with lifeless eyes.

Anne sat in St. Edward's Chair upon a scaffold draped with the finest cloth of gold. Across from her on another throne was her husband, beaming at her from beneath his crown. Archbishop Cranmer, looking ill at ease with the responsibility, anointed Anne with the oil and balsam, making a fumbling form of the cross on her head. He began to chant in Latin. *"Veni, Creator Spiritus, mentes tuorum visita . . ."*

A bishop stood by holding a pillow bearing a crown set with the royal jewels, a crown that would transform the Lady Anne into Queen Anne.

"Tu, septiformis munere . . ."

Anne looked at Henry. The king was watching the archbishop with the intensity of a hawk watching a mouse.

". . . infirma nostri corporis virtute firmans perpeti."

The bishop passed the pillow to Cranmer, who lifted the crown and nearly dropped it. He gasped, and Henry rose to his feet.

"Wait!"

Henry rushed toward Cranmer, who looked for a moment as if he feared the king would strike him. Those in audience stared, stunned at the breach of protocol.

"Give it to me!" Henry held out his hand. Cranmer gave the crown to the king.

Holding the jeweled headpiece in both hands, Henry crossed to his lady, smiled, and held it over her head.

"With this, St. Edward's crown, I do solemnly crown you queen of England," said Henry. He put the crown on Anne's head.

Her first thought was *It is much heavier than I imagined!*

Her second, *It is mine, at last!*

When Henry had returned to his throne, Cranmer continued the investiture, this time seeming to have regained his composure, blessing and then presenting Queen Anne with the scepters of her station. The boys of the choir began to chant the *Veni Creator.* The music was at once dignified and joyful.

It was done. "She" was now a royal "We."

* * * *

Anne couldn't wait to see Henry. It had been the longest day of her life, and she was exhausted—the preparations, the procession from the Tower, the ceremony, and the obligatory greetings that followed. She had her ladies dress her in a fresh gown for the evening festivities, brush her hair, and spray her with sweet waters. Then she hurried to Henry's private chamber. The child in her was resting, for which Anne was grateful.

Henry greeted her with a kiss and an affectionate cupping of her belly. "How was the day, sweetheart? Was not everything well done?"

Anne nodded. "Yes, it was beautiful!" She hesitated. "But there were so few people along the streets. They kept their hats on. And no one shouted." Henry's eyes darkened, but she continued. "It was more like, like a funeral than a parade."

Henry took her arms in a firm grip. It felt more angry than reassuring. However, his voice was even. "You have a party to go to," he said. "I want you to be happy. I want you to smile. You are my queen now."

"I know, but . . ."

The grip was even tighter, making Anne flinch. "I said, you are my queen. And everyone is waiting for you."

Henry leaned against a marble column on the viewers' gallery above the banquet hall, watching his queen from a distance. It was a splendid affair, indeed, with Anne upon the king's throne on the dais, attended by nobles, courtiers, servants, and members of her family. Smeaton upon his violin and other musicians on virginal and harp accompanied the gala with cheerful tunes composed especially for the occasion. Large ships made of wax and bearing the *H & A* initials were carried into the hall to rousing applause, and placed on the floor, giving the room the aura of a vast ocean. Charles Brandon, serving as High Constable, rode among the tables on his horse, monitoring the behavior of the guests.

Two faces were notably absent. Bishop Fisher. Sir Thomas More. They had been invited but had not come.

Henry's eyes narrowed and he strummed the column with his fingers. Fisher and More had ignored the royal invitation.

Boleyn and George stood near the dais, watching as Brandon, clearly unhappy with his role as overseer, climbed from his horse, gave the reins to a servant, then strolled past in search, most likely, of a greatly needed goblet of wine.

"Your Grace," called Boleyn, motioning Brandon over.

"Since you were appointed high constable today," said Boleyn quietly, "I must point out that what happened in the procession was your fault."

Brandon glared at him.

"We want to know who fired that shot," added George.

Brandon said, "I am already endeavoring to find out." He paused, then added sourly, "My lord."

"Oh," said Boleyn, drawing out the word to further drive in the sword. "I sincerely trust that you *are*, Your Grace."

Brandon leaned in and said quietly, "I have not forgotten Pennington. For I think that was *your* fault." Then he walked away.

Boleyn felt the pleasing stir of power and strong drink in his belly. He raised his glass and his voice, and said, "Here's to the Boleyns!"

George clinked his glass with his father's and the two drank with great satisfaction.

The ebony sky was laced with trails of smoke from the chimneys of countless London shops and homes. Tall iron braziers filled with sputtering logs lit the entrance gate to Whitehall Palace. A line of servants, who had tended the royal couple and the nobles throughout the day, filed one by one through the gate past the guards. They talked quietly among themselves about the procession, the performances, and most of all, the death of one of their own to an apparent shooting.

A king's groom stood in the queue, waiting his turn to return to his quarters. But then, with horror, he noted that the guards were studying each man's hands, holding a torch over them, looking for . . . what?

Brereton knew. They were checking for traces of gunpowder.

Dear God!

Brereton looked at his own hands and saw the dark stains there. He tried to wipe his hands on his tunic without drawing attention, but the powder remained in the creases of his skin.

The servant in front of him was examined and allowed to pass. Brereton was next.

A shout came from behind, "Make way there!"

Everyone stepped aside, allowing two haughty courtiers to ride out through the gate. And in that moment, in the commotion, Brereton slipped through the gate to safety.

Lady Mary, daughter to King Henry and Lady Katherine, the Princess Dowager of Wales, had grown into a lovely, dark-haired young woman in her teen years, a pious lady who, like her mother, took great comfort in prayer and devotion to God. Her home was Ludlow Castle, a bleak fortress upon a wind-battered hillside in the Welsh marches. Thomas Boleyn wasn't keen on having to make the trip. It had been unforgiving, offering up rough roads, stormy weather, and a carriage horse gone lame. But it had been the king's command.

Katherine's daughter appeared in some ways older than her years yet in others younger, so much a child. She stood in the center of the main hall, head down, clutching a string of rosary beads and listening to the pronouncements sent her by way of Boleyn. With each statement he made, she turned the beads over in her fingers as if trying to pray them away. Her father's marriage to her mother was null and void. Her mother was never the true queen of England. Henry's marriage to Anne was legal and valid.

When Boleyn was through, Mary looked up and said, "I know of no queen of England save my mother. And I will accept no other queen except my mother."

Boleyn's jaw clenched. He did not want this nor need this. "In which case," he said coldly, "I have to tell you that you are forbidden to communicate with your mother from this day forward."

Lady Mary's eyes flashed, though she did not break down. "May I not even write to her?"

"No. Not even a farewell note, considering your intransigence."

Boleyn waited, expecting Mary to say something, but she just stared at him. As he bowed and walked out, he could feel her dark, anguished eyes following him.

"How was the coronation?" Thomas More asked of Ambassador Chapuys as the two sat in More's study at Chelsea. He did not really care to know but needed to, and need at that moment was the more important emotion.

"It was a meager, uncomfortable thing," said Chapuys, rubbing his chin and looking for a moment out the window at More's youngest children playing in the summer sun of the rose garden. "Your absence was noted, Sir Thomas."

More sighed. "How is Her Majesty bearing up under all this?"

"I am no longer allowed to see her. And it is increasingly difficult for us to exchange letters. But I've heard that her household has been severely reduced. Her days are more than ever devoted to prayer. She has a room with a window looking over the chapel, and she will often pray there, day and night. Afterward her ladies will find the sill wet with her tears. For now, poor lady, she has lost both her husband and her child."

More's heart clenched. "I will try to see her."

"That would be dangerous."

"Nevertheless." More looked away, to the cross upon his mantle. "I have been thinking of the past, when I thought the king the most enlightened and promising prince in Christendom. I was sure his reign would be a golden age. I had such hopes." He looked at Chapuys. "Bishop Fisher has been placed under house arrest. You should beware yourself, Eustace."

Anne's royal chambers in Whitehall Palace were even larger and more elegant than those she'd had as Lady Anne. The number of servants

King Takes Queen   101

had increased twofold, bringing in new young women as ladies-in-waiting from around the empire as well as young, handsome serving men.

The queen had gathered them all together in her presence chamber, pleased to see them dressed in her livery of blue and purple, waiting for her orders. She sat in her chair upon the dais, holding in her hands a book of devotion.

"I wanted to speak today to all of you. As members of my household, I wanted to remind you of your duties." She glanced at her sister, Mary, who stood nearby. Mary gave Anne a small smile. Then Anne turned her attention back to the servants, in particular the most lovely of the young ladies in attendance. "You will all be honorable, discreet, just, and thrifty in your conduct. You will present a godly spectacle to others, attend Mass daily, and display a virtuous demeanor. On pain of instant dismissal and banishment, you must not quarrel, swear, nor ever speak or behave lewdly. Do you understand?"

In unison the ladies said, "Yes, Your Majesty." They curtsied.

Anne looked at the men. "And *you* don't go to brothels!"

The men bowed, some of them appearing to smile at the thought.

Anne pointed to a large table at the foot of the dais upon which rested a thick, leather-bound volume. "I will keep a copy here of Tyndale's English Bible. All of you are free to read it, and draw spiritual nourishment from it, for the old days are gone." She waited for a reaction but got none, so she continued. "Everything is changed now. Thanks to His Majesty you have all been delivered from the bondage of papal thralldom, idolatry, and superstition. This is a new beginning for me. For you. And for England."

"Anne, sweetheart." Henry, lying next to his sleeping queen, turned onto his side and caressed her swollen belly. The warmth of her tender flesh brought on an urgent burn that needed sating. His hand traveled from the rise of her abdomen to the soft rise of her breast. He rubbed the nipple with his thumb, and felt it harden instinctively.

But then Anne's hand gently covered his. She spoke, her words soft with the grogginess of dreams interrupted. "I can't . . . not now. While the baby is . . ." Her words faded away as she slipped back into sleep.

Henry looked at the lovely dark hair upon the pillow, rolled over, and sighed heavily.

It broke More's heart to see the great lady in such a state. She had received him from her bed, too ill to get up. The chilly, poorly lit room smelled of sickness and sadness.

"It seems," Katherine said to More, her hands pale upon the bed-covers, "I must cease to call myself queen, even though I was crowned so. They say that if I refuse, the king will withdraw his fatherly love for my daughter."

More could see the tears upon Katherine's cheeks, but was unable to say anything to console her.

"But," Katherine continued, "I shall not yield, neither for my daughter's sake nor anyone else's. Nor for a thousand deaths will I consent to damn my soul or that of my husband, the king."

"Madam, I—"

"There is still more," Katherine said, choking back a sob. "Lady Anne Boleyn has written me demanding that I surrender the christening gown I brought from Spain! God forbid I should ever give help in a case as horrible as this!" She sobbed aloud and More reached for her hand, wanting to hold it, but fearing it was too intimate for such a noble woman. He drew his hand back.

"God forbid, indeed," he said.

Katherine wiped her face, regaining her composure. "Forgive me. I am not used to visitors anymore as they are mostly forbidden. How did you get permission?"

"I wrote personally to Mr. Cromwell."

"You are a brave man."

"I cannot pretend to be detached from these events. I am encouraging all your supporters in Parliament and elsewhere to speak their minds and stand up for you."

Katherine coughed, touched her mouth as if embarrassed for the crudeness, and whispered, "Thank you, Sir Thomas. Thank you."

The dance was a new one, created especially for this evening's entertainment of the royal couple. The steps were intricate and mesmerizing, and the dancers weaved in and out among one another without a misstep, keeping perfect rhythm. Anne and Henry, upon their thrones, spoke to each other in quiet lovers' voices as the music directed the ladies and gentlemen around the floor, bowing, curtsying, touching hands, shoulders, and moving apart then together again. The accompanying stringed quartet, consisting of a lute, harp, lyre, and violin and seated in a corner near a window, was led by Mark Smeaton, dressed handsomely in dark green jerkin and flat velvet cap.

Among the dancers were Mary Boleyn and several of Anne's ladies-in-waiting. Mary had not been keen on joining the dancers but Anne had insisted, so Mary had obeyed. Though she struggled to smile and appear to enjoy the dance, she was humiliated by several of the male dancers who used the opportunity to whisper crude propositions to her as they stepped in time, bowed, and spun to meet their next partner. One man even let his hand slide from her shoulder to her breast, and chuckled at her when she gasped. Mary glanced at Anne upon her throne. She apparently had no idea what was transpiring on the floor.

I am known as the "great prostitute," Mary thought as she moved to her next partner and smiled at him to hide her discomfort. *Is this my fate forever?*

Quickly and discreetly, Brandon stepped close to Henry's chair and nodded toward the blond lady-in-waiting the king had been eyeing on the dance floor. "She's exquisite, isn't she?" he whispered.

Henry glanced at Anne, who was chatting gaily with her father, and then at Brandon. The question on the king's mind was easy to discern.

"She is Lady Eleanor Luke," answered Brandon. "Her family has an estate in Oxfordshire. Shall I—talk to her, on your behalf?"

The king looked again at Anne, then out at the enchanting Lady Eleanor, then back at Brandon. He did not speak and he did not nod. But the look in his eyes answered *Yes*.

George Boleyn made a point of flirting with all the lady dancers as he took part in the performance. He could make them all giggle, grin, and swoon, and enjoyed being able to do so. Yet when the dance was done, he was more than ready to leave them to their silliness. He had been watching another during the dance, someone with much more elegance, dignity, and appeal, someone who had, in turn, been watching him.

He strode toward the quartet, which was breaking now, standing and rubbing their arms and their necks, their instruments propped against their chairs. George smiled and nodded to Smeaton. "How do you like life at court?"

Smeaton bowed graciously. "I am most fortunate, my lord. I am thankful for the kindness and acceptance by the king and queen and for the patronage of your family."

George drew Smeaton aside, guiding him toward the long, carpeted table on which a spread of meats, puddings, and breads awaited. "Oh," he said, "we like to patronize artists, men of talent. The painter Holbein stayed with us, and my sister supports many musicians and choirs."

They paused in their walking to look across the room at Anne.

"The queen is a fine musician herself," said Smeaton. "As well as a very beautiful young woman. Even though—"

George felt his heart catch, and then begin beating again. "Even though—?"

Smeaton looked at George and his voice lowered to a near whisper. "Not as beautiful as her brother."

*   *   *   *

Henry invited Lady Eleanor to his bedchamber late in the evening following the party. She was nearly terrified as he invited her to play chess on the foot of his bed. Yet, ever the loyal subject, she obeyed.

Anne stood before her mirror the following morning, studying her growing belly and wondering why Henry had not visited her bed the night before. For even though she dared not let him know her, she enjoyed pleasuring him in other ways.

"It's ruining my figure," she told her father, who stood with her.

Boleyn took her arm and turned her to face him. "You ought to thank God you find yourself in such a condition! What's wrong with you?"

Anne looked back at the mirror as she felt the baby turn over, slowly.

The early September day was rainy and gray, with winds shaking the windows and old men creaking about, complaining of pains in their joints. At his desk in his outer chamber, Henry went about his morning routine of signing documents and reading petitions handed him by Cromwell. He glanced out at the rain every so often, feeling an odd sense of impending gloom. He needed a day of sport. When he was done with his duties, he would go hunting, the weather be damned.

Cromwell placed an impressive-looking document on the desk. Henry frowned and held it up. "What's this?"

"The final decision of the Curia in Rome."

Henry took a deep, silent breath, then read the paper slowly, carefully. One hand drew up around the corner, crushing it as the words came clear to him. He looked up at Cromwell, his jaw tight. "They've found for Katherine. They declare that my new marriage is invalid and any children produced from it, illegitimate."

"Yes, Majesty."

Henry spit out the words. "The pope threatens to excommunicate me unless I return to Katherine."

Cromwell nodded.

Henry shook his head and said quietly, deliberately, "He's too late." With that, he tore the papal bull in half.

The day had at long last arrived. Anne's labor had begun. Henry strode briskly and cheerfully through the court, Boleyn and George trying to keep up.

"I want you to organize jousts, banquets, and masques," the king said, "to celebrate my son's birth!" He laughed and shook his fists at the ceiling. "I can't decide between the names Henry or Edward."

Boleyn and George nodded, trotting along.

"I've already asked the French ambassador to hold him at the font at his christening. If he drops him, it's war!"

All three laughed. Then Henry suddenly stopped and looked at Boleyn and George, his face registering sudden seriousness. "We've consulted everyone," he said. "Physicians, astrologers, seers. They've all told us the same thing. We are expecting a prince!"

Boleyn and George both nodded. Of course it would be a boy.

Anne squeezed Mary's hand as hard as she could, caught in the grips of relentless, suffocating pain, unable to think but only to push and push again at the instructions of her sister. The room was hot and damp, the air filled with great urgency. Anne's ladies were about the bed, watching, their eyes dark and blinking like those of anxious starlings. The midwife knelt between Anne's knees and pressed Anne's belly.

Anne's hair was plastered to her forehead, her heels dug against the mattress. Her breaths came in loud, throaty grunts.

It must be over soon! This can't go on!

"Push, Anne!" urged Mary.

"Push, Majesty," said the midwife.

With a strangled scream, Anne pushed yet again, again, again, and felt something free itself from her, moving out and away. Was it done? Please God, was it over?

Mary leaned into Anne and kissed her damp cheek. Her voice was pitched with excitement. "It's here, Anne!"

Anne could hear a smack and a soft cry. The ladies gathered around the foot of the bed. And then there was silence.

"What is it?" Anne asked through chapped lips.

More silence.

"What's happened?" she demanded.

Mary looked from Anne to the midwife. Then she looked at Anne. "Nothing," she said. "Your Majesty has been delivered of a very healthy . . . girl."

Cromwell had broken the news. Henry had sat for a long time before he could make himself get up to see his wife. And his child.

He went alone, taking the private corridor from his chamber to hers, his steps measured and slow. The ladies-in-waiting curtsied and moved out of the way as he entered Anne's room. He found her with Mary, who stood with her head down.

Anne was in bed, her face drawn from the long hours of childbirth, holding the new child in soft white cloth. The infant had a crown of soft reddish hair, and the tips of her ears were pink.

Henry could not speak. How could this have happened? This could *not* have happened!

"I'm so sorry," Anne whispered in a raspy voice.

Henry shook his head, and gathered his resolve. "We are both young," he said. "By God's good grace, boys will follow."

Anne tried to smile, though all she could manage was a slight twitching at the corners of her mouth.

And then Henry walked away.

CHAPTER EIGHT

The christening ceremony was held in the Chapel Royal of Whitehall Palace several days after the infant's birth. The naked child, her eyes squinting and legs flailing, was placed by her godfather, Archbishop Cranmer, into the silver font. He blessed the child in the name of God, making the sign of the cross over her squirming body. Henry watched on, his face unmoved.

Charles Brandon slipped into the congregation next to Cromwell as Cranmer lifted the dripping baby from the font and handed her to a priest. The priest dried the child, placed her upon a table, and dressed her in a tiny purple mantle.

"A happy day, Your Eminence," said Brandon.

Cromwell raised a brow. "'Eminence,' Your Grace?"

Brandon smiled. "I understand His Majesty has made you his chancellor."

"I would still rather be called Mr. Secretary. And yes, Your Grace, it is a happy day when the king's first legitimate child is welcomed to the world."

The infant, now properly adorned, was held aloft by the priest as the garter king of arms proclaimed loudly, "God, of His infinite goodness, send prosperous life to the high and mighty Princess of England, *Elizabeth*!"

Trumpeters raised their horns and blew a fanfare as those in attendance applauded. Mary Boleyn, who had been standing, waiting, took the baby from the priest and carried her out of the chapel.

Anne waited in the dim candlelight of her bedchamber, listening to the approaching footsteps, her hands clasped tightly in expectation. Then, with a hush of quiet respect, the door opened and her little child, the duly christened Elizabeth, Princess of England, was brought into the room, carried by a smiling Mary. Following Mary were nobles and gentlemen bearing torches, a silent and reverential entourage who had come to witness the presentation of princess to queen in accordance with tradition and protocol.

Anne, her heart moved by the dignity of the moment, motioned them forward. Mary came first, and with great care handed the child to Anne, who kissed the baby on the forehead. The men bowed their heads.

Yes, the child was a girl. But she was *her* girl child, *her* daughter. Anne had never felt such complete love in her entire life. And at that moment and for the first time in months, Anne was awash in utter joy.

"Now that the queen and I have a child, with others to follow," said Henry, pacing back and forth in his outer chambers, "we must make the line of succession very clear. There must be no question of her illegitimacy."

Cromwell, ever unemotional and dutiful, inclined his head but did not speak.

"You will prepare a bill to put that before Parliament. It will state that the succession to the crown is now vested in *our* children, and no others."

"Yes, Your Majesty."

Henry stopped, rubbed his chin, trying to consider all the implications of his daughter's birth. "I am mindful," he said, raising a finger, "that some wrong-headed people are still unwilling to accept the validity of my marriage to the queen. In view of that, I think it appropriate there should be some . . . sanction against them. Everyone should be given the opportunity to demonstrate their loyalty."

Cromwell nodded, and Henry knew he had chosen his new chancellor wisely.

"Sir Thomas."

More looked up from his desk and squinted. Even though the day was bright, with warm sunlight filling the room, his eyes were tired, and it was difficult to focus.

"Bishop Tunstall is here." The servant stood back from the door to allow the visitor to enter.

More rubbed his eyes, stood, and held out his hand. This was not a visit he relished; Tunstall had once been used by King Henry to threaten Katherine when she refused to relinquish her crown. "My lord."

"Sir Thomas," said Tunstall.

"Please, be seated."

Tunstall, an elderly cleric with a large belly and chin to match, lowered himself into a chair beside More's desk.

"To what do I owe this honor?" asked More.

Tunstall wiped his brow with a cloth from his sleeve. "We've known each other a long time, Sir Thomas. Now you have retired from public life. I never see you. I am concerned about your welfare."

"I am well. Don't worry about me." More took his seat. "But I am concerned about Bishop Fisher. I hear he is still under house arrest and has been stripped of his bishopric."

Tunstall nodded. "Yes, the outcome of his intransigence is regrettable."

"I see," More replied. Then he asked the question for which he suspected the answer. "Has the king sent you here to see me?"

Tunstall smiled, though the smile was not one of reassurance. "His Majesty wondered why you did not attend the queen's coronation, as you were invited to do?"

More paused and linked his fingers atop his desk. He stared past Tunstall's shoulder for a moment, then back at the man. "I have a story to tell you," he said. "It is about the Emperor Tiberius. He enacted a law

King Takes Queen 111

that exacted death for a certain crime, unless the offender was a virgin. When a virgin eventually appeared on that charge, the emperor didn't know how to proceed. The solution? Let her first be deflowered and then she could be devoured."

More chuckled, wondering if Tunstall had heard the tale before and could understand his point in telling it. Tunstall chuckled as well, obviously not knowing the reason for the story.

"So your lordships," More continued, "in the matter of the matrimony, kept yourselves virgins. You should be careful to keep your virginity. For there are some, I won't name them, who first procure you for the coronation, and next to preach at it, and finally to write books defending it!"

Tunstall flinched.

"Thus they deflower you, and will not fail soon afterward to devour you. But they shall never deflower me."

Tunstall's face bunched up and his voice was no longer cordial. "Do you then deny the validity of the royal marriage?"

More did not answer.

After Tunstall had left Chelsea, More instructed his extended family, who now numbered a loving sixteen, to gather in the dining room. Before More went into the room to join them, his eldest son John asked him privately of the purpose of the Bishop's visit.

"Our loyalty is to be questioned," More replied. "God give grace that these matters never have to be confirmed by oath."

John and his father entered the dining room. Sir Thomas stood at the head of the table around which his family sat and explained to them that he was no longer in the king's good graces and his income was now greatly reduced. He requested that those who could should live in their own houses and eat at their own tables.

Several members of the family looked at each other with alarm, but More held up a hand to stop them before they could complain. "Why do you suppose things can never change?" he asked, exasperation edging his voice. "That you will be supported forever? Life is not like that. Real life is raw and difficult. And now you must face up to that fact." More paused and added softly, "If not to even worse things."

Fourteen-year-old Lady Mary, daughter of Katherine, Princess Dowager of Wales, strolled with Ambassador Chapuys in the tangled garden of Ludlow Castle, carrying a letter from the emperor.

"The emperor tells me that in every Catholic country the baby Elizabeth will never be anything but a bastard," said Mary, the words delicious on her tongue. *She* was the rightful daughter of Henry, not that red-haired daughter of a courtesan.

Chapuys nodded. "I'm told the lady is dismayed at having given birth to a girl rather than a son. That is proof that God has abandoned her."

Mary said nothing for a moment. She continued to walk, drawing her hand along an untrimmed hedge, knocking dew from the leaves. Then, "How is my mother?"

"I cannot visit nor speak to her. Her ladies say she is still strong, but always begs the king to be allowed to see you."

Mary touched her rosary. "I am sure His Majesty will one day relent, for I think . . . I believe . . . that he still loves and cares for me."

Chapuys smiled, though Mary thought the smile strained and sad. "I'm sure he does."

Anne lifted her child to her cheek and kissed her, then tickled her chin to see the child smile. Elizabeth kicked her feet and babbled softly. All the ladies in Anne's bedchamber clapped their hands in joy. The baby was everyone's darling—sweet, innocent, and charming.

Henry watched the maternal scene from the door, unnoticed. It warmed his heart to see the love in this room. Then Anne began to unlace the front of her gown.

"What are you doing?" called Henry as he strode into the chamber.

The ladies spun about and curtsied, going instantly silent. Anne's eyes widened in surprise. "Can I not feed her from my own breast?"

"Queens don't do that. Give her back to the wet nurse."

Anne reluctantly passed the baby to a stout and matronly woman, and Henry kissed the baby's head.

"The princess will shortly be given her own establishment at Hatfield," Henry said. "Among others, the Lady Mary will attend and wait on her."

Anne blinked. "Katherine's daughter?"

"Yes. It is as well she knows her new place. Cromwell is arranging it."

Henry smiled, leaned over, and kissed Anne softly on her lips. When he made to pull back, Anne drew him close again and whispered in his ear. "I will still give you a son. Come soon, my darling, to my hot bed."

Henry nodded then raised his head. But Anne saw him catch a lingering glimpse of her lady, Eleanor Luke, before he left.

Charles Brandon chuckled as his five-year-old son, Edward, fumbled with the bow and arrow, aimed at the target on a distant tree, and let the arrow fly. It went wide of the target and landed in some brush. *No matter,* Brandon thought, ruffling his boy's hair. *He will master it soon!*

A rider galloped across the field toward them. Brandon turned, squinting through the sunlight and gnats, and waited as the rider dismounted and bowed.

"Mr. Secretary," said Brandon.

"Your Grace," said Cromwell. "Is this your son?"

"Yes," said Brandon. The boy bowed, then went back to tackling the bow and arrow. "I'm teaching him to sport before I get too old for it. Do you shoot, Mr. Cromwell?"

"Sometimes."

Brandon took the bow from his son and handed it to Cromwell. Cromwell snatched an arrow from the quiver on the ground, threaded it, and fired in a single motion. The arrow struck the target on the tree dead center.

Brandon and Edward nodded in admiration.

"Shall we walk?" asked Brandon.

Leaving his son to practice, Brandon and Cromwell strolled through the tall grasses of the field. Meadowlarks, startled from their nests, flew up in a spray before them.

"What does the king want?" Brandon asked.

"He sends his love. He would like to see you back at court with your wife."

"And?"

Cromwell stopped. "His Majesty is aware that Your Grace favors the Imperialist cause. You say so openly in court. And you have, perhaps, a great sympathy for the Dowager Princess."

Brandon bristled. "Don't you? When you think of what has happened to her?"

"Actually, I do. Whatever people might think, I'm not heartless. Quite the contrary." He paused. "But I do serve the king."

They began to walk, over a knoll, toward Brandon's house on the hillside.

"His Majesty intends to vest the succession in the children he has with Queen Anne. A bill will go before Parliament. The king wants assurance that you will support it."

Brandon did not answer as he continued across the field.

In her humble bedchamber in Whitehall Palace, Lady Eleanor waited as King Henry unfastened her knotted hair and let it free. He ran his fingers through the strands, then took her in his arms and kissed her, his tongue relishing the taste of her mouth. Outside, beyond the walls, the November night was chilling. Yet the chamber itself was warmed with the pressing of their bodies and the heat of their desire.

In another humble bedchamber, Mark Smeaton sat upon his bed, trying a new piece on his violin, a sweet and mournful tune that stirred his heart and eased his soul. Though the air beyond the castle was chilly, his room was warm, and he was dressed in only his trousers.

"That was beautiful."

Smeaton looked up to find George Boleyn lounging in his doorway, his arms crossed.

"Do you play?" asked Smeaton, shifting on the bed and holding the violin out.

George crossed the floor and stood beside the young musician. He took the violin and put it on the bed. Then he placed his hand on Smeaton's broad bare shoulder and smiled.

"All the time," he said.

Hatfield House occupied a vast and beautiful plot of land just outside London. The house was one of King Henry's favorites, and he had given it to his infant daughter, Princess Elizabeth, for her household.

The day of Elizabeth's arrival was filled with a flurry of activity as servants, maids, wet nurses, and tutors settled in with their trunks and crates. Yet there was one unhappy soul that day, one who, on her arrival, was ushered to a lobby to meet the formidable Lady Margaret Bryan.

"Lady Mary," said Lady Bryan, looking Katherine's daughter up and down coolly. "Welcome to Hatfield, your new home. I am Lady Margaret Bryan, the princess's governess. These other ladies"—Lady Bryan nodded to several silent women in the room—"are also here to attend the princess, as are you."

Mary said nothing. Lady Bryan signaled and one of the women came forward, revealing a tiny baby wrapped in gold cloth.

"Lady Mary," said Lady Bryan, "I present to you Her Highness Princess Elizabeth."

Mary was silent, her face stony.

"You will be shown to your room," said the governess. "You will begin your duties in the morning, after prayers."

At last Mary spoke. "I shall say my prayers alone."

Lady Bryan seemed to note the defiance in the words, but let it go. Then a serving girl took Mary to her room, a small, bleak chamber down a long corridor. There was a tiny window and a stuffed pallet on the floor. Mary was silent until the servant left, and then she turned to the wall, folded her hands to God, and cried.

Christmas had come again, and this year the mood of the court was high and festive. A dance was held in the Great Hall of Whitehall Palace, attended by courtiers in the rich greens and golds of the season. The couples whirled about in graceful pavanes, creating kaleidoscopic patterns about the floor. Henry and Anne were among the dancers, spinning in good spirits, laughing with abandon.

Thomas Wyatt entered the Great Hall, looked at the lavish decorations, and moved to where George Boleyn stood watching the dance.

"Christmas," said Wyatt. "Why is it, that as you get older, it's *always* Christmas? Of course, it is always Christmas for you, isn't it, my lord? A baron in your own right now, and some new titles! Remind me."

George smiled smugly. "Master of Buckhounds. Lord Warden of the Cinque Ports."

"Hmm," said Wyatt. "Was there not another? Master of the Bedlam Hospital for the Insane?"

George's smile dimmed. "Yes."

"Do you plan to visit it?" Wyatt chided. "Though I don't mean as an inmate."

George took Wyatt's arm. His voice was cold. "I read one of your satires about life here at court," he said. "If I were you, I would be more careful about poking fun at those who have the power to hurt you." Then he turned up his hand. "Just some friendly advice."

Across the room, Henry and Anne left the dance floor, laughing and panting from the exertion. Anne, holding Henry's hand, said, "I have a gift for you!"

Courtiers parted as she led him to a table, upon which sat an exquisite fountain of gold, rubies, diamonds, and pearls. At the foot of the fountain were the marble figures of three naked women with water pouring from their breasts.

Henry clapped his hands. "It's fantastic! Who made it?"

Anne was thrilled with Henry's reaction. "Master Holbein!" she said.

"The man's a genius." Henry turned Anne to face him. "But so are you, my beautiful queen." He pulled her close and in full view of the partiers, kissed her ravenously.

Henry's groom Brereton stared at the gaudy fountain and at the royal couple grasping and groping before their subjects. He leaned to Ambassador Chapuys who stood beside him.

"Look at that common-stewed whore!" he snarled. "I could still do it! I could find a way to poison her."

"No!" Chapuys whispered sharply. "It would be blamed on my master. At the moment he doesn't need that. He has a war with the Turks to contend with."

Brereton continued to stare angrily at Anne as she flipped back her hair and laughed. "But why should anyone know?"

"Don't be stupid. They would find you and torture you, and you would tell them everything."

"No, I wouldn't. I'd die a martyr's death."

"You've never seen a man being tortured. Do you understand? You don't act alone!"

Henry found Brandon among the crowd, and hurried to him. "Charles! I'm so happy you came back to court. Happy Christmas!"

Brandon bowed. "And to Your Majesty. I came to give you a gift."

Henry glanced about, clearly enjoying the mystery but wanting to have his gift. "Where is it?"

"It must wait until the new session of Parliament," said Brandon. "For it's my vote."

"Ah!" Henry grinned broadly and put his hands on Brandon's shoulders. "I don't know how I *ever* doubted you!"

When Henry moved away, Brandon glanced toward a cluster of ladies that included his wife, Catherine. He caught her eye, and she smiled. He'd made the right move.

* * * *

Anne and Henry left the fountain and rejoined the dancers on the floor. Partners were traded, and Anne, for the moment, found herself dancing with her brother George as Henry circled Anne's lovely lady-in-waiting, Eleanor Luke.

Anne leaned to George's ear and said, "You see that girl? And the way the king looks at her?"

George nodded. "Is she his mistress?"

"Yes. Find a way to get rid of her."

They parted, breaking into single file lines, parading in rhythm to another partner. As Anne passed her sister, Mary, she said, "We must find you a new husband!" Mary smiled and then was gone with a dip and turn.

Anne and Henry came together again. Anne touched his arm. "I have another gift for you," she said. "I am with child again."

Henry drew his wife close. "Then my joy overfloweth!"

Henry called for a select group of his Privy Councilors to meet in his private outer chamber. They came quietly, obediently, as Henry had wanted and expected. He could not know the minds and hearts of all the councilors, but these men, including the Boleyns, Thomas Cranmer, Thomas Wyatt, and Charles Brandon, had proved themselves to the king on the most important matters.

Cromwell had a table prepared, spread with papers, quills, and inkwells. Once the men had settled in their seats, he rose to address them, holding a document.

"Majesty, Councilors, here is the new Act of Succession, which I am commanded to present shortly to the Houses of Parliament. The act nominates the children born of His Majesty and Queen Anne as first rightful heirs. By so doing it protects this nation from the great divisions it has suffered in the past when several titles have been presented to the throne."

Henry watched, pleased, as the councilors nodded.

King Takes Queen 119

"Also in past times," continued Cromwell, "the bishop of Rome, contrary to the great and inviolable powers of jurisdiction given by God to kings and princes, has taken it upon himself to invest whom he pleases in other men's kingdoms. This is something we most abhor and *detest*."

"Hear, hear!" said some of the councilors.

Cromwell continued. "The act warns that anyone saying or writing anything to the prejudice or slander of the lawful matrimony between the king and his beloved wife Queen Anne, or against his heirs, would be guilty of high treason, for which the penalty is death and forfeiture of goods to the Crown . . ."

"Furthermore, it is proclaimed that the new Act requires all the king's subjects, if so commanded . . ."

Sir Thomas More hesitated in his reading and looked up at his family, who had gathered in his study at Chelsea. He had obtained a copy of the act that was being presented in private to the select councilors and felt it only right that his wife and children know what they might be facing.

"Pray go on, Father," directed his son John, his face shadowed with worry.

More took a painful breath. The walls of the room seemed unduly ominous at that moment, as if closing in on him with cold and crushing hands. He read, "if so commanded to swear an oath that they shall truly, firmly, constantly, without fraud or guile, observe, fulfill, defend, and keep the whole contents of the bill . . ."

Cromwell continued reading to the councilors. "This oath will also require recognition of the king's supremacy in all matters, spiritual and temporal. Those who refuse to take it will be accounted guilty of treason and sent to prison."

Henry looked at each councilor in turn. They all nodded in agreement, even Charles Brandon. Satisfied, Henry sat back in his chair. "That is all well done, Mr. Secretary. I'm pleased."

Cromwell bowed. "Thank you, Your Majesty."

* * * *

Thomas More put the paper down and gazed at his family. He could see his own anguish reflected in their eyes.

"So," he said. "It must be sworn by oath after all. God save us."

The drum of the horse's hooves beneath Henry matched the rhythm of his heartbeat. Grit and thistledown rushed past on the wind; shadows from the trees lining the road cut the ground like the dark lances of forest spirits. Hatfield House was ahead, on the rise. Soon, he would see his daughter! He planted his weight more solidly in the stirrups and leaned forward.

Behind Henry rode Mark Smeaton and two yeomen of the guard. They kept Henry's pace, though at a length behind to allow the king not only the respect of leading the way, but to keep His Royal Majesty out of their dust.

The three rose out of the trees and up the hill to the house, passing lazy cows and sheep, which glanced up momentarily as the men rode by. Reaching the cobblestoned yard, Henry drew up his horse and jumped to the ground. A frantic page grappled for the leather reins as the horse skittered sideways. Without waiting for the others, Henry strode into the house.

Lady Bryan and several servants in the front hallway curtsied at his entrance.

"Mistress Bryan!" said Henry. "Good morning to you!"

"Your Majesty," said Lady Bryan, her eyes downcast.

"I'm on progress," said Henry, rubbing his hands together enthusiastically. "I came to see my daughter. How is she?"

"A credit to Your Majesty in every way." With that Lady Bryan gestured, and a wet nurse brought the baby forward and placed her in Henry's arms. Elizabeth looked much like a miniature adult in her velvet gown and silver circlet.

"My Elizabeth!" said Henry, nuzzling the child. "Who knows, Lady Bryan, perhaps one day this little girl will preside over the empires?"

Lady Bryan laughed along with the king.

Henry handed the child to Lady Bryan. "Forgive me. I have little time. But thank you for all your care toward our beloved princess."

Lady Bryan curtsied. "Your Majesty."

Henry swept back out of the house to where Smeaton and the yeomen, still mounted, waited. He snatched the reins from the page, but then he sensed something behind him and looked back.

Outside upon one of the tall stone battlements was a small, lone figure kneeling in supplication, her hand to the bodice of her plain gray dress. It was Henry's daughter Mary. The sight of his child so rejected yet still so loyal moved and stung Henry's heart. He bowed and touched his hat. The men with him did the same. After a long pause, Henry swung into his saddle and rode away.

George Boleyn stopped Lady Eleanor Luke on her way to her chamber, taking her arm and turning her about.

"How did you suppose no one would find out your secret?" he said, darkly.

Lady Luke stared at George, clearly confused and terrified. Her mouth opened but in that moment, she could not speak.

"You chamber was searched today," said George. "The jewels were found. You did not hide them well enough."

Lady Luke at last found her voice. "Jewels? I don't . . ."

"Her Majesty's jewels. The ones you stole."

"It's not true!"

"I say it is true. And so does my sister. If your crimes were ever reported, who do you suppose would believe *you*? After all, no one could accuse you of being innocent . . . could they?"

Lady Eleanor put her hand to her mouth. Clearly she saw the hopelessness of her position. "What—am I to do?"

"Leave court. Go back to your family. See if they will have you." Satisfied that the job had been done, George stalked away.

The king's commissioners traveled the country over the next weeks, visiting towns, hamlets, and parishes, carrying with them satchels filled with copies of the king's oath, quills, and pouches of ink powder, and a copy of Tyndale's Bible.

At a table in a small parish church, black-robed commissioners, looking much like large ravens, oversaw the interrogations and the signings. Englishmen were lined up out the door, waiting their turn to prove their loyalty to King Henry.

A nervous laborer stepped to the table, his hat in his hand.

"Name?" asked a commissioner.

"Seth Martins, Your Honor."

The commissioner stretched his shoulders, checked for Martins's name on the list, and nodded. "Will you take the oath, recognizing the king's supremacy in all matters of religion, and his marriage to Queen Anne?"

"Yes, Your Honor."

"Then place your hand upon the Bible." Martins did so. The commissioner spoke the oath and Martins repeated it, and made his mark.

Anne had taken to bed for a nap, exhausted from a long morning of royal audiences, needlework, and wondering about her child so far away. But from the next chamber came bursts of giggling, loud enough to bring the queen off her bed and to the door. She found two of her ladies looking at a small book, pointing to the text, and smirking. One was Anne's cousin, Madge Sheldon, a pretty girl with deep dimples.

"Lady Madge!" said Anne.

The young woman stopped, lowered the book, and blushed.

"What are you reading?"

Madge tried to hide the book behind her, though it was a futile attempt. Then she held it up reluctantly. "Just some . . . poetry. By Sir Thomas Wyatt."

"Give it here!"

Anne took the book and glanced at it scornfully. "You should not be wasting your time on such trifles. If you must read, when you are supposed to be attending on *me*, then you should read that book!" She pointed to the Bible still displayed upon its table. "You will learn a great deal more from it, including perhaps some wisdom."

"Yes, Madam." Madge lowered her eyes. The other lady followed suit.

"Now, go about your business."

The ladies curtsied and scurried from the room. As they did, a servant stepped in to announce, "The Earl of Wiltshire, Your Majesty."

Anne smiled, her spirits instantly lifted. She had not seen her father since he'd gone to France.

"Papa!" she said as he entered.

Boleyn bowed and kissed Anne's hand. "Your Majesty."

The servant exited, leaving them alone.

"You look well," said Boleyn, taking Anne's arm. "And I believe you're already showing."

Anne touched her stomach. "A little. How was your trip to Paris?"

Boleyn sighed. "King Francis is not the easiest man to deal with. He sends you wedding presents yet he pretends he cannot officially recognize you as queen." He paused. "As long as Katherine is alive."

Anne looked at her father. What might he be suggesting?

Boleyn's voice brightened, and he changed the subject. "How is the king? Is he pleased at your condition?"

"He is, but . . ."

Boleyn's brows drew together. "But . . . ?"

"Everything is fine. But when I was last with child, His Majesty took a mistress. And now I fear he may take another since I must be careful for the sake of the child and not let him enjoy his conjugal rights."

Boleyn guided Anne to the chairs by the window. After they were seated, he took her hand and said, "It's natural for a man, when his wife is big with child, to find temporary consolation elsewhere. And for kings, it is properly expected."

The words stung Anne and she looked away. But Boleyn cupped her face and brought it back around.

"Sweetheart. The danger to you, and to us, is not that the king takes a mistress, but that he takes the wrong one. Someone, for example, whose family is against our reformation and who can whisper in his ears to stop it, or prosper someone else who is against it. Someone we can't control, or who would seek to control the king. But if you suppose the king is sure to take a mistress, then make sure she is *your* choice, not his."

Boleyn said nothing for a moment, then kissed his daughter on the forehead and stood to leave. "I must make my report to the king. Just take heed of what I've said."

After her father had gone, Anne sat, thinking. Then she walked to the door he'd left open. She saw Madge Sheldon in the corridor, gathering clean linens for the queen's bed. A pretty girl, to be certain. A very pretty girl.

The cold and damp of the Tower had been brutal on Fisher's joints, but he did not complain. There were worse cells, God knew. There were worse pains.

The locked door rattled, and Thomas Cromwell entered the room. He gazed at the tiny window and the grimy walls, almost as if he were sad to see the ex-bishop in such a place. Fisher rose with great effort and bowed.

"Mr. Secretary."

"Reverend Fisher," said Cromwell. "I came to discover if you were being well treated."

Fisher shrugged. "My aged stomach cannot cope with the rank food, but that is nothing. It pertains to my body, not my soul."

Cromwell smiled a little. "You have not taken the oath."

"No."

"Do you refuse to accept that the king's marriage is proper and legal?"

"I believe His Majesty thinks so."

"You don't?"

"I believe as I have always believed. The marriage to Queen Katherine is valid and can be undone by no man. Not even Archbishop Cranmer."

"And do you dispute that the king is now Supreme Head of the Church?"

"Most emphatically. The King our Sovereign Lord is *not* the Supreme Head of the Church of England."

Cromwell sighed silently and nodded.

"Tell me," asked Fisher. "How is Sir Thomas More?"

Cromwell considered the question but let it go. As he turned to leave he said, "I will see if the quality of your food can be improved."

"Thank you."

Cromwell knocked on the door and the guard opened it to let him out. Then it was sealed again with an echoing clank.

There was a moment of silence and then a soft voice whispered from beyond the bars of Fisher's window. "Your Grace! Your Grace!"

Fisher moved slowly to the window and looked through the bars. A young couple, dressed in simple clothing, stood below on the gravel, their hands shading their faces against the sun.

"Your Grace?" said the young man. "Will you bless us?"

Fisher smiled and made the sign of the cross over them.

"God's blessings on you, my children," he said, feeling in that moment the respect and love he'd felt in the former life, before his world had been stripped down to just himself, God, and the black insects that lived in the walls. "Go in peace."

"Why did you get rid of Lady Eleanor?"

Anne, who had been seated at her window, embroidering intricate blackwork patterns to an infant's gown, looked up at Henry with a coy pursing of her lips. He had known his wife several years now, but still she could be an enigma.

"She stole something from me."

Henry knew, then, Anne's intent. But he pressed. "Are you sure she stole it?"

"Yes. I had evidence. I had no choice." She put the dress on the corner of the table beside her. "I hope Your Majesty is not *too* disappointed?"

Henry tried to look cross, but the teasing on his queen's face softened his expression.

"In any case," said Anne, "I have . . . something for you."

Henry tilted his head, waiting. Anne called to the chamber next door, and a lovely, dimple-faced young lady came in and stood before Henry. She curtsied, then handed the king a small silver locket. Henry opened it. It was a tiny portrait of his young daughter.

"Elizabeth," he said, pleased.

Then he looked at the Lady Madge, Anne's cousin, noting what a charming and lovely young lady she was.

Chapter Nine

When he prayed, Pope Paul III wrestled with God much like Jacob had wrestled with the angel. The pontiff grunted and rocked with effort, hands clasped so tightly the skin was stretched shiny, his words intelligible only to himself and his Maker.

Cardinal Campeggio waited patiently in the private chamber until the pope crossed himself and went silent, the prayers done. After a long moment, the pontiff stood, rubbed the stiffness from his knees, and acknowledged the cardinal with a question.

"Does the king remain obdurate?"

"Yes, Holiness," said Campeggio. "He refuses to listen to advice. He forces all true believers to perjure their immortal souls."

"How so?"

"They must swear an oath that the king is head of the English Church. Those who refuse are put into prison."

"Like our poor Bishop Fisher."

"Yes, Holy Father."

The pope moved to the desk on which sat his papers, his seal, and a large red hat. "This is unacceptable," he said. "The shepherd cannot stand idly by while the wolf enters the fold and threatens the flock." The pope picked up the red hat. "I have decided to make Fisher a cardinal. You will send his hat to England. Let's see if the king is still prepared to prosecute and torture a prince of the Church!"

*   *   *   *

It was a most precious moment for the queen, visiting Hatfield House, sitting on the parlor floor and playing with her infant daughter and making the child laugh. Princess Elizabeth's servants hovered nearby, as did Lady Bryan, watching the queen's every move to assure that the reunion was nothing less than perfect.

"How is she?" asked Anne. "Does she feed well?"

"She is good in every way, Your Majesty. She hardly cries, as if she knows already she is a princess."

Anne kissed the baby's feet. "I love you, Elizabeth. With all my heart, I love you. And I bid you never forget it!" Then, to Lady Bryan, "Before I leave, I wish to speak to Lady Mary."

Lady Bryan nodded and sent a servant off with a curt nod of the head. Anne kissed her baby once more, then stood and handed the child to the wet nurse.

After a moment Katherine's daughter entered the room, her eyes downcast. Anne was taken by surprise at how much she had grown, as tall as Anne now, and with a woman's figure.

"Lady Mary . . ."

Mary said nothing.

"I am here in kindness," Anne continued. "I would welcome you back to court and reconcile you with your father . . . if you will accept me as queen. More than that I don't ask."

Mary looked up. The venom in the eyes startled Anne. "I recognize no queen but my mother. But if the king's mistress would intercede with the king on my behalf, then I would be grateful."

It was as though Mary had struck Anne across the face. She stared, her mouth open, unable to speak. Mary stared back, youthful defiance holding her straight.

Lady Bryan, horrified, watched and waited for her orders. But instead of demanding Mary be beaten, Anne only flicked her hand to send the girl away. Mary curtsied, and walked out.

* * * *

Cromwell's office always smelled of cleanliness, efficiency, and duty. It was a large room, tidily arranged with bookshelves, cabinets, and bureaus stocked with books on politics, religion, geography, and languages. The windows, which looked out over one of the palace gardens, more often than not had the drapes pulled across them, as if Cromwell had little time or interest in anything beyond the business at hand.

As Sir Thomas More entered the office, Cromwell rose from his desk and smiled with forced cheerfulness. More knew the poison behind the smile.

"Sir Thomas!" he said. "Please be seated. This is but an informal occasion."

Cromwell motioned to a comfortable chair next to the desk. More sat and clasped his hands, waiting for the worst.

"Ale?" offered Cromwell.

"No, thank you."

Cromwell nodded, took a breath. "I'm sure we both know the object that has brought us together. It is very widely rumored, Sir Thomas, that you will refuse to take the Oath of Succession."

More didn't reply.

"I say this to you sincerely. I wish no harm to come to the great man who has for years enjoyed and deserved His Majesty's good graces. I would rather lose my own son than see you hurt."

More nodded, acknowledging the compliment.

"May I ask your opinion on the king's new marriage?"

"I have no opinion. I neither murmur at it nor dispute it. I never did and never will."

"Then, what is your opinion on the king's claim to supremacy over the Church of England?"

It was time to be most careful. "I was unsure about this matter," said More, "until I reread His Majesty's own pamphlet, *Assertio Septem Sacramentorum*. In fact, I have a copy here." More pulled a paper from his coat, a paper he and Henry had worked on together once, long ago.

"In the pamphlet, the king asserts the divine origin of the papacy. His arguments are as persuasive and powerful now as they were when he first wrote them."

Cromwell looked at the paper but did not reach for it. It was a shrewd move, to bring up the king's earlier, vehement support of the Catholic Church.

Cromwell said simply, "Will you take the oath?"

More was silent.

"I don't need to remind you of the consequences of not doing so."

More raised a brow. "I am the king's faithful subject. I say no harm and think no harm. I wish everybody good. And if this be not enough to keep a man alive, I long not to live."

They considered each other silently for a long, challenging moment. Then More stood.

"You should know," said Cromwell, "the king has no mind to coerce you."

More bowed. "Mr. Cromwell, please impart to the king my utter faithfulness, truthfulness, and loyalty to him."

And he left.

The embroidery on the infant's dress was nearly done. Anne sat by the fire in her chamber, putting on the finishing touches with red thread, imagining how lovely her daughter would look in the gown.

Lady Madge Sheldon entered the room with a sling of firewood. She curtsied and went about her business. Anne put her needlework down.

"Lady Sheldon . . ." she said. "Cousin Madge."

Madge, kneeling at the hearth, looked up. "Yes, Madam?"

"Come, sit with me." Anne patted the seat next to her.

Madge left the fireplace and sat obediently.

"You're very beautiful," Anne said at last.

Madge blushed.

"I suppose you have many admirers?"

Madge glanced at her cousin. "Yes, but I always remember what Your Majesty told us, about not being lewd, and setting a standard."

Anne smiled. "I'm sure you do. But . . . would it surprise you to learn that one of your 'admirers' is the king, himself?"

Madge's eyes flashed wide with fear. "It's not true!"

"It is true. Now, would it surprise you even more if I told you that you would have my blessing to become his mistress?"

Madge stared, confused.

"While I am with child, His Majesty needs to be able to lie with another woman. He is a passionate man." Anne took her cousin's hand. "But she must be someone I can trust. Whose family I can trust, like yours. After all, we are family. And you are a reformer."

"Yes, Your Majesty. We all gladly took the oath."

"And now will you gladly take the king to your bed?"

Madge looked at the queen, her mouth open but finding no words to speak.

Later that night, alone in her great bed carved with the initials *H & A*, Anne stared at the light of the candle on the stand. And she cried.

"What's this?" The king, at his desk, indicated a paper that Secretary Cromwell had handed him to sign.

"Majesty," said Cromwell. "There are some small monastic institutions which I've had cause to investigate. The monks refuse to take the oath. They prefer to serve the Vicar of Rome than you. This is a bill for their dissolution. All the considerable wealth of these houses will be transferred to Your Majesty's exchequer."

Henry nodded and signed the bill. Then waited for the next. Cromwell hesitated.

"Well?"

"Your Majesty," said Cromwell, clearly uncomfortable with what he had to say. "I've heard that the pope intends to make Reverend Fisher a cardinal. He has already dispatched a cardinal's hat."

Henry was furious. He pounded the desk. "Then Fisher will have to wear it upon his shoulders! For by the time it arrives, he will not have a head to put it on!" Henry sat back, hard, in his chair. "And what of More? Will he take the oath? Will he?"

Sir Thomas More stood before a seated committee in a chamber at White-hall Palace. His head was high, his hands folded. He knew what he would face. Perhaps not iron thumbscrews today, but thumbscrews of the mind and soul, pressure exerted by men who claimed to love God—Arch-bishop Cranmer, Bishop Tunstall, the Bishop of London, and Thomas Cromwell—in an attempt to make More do what he could not do.

"I have a list here," said Cranmer, examining his notes, "of all the great honors and privileges granted to you in the past by His Majesty."

More nodded. "I believe there is no man alive who would more will-ingly serve the king than I."

"Except in this current matter."

There was a long silence. Then Tunstall said, "Tell us what you make of the king's marriage to Anne Boleyn?"

"What I make of it I have plainly declared to His Majesty, who seemed to graciously accept my view."

"That is a false statement, and you know it!" declared Tunstall.

"Sir Thomas," said Cranmer, "we have come to the conclusion that, far from being a true servant, there never *was* a servant so villainous or traitorous as you."

More glanced at Cromwell, whose expression was blank.

Tunstall jabbed a finger in More's direction. "If you refuse to take the oath, not only will you be imprisoned but the most horrible things imaginable will be done to you!"

"My lords," More said gently, "these threats are for children, not me."

The men thundered at More. Cranmer snatched up a copy of the *Assertio* and waved it. "Do you deny you bullied and persuaded the king against his conscience to write this pamphlet against Luther?"

"Of course I deny it. I would never ask anyone to act against his con-science. And I remember that His Majesty rather persuaded *me* of the paramount importance of the papacy."

The men threw up their hands in horror, while Cromwell, for a brief moment, seemed to hide a smile.

Henry's first daughter, Lady Mary, had fallen ill. Henry sat in his pres-ence chamber, frowning and stroking his chin as Ambassador Chapuys read a letter from Katherine, requesting she be allowed to visit her daughter.

"'A little comfort and mirth with me would be a half health to her,'" read Chapuys. "'I would care for her with my own hands and put her in my own bed and watch with her when needful . . .'"

Henry stepped from his throne and paced about. "I will send my own physician to examine and help her." He looked at Chapuys. "But I can-not allow Mary and her mother to be together."

"But, Your Majesty," said Chapuys respectfully. "It is just the cry of *any* mother for *any* daughter."

Henry strode to Chapuys, his eyes narrowed. "But they are not just any mother and daughter! Do you not suppose they would conspire and plot against me?"

Chapuys took a sharp breath. "I cannot believe it."

"Of course you can believe it! You know it happens! Katherine is a proud, stubborn woman of very great and high courage. She could easily take the field, muster an army, and wage war against me as fierce as any other Isabella ever waged in Spain!"

Chapuys fell silent.

In the warm, green shadows at Chelsea's front gate, Sir Thomas More bid his family good-bye. He had been summoned to Lambeth Palace to take the oath. More's wife Alice, his son John and daughter Margaret, and the younger children kissed him in turn, and weeping, stepped back to hold one another as More walked down to the riverfront, glancing back one more time at the home and family he knew in his heart he would never see again.

The room in Lambeth Palace was cold, dark, oppressive, and chosen, More suspected, for those very reasons. The bishop of London, Thomas Cromwell, and Archbishop Cranmer were gathered in their chairs, watching accusingly as Thomas More perused the oath they'd asked him to sign. More had not been invited to sit.

After reading the oath carefully, More handed it back to Cranmer. "I don't mean to put at fault this oath, nor its makers, nor any man who swears to it. And I will never condemn the conscience of any other man. But for myself, my own conscience so moves me that I will swear to the validity of succession yet not the rest of it without jeopardizing my soul to perpetual damnation."

The bishop scowled and shook his head. "We are sorry to hear you say this. You are almost the first to refuse it, and your refusal will cause the king to be both indignant and suspicious of you." The bishop held up a list, showing More hundreds of signatures of those who had sworn to the oath.

More said simply, "I cannot swear, but I do not blame any man who has sworn."

Cranmer spoke through tight jaws. "What particular aspect of the oath disturbs you?"

"You say I have already offended the king. So if I should open and disclose the causes of my refusal I could only offend him more. And that I won't do. I would rather accept all the danger and harm that might come to me, rather than give him cause for further displeasure."

"You have not answered the question!" shouted Cranmer.

"No, sir," said More. "But in law, no man is obliged to condemn himself."

Cranmer's face was red, his cap quivering on his head. "I ask you a final time, before the awful penalties are exacted upon you, why will you not swear?"

But More would not answer.

* * * *

Henry sat upon his dun thoroughbred, shifting slightly in the new saddle, testing its fit and feel. The saddle bore the entwined monograms *H & A,* as did the saddle now being adjusted and cinched on the back of Queen Anne's dappled mare. They were fine saddles of soft leather, gifts from some courtier whose name, at the moment, he could not remember.

He glanced up the path leading from the stable yard. Where was Anne? She was to have been here by now, ready for their ride.

A pretty young woman dressed in dark green riding attire approached the yard. It was Lady Madge Sheldon.

"Lady Sheldon," said the king. "Where is the queen?"

Madge curtsied. "Your Majesty, the queen is feeling indisposed and asks you to forgive her for not riding this morning."

"Of course," said Henry.

"She—" began Madge. "She wondered if your Majesty would be pleased if—if I took her place, riding."

Henry smiled and gestured toward the mare. "If the queen gives her permission, then why not? Lady Sheldon."

They rode in near silence for a while, beyond Whitehall Palace and into the countryside outside London. The king's hunting lands were vast and beautiful, filled with deer and birds, rabbits and foxes. Several guards followed at a respectful distance.

Henry thought about Anne, back at court, and of this lovely lady she sent to be his companion for the day. Then he smiled. Perhaps it would be for more than the day.

"What is your name, Lady Sheldon?" he asked.

"Margaret, Your Majesty. Though people call me Madge."

"Then I shall call you Madge, if you'll allow?"

Madge looked at the king, and he could see the pretty dimples in her cheeks. He thought those dimples needed caressing. "Of course, Your Majesty."

Later, in the king's rustic hunting lodge, Henry and Lady Sheldon sat alone at a small table to enjoy the food and wine that had been brought on their ride. Madge finished her third glass of wine and put the glass on the table. She hiccupped, and began to giggle.

"Madge!" said Henry, grinning.

"What?"

"Madge, I don't know, it's just . . . funny."

Madge's brows drew together, but she continued to giggle.

"I like your dimples," said Henry. "When you laugh, Madge." He reached for her. Madge lowered her eyes and grew quiet.

"Madge."

"Your Majesty."

The king pulled the lady close and began to kiss her dimples, her neck, her lips.

The constable of the Tower of London rattled the key in the lock and opened the door to a musty cell that held only a chair, a stuffed pallet, a small stove, and a desk with a single candle. The constable escorted More inside. More did not complain, but was glad his family could not see his new abode.

"Sir Thomas . . ." said the constable, his voice pained, as if he wanted to say more but could not.

"Thank you," said More.

The constable bowed and began to withdraw. Then he turned back. "Oh," he said. "Your Highness might like to know that the Reverend Fisher is lodged in the room below. Good day to you."

Then the constable was gone. The door was locked.

More walked to the window and looked out through the narrow slit. He looked at the rolling clouds and the streaks of sunlight pouring through them to the earth. The sight reminded him of Jacob's ladder in Genesis, and the angels that descended and ascended it into Heaven. He looked at the spires of the churches on the London hillsides and folded his hands to pray.

It was difficult to write in his cell, but composing his thoughts gave Sir Thomas More some comfort and a sense of purpose. On this damp evening he was creating an essay on the Passion of Christ, the Lord's suffering. He was allowed paper and ink with which to write, and a small crucifix, which gave him courage.

There was a soft whispering at his door. "Sir Thomas!"

More inclined his head, listening.

"Sir Thomas!"

More stood with his candle and walked to the door. He knelt on the cold, uneven floor and listened through the gap beneath it.

"I'm here," he whispered. "Who are you?"

"John. A servant to Bishop Fisher, who is kept below here. He asks you to be of good cheer."

"How is he?"

"He is old, sir, and not well. He cannot eat the food. But his spirit is ever unbroken."

More closed his eyes thankfully. "I'm glad to hear it."

"He . . . he asks if you would ever contemplate taking the oath, and under what circumstances?"

More hesitated. "Tell him . . . tell him that I cannot take the oath without jeopardizing my soul to perpetual damnation. And *that* I cannot do."

There was an audible sigh. "Thank you, sir. I know it will renew my master's courage. Now I must go."

"God bless you," said More, but there was no reply. John had moved away.

Queen Anne squeezed the silver scissors carefully, snipping the last stray thread from the blue coverlet. She held the coverlet up, and, pleased with her handiwork, placed it carefully into a mahogany cradle beside her chair. There were only a few more months before Henry's son was born, and what a joyous day that would be.

Glancing over at her bed, Anne watched Lady Sheldon smooth the pillows and adjust the curtains. When Madge saw Anne looking, she curtsied and made to leave.

"Madge," said Anne. "Tell me. Did you . . . console the king?"

Madge blushed, but nodded.

Anne stood. "I told you, I'm not angry with you. It's all right."

Madge could not look at her mistress.

"Say something."

Madge took several breaths. "I . . ." she began but could say no more.

Exasperated, Anne waved the lady out. She sat alone for a moment, then placed her hand on the cradle, and sighed.

Archbishop Cranmer reported that there had been great success throughout the country in the swearing of allegiance to King Henry as head of the Church and in favor of his marriage to Queen Anne.

"But?" Henry asked, pausing with his knife in hand, a boiled leg of lamb in his bowl. Cranmer stood before him in the king's private dining chamber, hesitating to give the rest of the report, knowing the king could read the worry on his face.

"But," said Cranmer carefully, "we cannot persuade either Fisher or More to swear." He glanced at Cromwell, who stood at the end of the table, and then back at Henry. "However, Your Majesty, they may swear to part of it. Sir Thomas has already told us he has no argument with the Act of Succession, and . . ."

"No!" said Henry, slamming his knife into the table. The servants and Cranmer flinched, though Cromwell was unmoved. "There will be no compromise! For if we allow them, of all men, to swear to only what they like, then a precedent is set for others to follow. In this matter, Your Grace, it is all or nothing. You will have to be more persuasive."

Cranmer bowed, then stepped to the king's chair, presenting a letter. "Your Majesty, Dame Alice, wife of Sir Thomas More, has written you, asking to remind you of her husband's long service, and says he does nothing now out of malice but only the imperatives of his conscience."

Henry pulled the knife from the table and let out a long breath. His voice softened. "I know all about his conscience. He's worn it on his sleeve for years." He looked at Cromwell. "When he resigned as chancellor, he made a promise that he would retire from the world and live privately, to attend his soul. But it wasn't true. He continued to write and publish pamphlets about my matter and my conscience. He visited Katherine and cajoled others to support her."

Cromwell and Cranmer said nothing, waiting for the king's last word.

It came after the king had licked the knife and had driven it into the lamb. "He broke his promise. He must accept the consequence."

When Cranmer and Cromwell had left the dining chamber, Cromwell took Cranmer aside to speak quietly.

"We will have to find another way. It is imperative we do not create martyrs out of men who in every other way no longer matter to the world. I will visit More's wife and family. They can be encouraged to persuade him, more than anyone else. After all, if he is charged with treason, they stand to lose everything."

Within the grim and lonely walls of The More, the Lady Katherine, Dowager Princess, waited, her illness having drained her strength for many months. Days flowed into one another with nothing to differentiate them, fall into winter into spring, her prayers the one comforting constant in a gray world.

Ambassador Chapuys was dismayed to find the lady pale and wan, lying beneath a blanket on a daybed.

Katherine greeted the ambassador with a nod and weak smile. "Is my condition so surprising?" she asked. "I've had visits from the Earl of Wiltshire and others, trying to make me take the oath and threatening me when I did not. Boleyn told me I should be sent to the scaffold. So I asked him who would be the hangman? I said I would readily die if I was allowed to do so in full view of the people."

Chapuys shook his head slowly. "I truly believe Boleyn to be an emissary of Satan."

Katherine adjusted her coverlet. "Tell me. What news of poor Bishop Fisher?"

Chapuys retrieved a folded paper from a leather satchel. "I received this letter. The bishop's servant smuggled it out." He took a breath, and read, "'My friends, forgive me if I write of my wretched condition, but my cell is so cold and damp that I shiver even at midday. I fear I am fallen into decay and diseases of the body and can no longer take care of myself. I've neither shirt nor sheet nor other clothes that are necessary for me to wear. All I have are ragged and rent too shamefully. Notwithstanding, I would happily stand ashamed if only they would keep my body warm.'"

Katherine crossed herself. Her voice was ragged with emotion. "You see how we suffer, who keep the faith and the truth? Poor Fisher. He was like a lion in my defense. Now he will die alone and ashamed in prison."

"It . . . may be worse."

Katherine's trembling hand went to her breast.

"Parliament has passed a new Treasons Act. It makes 'malicious' denial of the king's supremacy punishable by death."

"He *wouldn't* do that!"

Chapuys bowed his head.

"Sir Thomas, you have visitors."

More looked up from his desk, squinting, his neck knotted and hot from hours leaning over his writings. The cell door opened with a grinding squeal, and his wife, Alice, and daughter Margaret came in.

More clambered up, gathering his family in his arms, for the briefest and sweetest moment aware of nothing but their presence and their love.

Then Alice stepped back to survey her husband's cell. "Well, Thomas More," she said softly, trying to hide her dismay. "I marvel that you've always been taken for so wise a man that you will now play the fool here in this filthy prison and be content apparently to be shut up among mice and rats."

The look in his wife's and daughter's eyes nearly broke his heart, and he said, "Don't look like that. I assure you this is one of the best rooms in the Tower. I am a guest of the constable who brought you here. I told him before that if I showed any signs of ingratitude for his great generosity then he should just throw me out of the Tower altogether!" He laughed. Alice and Margaret did not.

Alice took More's hand and squeezed it gently. "You know why we have come here."

"I thought it was to see me."

"Yes. But beyond that, we have come to ask you to swear the oath, so you can come home with us. We have such a marvelous, comfortable home compared to this!"

"Yes, but tell me one thing, Alice."

"Yes?"

"Is not this house as close to Heaven as my own?"

Alice dropped her husband's hand. "Good God, man. Is that all you can say?"

More took a slow breath. "You were always plainspoken, Alice. I admire that."

"Then," said Alice, "let me tell you plainly, husband, that I, and Margaret, and all our other family, have taken the oath and feel no worse for it!"

"I've always said I do not blame any other man, or woman, that has sworn. I only say I, myself, cannot."

Alice's face was pleading now. "We could swear in the certain knowledge that God regardeth the heart, and *not* the tongue. Therefore the meaning of the oath depends upon what you think, not what you say."

Dear Alice, always prepared for an argument. "Perhaps so. But still, I account that dissimulation, and I am afraid I cannot do it."

Alice's face went red. "You are thinking only about yourself!"

"How so?"

"If you are proceeded against, then all your possessions are forfeited to the crown. We would be forced into penury."

More's heart was cut. His voice lowered. "I have had more sleepless nights over that issue than over *anything* else."

"Still you will not swear?"

"Alice . . ."

His wife turned away. More saw that Margaret was crying silently. He put his arm around her.

"I want you to understand," he said as gently as he could. "I do not willingly seek martyrdom. In our faith it is considered a great sin to do so. I will try in every way to accommodate the king and his desires. Remember, he once made me a promise that he would not force me to do anything against my conscience, to look first unto God, and only after unto him. I am certain we shall come at last to a compromise." More took a piece of cloth from his desk and handed it to Margaret. "There now, dry your eyes. And you, Alice, say you are not angry with me. If you left and I thought so I would feel even more lonely than before."

Alice stepped back and touched More's face. "I am not angry with you. But I am frightened. So very frightened."

More's stoic wife, so brave and strong, began to tremble madly. More held her close, trying to soothe away the fear, knowing it was impossible.

Anne walked through the court, accompanied by Madge Sheldon and several of her other ladies, her head high, aware that though courtiers bowed to her, they did not show the warmth they used to show Katherine. *No matter*, Anne thought, *I am queen! I am soon to give birth to the Prince of England. Let them be sour. Their attitudes change nothing!*

Madge opened the door to Anne's private chamber and Anne entered the room.

And then a sharp, hot pain drove into her abdomen.

"Ah . . . !" she gasped.

"My lady?" asked Madge.

Anne clutched her stomach, terrified as the pain came again. With Madge holding her arm, Anne reached beneath her skirt. When she withdrew her hand, it was covered with blood.

"Oh, my God!" she wailed. "Oh, my God!"

* * * *

Henry came to his wife's bedchamber that evening. Anne dreaded the visit, yet longed for his arms to comfort her. The room was dark except for several candles burning on a table by the wall.

The king stood by the bed without speaking. Anne could not read his face in the shadows. She said, "I lost the child."

"Yes," said Henry. "They told me."

Anne waited, hoping he would come to her.

Henry said, "We will make no public announcement of the fact."

Was that all he would say? Was that it? "No," Anne managed. "Thank you, Your Majesty."

Henry walked out and shut the door. Anne burst into tears.

If Thomas Cromwell didn't know who occupied the Tower cell, he thought he would not have recognized the prisoner. Fisher had lost a great deal of weight and his body reeked of filth. The old man, sitting upon his mattress in thin trousers, shivered constantly.

"I came to give you two pieces of news," said Cromwell, staring hard at Fisher. "First, the pope has made you a cardinal . . ."

Fisher's eyes widened and he crossed himself joyously with a thin, crusted hand.

"But the second is that Parliament has decreed that to maliciously deny the king's supremacy in all matters is now a treasonable offense, punishable by death. So I ask you again, will you take the oath?"

Fisher sighed. "You already know my answer."

"Yes." Cromwell took a letter from a pouch at his waist. "My agents intercepted this. It was written to the emperor. The writer begs the emperor to invade England and restore what he calls 'the true queen and true faith.' Did you write this letter?"

Fisher said nothing. There was nothing to say. His signature was on the paper.

"In due course, Mr. Fisher, you are to be arraigned for treason and will be tried according to His Majesty's pleasure."

Fisher took a raspy breath, then another. "I must thank you, Mr.

Secretary, for bringing me news of my new hat. At least it was not all bad news." And with that, he managed a smile.

Anne stared at her father from her bed, shocked at his accusation, her hands shaking, her body still wrung out from the agonizing miscarriage.

"I did nothing to kill the child!" she pleaded. "I don't know what happened! Father, believe me, I was so careful!"

Boleyn crossed his arms and frowned, his eyes cold and icy as the Thames in February. "Not careful enough. We must *all* be careful. But you, *especially*, not to lose the king's love. Or *everything* is lost. Everything! For all of us!" He strode angrily from the room.

Afternoon winds blew hard from the west. The windowpanes of Pope Paul III's study shook as if angry spirits demanded entry.

The pope smoothed a paper out on his desk. "Our English friend writes that 'the lady is not to have a child after all.'" He looked across at Campeggio, now his secretary, who sat with his gout-afflicted foot propped on a pillow. "He also says that the king has already been unfaithful to her and that his love 'daily increases' for another 'very beautiful and adroit young woman.'" The pope touched his chin. "Those are his words, a beautiful and adroit young woman. I don't know about you but when I was younger, I knew all about adroit young women."

Campeggio nodded thoughtfully. "Yes, Holy Father."

The pope considered his secretary. "You have a son, I know. And I am not ashamed to say that I had four illegitimate children, before God made me turn away from beautiful and . . . adroit . . . young women."

Campeggio crossed himself.

"But," said the pope, looking back at the letter. "He also says that all this may mean nothing, 'considering the changeable character of the king and the craft of the lady, who well knows how to manage him.' You and I, Campeggio, have done well to escape the craft of women. Celibacy is an immense relief."

"Yes, Holy Father. But our friend is still fearful for the lives of Queen Katherine and her daughter. Neither is safe as long as the concubine has power."

"I will order prayers to be said for their safekeeping. Also for Cardinal Fisher. God grant him the courage to endure his tribulations."

Gazing at the torrent against the window, Campeggio said, "Yes, Holy Father."

"On the other hand, in the days of the founders of our church, it was considered a privilege to be martyred, like St. Peter and the other apostles. Our Church was founded upon the blood of martyrs. So perhaps it is a pity that you and I, Campeggio, unlike Cardinal Fisher, no longer have the opportunity to die for Christ."

Campeggio looked from the rain and back at the Holy Father.

Thomas Cromwell fingered the long, dirty beard on Thomas More's face and wrinkled his nose at the sour odor of the cell. Then he motioned for More to have a seat upon the chair. More chose to stand.

"How may I please you, Mr. Cromwell?" More asked. His voice bore the hoarse traces of his imprisonment.

"It would please me to know why you will not take the oath."

More sighed, amazed at Cromwell's persistence. "Mr. Cromwell, I have in good faith discharged my mind of all such matters and will no more dispute king's titles, nor pope's."

"The king accused you of obstinacy for not giving your reasons. You must have some view of the statute?"

"I have this view, that the act of Parliament is like a double-edged sword. If a man answers one way, it will confound his body. If he answers the other, it will confound his soul."

"But by not answering at all, you incur penalties. His Majesty has commanded me to draw up an act that will make your imprisonment permanent and lead to the confiscation of all your goods."

More closed his eyes for a moment. "Poor Alice."

"Sir Thomas, thousands have taken the oath. Many, I am sure, still share your faith and your beliefs. And yet, not your scruples."

"Well, as to that, some may do it for favor, some for fear. And some may think they can later repent and be shriven, and God will forgive them. And some may be of a mind that if they say one thing but think another, then their oath goeth upon what they think and not what they say." He paused. "But I cannot use such ways in so great a matter."

Cromwell shook his head. "In which case, and in all honesty, Sir Thomas, you are likely to pay the ultimate price."

"Is that all?" asked More sympathetically. "Then in good faith there is no difference between us, except that I shall die today and you tomorrow."

Chapter Ten

Madge Sheldon opened the door to Queen Anne's private chamber and curtsied. "My Lady, your sister is come."

Anne clapped her hands with great joy, and smiled at her father, who was visiting with her. She'd not seen her sister in many months. But then when Mary entered, Anne's heart fell. Mary was heavy with child.

Mary stooped, clumsily, in obedient supplication as Anne jumped to her feet and stared with a mixture of joy and trepidation. Boleyn remained seated, his arms crossed, and watched the scene with narrowed eyes.

"How has it happened?" Anne asked, touching her sister's belly. "We knew nothing!"

"I'm—married."

"Married?"

Mary looked from Anne to Boleyn, embarrassment etching her features.

"So," said Anne, "who is your husband?"

"His name is Mr. William Stafford."

"Is he at court? I haven't heard of him."

"He—William is a man of little standing and no fortune. He is now a serving soldier in Calais."

"Then why did you marry him?"

"I—I married him for love."

This was more than Boleyn could stand. He roared to his feet and went to Mary, his finger in her face. "You think him worthy to be the husband of the queen of England's sister?"

"Yes, Father. Since I love him and I—"

"You are much mistaken! You married him in secret, without asking approval! He is such a nothing we could never have given our permission—"

Mary tried to smile. "You should meet him. He is a fine, good, honest man! I—"

Boleyn grabbed his daughter's arms and shook her. "Since you acted brazenly and in spite of me, I shall cut off your allowance. You and your fine, honest man can rot in hell as far as I'm concerned!"

Mary cried out and pulled back from her father. She looked at Anne, her lips trembling. "Anne? How easy do you think it was for me to find a proper husband, when I was called the 'great prostitute'! I think myself fortunate to have found William and to be loved by him."

Her sister's anguish broke Anne's heart. She wanted to gather her and soothe her, yet her father's anger commanded her tongue. "You did not ask my permission," she said.

"Do I have to ask your permission to fall in love?"

"Yes!" roared Boleyn. "Now we are royalty. Everything is different!"

"Anne?" said Mary, her voice pinched and quivering. "Please, sister. If only you knew how much this meant to me."

Anne glanced again at her father. "No," she said slowly. "You and your husband are banished from court."

Mary covered her face, curtsied, and left the chamber in tears.

The trees of the royal forest were heavy with foliage, branches arching out to weave green canopies overhead, shading King Henry and his companion, Charles Brandon, as they reined their mounts to a walk, ending an invigorating morning hunt.

Henry leaned back in his saddle and slipped his feet from the stirrups to let them dangle freely. "Charles," he said casually, "we must go hunting again soon. I have some new boar spears. They were given me as a present. Then I forgot about them."

Brandon nodded, then pulled his own feet from his stirrups. He sensed the king wanted to say more, so he waited.

"I want to ask you a personal question," said Henry.

"Yes?"

"Have any of the women you've bedded ever lied about their virginity?"

Brandon couldn't help but smile. "Their virginity? I'd put it the other way around. Did any of them *not* lie about it? Why do you ask?"

Brandon saw immediately the king was not happy with the answer.

"I ask Your Majesty's forgiveness," he said.

But Henry shook his head. "It doesn't matter. I asked for the truth and you told me."

"I was exaggerating."

"No," said Henry, returning his feet to the stirrups. "I don't think so."

They rode on in silence, followed at a distance by several dutiful guards. Then Brandon noted, up ahead and coming in their direction, a man and a woman astride two horses. As they got closer, Henry muttered, "What's this?"

They were commoners, the man rough-hewn and coarse, the woman young and clearly pretty even though her mouth was covered with a scarf.

Henry dismounted and approached the pair. When they realized who it was, they bowed their heads.

"Good morrow," Henry said.

"Your Majesty," said the man nervously. "I assure Your Majesty I have a permit to ride through Your Majesty's forest. I swear and I could easily prove it."

"What's your name?"

"W—William Webbe, Your Grace."

"And your sweetheart's?"

"Bess, Your Grace."

Henry flicked his hand. "Come here, Bess."

He reached up and pulled the young woman down from her saddle. She glanced at William but said nothing. Henry slowly unwound the scarf to reveal the quivering beauty beneath.

"Hello, Bess."

Bess glanced down. "Your . . . Majesty."

To Brandon's delight, Henry leaned in and kissed Bess fully and urgently. Webbe looked away, stunned and unable to watch.

Then the king said to Bess, "Come with me." As Webbe shifted uneasily in his saddle, Henry led Bess to his own mount and helped her astride. Brandon smiled as the king reined his horse toward the hunting lodge.

Let Henry take her, he thought. *Let him find the beauty in another flower! Let his heart be moved even further away from Anne Boleyn!*

Her heart beat relentlessly and her legs refused to be still. Back and forth she walked, back and forth again, through the light of the candles on the table and into the shadows by the windows. Her hair was tangled and her gown wrinkled, but she could not care. There were demons taunting her.

"Sister?"

Anne looked up and squinted to find George standing in her room, staring at her.

"I—couldn't sleep," she managed. She began to pace again, reaching the windows and turning, her hands out to keep her balance. Yes, she had been drinking. She had to do something to make them leave her alone.

"Why could you not sleep?"

"For thinking of her!" Anne snapped.

"Who?"

"The Lady Mary, of course! And . . . her mother."

"Katherine?"

Anne stopped and stared at George. "Yes! Katherine!"

George frowned. "I don't understand. What harm can they do you now?"

"Every harm!" Anne grabbed for the flagon on the table and refilled her cup with wine. She took a long, noisy drink. George poured himself a drink, then held it, watching his sister.

Anne shook her cup at her brother, sending spatters to the floor. "I hate Katherine for all that proud Spanish blood! But Mary is worse. As long as Mary is alive, she could be queen!"

"No. The Act of Succession makes it impossible. Elizabeth, *your* daughter, is made heir to the throne."

Anne began to pace again. "The king can change his mind! He has absolute power! And what he has given, he can take away, and what taken away, he can give back. He could still make Mary queen above my daughter."

"But why should he?"

"I don't know. I just fear it. And my fear murders sleep. This is all I know of Mary, that she is *my* death, and I am *hers*!"

"Tell me, Mr. Cromwell," said Henry, standing at the window of his private chamber, gazing down at the gardens and the single-minded business of the gardeners with their carts, spades, and scythes. "Does Sir Thomas continue in his stubbornness?"

"Yes, Majesty."

"Then you will visit him again. You will force him to give his reasons for not taking the oath. Or I will deem his silence on the matter to be malicious."

Henry pushed away from the window. "I have done a great deal of thinking about the reforms we are making to religious practice in the kingdom," he said, crossing the floor, his hands behind his back. "Our intention has always been to purge the Church of its corrupt ways. Not to destroy faith, but to make it honest. I am charging you, Mr. Cromwell, to appoint commissioners to make a thorough survey of all the monasteries and religious houses in England, in order to uncover and investigate any abuses within them. And at the same time to establish their possessions, in land and wealth and so on."

Cromwell nodded.

"I am appointing you vice-regent in spiritual matters. Yes, you are a layman, not a churchman. But in this matter I cannot trust the prejudice of any churchman. You will begin the survey immediately."

Cromwell bowed and left. Henry walked back to the window, and removed a small silver locket from the pouch at his waist. He opened it, revealing the tiny picture of his wife Anne, the portrait she had sent him so long ago, when he desired her most fiercely.

Ambassador Chapuys stood amid the partyers, watching the festive dancing in the Great Hall, feeling less than festive himself. The king and queen moved about in the proscribed steps, dancing with and among Madge Sheldon, George Boleyn, Mark Smeaton, and other ladies and courtiers. Henry and Anne appeared happy with each other, exchanging warm smiles when they were close.

Then Chapuys noticed another near him, a young lady observing the dancing with a solemn face. Chapuys moved to her.

"Excuse me. Aren't you Margaret More, Sir Thomas's daughter?"

The young woman glanced up. "Yes, sir."

"I am Eustace Chapuys, the emperor's ambassador," Chapuys said quietly. "It is a great pleasure to meet anyone associated with Thomas More. He's a very special man."

Margaret curtsied. "Thank you, Your Excellency."

"May I ask why you have come to court?"

Margaret held out a paper. "I've come to petition Mr. Secretary Cromwell. Lately most of our lands have been sold. My family is near poverty. I must beg Mr. Cromwell for pity and help. Things go very hard with my mother. There is no other recourse."

"I'm sorry to hear it. I'm sorry for many things that are occurring in this kingdom. The good seem to suffer and the wicked to prosper."

Margaret nodded. She knew firsthand.

* * * *

Anne knew her father was watching her closely, but it didn't dampen the evening. He could worry all he wanted. She wanted to be happy, and she would be so.

She stepped and turned, coming to partner for a moment with Mark Smeaton. She smiled as he took her hand. "Mark?" she said, brows raised.

"Majesty?"

"You're a free spirit. I love that. Everyone else . . . constrains me. Nobody understands." She took a step right, then left in rhythm to the music. "Never leave me."

Mark smiled broadly. "I would rather die." And with that, he whirled away.

Far removed from the good food, fine clothing, and bright halls of the palace, Thomas More stood in the center of his cell, holding his daughter in an embrace that at once eased his soul and tormented his heart. The warmth of her body was a precious balm against the relentless chill of the Tower; the warmth of her love was a painful and priceless gift.

"How did you find court?" he asked softly.

Margaret stepped back and shook her head. Her voice was thick with disgust. "It seemed to me they never do anything but sporting and dancing! And as far as Anne Boleyn is concerned, I think she never did better."

More touched his daughter's arm. "I am full of pity to think what misery that woman will shortly come to. Those dances of hers are such dances they might take all our heads off like footballs. But it won't be long before her own head will dance the same dance."

Margaret looked closely at her father, at his bony frame and thread-bare clothing, at the sallow skin and hollow eyes. "What has happened here? It seems they are treating you worse than before."

"They have taken away the stove and some clothing. My food is reduced."

Margaret's face drew up, but More shook his head. "For the love of God, do not be concerned about me. I think often and hard about Christ's Passion and agony. I am not afraid of death." He hesitated. "I am only afraid of torture. In case they use violent ways to make me swear. I don't know how brave I would be. My flesh shrinks away from pain."

"But you do not have to suffer! Just take the oath, like I did. Like everyone has done. Just say it and your body will be saved!"

"But the saving of my body will be at the expense of my soul."

"No!"

"Yes."

"No! None of us believes that. Father, please! For the love I know you bear us, don't do this to us!"

More looked at Margaret's face, at the terror, love, and anguish etched there, and he burst into tears. The tears he had held back and had prayed into the shadows for so long rushed forward and poured out, wracking his body. Margaret took her father in her arms and held him as he sobbed.

Lady Mary Boleyn stepped into Secretary Cromwell's chamber, her hands folded over her rounded belly, trying her best to look composed.

"Lady Mary," said Cromwell, putting down his quill, a sympathetic look on his face. "What can I do for you?"

"I came because I wish to be reconciled to the queen. I confess that in my dealings with the world, love overcame reason. I beg my sister's forgiveness." She paused as the child within her kicked tenuously. "After all, she above everyone else should know about marrying for love."

"Forgive me, but you should not presume upon the queen's good graces, or ever assume that forgiveness is lightly given."

"I do not so presume. I only—"

Cromwell held up his hand. "I cannot say," he said. "But it may be that the queen is not minded in the matter."

"But you must ask her!"

Cromwell said nothing, but in his eyes Mary could see that her request was futile. At first she was terrified, but then something shifted inside her.

She felt a surprising new strength, a relief, at realizing the truth. She let out the breath she'd been holding, and said, "Then, perhaps, Mr. Cromwell, you can tell Her Majesty that I might have had a greater man of birth, but I could never have had a man who loved me so well. And—"

Cromwell's eyes were hooded. "Yes?"

"And tell her that I would rather beg my bread with him than be the greatest queen alive."

With that, she with her unborn child turned, and walked away, confident, into their future.

Katherine coughed, and touched her lips with her handkerchief. Each breath drew a pain in her chest, though she would not show the hurt to her visitor. A queen was dignified at all times, even in her sickbed. On the stand beside her bed were candles, brass icons, and small figures of saints. They comforted her greatly and were a constant reminder of God's steadfast love during tribulation.

Ambassador Chapuys bowed and spoke in a near whisper, as if loud words might injure Katherine. "Majesty."

"Forgive me receiving you this way," said Katherine. "I am still not well."

"I understand," said the ambassador. "But it may give you cheer to know that Princess Mary is much improved after the king sent his own physician to her."

Katherine smiled as best she could. "Thank God."

Chapuys looked away as if struggling with something terrible he needed to say.

"What is it?" asked Katherine, not certain she wanted to know.

Chapuys looked back. His eyes were pinched. "Bishop Fisher has been convicted of treason. He's to be martyred in a few days' time."

Elizabeth Darrell, Katherine's lone servant, could not slow her thoughts. Her mind moved back and forth as furiously as the rag she was using to scrub the tile floor of the parlor. She feared more for Katherine; no, she feared for herself. It would be best to try to cheer the queen; no, it would be best to be truthful and acknowledge the hopelessness of the situation. Elizabeth's head hurt with it all, and she scrubbed harder.

There was a scuffing in the room and she glanced up. Thomas Wyatt stood near the door looking at her. Elizabeth stood and wiped her hands on her apron.

"Why are you here?" she asked. "To see the degradation that we've been forced to?"

Wyatt shook his head sadly. "No. I don't like to see it. Why do you stay? Why don't you come back to court?"

"I love the queen. Nothing in this world will make me leave her, since I am her last servant. I would rather die."

Wyatt stepped toward Elizabeth, but she held her hands up to stop him. "I am a Catholic. I believe in my faith. Perhaps you poets don't believe in anything?"

Wyatt considered this. Then, "In love, perhaps."

"Love is nothing."

"Love is *everything*."

They stared at each other for a long moment. Then Elizabeth said, "You may kiss me. Then you will leave me alone. Forever. I don't want your pity, Thomas."

Wyatt took her at her word and into his arms. He kissed her, and she found herself kissing him back, the feelings she'd once had trying to return. But then she turned away to stare at the wall.

"Elizabeth?" His voice was filled with genuine anguish.

She said nothing. And after a moment, she heard him leave.

King Henry's hands were clasped tightly as he knelt before the figure of the crucified Christ in the Chapel Royal. He was alone on his order, and there, by himself, prayed fervently.

"There is something I need to ask you," he asked, pleading with the Christ. "It is on my conscience. It troubles me. My heart is heavy and full and sore."

The marble face of the Lord seemed to look down at him, into his soul. But was there compassion in the face? Henry could not tell, and it wounded him.

"God knows how I love him," he said, his throat tight, his face bathed in sweat. "I say this only to you. I confess only to you. I love him. And I hate him. I hate in equal measure to my love, for he is the spirit that denies. Only you can know or judge, whether he be on my conscience or not!"

Henry's heart kicked painfully. "Why?" he demanded of the Lord. "Why can he not be as others? Why does he cross me? Why can his vanity be greater than a king's? Vanity of vanities, sayeth the preacher, all is vanity! And behold, I have seen all the works of many under the sun, and all is vanity!"

Henry stood then, before Christ, and shouted through his tears, "All is vanity!"

Sir Thomas More knelt in prayer beside his pallet, his knees raw, his hands chapped. His time on earth was not long now, and the Lord's hand on his heart was a sweet and terrible solace.

"Sir Thomas!" The voice came from beneath the door.

More took his candle and sat with effort on the floor by the door. "Is that John?"

"Yes, sir. My master is called forth tomorrow. He hopes you and he shall soon meet in Heaven."

"Tell him that will be the way, for it is a very straight gate we are in." He paused. "And tell him he deserves and will receive all of Heaven's graces."

John's footsteps moved away, and More leaned heavily against the door, his head in his hands, his heart breaking.

A large crowd had gathered to witness the beheading of Bishop Fisher in the Tower courtyard. The sunlight was bright and warm, as if offering the old cleric the only thing it could on his last day upon the earth.

Cardinal Fisher was shrunken and frail, his skin drawn tight upon his skull. He had been given a new simple black vest and cap to wear, a small concession.

Followed by two guards, he climbed the scaffold with great effort, his body aching with age, stiffness, and fear. When he reached the top, he nodded at the swordsman, and turned to the crowd below.

"Good people," he said. "You see that today I am wearing my finest clothes, for today is my wedding day!"

There were murmurs of sympathy through the crowd. Brandon, Wyatt, and Boleyn, near the front of the gathering, watched in silence.

Fisher took a breath, looked down at the chopping block, then out again at the upturned faces. "Good people. I ask you to love the king and obey him, for he is good by nature, even if he is not right in his religious policies. Of my own deeds and life, I have nothing to say, except I am condemned for wishing to preserve the honor of God and the Holy See . . ."

More in the crowd muttered their sympathies and approval.

"And now, I ask for your prayers. I am only flesh and fear death as any man does. It's true that I have long since made up my mind to die for Christ and his Church, but now that the moment is at hand, my body rebels in terror. I need your help."

The crowd began to call out.

"God bless you, Cardinal Fisher!"

"God be with you!"

The crowd's voices rose together, and the voices strengthened him. Humbly, Fisher kneeled and stretched out his arms. He uttered forgiveness to the swordsman, and, without trembling, lowered his head over the block.

Curiosity had the best of Pope Paul, and he leaned over, carefully, to catch a glimpse of the goings-on behind the tall, drape-covered scaffolding on the floor of St. Peter's. But then he heard the tap-tap-tapping of Campeggio's walking stick on the marble floor, and he quickly stood straight.

"Holy Father!" Campeggio called.

Behind the drapes, there was a shout. "Not like that, assholes! Moses looks like a pile of crap!"

An old man emerged from the drapes, covered in dust and smears of paint. He glanced at the pontiff with apparent disgust and stormed off.

"Do you know who that was?" the pope asked Campeggio, his voice pitched with excitement. "Michelagniolo di Lodovico di Lionardo di Bounarroti Simoni."

Campeggio's eyes widened. "Michelangelo? That was *him*?"

"Yes. We forgive him because people say he's a genius. Now what did you say to me?"

"Holiness, we have heard from England of the murder of Cardinal Fisher."

The pope nodded, then tried again to look behind the drapes. "I've heard of it. It's an outrage. I made Fisher a prince of our Holy Church but it mattered nothing to the king, who is so mired in vice and lust that he is beyond reason."

Tired of trying to sneak a peek, Pope Paul caught a corner of the drape in his fingers and tugged it aside several inches. The painted visions that were revealed made him smile with appreciation—vibrant colors, rich tones, and the smooth hues of naked flesh.

Anne lay abed, staring at the bedside candle. She had tried to sleep, but her body, like a willful servant, disobeyed her. So she stared at the flame, exhausted and tormented, letting the flickering light create images in her mind, images that danced for a moment then faded away.

The back door to her chamber opened, and Henry was there, his chest bare and bathed in sweat, his face etched with shadow and light.

Anne looked from the flame to her husband and saw a fierce compassion in his eyes, and her heart clenched with hope.

"My lady," he said. He climbed into bed with Anne and drew her close.

Anne at first could not speak. And then she whispered, "Do you . . . still have a passion for me?"

"I do, sweetheart." He cradled Anne against his chest.

The torrent inside her soul swelled and broke. She began to sob.

"There," said Henry, holding her even closer, rocking her. "Don't weep. It's all right. Everything is all right."

All the writings he had done, all the heart's blood he had poured onto paper, was being taken away. Sir Thomas More watched as Sir Richard Rich, the solicitor-general, gathered the stacks of paper, pens, packets of ink powders, inkwell, and books and, on Cromwell's orders, placed them into a large chest. More's life was being reduced yet again.

As Rich continued to strip More's desk of the last of his human comforts, More turned to gaze out the window of his cell. It was best not to watch.

"May I ask you a question?" asked Rich.

More didn't look back. "Only if it's hypothetical, Richie. It's better that way."

Rich chuckled, almost sympathetically. "Suppose that Parliament enacted a bill to say that I, Richard Rich, was king and that it would be treason to deny it. Would you accept me as king?"

More turned and smiled sadly. "Yes. But let me counter with another hypothetical case. Suppose Parliament enacted that God should not be God, and opposing the act would be treason. Would you say that God was not God?"

Rich weighed one of More's particularly hefty manuscripts in his hands and, impressed, raised a brow. He put the manuscript in with the others in the chest. "No," he said. "Since Parliament cannot make any such law."

"And no more can Parliament make the king supreme head of the Church!" said More.

"There, Thomas," said Rich, closing the lid of the chest. "I think my work here is done."

Fisher had been dead a week, his head stuck upon a spike of the iron railing outside Whitehall Palace, where those faithful to the king had come to scowl, and those faithful to the Catholic Church had come to pray. Henry did not enter or leave the palace by the gate nearest the head; he did not care to see it. He did not need to.

The king was at work at his desk, reading, when he heard Cromwell enter his outer chamber. He did not look up. He did not care to see Cromwell's face. He did not need to.

"Majesty," said Cromwell after a moment. "Now that Fisher is dead, what should be done about More?"

Henry continued his reading, though his thoughts were not on the words. "We should press ahead, Mr. Cromwell. We should press ahead."

After another moment, Cromwell bowed and left.

Dust spun on the sunlight filtering through the tall windows of the Westminster Hall council gallery, and a fly that had gained entrance into the room was cheerfully landing on the drapes, the chairs, and the floor, crawling and hopping about. The dust and the fly, however, offered the only sense of abandon in the room. The five commissioners seated at the cloth-covered table stared gravely at Sir Thomas More, who stood before them, painfully thin, unkempt, unshaven. Upon the walls hung paintings of commissioners long dead, men who could no longer speak but whose expressions seemed to mirror the critical attitudes of those at the table.

At last, one commissioner, dressed as they all were in robe and cap of black, broke the silence. "Sir Thomas More, you are arraigned before this commission on charges of high treason. How do you answer the charges?"

More made an effort to ease his breathing. Around and behind him sat an audience of interested noblemen, including Thomas Cromwell and Thomas Boleyn. More could feel their curiosity, their morbid fascination burning into the back of his neck. Nothing he could say would matter. But speak, he must.

"I begin by denying that I ever maliciously opposed the king's marriage to Anne Boleyn. I have never spoken maliciously against it, but only sometimes according to my mind, opinion, and conscience, and have suffered as a result."

A second commissioner leaned over the table. "But you *have* maliciously denied the Act of Supremacy!"

"No. I have been silent upon it. And for all my silence, neither your law nor any law in the world is able to justly and rightly punish me, unless you may also lay to my charge either some word, or some deed."

"Your continued silence can easily be construed as an action."

"Ah, but even in that case, the presumption that silence gives consent precludes the charge against me."

The commissioners whispered among themselves, their voices low like distant growls in a forest.

A third commissioner pointed at More. "What of the charge that you conspired in prison with Bishop Fisher, a convicted traitor?"

More shook his head. "I never met him in prison but talked a little to his servant about familiar things and recommendations, such as were seemly to our long acquaintance."

The commissioners whispered again. Then the first said, "We go back to your supposed silence on the Act of Supremacy. We think you have in fact spoken about it. And we have a witness. Call the solicitor-general. Call Mr. Richard Rich."

More turned quickly about to see Rich entering the chamber, avoiding More's gaze, to stand before the commission.

"Sir Richard," said the commissioner. "You are under oath. Do you tell this commission, truthfully, what the accused said to you on the matter?"

"Yes, sirs."

More thought back to their talk in his cell, recalled their hypothetical conversation. His heart picked up a fast, painful rhythm. *My Dear God, no—*

"We agreed that Parliament might not make such a law that God was not God, to which Sir Thomas said, 'no more could Parliament make the king supreme head of the Church.'"

"So he maliciously denied the king's authority, in those words?" asked the second commissioner.

"Yes, sirs."

A loud murmur broke out in the audience, some men sounding pleased, others shocked. More's hands, clasped before him, tightened on themselves.

The first commissioner raised his finger. "Then I will charge this commission to return a true verdict, to determine whether Sir Thomas More did converse with Sir Richard Rich in the manner alleged?"

The commissioners nodded. Their agreement was unanimous.

"You do so find him guilty? Then I will proceed in judgment against the prisoner."

"My lord," said More. "When I was a lawyer the convention was to ask the prisoner before judgment why judgment should not be given against him."

The commissioners shook their heads, irritated. The first commissioner said, "What, then, are you able to say to the contrary?"

"Seeing that you are determined to condemn me, God knows how, I will now discharge my conscience and speak my mind plainly and freely." He could hear the frisson of expectation stirring behind him. "This indictment is ground upon an act of Parliament directly repugnant to the laws of God and his Holy Church, the supreme governance of which may no temporal prince presume by *any* law to take unto himself. It belongs by right to the See of Rome, to St. Peter and his successors, as our Savior said from his own mouth when he was on this earth." Hearing his convictions, his own words, at long last on the air restored his courage, and his voice rose with passion. "This realm, being but one small part of the Church, cannot make any particular law disagreeable to the general laws of Christ's universal Catholic Church. No more can this realm of England refuse obedience to Rome than can a child refuse obedience to his own natural father."

There was an uproar in the gallery. Men shouted at More, screaming that he was, indeed, a traitor. The commissioners banged their gavels.

"Now we plainly see that you are maliciously bent!" cried the second commissioner.

"No," said More. "Not maliciously. I hope we may all meet merrily in Heaven hereafter, and I desire Almighty God to preserve and defend the King's Majesty, and send him good counsel."

The commissioners continued to bang their gavels until there was silence. The first commissioner narrowed his eyes, leaned forward, and said, "Sir Thomas More, you are to be drawn on a hurdle through the City of London to Tyburn, there to be hanged till you be half dead, then cut down alive, your bowels to be taken out of your body and burned before you, your privy parts cut off, your head cut off, and your body divided into four parts . . ."

More looked at the fly, now on the window glass, and thought how easy to be a fly, one of God's simplest creatures, so ignored and overlooked by men.

He was returned to the Tower of London to await his terrible sentence, surrounded by guards with halberds and swords. A crowd had gathered at the street to watch the famous prisoner, some to chide, some to weep. With a mixture of ecstasy and anguish, More saw his family amid the gathering. John and Margaret, their faces torn with terror and devotion, knelt on the road to ask his blessing.

More raised his chained hands as best he could. "I bless you, my children. Be of good cheer, for I will pray for you, and Dame Alice, that we may meet in Heaven together where we shall be merry forever and ever."

A guard grumbled and shoved More forward. Yet Margaret, overcome, rushed through the men and the swords to gather her father around the neck, and to lovingly kiss him again and again.

They had been discussing other business—new properties, new palaces, new horses—when Henry slammed back from his desk, stood, and walked to the window of his outer chamber. Cromwell stared after him.

After a long silence, Henry said, "When is the execution?"

"Tomorrow, Your Majesty."

"What date is that?"

"The sixth of July."

"At what time?"

"Ten in the morning."

Henry sighed. Down below, in the garden, he could see Anne, her brother, and her father, walking in the gardens and chatting happily. Anne had plucked springs of lavender and sage, and held them to her nose, taking in their fragrances.

"I have decided to commute the sentence to beheading. Tell the officials."

"Yes, Your Majesty."

Cromwell bowed and left. Henry continued to watch the happy family below, laughing amid the roses and lavender.

More's family had not been allowed to attend the execution. Hundreds of others had come, though, and stood pressed against one another beneath the scaffold and across the Tower green.

More climbed the scaffold steps steadily, accompanied by Humphrey Monmouth, the sheriff of London. The fear of pain that had so tormented him was gone, and he was lifted in his soul, praying, stepping ever closer to union with his Savior.

I pray to have the last things in remembrance. To have even before my eyes my death that is ever at hand. To make death no stranger to me . . .

A step wobbled, and Monmouth caught More's arm to steady him.

More smiled. "Thank you, Sir Humphrey. But when I come down again, let me shift for myself, as well as I can."

He stepped onto the platform and walked to the hooded headsman and the wooden block. More turned to the crowd and spoke calmly. "I ask you all to bear witness with me that I shall now suffer death in and for the faith of the Holy Catholic Church. I beg you to pray for the king, and tell him I died his good servant, but God's first."

At that, the headsman, holding his ax, kneeled before More and clasped his hands. "I ask for your pardon and blessing," he whispered.

More kissed the man and said, "You will give me this day a greater benefit than ever any mortal man can be able to give me. Pluck up your spirits and be not afraid to do your office."

The headsman stood, and More knelt before the block. He raised his face away from the crowd and to the sky, and he offered his last words as a mortal to his Heavenly king, "Have mercy upon me, oh God, according to thy loving kindness."

He put his head gently upon the block.

And it was done.

Henry watched the clock on the mantle as the hands moved slowly toward the hour of ten. He was alone in his private chamber. Every muscle in his body was racked with torment, and his mind reeled with what he'd had to do but what his heart did not want him to do.

The clock hands moved closer to the execution hour.

Henry looked away from the clock, to the wall, to his shadow on the wall. There, he could see a silhouette, but not himself. He could not see his face, nor his eyes. What would be there in his eyes at that moment?

He looked back at the clock. The hands reached ten.

Henry clenched his fists and screamed.

CHAPTER ELEVEN

The crowd in St. Peter's Square roared as Pope Paul III, in his golden robe, stepped through the velvet curtains onto the small balcony, blinking momentary in the sun, holding his hands out toward the vast and adoring crowd below. Bishop Campeggio and several other bishops, all dressed in scarlet robes, their hands folded piously, moved out to flank the pontiff on the balcony.

The pope made the sign of the cross and then blessed the joyous horde of humanity. *"Sancti Apostoli Petrus et Paulus, de quorum potestate et auctoritate confidimus ipsi intercedant pro nobis ad Dominum."*

The crowd responded, "Amen."

"Precibus et emitis Mariae semper Virginis . . . et omnium Sanctorum misereatur vestri omnipotens Deus et dimissis omnibus peccatis vestris, perducat vos Iesus Christus ad vitam æternam."

"Amen."

Then the pope said, "My beloved brothers and sisters, I offer you the blessings of God with all my heart. But today, forgive me, I shall speak in English."

The crowd stood, their gazes fixed expectantly upon him.

"To the faithful people of England," said Pope Paul, "your Holy Father offers you the hand of condolence, his tears of grief, and his anger at the martyrdom of Sir Thomas More and Cardinal Fisher. Their murders have shocked the whole of Christendom. It was an unpardonable sin against God and our Holy Church, in whose name these two noble men died. We pray for their souls but know that they are already received into Heaven with great joy.

"But we pray, too, for those in England who must continue to live under tyranny, in fear for their lives and their souls. We pray the king ceases to listen to evil counsel and returns to obedience and the true faith before it is too late. We pray to Mary, Mother of God, that England may be redeemed from heresy and all its evil ways, and from the clutches of the heretics who are even now leading her toward destruction and damnation!"

The crowd, together, replied, "Amen." Campeggio nodded, offering his own silent prayer to God for divine aid.

The brothel was dark and seductive, thick with the cloying scents of exotic perfumes and sex, lined with small chambers in which young ladies laid about, stretching and arching their bodies amid the shadows to entice, to please. Through this darkened place Henry moved silently, led by a gnarled little man who was helping him in his search, peering into the chambers, seeking out the one who might heal him, if not for a lifetime at least for an hour.

Then he found her, her lithe, unclothed body upon a bed of pillows, her face hidden by a veil. Her waist was narrow, her nipples erect, and her long hair shining upon her shoulders. She smiled and beckoned to Henry. He went to her to hold her, tears filling his eyes.

Another woman was suddenly there, her damp and naked body pressed against him, her breath in his ear. He caressed both women's breasts but did not kiss them.

After a moment the veiled woman whispered, softly, "Why?"

"I come here to forget," said Henry. "To forget the mortal ache of memory." He drew the women even closer, his fingers moving about their flesh in desperation, and then they faded away . . .

The tavern crawled with the drinking and the drunk, filled with those who sought respite from life's trials in spirits, song, and companionship.

Ambassador Chapuys and William Brereton had found a cramped corner away from prying eyes and ears and had ordered a round of ales.

"Tonight," said Chapuys, "we sup and think of those who are no longer with us. To More and Fisher, martyred men."

Both men raised their tankards.

"God bless them," added Brereton with a sad nod of his head.

They took long drinks, savoring the flavor and the heat. Then Chapuys put his cup down and leaned toward Brereton. "I am told," he whispered, "that many who initially supported the king's reforms are now forming a different opinion. The terrible murders of honest and faithful men have opened many eyes."

"I do not blame the king," said Brereton. "He is surrounded by false and evil counselors."

"Then he should not listen to them."

Brereton wiped the corners of his mouth with his fingers. "He would not, except for one thing. He has been seduced by witchcraft. I have always believed it, and now I have proof."

Chapuys glanced anxiously about, then back at Brereton. "You have proof?"

Brereton nodded. "I've befriended a maid of Anne's bedchamber, who has told me the harlot hides a secret. She has a deformed hand, an extra fingernail on her left hand which she is always at great pains to conceal."

Chapuys strummed his fingers, urging Brereton to continue.

"As well she has moles all over her body, which are known sometimes as the Devil's Teats. This maid has sworn to me that she has seen these upon Anne's naked skin, even though the lady constantly seeks to cover herself."

Chapuys crossed himself. "My God, is it so?"

"It's the truth," said Brereton, eyes aglow with ale and candlelight. "That's why she must die."

Henry, standing near the window of his outer chamber, glanced back at Cromwell, who was standing by the table in the middle of the room, holding the papers the king had just signed. "George Boleyn—Lord Rochford—is to marry Lord Morley's daughter."

"Yes, Your Majesty."

The king stroked his chin, forcing his mind onto the matters at hand even as his thoughts fought to return to a dark moment of the recent past.

"Lord Morley came to see me," Henry said. "He cannot meet Boleyn's demand for a dowry of three hundred pounds. I assured him I would make up the shortfall and also grant Lord Rochford the manor of Grimston in Norfolk as a wedding gift."

"Your Majesty is most generous."

Henry glanced at the window again, away from Cromwell, and he opened his fist. He had been clutching the little silver crucifix Sir Thomas More had given him for Christmas in a time long past. Henry closed his hand again tightly, the silver warm and accusing in his palm.

"How is your survey of the religious houses progressing?" the king asked.

"The commissioners have uncovered many enormities."

"What sort of enormities?"

"They have found what they did not at first expect. The monks in many places are so depraved, so licentious and corrupt that the commissioners already despair of any perfect reformation. They have also discovered innumerable cases of fraud."

Henry strode from the window and placed his closed hand atop the bronze globe that sat on the table and gave it an idle spin. "Fraud?"

"Yes. Take for example the case of the celebrated Holy Blood of Hailes, supposedly the blood of a saint, used for healing pilgrims who flock there hoping for a miracle. It turns out to be the blood of a duck, which the monks renew regularly."

"Duck's blood." Such cold deception! Then he noticed Cromwell had gone silent. "What else?"

"If Your Majesty will forgive me, I think we should be finding ways to promote Your Majesty's new monarchy."

This piqued Henry's interest. "What do you have in mind?"

"One way is through the production of plays."

"Why plays?"

"Plays are an ideal way of setting forth, in a lively way, the abomination and wickedness of the bishop of Rome. As well as the wickedness of monks, nuns, friars, and suchlike, to which your commissioners have attested. They're also a way to demonstrate to people the obedience that as subjects they owe, by God's and man's laws, to Your Majesty."

Henry nodded. "Good. Then, Mr. Secretary, I leave it to you to finance and produce some."

A flicker of hesitation crossed Cromwell's face, but he bowed and left.

Alone, Henry moved from the table to his favorite chair and sat. He leaned back, looked at his fist, and then slowly opened it. There, upon the flesh, he saw the red indentation of the crucifix, as if he had been branded.

A torch came forward through the stone passageway, the orange glow bathing the damp walls and floor—it was the constable, leading George Boleyn through the bowels of the Tower of London to the alcove where Archbishop Cranmer and Cromwell, holding his own torch, waited for him. George looked less than pleased to be where he was, but Cromwell knew that he would soon forget his discomfort.

"My lord," greeted Cromwell.

George let out a breath. "Mr. Secretary." And then to Cranmer, "Your Grace."

Cromwell motioned the others to follow. He led them along the corridor, down a narrow set of stairs, to a hallway even deeper in the Tower.

"Since your lordship makes no secret of your zeal for reform," Cromwell said to George, watching his steps and not looking back, "we were anxious to let you know our progress. His Grace has just informed me of an important appointment at Canterbury Cathedral."

"Dr. Simon Heyes has been made our new dean," Cranmer added.

"Dr. Heyes particularly detests the cult of images and is determined to remove them from the Cathedral, as well as introduce the new learning."

They passed cells and rooms with doors closed and fortified with iron bands and locks. The men turned right and then left into a colder, even narrower corridor.

"It's vital we place reformers in positions of responsibility inside the church. There's bound to be a reaction to the self-serving martyrdoms of Fisher and More."

"After all," said Cranmer, "the Catholic Church has depended for centuries upon the ignorance and credulity of the faithful. The last thing they want to see is an educated and evangelical population."

George spit air. "That won't stop ignorant people attacking both the queen and the evangelical movement, as they're doing even now!"

Cromwell stopped to gaze directly at George. "Which is why I'm letting it be known through the kingdom that if anyone hears their neighbor or friend criticizing the king, his marriage, or his reforms, then they have a duty to report it."

"At the same time," said Cranmer, "*we* have a duty to spread the good news. If the new monarchy is about anything at all, then it is about liberty! Liberty from old superstitions, from fear and guilt. We are moving from darkness into light."

They had reached the end of a long hallway where a low door was open, revealing a brightly lit chamber. They ducked under the doorframe and stepped into the room.

"I agree with Your Grace," said Cromwell. "Fortunately, we now have a new weapon with which to promote our ideas."

George turned his attention from his fellows to the activity in the room. Dozens of torches burned from brackets on the walls. Half as many people, dressed in simple workmen's clothing, moved about a large and peculiar wooden machine, checking gears, tightening bolts.

George stared at the machine in wonder. "What in God's name is that?"

Cromwell crossed his arms proudly. "It's a printing press, my lord. And it will change the world."

Anne watched as Henry took a bite of bread and put the rest back into his bowl. She picked at the venison in her own bowl, waiting for the right time to speak. They dined alone except for the ladies who stood at a respectful distance and the noble whose duty it was to serve the couple, but Henry seemed distracted, taken from her by whatever was on his mind.

At last she could hold it no longer. "May I—say something?"

Henry nodded without looking at her.

"There are many people abroad, and perhaps within this kingdom, who still question the legitimacy of our daughter."

Henry looked at her, his eyes flashing. She had his attention, and he wasn't happy.

"You know it's true," she pressed.

He took a breath. *Go on*, his expression said.

"If Elizabeth was betrothed to King Francis's youngest son, the Duke of Angouleme, then her legitimacy and station would no longer be questioned by anyone."

Henry spoke at last. "I've already thought it. I will speak to the French ambassador."

"Thank you," said Anne. She hesitated. "What are *you* thinking?"

"Nothing."

"Will—you come to my bed tonight?"

Henry stabbed a piece of venison. Then he shook his head. Anne's heart sank.

The bedchamber was dark, with candles burned to near stubs in their silver holders. Henry could not sleep. Every nerve was on edge, and try as he might he could not slow the relentless thoughts crawling back and forth, picking at his brain, tormenting him.

Turning onto his side, he opened his hand to find More's crucifix nestled inside. Had he gone to bed holding it? Had it come to him of its own accord, to plague him?

And then a shadow moved across the far wall. Henry gasped and stared. It was the silhouette of a man, a man in a wide cloak and flat hat—More's cloak, More's hat.

"Who's there?" Henry demanded.

There was no reply. Henry climbed out of bed, trembling, and crept toward the figure. He took a tremulous breath and whispered the name.

"Thomas?"

He reached the wall. There was no one there.

The Chapel Royal choir, dressed in robes of white and red, observed the choirmaster with single-minded dedication, raising their voices to herald the impending union of Jane Parker, daughter of Lord Morely, and George Boleyn, Lord Rochford and brother of Her Royal Majesty. Anne, her father, and Archbishop Cranmer stood at the altar. George, Mark Smeaton, and several other young men stood to the left of the altar, whispering and smiling as Jane Parker walked through the seated guests, up the aisle on her father's arm.

Jane watched George intently from beneath her thin veil, hoping he would favor her with a smile, but he continued his quiet bantering and laughing with his friends. She could not go on. She stopped and glanced at her father anxiously.

"What is it?" Lord Morely whispered.

"I've changed my mind," she said quietly yet decisively. "I don't want to go through with it."

"Now, sweetheart. Every woman has this moment of faintheartedness. It's natural." He squeezed her arm for support.

But Jane wailed, "No!"

The guests and wedding party stared at the young bride. George only shook his head and smirked.

Jane had embarrassed her father, but she couldn't help it. She could not marry a man who had no feelings for her.

But Lord Morley spoke sternly under his breath. "You are marrying into a great family. You *will* do it whether you like it or not!"

Jane took a breath, and another. Then, with her eyes fixed forward, she continued to the altar. She knelt before the rail and lowered her head.

George Boleyn knelt beside Jane, though he did not lower his head.

Archbishop Cranmer began the ceremony. *"Et benedictio Dei omnipotentis, Patris et Filii et Spiritus Sancti."*

Jane glanced at George. His head was still up, as if he felt he were too good to bow even to God.

But then Thomas Boleyn stepped forward and pushed his son's head down upon the railing.

"Get on with it," he said impatiently.

The wedding celebration was held in the Great Hall. Servants scurried in and out with chargers of food and flagons of wine and beer. Henry's musicians played lively music to inspire dancing and merriment. But in spite of the bounty, the glamour, and the song, the celebration was awkward and strained. While George sat with Mark Smeaton and his friends at one end of the table, Jane, his new bride, sat with her parents at the other end. George was just as happy to have it that way. He couldn't fathom pretending to fawn over the girl.

"So," asked Smeaton, leaning against George and inclining his head in Jane's direction. "Who is she?"

George swayed, light-headed with drink. "Jane Parker. Lord Morely's daughter. He's a distant cousin of the king . . ."

"Oh!" Smeaton nodded knowingly. "Now I understand."

George shrugged Smeaton off. "No, you don't, you bastard. He's also translated Petrarch."

Smeaton chuckled, and George wrinkled his eyes, confused. "Is that funny?"

Smeaton shrugged. "I don't know."

They both laughed and then looked down the table at Jane Parker, who lowered her head as if she thought her new husband was laughing at her.

"Your Majesty, Sir Henry Norris."

Henry sat upon the throne in the presence chamber, apart from the wedding festivities, studying the pleasant-looking man the chamberlain had just announced. Norris was light haired and thick shouldered, older than the king by a few years, a former jousting partner.

"Sir Henry," said Henry cordially.

Norris bowed. "Your Majesty."

Henry was curious; he'd not seen nor heard from Norris in quite some time. "What can I do for you?"

"As Your Majesty may know," said Norris, "I recently became a widower."

Henry nodded sympathetically.

"I am looking to wed again. My choice has fallen upon one of Her Majesty's ladies."

Henry wondered which of the young dainties had caught his friend's eye. "Who?"

"Lady Margaret Sheldon."

The name didn't immediately register, but then Henry said, "You mean Madge!"

"Yes. Some people call her that, if they are familiar with her."

Henry tried to suppress a smile. "Have you made your intentions plain to Mistress Sheldon?"

"No. I have admired her from a distance. But I now should like to take things further. If your Majesty can think of no . . . impediment?"

Henry looked into his old friend's eyes and wondered, *Does he know?*

But then he said, "No. None. You have my permission. I have known you a long time. She could not marry a more honest or more honorable man."

Norris was clearly touched, bowing again and holding his hand to his heart. "I am grateful to Your Majesty."

The chamberlain ushered Norris from the chamber.

Henry looked at the closed door for a moment and sat back and shut his eyes. His mind wandered, taking him back to the harem and the women, where they lay together, beckoning him, wanting to be chosen. Henry walked slowly toward a young naked woman whose back was to him. Her head turned. He did not know her, but she wore a veil much like the other woman—

"His Excellency the French Ambassador," called the chamberlain.

Henry opened his eyes.

The ambassador, a prissy man with curled hair and trim beard, bowed. "Your Majesty wanted to see me?"

"Yes," said Henry. "I wanted to ask after my brother, the king."

"His Majesty is very well, except for his hatred of the emperor, which is like a disease."

"So he still wants our friendship?"

The ambassador's mouth dropped open, and it was a moment before he could speak. *"Mon Dieu!"* he sputtered. "He loves you above all the princes in the world!"

Good. "Then," said Henry, "put this proposal to him. That his son Charles, Duke of Angouleme, should be betrothed to our beloved daughter Elizabeth."

Clearly pleased, the ambassador smiled and bowed.

Gathering the remaining scraps of her courage, Jane Perkins stood from the table, straightened the fall of her white gown, and walked over to her new husband. She curtsied.

"Ah, sweetheart," said George.

Jane looked at Smeaton, who stood, giving her his chair. Jane sat and leaned toward George, speaking quietly. "You do . . . love me . . . don't you, George?"

George put down his wine goblet and laughed. "Of course I love you. I married you, didn't I?" He grabbed her arm and pulled her closer, smelling strongly of lust, sweat, and spirits. "I can't wait for tonight!"

She looked at him and was afraid of what she saw in his eyes.

Anne left the party in the Great Hall, excusing herself to her father and hurrying out and up the stairs to the second floor. She followed several corridors, led by intuition and a sense that something was wrong. Henry had attended neither the wedding nor the celebration. He claimed he was too busy with matters of state. And as true as that might have been, Anne felt there was more going on.

She stopped at a tall window and gazed down into the courtyard, just in time to see Henry mount his horse and ride off, accompanied by two grooms. *Where are you going, Henry? Where?*

Anne watched until he was gone. When she turned back toward court, she found Madge and Nan waiting for her with puzzled looks on their faces.

Jane counted her breaths as she lay upon the rose-scented wedding bed, listening to George in the outer parlor with his friends, still drinking and laughing. She was dressed in a white gown, which she had tucked and arranged as she thought it should be, her hair brushed out, propped upon down-filled pillows.

At last George entered the chamber, slamming the door behind him and hopping first out of his boots and trousers, and then shedding his shirt. Jane could hear his panting. Frightened, her breathing picked up its pace.

George fell into the bed and immediately fondled her breasts through the fabric of her gown. He muttered, "Ah, sweetheart, my love," and kissed her mouth and her neck. Jane, never having had a man before, tried to kiss him back but her efforts were clumsy. This irritated the drunken George.

He cursed loudly, tore open her gown, and shoved her legs apart. Jane gasped and began to cry. "No, please don't! Please, no!"

George poised himself between her legs and entered her with a force that drove her backward. Jane wailed with the pain. Her heart and mind reeled as her husband brutally had his way with her.

I can't bear this! I can't!

Jane's scalding tears went unnoticed. To George, she could have been any woman, any whore, there for his pleasure alone.

Then, at last, he was done. He rolled off her and was asleep in just moments.

Drawing her quivering legs to her chest, Jane curled up on the bed's edge and buried her face in her hands.

The actor representing Pope Paul III had a round face and crooked nose; the man acting as Cardinal Campeggio was white-wigged and hunched so far over a walking stick that he was nearly bent double. The audience attending the play on the palace grounds loved the caricatures, and howled in laugher as the two hobbled about on the stage and addressed each other in clever rhyme.

"Now," said the pope, "as much as King John does Holy Church so handle, so here I curse him with cross, book, bell, and candle." He farted loudly, causing the cardinal to reel back from the smell.

The pope then crossed himself. "I will ask God to put him from his eternal light. I will take him from Christ and after the sound of this bell . . ."

He waited, looking about, and his face drew up into a scowl. "The bell, you buggers!"

A bell sounded offstage and the audience laughed again.

"And after the sound of this bell . . ."

The bell continued to ring and the pope waved his hands dramatically. "I said *after* the sound of this bell . . . !"

The ringing stopped. "Both body and soul, I will give him to the devil in Hell!"

The pope grinned and then farted again. Campeggio fell over backward, howling from the stench.

Charles Brandon, seated in the audience, watched the play with little reaction. His wife, Catherine, was seated next to him, smiling blandly but enjoying it little. Also in attendance were the king and queen, the Boleyns, poet and Privy Council member Thomas Wyatt, Secretary Cromwell, Ambassador Chapuys, and numerous other men of importance accompanied by their ladies.

Halfway through the performance, Chapuys moved over to where Brandon was sitting. Brandon glanced about furtively and asked, "How is Queen Katherine?"

"Very unwell. She is sinking. Not only are her circumstances greatly reduced, but she has been separated from her daughter for the last four years."

Catherine had turned to listen. "That's very cruel!"

Chapuys nodded. "But her faith is astonishing."

"And the Lady Mary?" asked Brandon.

"As long as the concubine has power, I fear for her life." With that, Chapuys moved away.

"Meanwhile, I will such rubbish advance, as will be for us a source of perpetual finance," said the pope onstage. He counted on his fingers, "Hearing confessions, pardons, worshipping of saints, seeing of images, and so on! You get the picture."

Campeggio did indeed, and he rubbed his fat hands gleefully, seeming to imagine all the money. The audience laughed in unison.

Thomas Boleyn, seated with George and his new wife Jane, stood and walked over to Thomas Cromwell, who was clearly enthralled with the production.

"A fine piece of work, Mr. Secretary," Boleyn said. "And educative. I wonder who wrote it?"

"A Mr. Bale," said Cromwell, keeping his eyes on the actors. "He was once a priest of the old faith, but seeing for himself how it went on, became a most passionate reformer."

Boleyn nodded, then leaned in. "I think our family never did anything better than facilitate your own rise, Mr. Secretary. And I trust you never forget that we did so." With a smile, he walked off.

The play continued. Anne, seated close to the stage, watched anxiously as Henry moved about through the audience. Each time he paused to speak to another woman, her heart sank. She was losing him, and she didn't know how to stop it from happening.

Onstage, an actor playing King John addressed a priestly character named Treason.

"Let's hear something on behalf of the old Church," demanded King John.

Treason tipped his head. "Well, in the old Church you can have your gilded images to call upon when necessary! You have your crawling, your kissing, setting up of lights, money in the box, prayers for toothaches, pestilence, and the pox."

The audience laughed. Anne watched Henry laugh, too. Clearly King John represented her husband.

"But," said King John, "what is there of Christ in your Church?"

"Well, nothing at all, except the Epistles and the Gospels. But since they're in Latin, no one can understand them at all."

More laughter. King John's face darkened. "Have you known such things, and never sought a reformation? It is life to the whole congregation. If ceremonies and superstitions from us fall, then farewell monks, canons, priest, friar, bishop, and *all*!"

There was loud applause from the audience. Anne joined them in showing her appreciation. Then Henry was back beside her, smiling, taking her arm.

"I spoke to the French ambassador," he said. "Francis is sending the Admiral of France to arrange the marriage."

Anne's heart eased. "Thank you," she said.

Henry waved Brandon over to join them. Anne tensed again.

"Your Grace," said Henry.

"Majesties," said Brandon, arriving with a bow.

"The Admiral of France is coming to pay an official visit. I want you to receive and entertain him on my behalf."

Anne couldn't contain her suspicion. "Why *him*? Surely my father would be a better choice."

Henry's expression was suddenly hard, and Anne flinched. Henry spoke to Brandon, "I trust Your Grace will carry out my commands." Brandon bowed and moved away.

Henry considered Anne for a moment. His words were terse. "That was unnecessary,"

"He hates me." It was all she could say.

"But he *loves* me." Henry left Anne to sit in the crowd, biting her lip.

Upon the stage, the play was concluding. An actor playing England, donned in red, white, and blue and holding a staff, had taken center stage. He raised his hands to the audience. "Pray unto the Lord that the king may continue to rule over us, to our souls' consolation. And that his offspring may rein, too, to subdue the great Antichrist in Rome, to the comfort of this nation!"

The audience clapped again, enthusiastically while some called out their approval. Anne applauded as well, though her troubled mind was elsewhere.

Lady Mary, daughter of King Henry and Katherine, paused in her bedtime prayers to listen to girlish giggles outside her door. She turned on her knees, frowning, wondering what mischief was afoot.

Following the giggles were footsteps receding, moving down the hallway.

Mary crossed herself and stood, moving to the door quietly. She peered outside. She had recognized the voices as those of the girls who sat with the infant Elizabeth during the night. They had snuck out, leaving their duties behind.

Leaving the baby behind.

Mary stepped into the corridor silently, pulling her door shut behind her. Then she slipped up the hallway to the baby's nursery and went inside.

The child was asleep in a gilded cot with a silken canopy. The features of her tiny face were visible in the moonlight through the window.

Princess Elizabeth.

Mary closed the nursery door and moved to the cot, gazing down at the child who had stolen everything from her. She lifted the child and stared at her, then drew her close. Closer.

The door burst open, and Lady Bryan rushed in, her face twisted in fear. She stopped short and watched as Mary walked back and forth, the child nestled to her neck, singing softly. Mary looked at the lady and said simply, "She woke and I took care of her. She's asleep now."

Mary gently placed the child back into the cot, and Lady Bryan hurried to check on the child. Elizabeth was sleeping peacefully, a small smile on her lips.

With a curtsy, Mary excused herself and left the nursery. She could feel Lady Bryan's gaze follow her out.

"I like you, Excellency. You're very clever." Henry and Ambassador Chapuys were walking together in the royal forest. The spring day was pleasant, filled with the coos of doves and the scents of white lilacs. Two guards followed behind at a discreet distance. "But I don't always like the way the emperor treats me. He seems to think that, as far as Katherine is concerned, I act out of spite. But I swear it's not true."

Chapuys said nothing.

"I suppose," said Henry, gesturing, his voice rising passionately, "I ought to be content with the knowledge that the world knows the many wrongs that have been done to me."

Still, Chapuys remained silent.

Henry stopped. "You don't approve of the changes I'm making. Cromwell intercepts some of your letters."

Chapuys pressed his lips together but looked at the king.

"We used to call it 'humanism,'" Henry continued. "Wolsey, More, and me. We were all humanists. People think I've changed but I haven't. Chapuys, I promise you that I am going to make such a reformation in this kingdom that I shall be eternally remembered throughout all Christendom."

At last Chapuys nodded, and he almost smiled. "I have no doubt whatsoever that Your Majesty will always be remembered."

Anne sat at the virginal, her fingers moving up and down the ivory keys, playing a melancholy melody that matched her mood.

George was announced by Nan, who quietly retreated from the chamber. After watching his sister silently for a moment, George went to her and put his hand over hers. Anne stopped her playing, took George's hand, and kissed it.

"What is it?" he asked.

"He's having more affairs."

"Are you sure?"

"Of course I'm sure. Often I can't find him. No one will tell me where he is. He leaves the palace and is gone for hours sometimes." She uttered a sour laugh. "I think he has a harem somewhere."

"Anne." George tried to put his arm around Anne but she shrugged him off. Anxiety rose in her veins like a blaze up a tree, and she could not stop it.

"Something's going to happen to me. You know there's an old prophecy, one everybody knows. It says that a queen of England will be burned!" Anne began to cry, and this time she let George comfort her.

"Don't talk like this," he said. "Nothing is going to happen to you."

Anne shivered and wiped her eyes. "I am not able to give the king a son to be the living image of his father."

George held and kissed her. "Everything is going to be all right. Please don't cry. I love you. I'll look after you, I swear. Please, don't cry."

Through the open door to the adjoining chamber, Lady Madge Sheldon watched as George Boleyn kissed and caressed his sister. She frowned, uncertain of the show of affection from brother to sister.

Thomas Cromwell had a new duty as secretary, that of collecting, reading, and recording the status of cases of illegal conversations and statements uttered by English citizens. These were conversations and statements counter to the will of the king, conversations and statements that could be deemed treasonous. Ever since the notice had gone out to the people, hundreds of reports had come in with hundreds of names. Cromwell's desk was weighed down, and he spent hours each day reading and noting upon the reports that the case either showed "Malice" or it was "Unfounded." The work was tiring and yet invigorating. His Majesty's New Monarchy was unfolding.

"Mr. Secretary."

Cromwell looked up, not having heard Thomas Wyatt enter his study. "Sir Thomas."

Wyatt moved to the desk and looked at the piles of paperwork, the lists of names. "What are these?"

"Denunciations."

Wyatt frowned slightly.

Cromwell tapped a paper with his finger. "It is reported here that a canon at Tewksbury, mistaken or otherwise, offered prayers to Katherine the Queen instead of to Anne."

"What will you do to him?"

Cromwell waved his hand. "Nothing. He's near eighty years old. An absentminded slip of the tongue in such an old man is forgivable. Some of the other reports, however, are more serious." With that, he nodded at another pile of papers.

It was clear from the furrowing of his brow that Wyatt found the information chilling. Cromwell stood and crossed the room to a large table. He motioned Wyatt to join him. "Look at these," he said.

Stacks of paper covered the tabletop. These were not handwritten, but machine-printed documents. The type was dark and even. Wyatt held a paper up, marveling at the quality.

"These are tracts praising His Majesty," said Cromwell, "his new monarchy and his reformation. They explain to people why the reformation is necessary, and the liberties and opportunities it brings, even to the king's humblest subject."

Wyatt nodded. "They are impressive. You are to be congratulated on your industry, Mr. Secretary. But . . . does it never concern you that the king has taken to himself an absolute power, without any constraint, to remake the law?"

Cromwell spoke evenly. "Is not that which pleases the king the law?"

Wyatt looked trapped. "I was only observing . . ."

"Wyatt," said the secretary. "I like you. But you have a reputation. You gamble and you whore. You sail close to the wind. God forbid it should ever blow you onto the rocks."

"Where are you going?"

King Henry, sitting upon his horse and adjusting the stirrups, looked over to see Anne hurrying across the courtyard in his direction. Henry and two of his grooms were preparing to leave the palace. He did not need the queen's interference. "Out," he replied simply, then picking up the reins and threading them through his fingers.

Anne stopped close to the horse. Her face was troubled. "Where?"

Henry glared at his wife. "Go back inside."

Anne's lips tightened. "Where are you going? I want to know."

"It's none of your business." Anger rose in him, that his grooms would see such a display. "It is my pleasure that you go back inside. Now."

Anne stared at Henry, and he stared at her. Then her face fell, and she managed a small curtsy. She spun about and went back into the palace.

Henry squared his shoulders, nodded to his grooms, and they rode off.

Brereton's moment had come. Anne was alone, walking through the Great Hall. Brereton could see the distress on her face, and what he was going to do was made all the more delicious for it. Glancing right and left, Brereton stepped up to Anne, who blinked, startled, and opened her mouth to speak. But the words were never uttered, for Brereton raised the knife he was holding and drove it into her chest. Again, again, again. Anne's knees buckled and she fell to the tile floor, scarlet blood gushing from the wounds.

"Jezebel!" he cried. "Whore!"

Anne writhed upon the tiles and went still.

A smile crept onto Brereton's face. He was proud of his handiwork.

Then he watched as Anne, followed by her ladies, walked through the Great Hall on her way to whatever it was the concubine did with her time. Though he'd only imagined her murder, his heart pounded with the divine ecstasy of it all.

The country home of Charles Brandon and Catherine was decorated especially for the visit of the French admiral. The couple donned their finest clothing to welcome the guests, and the servants were likewise elegantly dressed and properly coiffed. Vases of flowers and bowls of exotic fruits sat about on sideboards and tables, and new and numerous candles burned in brass sconces along the walls and in tall stands.

The doors opened, and a servant announced, "His Highness Philippe Chabot de Brion, Admiral of France."

The admiral entered, a bearded man in his middle years, his uniform most elegant with a high collar and ruff, jeweled buttons and gold trim. He was followed by an elderly man and a lovely young woman. The admiral bowed to Brandon. "Your Grace."

Brandon returned the bow. "Admiral Chabot. It is my privilege and pleasure to welcome you and your party to my house and to England. May I present my wife, the Duchess."

Admiral Chabot smiled and kissed Catherine's hand. *"Enchantez, madam."* Then he indicated those who had come with him. "With your permission, may I present my secretary, Monsieur Alfonse Gontier . . ."

"Madam. Your Grace," said the secretary, stooping low and sweeping out his arm.

"And my niece, Mademoiselle Germaine."

Catherine considered the young woman. "You are very pretty," she said.

Germaine blushed and smiled. Then she looked at Brandon, tipping her head coquettishly and blinking her long lashes. Brandon ignored the flirting.

"Tell me, Your Grace," said the admiral, looking about the room as if deciding whether it was fit for him or not. "What are we to expect?"

"Your Highness," said Brandon, "I am to entertain you and your staff for a few days. Then the king invites you to dine at court."

The admiral nodded. "Very good."

"There is . . . one other thing. I am told that Queen Anne has planned a banquet in your honor. And a tennis match."

The admiral looked at Brandon, his expression unreadable, saying nothing.

Brandon rushed on. "I believe you met Her Majesty before, in Calais, when she accompanied His Majesty. Before her coronation."

Admiral Chabot gave a small shrug. "Perhaps, but I've no recollection of any such meeting. And, alas, I don't play tennis." He smiled, though the smile held no warmth.

The following morning, Brandon found respite from the overbearing admiral by taking on the chores of a stable boy. Sleeves rolled up, he took pleasure in rubbing down his favorite horse with a cloth, combing out its mane and tail, and treating it with lumps of sugar.

As he was working he became aware of someone in the stable with him. He turned to see the beautiful Germaine, her cheeks pink, a seductive pout on her lips. Her hair had been freed of its combs, and hung like a satin curtain down her arms and over her ample breasts. Brandon dropped the cloth on the stall railing and stepped over to the mademoiselle. He hesitated, but then reached out for her cheek. She responded immediately with a soft sigh.

Brandon ran his fingers through the fine strands of soft hair, then pushed them back behind her shoulders, exposing the pale, tender flesh just above her low neckline. Germaine moved in to Brandon and he in to her, and they kissed passionately.

"I had planned a banquet in *his* honor," said Anne, pacing back and forth in her private chamber. Mark Smeaton was with her, seated on a mahogany chair, holding his violin, running his finger absently along a length of catgut.

"Whose honor?"

"The Admiral of France. He's been here two weeks already, staying with the Duke of Suffolk, and he has not even sent me a message of goodwill! Every other French envoy has always done so."

Smeaton laid his violin aside. It was clear he did not know what to say. This frustrated Anne even further. Hot tears pricked the corners of her eyes. "Neither has he requested an audience with me," she said. "With *me*, the queen of England. When we are discussing the future of my own *child*! They also tell me he has struck up an acquaintance with the Imperial ambassador, Chapuys. Why should he do such a thing?"

Again, Smeaton remained silent. Anne stopped her pacing and put her hands on her hips. "Why do you not say anything, Mark?"

"Your Majesty must forgive me. I don't know what to say. These matters are beyond my competence. I'm only a dancing master."

Anne shook her head and paced again. "There's something else. Someone, probably some bitch who hates me, told me that the king has deliberately invited many beautiful women to court for the admiral's visit. Can you believe *that*?"

Her tears of anguish began to fall in earnest.

Admiral Chabot came at last to court to attend a ball and banquet hosted by both the Royal Majesties. Brandon escorted the admiral and his party into the Great Hall. The tables were covered with newly woven silk cloths, ordered by Anne for the occasion, each bearing the large, embroidered initials *H & A*. Atop the cloths sat glimmering gold and silver bowls, candlesticks, flagons, and goblets, fashioned by the best smiths for the event, also featuring the king and queen's initials. Musicians, set in quartets about the hall, took turns playing selections of both English and French tunes.

"Your Majesty," Brandon said, bowing to Henry. "May I present His Highness Philippe Chabot de Brion, Admiral of France."

Chabot stepped forward and bowed with a flourish. "Majesty."

Henry nodded. "You are very welcome to our court. May I present my wife, Queen Anne."

Anne was painfully aware of the stiff formality of Chabot's greeting as he addressed her and kissed her hand. She looked at Henry to see if he'd noticed, but he was already gesturing toward the dais.

"Come and be seated, Your Highness," he said.

Henry led the way to the High Table, where the royal couple took their chairs. The admiral was seated next to Anne, with Thomas and George Boleyn taking chairs at each end of the table.

With a nod of the king's head, the banquet began. Servants scuttled in and out, bearing huge platters of fish, fowl, and game animals, each adorned and presented as a sculptured piece of art with flowers, feathers, and beads.

Henry watched his guest's face carefully. Anne knew her husband was trying to impress the Frenchman, but it didn't seem to be working. Chabot waved away most of the dishes, and even hesitated to taste English wine. When Henry insisted, Chabot sniffed it suspiciously, took a sip, and made a face. Then he laughed loudly and declared, "It's very fruity. And strong. Like gladiator's sweat!" Henry joined him, chuckling, though Anne knew the gaiety was forced.

As Anne sipped her wine, her gaze moved from Chabot to the people in the Hall, wondering what she should say that the admiral might notice her. It was as though he were deliberately ignoring her.

Henry squeezed Anne's hand, indicating that he sensed her discomfort. He pointed to a man in the crowd and said, "Highness, who is that gentleman there?"

"My secretary, Monsieur Gontier," said Chabot.

Henry stood. "Then I must introduce him to the queen." Henry gave Anne a quick smile and left the dais.

After a moment, the admiral turned toward Anne. "Your Majesty must forgive me for not attending the banquet you arranged in my honor. It was most unfortunate, but his Grace the Duke of Suffolk and his charming wife have kept me a virtual prisoner in their castle. I was—how shall I say, imprisoned by affection."

Anne nodded, not believing him but pretending to. Then she looked out at the gathering and burst out laughing. Henry had not found the secretary, but instead the young French maiden who had accompanied Chabot to England. The king was engaged in some intimate discussion with the delicate beauty.

Chabot gasped, offended. "How now, Madam? Are you amusing yourself at my expense?"

Anne shook her head and tried to subdue the painful laughter that forced its way up from her soul. Yet she was helpless to it, to the hopelessness and loneliness. "Forgive me," she said, wiping her eyes. "I could not help laughing at the king's proposition of introducing your secretary to me. For whilst he was looking for him, he met that pretty lady and forgot the whole thing!"

The admiral stared at Anne stonily. He was obviously unimpressed with her candor. Anne could do nothing about it, however. She just sat and watched as the French lady gave Henry, and then Charles Brandon, her lift of the chin and wink of the eye. Ah, the joys of being a woman of nobility, of being a queen. How easily nobles slipped through her fingers. How easily she could lose her king.

Festivities were over for Henry although the music, dancing, and dining continued on in the Great Hall. That was good; let the courtiers get drunk and fat on into the night. Henry was ready to conduct some important and most personal business. He invited Admiral Chabot and Cromwell into his private chambers, with one purpose only.

"What instructions do you have from your master, with regard to the betrothal of my daughter Elizabeth to the Duke of Angouleme?" Henry asked.

Admiral Chabot glanced from Cromwell to the king. "His Majesty regrets that such a proposition is impossible."

Henry stared at the man, stunned. "Why impossible?"

"Much as he loves Your Majesty, the king cannot agree to betroth his beloved son to a—a bride whose legitimacy is not accepted by His Holiness Pope Paul, by the Holy Church itself, nor even by the emperor."

The backs of Henry's hands flushed cold with rage and humiliation. It was all he could do to keep from ordering the admiral from his chamber.

"However," continued Chabot, "His Majesty, to demonstrate his love, proposes another match. He would consent to the betrothal of the dauphin to Lady Mary."

Henry's heart pounded. He drew heated breaths through his teeth.

"If you don't agree to the match, my master will marry his son to the emperor's daughter, leaving your country isolated in Europe." Chabot cocked his head to the side, almost tauntingly, and waited for a response.

There was a long, tense, and silent moment before Cromwell said, "Highness, your audience with His Majesty is over."

Chabot, seemingly unfazed, bowed and left. Henry looked at Cromwell, enraged, incredulous, but sensing something profound taking a turn inside him.

* * * *

"I have no excuses, Catherine. I thought those days were behind me."

Catherine glanced out from the small alcove in the Great Hall, to where other couples were enjoying merriment and music. She had seen the looks Mademoiselle Germaine had given her husband, and the gazes he had given her. And in that moment, she realized the truth of her husband's infidelity. "Perhaps human nature can never change."

Brandon took her arm. "I swear to you it won't happen again. I love you too much."

Catherine lowered her eyes and sighed.

"I have no right to ask you to believe me, but it's true."

Catherine looked up again, and slowly reached out toward his hand, though she did not take it. "You see," she said. "You *did* make me cry after all."

Anne had to ask. She had been waiting for hours since the banquet was over, waiting for a private moment with her husband, and even though it was nearing three in the morning, she could not sleep until she knew the answer, even if she did not relish the truth. Now, in the king's private chambers, she stood in the middle of the floor, her head held high.

"Who *was* she?" she demanded.

Henry looked at Anne. He sat in his chair, his fingers linked, one leg thrown over the chair's arm as if in a passive, casual challenge.

Finally he answered dryly. "Who was who?"

"The lady you spoke to when you were supposed to be finding Monsieur Gontier."

"I don't know."

Anne stepped closer, leaning one hand on the edge of the king's desk. "Is she one of your mistresses?"

Henry's eyes flashed, dangerously. Still, Anne pressed.

"How many do you have? What are their names? Where do you keep them? Someone told me that your nobles, like Brandon, are assisting you in having your affairs."

Henry stood, hands flexing. "That's enough."

"No. You've always told me we should be truthful to each other. You said it was a definition of love."

"Then here's the *truth*," said Henry, stepping closer to his wife, his face taut, reddened. "You must *shut* your eyes and endure, as your *betters* have done before you!"

Anne gasped. "How can you say that? Don't you know I love you a thousand times more than Katherine ever did?"

"And don't you know I can bring you down as quickly as I raised you? You should thank God you have your bed already, because if you hadn't I wouldn't give it to you again!"

Anne broke into sobs. Henry walked past her toward his bedchamber. He paused and said, "Francis won't agree to the betrothal."

Anne stared. "Why?"

"Why do you *think*?" Henry leaned toward Anne, snarling. She took an involuntary step backward. "Because he and the pope and the emperor all agree that she's a bastard! And that you are not my wife!" Henry spun about and entered his bedchamber, slamming the door. Portraits on the wall clattered with the force, then went still.

The private gardens hummed with early summer—butterflies lighting upon newly opening buds, birds gathering grasses to build their nests, water striders skating the water of the canal. The royal couple strolled the grounds, Henry walking with Brandon, and Anne walking at a distance with her ladies and her newest pet, a small white dog.

"Tell me," Henry asked Brandon, "how is your Catherine?"

Brandon broke a small branch as he passed. "She's fine. In fact, she's with child."

"You're a happily married man, Charles. I envy you." Henry rolled a small object in his hand and walked on. Then he said, "Do you think the planets influence our lives?"

Brandon thought for a moment, then said, "I don't know."

"I would often discuss the issue with More. We used to stand on the

King Takes Queen   195

roof of an evening and study the heavens. More had a great knowledge of the stars and how they affected our humors." Henry opened his hand and looked at the object he was carrying—More's silver crucifix. His voice softened. "I regret now what happened to More. I wish it hadn't happened. But it wasn't all my fault. Whenever my resolve weakened, whenever I was inclined to save him, a certain person privately urged me on to his destruction."

Brandon stopped and frowned. "Who?"

Henry glanced up the path to where Anne was stooped, rubbing her little dog's ears. "You know who she is, Charles."

Suddenly, Henry raised his arm and hurled More's crucifix into the canal. It held at the surface for a moment, then spun and sank into the depths.

Chapter Twelve

The forest was bathed in silvery twilight, and the air was filled with the familiar yet haunting sound of tawny owls in the trees. Anne rode with Nan and Madge along an earthen path, not certain where she was going but feeling safe with her ladies beside her. They reached a clearing, and Anne dismounted, happy to see others she cared for—her father, her brother, Mark Smeaton, and Thomas Wyatt—waiting for her. Mark offered her an apple, but she refused it with a lighthearted laugh.

Suddenly, a bent old woman stepped out from the trees. Her skin was pale and wrinkled, her eyes black as the bottom of a well. Anne caught her breath. But her father took her arm and led her to the old woman. Anne obeyed, trying not to look at the old woman yet unable to resist.

Three masked figures joined the old woman. They took hold of Anne, removing her outer garments and dressing her in a red shift. Anne looked desperately about to find her father, brother, and friends, but they had vanished.

Anne's terror grew. The masked figures bound her hands and led her to a river where stood a huge and hideous wicker man made of tightly woven branches. Anne tried to scream but could make no sound. The door in the belly of the ghastly wooden effigy was opened and Anne was forced inside. The door was latched.

The old woman and masked figures lowered the wicker man into the water. There were strange, white-eyed men and women standing in the river, and they rocked the wicker man along with the current. Anne struggled and splashed as water poured in through the sides. Moments later, others on the riverbank reached down and pulled the wicker man out. And then Anne saw what was coming toward her—a flaming torch.

Anne's voice unlocked and she screamed. She grabbed the splintery, wooden bars and shook them with all her strength, but they held tightly. The torch came closer. The glow revealed the face of she who bore the torch. It was Katherine's daughter, Mary. Mary, with an expression of ecstasy, put the torch to the wicker man and set it aflame.

Oh, God, no! I don't want to die! I don't deserve to die!

The flames roared around her, against her, singeing her flesh, then catching her hair—

She sat upright in bed, clutching her heart, her face bathed in sweat. She did not let herself cry out, but curled up to hold it in. In this, for a moment at least, she had power.

She did not mean to awaken her sleeping mistress, but Katherine's state was such now that at times her senses were dulled and at other times, heightened. The room stank of decay and impending death. There was nothing Elizabeth could do to cure the room of its disrepair, nor her mistress of her malady.

"Mary?" muttered Katherine, her eyes closed.

Elizabeth went to her bed and touched her hand. "It's Elizabeth."

Katherine opened her eyes. She sighed and turned her face away. "I've not seen my daughter for more than four years. Do you not think it cruel of them to keep her away from me?"

"Gentle Madam, yes."

"It burns my heart."

Elizabeth had no words to ease the burning.

"Read the Curia's judgment to me again," said Katherine. "Please."

Elizabeth took the old parchment bearing the papal seal from a drawer in the bedside table. She read, "We pronounce that the marriage between Henry VIII and Katherine of Aragon stands firm and canonical, and their issue still stands lawful and legitimate."

A rare smile crossed the lady's lips and she reached out for the paper, took it, and kissed the seal. "You see?" she said. "That is eternal truth, which no *man* can *ever* deny."

Henry opened the large, leather volume eagerly. The book was the *Valor Ecclesiasticus,* the results of the commissioners' investigations into the wealth and practices of all the religious houses in England. Cranmer, along with Cromwell and Boleyn, had brought it to the king's private chambers for his perusal.

As Henry flipped through the book, looking at random pages, Cromwell explained, "It lists all the treasures and properties, the wealthy and vast private lands, of the monasteries, priories, and other religious establishments."

Cranmer added, "It as well lists the innumerable cases of laxity, corruption, and fraud which have flourished, unchecked, and in some cases for hundreds of years, in these same institutions."

Henry continued to turn the pages, dense with their lists and computations.

"Meanwhile," said Boleyn, drawing closer to the king, "your own treasury is much depleted. Is it not a thing to marvel at, the richness of those who ought to be your subjects, and the poverty and debt of the English crown?"

Slowly, Henry closed the book, thinking a king should never hear such words, thinking it should and it would be rectified. "Is it, indeed," he said. "It is something to marvel at, my lord."

The mirror reflected a woman with clear skin and silky hair, not much older than she'd been when she'd first met the king. But what did Henry see when he looked at Anne? An aging woman, etched with strain and worry? Anne touched her face, forlorn, wondering.

A man's voice could be heard in Anne's outer chamber. She hurried from her bedchamber, calling, "George?"

But it was Sir Henry Norris, the king's friend. Anne did her best to hide her disappointment. "Sir Henry," she said as he bowed.

"Your Majesty," said Norris, "I came again to pay court to Lady Sheldon, with the king's permission."

"Yes," said Anne, looking over at Madge, who smiled and lowered her eyes.

"I—I also wanted the opportunity to express my love and devotion for Your Majesty," said Norris.

Anne looked back at him.

"As a reformer, myself," continued Norris, "I know the good works you do, without asking for praise but always deserving it."

"I don't seek praise," said Anne, touched by Norris's heartfelt declaration. "When I visit religious houses, it is to urge those inside to cleanse and purify their corrupt lives and doctrines, or else they will surely be destroyed."

Norris nodded. "We evangelicals must breathe new life into dead bones and encourage the ignorant to accept the priority of faith and the word of God."

The queen nodded and smiled. "I see we understand each other, Sir Henry." Then she motioned toward Madge. "Lady Sheldon, Sir Henry Norris has come courting."

Madge came forward shyly, a young woman half the age of her suitor, yet seeming happy with the match. She curtsied. "My lord."

As Norris and Madge left, George came in. He watched the couple leave, then turned to Anne. "You wanted to see me?"

Anne felt her body droop, her smile fall away, the weight of trouble settle on her again as a heavy, oppressive cloak. She beckoned George into her bedchamber and closed the door.

Taking her brother by the hand, Anne led George to her large oak bed by the far wall. They sat on the linen-covered down mattress. The little white dog, asleep on the pillows, made a tiny grunting sound and turned over. Anne grabbed both his hands now, needing the comfort his touch offered.

"I had the dream again," she whispered urgently.

"Anne!" George stared at her and shook his head.

"I told you before, I am her death and she is mine. So long as they are both alive, I can never be safe. Why doesn't Katherine just die? They keep saying how ill she is. Why doesn't she just die?"

"Stop it!"

Anne drew herself up. "I had a thought. The next time Henry goes abroad, I shall be left as regent. Then I can order their deaths."

George was shocked, and he grabbed her shoulders. "You're crazy! Stop it! Stop, and listen to me! Never let anyone, not even your ladies, ever see or hear you like this. You're the queen of England! For the love of God, act like it!" George caught his breath, lowered his voice. "After all, you were a lady to Queen Katherine. You saw and heard how she behaved. It seemed to me she never betrayed her real feelings. Can you not be more like her?"

Anne stared at her brother. She could barely speak the words. "More—like Katherine?"

"Yes. You heard me! At least *seem* happy. Contented. Not a heap of misery!" George let go of his sister and left the bedchamber, slamming through the door, leaving it partially open and nearly knocking over Nan, who had a broom in her hand but was not sweeping.

The Priory of Syon Abbey was a stately, ivy-laced stone fortress built to the glory of God along the Thames River. Moved from swampy acreage in London to more solid ground southwest of the city one hundred years earlier, it was home to men who had dedicated their lives to the Catholic Church, monks whose passion was gardening, tending bees, and praying.

As the Priory abbot knelt in silent supplication before a statue of the Virgin in a peaceful garden grotto, he was interrupted by a panting, frantic monk.

"Father Abbot!" the monk said, waving a letter.

The Abbot crossed himself, rose, and squinted at the paper the monk was holding. "The king's seal?"

The monk's face was ashen. "Yes, Father. We are to be suppressed! The whole priory, by orders of Mr. Cromwell."

The abbot crossed himself, anxiously. "Show me the letter." The monk handed the letter over, and the abbot read it, his face falling.

"What have we done, Father?"

"I don't know." The abbot opened his fingers, letting the letter drift to the ground. He walked from the grotto, hands folded, head shaking.

A monk in the herb garden had heard the commotion. As the abbot passed him, he asked, "What's to become of us?"

The abbot had no answer.

The royal taster for the evening was William Brereton. The servant brought the platter of apple-garnished fish to the sideboard; Brereton stepped forward, took a small portion on his knife, smelled it, and put it in his mouth. After a moment he nodded; the fish was safe for the king and queen. The noble in charge of serving for the evening carried the platter to the dining table, bowed, and withdrew.

Henry smiled at Anne, who tried her best to smile back. Then she asked quietly, "Will you ask the French ambassador again if Francis will not relent and agree to the marriage of Elizabeth to his son?"

Henry picked up a piece of fish. "I might." He smiled again, though it was clear he didn't care to discuss it further.

Still, Anne pressed, "Don't you think our daughter's future is important?"

"Of course I do." Henry put his knife down. "Surely you understand that Francis's refusal to agree to the marriage in the first place was insulting? Do you want me to beg?"

"No! Of course not." Anne lifted a piece of fish to her lips, then paused, smelling it.

"Sweetheart," said Henry. "It's been tasted. It's not poisoned."

Anne put the morsel into her mouth. It had little taste, but she forced it down.

"The fact is," Henry said, "it might be better for us to pursue an alliance with the emperor."

Anne scowled. "That would suit Katherine."

"It has nothing to do with Katherine. It has to do with England, and England's interests. After all, I am supposed to be concerned with that!"

Anne glanced at the noble at the far end of the table, aware that he might be enjoying the argument. "I'm sorry," she said. "Forgive me."

"You have no reason to be sorry. You care about our daughter, and you should. But," he added, giving her a look that was not to be challenged, "leave the greater things to *my* care. Do you understand?"

Anne nodded, and meekly lowered her eyes.

That same evening, Thomas Cromwell entertained Archbishop Cranmer and his wife, Katharina, at dinner. The room was bright and pleasant, and the food plentiful.

"So tell me," Katharina addressed Cromwell, her hair free about her shoulders, her elbows on the table, "you are suppressing some religious houses?"

"We are starting to do so."

"What else?"

"I intend to abolish almost all the holy days which fall in the law terms or during the harvest. These enforced holidays damage the country's economy and stop vital works. And, in fact, they also impoverish workers."

Katharina nodded and took a bite of venison. "And the priests?"

Cranmer joined in, leaning on his elbow. "As far as the clergy are concerned, we mean to issue a set of injunctions requiring them to preach the Supremacy. There will also be an injunction requiring parents and employers to teach their children and servants the Lord's Prayer, Creed, and Ten Commandments in English rather than Latin."

Cromwell added that clerics would be required to attack the cult of images and pilgrimages, and that the money previously wasted on relics would go to the poor.

Katharina smiled. "That's very good, but, gentlemen, I don't believe you're going far enough or fast enough!"

Cromwell glanced at Cranmer. "Your wife is a great radical, Thomas."

Cranmer nodded. "She is. Give her a cart, any cart, and she'll overturn it!"

The men laughed. Katharina didn't join them. Her eyes narrowed. "Being carried around in a box does not make you laugh."

Cranmer reached for his wife. "My dear, I'm sorry about that."

Katharina pulled away. "I'm not 'your dear.' I'm nobody's 'dear.' I am a woman and I demand equal respect for my ideas! It may seem strange to you here, but in Germany it's already different! For me, the practices of the Catholic Church are *evil*. People are kept in total ignorance and made to feel guilty about their own bodies and their own thoughts. Even worse, the idea that the rich are able to purchase a plot in heaven for their souls!"

Cromwell inclined his head. "I agree with you. The Catholic Church is corrupted and irredeemable."

"Then," said Katharina, "you should smash and destroy it utterly and without pity. That is my advice to you, Mr. Cromwell." She wiped her mouth and gave him a wide and confident smile. "Now, you can put me back into my box!"

Dinner continued, cordially, and when the meal and visit were over, Cranmer left for home in his carriage, with Katharina stowed safely in her large wooden crate.

William Brereton stood at a palace window, gazing down into the private gardens, clutching his fists and breathing through his teeth. Queen Anne was in the garden, holding her toddler daughter, Elizabeth. The child was beautiful, her fiery red hair adorned with a miniature coif of pearls and satin.

Lady Bryan, the child's guardian, stood by as Anne scooped the child into her arms and kissed her. "My darling girl, my angel! My own heart!"

"Mama," cooed Elizabeth.

Anne dismissed Lady Bryan, and continued to caress and kiss her child.

"Have you missed me?"

The little girl nodded. "Yes, Mama."

"I've missed you! I'm going to have lots of new clothes made for you! Would you like beautiful new clothes to wear?"

Elizabeth nodded, and her mother held her close.

Brereton turned from the window, his mind reeling and his blood chilled. Then he looked back at the garden. There was no queen, no princess. He'd only imagined the future. But it was a future he could not allow to come true.

The abbot of Syon Priory was shocked to see a stranger in the Scriptorum, standing amid the silent monks as they slowly and scrupulously copied out religious texts, examining the works as if he, himself, was abbot.

"Sir?"

The man looked up from the text he was inspecting, with not a trace of embarrassment on his face. "Ah, I should have warned you of my impending visit," he said with an unnaturally broad grin.

"Who are you?"

"My name is John Leland. I am His Majesty's librarian. You keep a library in the priory, I believe."

The abbot frowned slightly. "Yes. It contains many old and fine manuscripts and texts. We are very proud of it."

Leland pursed his lips. "The king has commissioned me to diligently search all the libraries belonging to those religious houses about to be suppressed. He is anxious to preserve all their literary treasures."

"You—you mean you intend to remove them from here?"

"Naturally. They will be housed in the royal libraries."

The abbot was speechless. Leland seemed pleased with the cleric's dismay.

"His Majesty has also ordered me to find texts that would emphasize the royal supremacy and the new monarchy."

The abbot found his tongue. "I do not think, Mr. Leland, that you will find many such texts here!"

George's father's face was lined with frustration. "Have you talked to the queen lately?"

"Yes," said George.

Boleyn glanced up and down the corridor, making sure none of the courtiers were within hearing. "She gives me cause for concern. Everyone can see that the king is not so much in love with her as he used to be. What's wrong with her?"

"I don't know. Perhaps she's afraid."

Boleyn's frustration turned to barely contained anger. "Poor George! Have you gone softheaded?"

"No!"

"I hope not! You see, the stakes are too high. Whoever is a coward now will soon rue the day and regret his misfortune. Successful people only recognize fear in others." He took George's arm, roughly. "Go and talk to your sister again." And with that, he was gone.

The queen's private chamber pulsed with jaunty music and loud conversation. There was barely room to move with all the servants and the courtiers, some of whom George barely knew. Mark Smeaton sat on the back of a chair, playing his violin. In the center of the room, Nan and Madge twirled about as Wyatt and the other men clapped. Brereton, the king's groom, watched on, silently.

When Anne saw George, she pushed through to him. Her eyes were unnaturally bright, as if she'd been drinking.

"This is better, isn't it, George?" she cooed, too loudly, putting her arms around her brother's neck.

"Much better."

"Will you dance?"

"No. Not now."

Anne pouted, but then joined Nan and Madge in the middle of the floor. She waved her hand for others to join. Some men obeyed cheerfully; Brereton did so without smiling.

George moved to Wyatt, who was staring fixedly at Anne. "All this time," George said. "You're still in love with her."

Wyatt smiled wryly. "You're mistaken, my lord. My love is all sprung and spent. A long time ago."

"Hmm," said George. He looked out at the dancing. It was a wild revelry, yet it seemed forced, staged, a play created to belie the queen's fear. Anne's enjoyment seemed more desperation, and her smile a mask.

Anne moved from partner to partner, studying faces to make sure everyone was having a good time. They had to see that she was free and merry, that they had no reason to wonder if the queen was unhappy.

Brereton's gaze was cold, however. Anne danced closer to him. "Why do you look at me like that?" she demanded. But he danced away without answering.

The great doors were flung open, and Anne heard, "The king!"

The violin music stopped abruptly, as did the dancing. Everyone dropped into bows and curtsies. With the courtiers down, Anne could see her husband clearly. He looked displeased, as if catching children in mischief.

Anne tossed her head and walked to Henry, her lips parted, seductive. The look in Henry's eyes shifted in an instant, from angry to aroused. Taking Anne's hand he said, "Mark, play a Volta."

Smeaton nodded, bent over his instrument, and began to bow a fast-paced Italian tune in a mesmerizing, minor key.

As everyone else moved back, Henry drew Anne close, moving his body against hers in rhythm to the music. They touched hands, stepped and whirled, Henry sliding his hand in a tantalizing motion along Anne's hip and tossing her into the air, catching her, and lowering her to the floor. Around the floor they moved, touching, caressing, lifting, and falling. Anne's heart pounded; her mouth was wet with desire. She felt countless eyes upon her, and it was wonderful. These eyes were witnesses to the truth. They could see the great love the king and queen had for each other, how their passion lived and burned.

They danced until they could dance no more, and then moved into Anne's bedchamber.

The lovemaking had never been so intense. Anne clawed at Henry, biting his skin, wrapping her limbs about him with great force. She needed to take him, consume him, and in doing so, bring him back to her. Henry reciprocated, mounting her with an urgency that both bruised and pleased her.

At last, both spent, they collapsed upon the mattress. Anne continued to kiss her husband, and she said, "I want to conceive again. I want to give you a son who'll be your mirror image. But—I can't."

"What?"

"I can't conceive a son while they're alive."

"What are you saying?"

"Katherine and her daughter."

Henry drew back from Anne's kisses. "Are you saying you want me to *kill* them?"

Anne didn't answer, but the king had heard her. She placed her head gently on his chest and sighed.

The boy was about fourteen, and dressed in fur-trimmed jerkin and broad-brimmed hat. Pope Paul, seated with Campeggio and several other cardinals, stopped the meeting to wave the boy into the chamber.

"Alesssandro!"

The boy came forward, knelt, and kissed the pope's hand. The pope lifted his head up and kissed the boy's cheeks affectionately.

"Let me look at you," he said. "How you've grown. You're almost a man."

The boy nodded.

"Are you honest and clean?"

"*Sì*, Grandfather."

"Do you pray to God? When you pray, are you truly humble?"

The boy shrugged, amused. "Sure."

"Good boy." The pope kissed him again. "Off you go."

As Alessandro left the chamber, the cardinals smiled and applauded.

"He'll make a great cardinal," said the pope, leaning back again in his chair, his hands clasped in satisfaction. "Don't you think?"

All the cardinals nodded. Then the pope drew a breath, turning his thoughts back to issues at hand. "Messeigneurs, we have other business. Firstly, I have invited the sculptor Michelangelo to paint a Last Judgment in the Sistine Chapel."

An olive-faced cardinal with ratty eyebrows touched his finger to his lips. "Holy Father, some people still object to his work on the ceiling."

"I did myself," said the pope. "But now I like it."

"Won't the Judgment be expensive?" asked Campeggio.

"No," said the pope. "We don't pay him much. He's only an artist, after all."

All the men laughed.

Campeggio then asked, "What of the king of England's Great Matter?"

The laugher faded. The pope said, "I will tell you a story. Once, when I was a boy, I went swimming. The tide carried me far from shore into the deepest water. I prayed aloud to God, and a friendly wave came and pushed me back to shore."

The cardinals' faces were rapt, listening.

"So it is with the king of England. He has been carried far from the shore but he doesn't know it. He doesn't ask for God's help. He doesn't ask for our help. He thinks he can swim alone. But very soon he will realize he is not swimming but drowning."

The crucifixes were flying, tossed into carts alongside statues of the saints, icons of the Virgin Mary, and every other religious figure and painting to be found in and around the Syon Priory. The workmen, sent to strip away all items representative of the Catholic Church, not only pillaged the artifacts, but went as far as to remove windows and roof tiles. All were flung to the ground and hurled onto the growing piles in the carts.

The abbot stood in the grass with several monks, staring in horror at the destruction. Several monks were crying.

"Father," said one, his voice tremulous. "Who are these men?"

"Bretons. From France," said the abbot. "Huguenots."

"Protestants?"

The abbot nodded, his heart clenched, his own eyes beginning to brim.

"But why them?"

The abbot watched as several Bretons stood over a large painted icon of the Virgin Mary and chopped it to pieces with an ax. Several others set fire to an altar cloth and whirled it about in triumph. "Perhaps," he said, "Mr. Secretary Cromwell felt he could not trust Englishmen to destroy their own heritage and besmirch their own faith."

The demolition continued until late afternoon, when the horses were whipped and the carts rattled away, weighed down with piles of smashed, twisted, and burned rubbish that was once priceless and precious treasures. The abbot collected his pilgrim's staff and the small bundle that carried his few personal items, forced himself to look one last time at the desecrated building, and, with tears in his eyes, turned and walked away.

Anne hurried along the corridor, courtiers bowing in her wake, to the doors of King Henry's private chambers. Nan and Madge trotted after her. As ever, the chamber doors were guarded by two scarlet uniformed yeomen of the guard, their battleaxes and pikes in hand. The chamberlain appeared and bowed to the queen.

"Your Majesty," he said.

Anne drew herself up. "I've come to see the king."

The chamberlain hesitated, slightly flustered. "Madam, His Majesty left to go hunting this morning, with the Duke of Suffolk . . . and other nobles."

Gone again! Anne tried to hide her surprise and disappointment. "Suffolk?"

The chamberlain nodded deeply. "Yes, Madam."

"Ah," Anne said, forcing herself to smile. "I remember now. He told me." She stared at the closed doors. Was he gone? Was he with someone else?

Anne turned sharply on her heels and moved back through court, followed by her ladies, the same courtiers bowing and making way.

But this time, it seemed to Anne that their bows mocked her and their gazes judged her.

The red stag buck was especially fine, with a thick neck and huge rack of antlers boasting twelve points. Henry had downed the animal with a crossbow and now knelt in the wet grasses of the field to finish the kill. Brandon held the horses as Henry made the final, fatal slash into the animal's neck with his knife.

"A good prize," said Brandon.

Henry nodded, and wiped the blood from his knife into the grass.

"Do you want to return to the palace?"

Henry stood and motioned to his servants, who had been riding behind, to collect the dead animal. "No," he said. "Is there somewhere near here we could stay?"

Brandon thought for a moment. "There's Wulfhall."

Henry took the reins from Brandon and mounted. "Wulfhall. Whose house is that?"

"Sir John Seymour and his family."

Henry stroked his chin. "I remember Sir John. He was with us in France." Then Henry got a playful look in his eye. "Let's surprise him!"

Wulfhall was several miles to the west, at the edge of Savernake Forest, and by the time the hunting party reached the estate it was nightfall. The house was ancient, its peaked roofs and stone chimneys having seen the turn of many hundreds of summers already. At Henry's signal, Brandon galloped ahead.

Brandon passed through the gateway and drew his horse up at the door. Quickly tethering his mount to an iron post, he entered without knocking and strode into the front hall calling, "Sir John! Sir John!"

John Seymour, a man of middle years and a balding head, appeared from one of the rooms. "Who is this shouting?" he called angrily.

"Sir John," said Brandon, "you have an unexpected guest."

Seymour's eyes widened, and he bowed. "If you mean yourself, my Lord Suffolk, then you are most welcomed!"

Brandon grinned. "No, sir, not me. Your guest is the king of England."

Seymour's eyes, already large, grew more so. "The—king of England? He is—"

"Yes, sir," said Brandon. "He is even now at your door."

At that moment, Henry was in the front doorway, hands on his hips, laughing.

John Seymour did his best to entertain his guests on such short notice, instructing his cooks to prepare and present the best meats and breads on hand, and to keep the flagons of wine filled. Several servants, skilled with instruments, entertained from the corner of the dining hall on lute and pipe.

Seymour had given Henry the head of the table, and sat to the king's right. Brandon was to the king's left. Seymour noted the dwindling food upon the platters and chargers, and ordered for more to be brought in.

"Your Majesty must forgive the tardiness of my kitchen," said Seymour.

Henry wiped a crumb from the corner of his mouth. "I think I am very well looked after, Sir John." He nodded at Brandon. "The Duke and I were reminiscing about our French campaign."

Seymour smiled. "Ah, yes."

"It's a pity we only fought one battle against them."

"Ah," said Seymour, "but what a battle! I remember how we charged at them, with His Grace"—he nodded at Brandon—"leading the vanguard with tremendous bravery. And how the French were broken and routed in the charge and fled the field before us."

Brandon slapped the table, grinning. "So all we saw were their spurs!"

The men laughed.

"And then," said Henry, leaning forward over his bowl, "the town of Therouanne fell!"

Brandon nodded and pointed his knife at Seymour. "You also won golden opinions that day, Sir John."

"Happy days!" said Henry. He lifted his tankard to his friends and drank.

"After the victory," said Seymour, "I remember the jousting, before Charles of Castile and Margaret of Savoy. Your Majesty ran many courses against His Grace and the French champion and broke many lances!" The man smiled and shook his head. "I must tell Your Majesty that the Milanese ambassador was amazed by you. He said to me, 'The king was fresher after his exertion than before. I don't know how he can stand it.'"

The men laughed again, but Henry quickly went silent. To Brandon, the king seemed nostalgic, almost sad.

"It was a long time ago," said Henry at last. "Alas, we are all older now."

Long after the dining was done, the men sat about the table, sharing old memories, complimenting one another on their acts of bravery and skill. Henry seemed more relaxed than Brandon had seen him in years. Candles flickered and were replaced by servants as the evening wore on.

Then Brandon noticed Henry's attention shifting to something across the room. Brandon turned to see a young woman in the doorway. She was tall and pale, with thick, golden-red hair. Her green gown set off her blue eyes and hair in a most stunning yet modest way. She appeared to Henry as an earth goddess, delicate, mysterious, and beautiful. His heart caught for a moment and then began beating again.

Seymour turned in his chair, also. The master of the house smiled, stood, and motioned the young woman to the table.

"Your Majesty," said Seymour, "may I present my daughter, Lady Jane."

Henry and Brandon stood. Jane approached the king, then knelt on the floor and kissed his hand.

Gently, Henry lifted her to her feet, and said softly, "Jane."

There was rustling in the darkness. Katherine opened her eyes and peered through the thin bed curtains to see a figure standing in her room. Candlelight defined the features vaguely, and Katherine pulled back the curtain with a trembling hand.

Her heart quickened. "Mary?"

It was her dear daughter!

Katherine struggled to sit up against the pillows. "Mary! Oh, Mary!"

Mary came forward, smiling, and fell tearfully onto the bed beside her mother. Katherine gathered her daughter in her now-strengthening arms, weeping with joy. "Oh, sweetheart—sweetheart! Is it you? Don't weep, don't weep."

The girl was warm in her mother's arms, soft, tender, smelling of spring and sunlight. Katherine breathed in her scent, thanking God for this miracle.

"Let me look at you." Tenderly, Katherine lifted her daughter's face. It was that of a beautiful and pious young woman, unravaged by care or illness. "There you are. I have not seen you for so long. For five years, an eternity! But here you are! Oh, Mary, my sweet child, my beloved, my angel, my world . . ." Katherine sank back into the pillows, her eyes closing.

Elizabeth knelt by the bedroom hearth, listening to her lady muttering words of affection to the empty air. She rose with her bucket of warm water and clean rags.

Katherine blinked and drew a sharp breath. "Elizabeth, she was here, she came to me."

"Yes, Madam, I know. Are you in pain?"

Katherine nodded with effort.

"Then let me summon a doctor."

"No," said Katherine. Even at a distance, Elizabeth could smell the sickness on the woman's breath. "I don't want a doctor. I've wholly committed myself to the pleasure of God."

Elizabeth nodded, and went about mopping her mistress' brow and cooling down her arms, though she knew it did nothing to help Katherine except, perhaps, to give her a brief distraction from her growing misery.

Mark Smeaton sat on a chair in Anne's bedchamber, playing a soft, poignant tune as Anne stood beside the fireplace and watched the embers dance. The glowing coals seemed bright and joyous, something a child might reach for to touch, to hold. Yet Anne had been burned before. She knew how pretty things could hurt.

The song ended. Anne looked over her shoulder at Smeaton.

"Oh, Mark, I am so sad."

"Why sad?"

She walked to him, head down. "If I had a son, it would bring about a golden world."

Smeaton looked at her with his beautiful eyes, eyes so full of compassion. Anne smiled through her tears, then leaned over to kiss Smeaton on the cheek.

*   *   *   *

Through the open doorway, Nan held the bundle of sticks and watched the queen smile, touch the musician's face, and then kiss it.

The reports were greatly troubling, and Anne meant to have her say. She called for Cromwell, who came, dutifully, to her outer chamber.

"Madam," he said as he bowed. "You wished to see me?"

Anne put her needlework aside and considered the king's secretary with a steady glare. "My father tells me you are determined to close down every religious house in England. Is that true?"

"Yes, Madam," said Cromwell, in his infuriating, matter-of-fact tone. "As Your Majesty knows, the church commissioners found that abuse, laxity, and fraud were commonplace."

Anne lifted her chin. "Yet some religious houses received good reports. Isn't that also true?"

Cromwell said nothing, but his expression remained impassive.

Anne rose and stepped closer to him. "I also hear that *all* the wealth and assets of the monasteries are to be transferred to the king's treasury."

"Indeed. I intend to make His Majesty the richest king that ever was in England."

Anne's anger grew. "But surely some of that wealth could be put to better use!"

"Better use, Madam?"

"Yes! For endowments to educational and charitable causes—which even Wolsey did!"

There was a hint of anger on Cromwell's face, now. Anne could see it flicker briefly across his features like the tongue of a snake. "Madam," he said, "I am surprised to hear you openly question the king's policy, which both your father and brother wholeheartedly support."

"I question the policy, *Mr. Secretary*, because I am not convinced it *is* the king's!"

Cromwell tightened his jaw. "Madam, I assure you—"

"You are far too high-handed, Mr. Cromwell!" Anne saw the challenge in his eyes, and she met it, subduing her voice but not her rage. "You ought to be careful, or I will have you cropped at the neck."

With a brush of her hand, she dismissed the secretary, who bowed and turned away, leaving a chilling void.

Elizabeth sat at the small table beside the bed, inscribing Katherine's last words as a somber-faced, black-robed priest drew out his vial of consecrated oil and made the sign of the cross over the dying woman.

"I know I must die," Katherine dictated in a voice so small that Elizabeth had to incline her head to hear. "I ask that my debts be cleared and my servant be recompensed for the good service she has done for me." Katherine took several raspy breaths. "I wish to be buried in the Convent of the Observant Friars. I would wish that five hundred masses be said for my soul and that someone should go to the shrine of our Lady at Walsingham to pray on my behalf.

"To my daughter, Mary, I leave the collar of gold I brought from Spain, and my furs—"

Katherine began to cough, clutching at her sunken chest.

"Madam," said Elizabeth, putting the quill down and standing from the table. "Let me help you." She slipped her arm beneath her mistress to help Katherine sit up.

"Thank you, my lady," Katherine said. "It is a great consolation to die in your arms, not totally abandoned like an animal."

Elizabeth swallowed back the tears and held the woman as closely as she could without further hurting her.

Then Katherine said, "I must write to the king."

Elizabeth carefully withdrew and returned to the table. She put the quill into the inkwell and the tip to the paper.

"My lord and dear husband, I commend me unto you," Katherine whispered, completing the missive. "The hour of my death draws fast on, and my case being such, the tender love I owe you forces me to put you in remembrance of the health and safeguard of your soul, which you ought to prefer before any consideration of the world of flesh whatso-ever, for which you have cast me into many miseries and yourself into many cares.

"For my part, I do pardon you. I do wish and dearly pray God that He will also pardon you. For the rest, I commend unto you Mary, our daughter, beseeching you to be a good father unto her, as I have always desired. Lastly, I vow that mine eyes desire you above all things."

Katherine's thin fingers rose and gestured for the quill. Elizabeth brought the paper and pen to her lady, and helped her sign *Katherine the Queen*.

Exhausted, Katherine slumped into her pillows, so pale, so weak now that she seemed to fade into the white of the linens.

As Elizabeth began to weep, the priest bent over Katherine, dabbed his finger atop the vial of oil, and tenderly anointed her eyelids.

"*Domine, in manus tuas, commendo spiritum meum,*" murmured Kath-erine. With the greatest of dignity, a smile appeared on her lips and she gave her spirit up to God.

Henry sat alone in his private chambers, reading the letter from Kather-ine. When finished, he let the paper fall to the floor and he put his hands over his eyes. Hot and bitter tears soaked his palms.

In his small and simple chamber in the palace, Brereton placed the point of a knife against his hand. The knife reflected light from the candle on the table and the smile that was on Brereton's lips. Then, sucking air through his teeth, he slashed the shape of a cross into his palm. He watched, transfixed, as the blood dripped onto the Bible and crucifix beside the candle.

Nan rushed into Anne's chamber, where the queen was sewing, alone.

Anne looked up to see the anxious expression on her servant's face. "What is it, child?"

Nan bowed and said, "Katherine has died."

Anne nodded and waved Nan out. Alone again, she smiled. "Now I am indeed queen."

The state into which The More had fallen over the years was both shocking and tragic. Thomas Wyatt secured his horse to the branch of a scrub tree that had grown in the courtyard, and pushed through the unbolted front door. Leaves blew in with him, and rats ran from his footsteps.

"Elizabeth?"

He hoped she was there, that he could, at last, give her an escape from the life to which she'd dedicated herself, the life that had drained so much from her. He moved through the parlor and into a narrow corridor. He pushed open a door and peered inside. It was a bedchamber with cracking, moldy walls, and a bed with threadbare linens. Katherine had died here. It still smelled of illness and long suffering.

"Elizabeth?"

He moved down the shadowy corridor, peeking into various rooms, finding nothing but more gloom, more rats.

Then he stopped. He'd heard a dry, creaking sound at the end of the hallway.

"Elizabeth?"

He moved quickly to the last chamber and stepped inside.

"Elizabeth! Oh, Jesus!"

Wyatt fell to his knees beside the overturned chair, burying his head in his hands, shutting off the dreadful sight. Elizabeth swung gently from a rope lashed to an overhead beam, her rosary beads caught upon stiffened fingers.

Lady Mary sat on her cot in her bedchamber, slowly opening the box that had been handed her by Lady Bryan with the dismissive words, "Your mother has died. This is from her."

Mother . . .

In the box, Mary found rosary beads and three silver, jewel-studded hair combs. There were also a collar of gold and two carefully folded furs. Then, at the bottom of the box, Mary discovered a document, yellowed and brittle. She drew it out and read it. It was the marriage certificate of her mother and father.

Mary put the rosary beads to her lips and kissed them, and she kissed the document.

Mother . . .

The Morris Men pranced in and out through the nobles and courtiers in the royal park of Whitehall Palace, banging tabors, blowing pipes, and shaking their legs so that the bells on their pantaloons jingled. The day was cool and pleasant, perfect for an outdoor holiday. Girls wandered about with baskets of fruits and pastries, and a minstrel with a hurdy-gurdy sat upon a wall and turned out a gay and whining tune.

Cromwell and his wife had joined George Boleyn and his wife to watch a pair of slathering, thick-shouldered dogs fight each other in a pit. The men placed their bets and cheered as the ladies watched on with little interest.

Sudden applause erupted, and the crowd parted, then bowed, welcoming the king and queen to the festival. Henry was dressed in a somber gray, but Anne wore a bright yellow gown stitched through with designs in gold thread. Behind the couple, carefully tended by her governess and several ladies, was the little Princess Elizabeth. The child had found a flower, and was clutching it in her hand. She giggled each time a courtier bowed to her.

Immediately, from his place beside the dog pit, George noted the strain between his sister and the king. Anne seemed to be celebrating Katherine's death, and Henry appeared none too pleased. How careless of his sister, if that was her intent.

George noted Mark Smeaton in the crowd, chewing an apple and watching the royal procession. George walked over to the musician.

"Not performing today, Mark?"

Smeaton smiled. "Not today, my lord. But perhaps . . . tonight?"

George glanced about, fearing someone might have heard. "I'm not sure."

Smeaton looked over George's shoulder toward Lady Jane, who was chatting with Lady Catherine. "Have you told her about me? About us?"

"No."

"Why not?" Smeaton nudged George with his elbow. "You're bloody George Boleyn. You're like a bloody god here!"

George sighed. "If you could read Greek, Master Smeaton, you would know that even the gods had problems with their wives!"

As Anne moved away to talk to several courtiers, Henry sought out the one person he'd hoped had accepted the invitation to the festival. He found Sir John Seymour under a tree with Charles Brandon, talking horses.

"Sir John!" said Henry, striding forward, smiling broadly.

Seymour bowed deeply. "Your Majesty."

Henry put his hands on his hips. "We wanted to thank you for your generous hospitality. All the more so because our visit was unexpected."

"Sire," said Seymour, lowering his head respectfully, "it was the greatest pleasure and privilege, and the room Your Majesty slept in will now forever be called the 'King's Bedroom.'"

Henry laughed lightly. He glanced at Brandon, then back at Seymour. "Your daughter Jane should come to court, as a lady to Her Majesty."

Seymour looked very pleased. "Thank you, Your Majesty. You do our family a great honor."

Henry nodded and turned away, a sense of expectation and joy in his heart. Then he saw his little daughter in the grass nearby, happily picking flower tops off stems.

"Sweetheart," he called, "come here!"

Elizabeth dropped the flowers and ran to her father. Henry lifted her to the blue sky and kissed her cheeks.

"My Elizabeth," he said.

"My Papa!" said the child.

They both laughed with delight.

Anne heard someone call her name and she looked up from the young courtier who had been entertaining her with clever riddles beside the wall on which the hurdy-gurdy man continued to play his tune. She saw it was her father, and he looked very stern indeed.

"Yes, Father?" she replied sweetly, hoping to alter his mood.

Boleyn motioned for Anne to walk with him. She came, grudgingly. Once they were apart from the milling crowd, Boleyn spoke his mind.

"I have heard reports which alarm me."

Anne pursed her lips. "What reports?"

"It seems that you have quarreled with Mr. Cromwell."

"We disagreed on an important and public issue."

Boleyn's eyes narrowed. "Anne, I did not bring you up to have opinions. Or to express them. Or to quarrel with those closest to the crown!"

Anne's eyes flashed. "But I am closest to the crown! I am the king's wife!"

"And you should remember how you got there."

The Morris Men passed by, jingling their bells and banging their drums, and they bowed deeply as they went by.

Anne stared at her father. "I *know* how I got there, and it was not all *you*. It was not all *you*, nor all *Norfolk*, or *George*, or any other *man*. It was also *me*. He fell in love with *me*. He respected *me* and my *opinions*."

With that Anne shook her head and abruptly began to laugh.

Boleyn was freshly dismayed. "Come!" he demanded. "What *is* it?"

Anne brushed a stray hair back from her face and looked at her father defiantly. "You have no need to worry," she said. "There is good news all around. Katherine is dead, and . . ." She paused.

Boleyn looked at his daughter, waiting.

"And I'm pregnant. Do you understand? I'm carrying the king's son." She held her head high and ran one hand down the fabric of her bright yellow dress. "We are on the edge of a golden world!"

Chapter Thirteen

A royal court is a place of beauty—gold and roses, tapestries and crowns, rubies and candelabras. So it went almost without notice when a beautiful young couple entered Whitehall Palace and moved through the meandering corridors that led to the queen's private chambers. The couple were brother and sister; he tall and finely featured, she tall and elegant, with hair the color of sunrise. Guards noted their papers and gave them pass, but then the couple was forgotten.

In spite of her outward composure, the young woman was quite nervous. As they reached the closed door to the queen's rooms, she took her brother's hand and squeezed it gently.

"Thank you, Edward," she said.

"Sister." Edward Seymour nodded reassuringly. Jane could read the message in his eyes. *Be careful. Here is your chance.*

A guard opened the door, admitting Queen Anne's newest lady-in-waiting.

A severe-looking chaplain in robe and black skullcap stood beside a table on which sat a Tyndale Bible. Five ladies-in-waiting sat about in chairs, sewing and waiting to attend on Her Majesty when she arrived. Most of them remained seated but glanced up to give Jane a cool, appraising look. One, however, stood, approached Jane, and introduced herself as Nan.

"You are Lady Jane?" Nan asked.

"Yes."

Nan's voice was stern, instructive. "Her Majesty is just coming. You are not to speak anything to her, until you are invited to."

"Yes," said Jane quietly.

The bedchamber door opened and the queen appeared, dressed in a solid green kirtle with a silver-threaded gown. Jane noticed immediately that Her Majesty was in the early stages of pregnancy.

All the ladies curtsied, deeply. Then Anne motioned to the chaplain, who picked up the Bible and turned toward Jane.

"Mistress Seymour," said the chaplain, his monotonic voice deep and almost chilling, "will you place your hand upon this Holy Bible."

Jane put her hand on the cover.

"And will you promise and swear to serve Her Majesty Queen Anne faithfully, honorably, and discreetly; and will you promise and swear that your conduct will always be modest, virtuous, and good, presenting at all times a godly spectacle to others?"

Jane glanced at the queen, whose face was expressionless.

"I do so promise and swear," said Jane.

The chaplain moved back and Anne came forward. Jane felt her skin prickle, as if the queen's gaze was full of tiny, hot daggers. "Lady Jane," said the queen.

"Your Majesty," said Jane, lowering her eyes.

Then the queen turned back into her bedchamber as the ladies curtsied. Jane held hers until she heard the door close.

William Brereton's face had changed, and it caught Ambassador Chapuys off-guard. The king's groom had lost weight, revealing ill-set cheekbones and defining his brow such that a permanent shadow seemed to cloak his eyes.

Chapuys caught sight of Brereton amid courtiers and milling subjects in the main corridor of Whitehall Palace. He took the groom aside to speak in an alcove behind a couple of grumbling petitioners who had, from their ripe smell, not cleaned themselves in perhaps a year.

Chapuys spoke in a hushed tone. "I managed with some difficulty to obtain a copy of the secret report of the autopsy on Queen Katherine."

Brereton's shadowed eyes widened. "What was discovered?"

"Most of the internal organs were normal, except for the heart. It had a black growth, hideous to behold, which clung closely to the outside."

"What could have caused it?"

"Her doctor, a Mr. de la Saa, who I trust completely, told me the growth was consistent with the evidence of poisoning. He said that her condition had suddenly worsened after she drank a certain Welsh beer."

Brereton let out an angry breath.

"I'm sure the beer was tampered with," said Chapuys. "I am also sure that, had the body been properly examined, traces of it would have been seen."

"Then," snarled Brereton, "her threats were not empty ones. She succeeded at last!" Brereton glanced up the corridor in the direction of the queen's chambers. "She-devil! Poor Katherine." He made a discreet sign of the cross.

"There is little need to pray for Katherine. Her holy soul is in eternal rest."

"But poor Mary," said Brereton.

Chapuys nodded and then peered around cautiously. "We shall talk later." He excused himself, backing away from the groom and moving into the milling crowd. Suddenly, his sleeve was grabbed from behind, yanking him backward. Chapuys spun about to chastise the jokester to find himself face to face with King Henry.

Henry laughed. "Excellence!"

Chapuys forced himself to look happy, and he bowed. "Your Majesty."

Henry nodded, indicating Chapuys should walk with him.

"I hear," the king said, "that your master is to be congratulated. He has taken Tunis from the Turks."

"Your Majesty is well informed," replied Chapuys. "The threat of the Turkish invasion has indeed been lifted by the emperor's victory. Peace will follow."

The king drew a breath. "Would that it followed everywhere."

"Yes, pray God. Perhaps one day there will be no more need for war, or war's alarms." *Yet that will never be*, he thought.

"In the meanwhile," said Henry, stopping to face the ambassador, "please send my love and congratulations to the emperor. Tell him that . . ." He paused, thinking. "That of all the princes in the world, I admire him most."

Henry was filled with energy and joyous expectation. His wife was pregnant with what he knew was his son, and the beautiful Jane Seymour had come to court. He called Cromwell into his private chamber to discuss current situations that needed his attention.

"Now that the emperor has dealt with the Turks," said Henry, seated on his chair, one leg over the arm, fingering the gold chain at his neck, "his armies are freed to turn upon us, and a while ago, I swear he would have done so." He let go of the chain. "But no longer. With Katherine's death the cause of our enmity is altogether taken away. And I have a new desire to renew my friendship with him." Henry dropped his leg from the chair arm. "You will talk to Chapuys. Find out the cost of friendship."

Cromwell nodded. "Yes, Your Majesty."

Henry stood and began to pace. "What of our reforms?"

"The bill for the dissolution of the larger monasteries will be laid before Parliament at the next session."

Henry nodded and gestured to dismiss the secretary. But then he said, "There was something else. I know you have family, a wife and son. What's your son's name?"

"Gregory, Your Majesty. I had two daughters also, but they died."

"Bring your family to court. I should like to meet them."

"Majesty," said Cromwell with a bow. He then turned, leaving the king in his state of joy, to ponder and to plan.

* * * *

Maundy Thursday commemorated the event of the Lord's Supper, when Christ washed his disciples' feet and dined with them one last time. It was tradition in court for the queen to humble herself and wash the feet of the poor, selected from the streets of London, and to present them with alms.

The destitute were herded into the Chapel Royal, where they removed their shoes and had their feet scrubbed by dutiful servants. Then they waited in queue for the queen, shifting back and forth, gazing in awe at the glory and grandeur around them.

Anne entered the chapel with her husband. In the loft, the choristers sang a *Te Deum*, their voices clear and heavenly. Anne knew her duties, and found them to be peaceful to her soul. She liked the smiles she received when she handed coins to the poor. She liked the appreciative submission when she washed and dried their feet. Of course, the feet had been thoroughly scoured prior to her handling them. It would not do for her to wash truly dirty feet.

The ranks of courtiers and ladies-in-waiting bowed and curtsied as the royal couple moved through the lines. Then Anne saw it. The look Henry gave to Jane Seymour, and the look Jane returned.

Anne's body stiffened.

Archbishop Cranmer met the couple at the altar with a bow. With the passing of time, the man no longer looked uncomfortable in his holy vestments, but appeared to have filled out the role with both his attitude and increasing bulk.

"Your Majesties," he said. Then, to Anne, "If Your Majesty will follow me."

Henry smiled at Anne, but she pretended not to see it. She followed Cranmer to the queue of the poor.

"Good people," said Cranmer, "here is the Queen's Majesty, come this Maundy Thursday to give you alms and wash your feet as did our Lord Jesus Christ to his disciples, commanding them to love one another."

A servant drew a large white apron over Anne's gown, then gave the queen a towel for drying and a nosegay to guard against infection. Anne knelt before the first of the poor, an old man with thin legs and gnarled toes. A basin of water was placed on the floor beside queen. She lifted the man's feet into the basin, rubbed the feet gently, then lifted them out and dried them with the towel. Holding the small bouquet to her nose, she kissed the wrinkled skin.

"God bless and keep you," Anne said quietly. "God in His mercy bless you and keep you. Amen."

As Anne moved to the next person in the line, Nan and Madge, bearing baskets of bread, wine, fish, and clothing, came forward to give the old man his gift. Then Nan handed him a red and white purse of coins. The old man crossed himself and blessed them for their generosity.

As Queen Anne continued down the line of poor, two old women who'd had their feet washed stood together, peering into their coin purses.

"Look!" said one, holding out the money. "This is twice as much as the old queen gave!"

The second woman watched down the line as Anne, on her knees, continued the rituals. "Perhaps," she said, "she means to buy our love."

George Boleyn didn't see his wife, Jane, now Lady Rochford, in the shadows of the corner of the room until she coughed, lightly. She'd been watching him as he came into their apartment, staring at him with accusatory eyes.

"Sweetheart," he said, caught in the unsteady grip of many glasses of wine. "What is it?"

"Where have you been?"

"I had meetings. Privy Council matters."

"Until this hour?"

"The king's affairs never sleep."

Lady Rochford stepped out of the shadows. George sat at the table and pulled off a boot.

"What of your affairs?"

George fumbled with his second boot. "My affairs?"

"You've just come from another's bed. Don't deny it!"

George leaned on the table. He could see in his wife's eyes that she would not accept another story. "Very well," he said. "I shan't."

Lady Rochford stepped even closer, eyes blazing. "What makes it worse is that you've not forsaken my bed for that of another woman, which perhaps I could understand, as I think myself the plainest Jane at court. But—for another man."

George just looked at her.

"It's true!" Lady Rochford wailed. "Oh, my God!"

George stood and reached for her, but she shrank back in utter revulsion. "It's disgusting! It's a sin against God. A sin against nature. And those who practice it are condemned by the Gospels to live forever in Purgatory!"

Neck tightening, George glowered at his wife. "Sometimes, my love, I think that with you I'm already condemned to live in Purgatory!" He left the apartment, slamming the door behind him.

The night had not treated Thomas Boleyn kindly. He had slept very little, tossing and fretting, thinking of the arrival of the lovely yet potentially dangerous Lady Seymour to court. The following morning he took his daughter into the garden for a talk.

"They tell me that Mistress Jane Seymour has been appointed one of your ladies," he said once they were beyond the ears of Anne's ladies, who strolled a fair distance behind.

Anne, walking beside him with a red rosebud in her hand, nodded. "Yes. At the king's command."

Boleyn could hear in his daughter's voice her discomfort with the subject. That was good. She needed to be very uncomfortable with the situation. "The Seymours are an old and interesting family," he said. "Sir

John fought beside the king during his French campaign. He also has two sons, Edward and Thomas. I hear the first is steady and cold, the other rash. But both are ambitious and greedy. Though they've all taken the oath, what is not known is how honestly or completely they have renounced the old religion. It is something we must hope, before too long, to discover."

Anne stopped and put the rosebud to her nose. "And if we can?"

"Then the tide of their ambitions can be turned, and will ebb away. We shall hear no more of them."

Ahead, the Princess Elizabeth and her governess entered the garden through a gate in the hedge. Both curtsied to the queen.

"Madam," said the child.

Anne laughed, threw the rose aside, and held out her arms. *"Vien ici, ma belle!"*

Elizabeth raced to her mother, holding her tiny skirts. Anne scooped her up and spun her toward Boleyn. "How pretty you look in your new clothes! Is she not very pretty, Papa?"

Boleyn nodded, but then looked at Anne's stomach. "Indeed, she is a pretty girl. But what you carry in your belly is our savior!"

Cromwell and Chapuys sat in large mahogany chairs with tall backs and thick cushions, sipping Cromwell's best wine as a warm fire on the hearth and candles in sconces chased back the night.

Placing his goblet aside, Cromwell linked his fingers together and said, "As I told you, His Majesty is most desirous to make an alliance with the emperor. And I believe also that such an alliance would be greatly to the benefit of this country."

Chapuys dabbed the corners of his mouth and nodded. "I've communicated with the emperor. He, also, is eager to find a way to make a new, strong alliance. And to show his goodwill, I can tell you that he is willing to persuade His Holiness, Pope Paul, not to publish the sentence of excommunication against the king, which would have deprived him of his throne."

"I'm sure His Majesty would wish to express his immense gratitude to your master."

Chapuys nodded.

Then came the more important issue. "And in return?"

The ambassador put his goblet down. "In the circumstances, after the death of his beloved aunt, the emperor is prepared to offer the king his support for the continuation of his marriage to Anne Boleyn. But—"

Cromwell waited.

"On condition that the king declares Princess Mary to be his legitimate heir."

There was a long moment of silence. Cromwell poured himself another goblet of wine. Then he said, "I accept that is, in many ways, a generous concession on behalf of the emperor."

"He begs the king to understand it is as far as he is prepared to go."

"I will certainly put the proposal to His Majesty."

Chapuys looked at Cromwell uncertainly. "With your approval?"

Cromwell sighed, silently. "Even with my approval, Excellency, it may not be easy."

The court was quieter in the evening, though always shifting with guards, courtiers, and ladies on the way to and from their respective duties. In an alcove, Mark Smeaton and Thomas Wyatt stood, apart from the nocturnal processions.

"She *is* pretty," said Smeaton.

"Who?" Wyatt looked up from the paper on which he'd been scribbling.

"Lady Jane Seymour. She's new at court." Smeaton pointed toward the lady, who was walking past them, her eyes lowered modestly. Smeaton winked at Wyatt.

But Wyatt did not return the wink. Instead, he handed Smeaton his paper. Lifting it up to the light of the nearest sconce, Smeaton read the first lines of a poem.

> *If thou wilt mighty be, flee from the rage*
> *Of cruel will;*
> *And see thou keep thee free*
> *From the foul yoke of sensual bondage.*

"'The foul yoke of sensual bondage,'" repeated Smeaton with a chuckle. "I like that!"

Wyatt snatched back the paper, scowling. "Then you don't understand it, or how cruel the will that drives it. Until you see the fruits of a sensual bondage swinging from a rope."

A groom had come to her in the corridor and told her a friend had wished to speak to her in private. Lady Jane Seymour could think of no friend she had in court, but hesitantly and obediently followed the groom down a side corridor to an empty chamber.

"Who—?" Jane began, but the groom said nothing more, stepped outside, and closed the door. Jane was alone. She held her breath and waited.

The door in the far wall opened, and the king entered. Jane immediately dropped into a curtsy and waited.

The king approached her and said softly, "Jane."

Jane looked up at the king. "Your Majesty."

The king held out his hand and lifted her up. He gazed at her deeply, causing Jane to shiver. At last he said, "I ask of you only one thing, that you should allow me to serve and worship you. Just as Lancelot served and worshipped Guinevere. Gentle sweet lady, will you let me so?"

Jane's breaths came more quickly, though she spoke in a quiet tone. "I will."

"May I kiss your hand?"

Jane offered the king her hand, and, closing his eyes, he kissed it tenderly, longingly. "My lady," he whispered. He bowed and left the room. Jane stood for long minutes afterward, feeling the tingle of the kiss upon her hand.

* * * *

"Puh!" said Anne, dropping her cards to the table. George had won another round, and he cheerfully scooped up his winnings—a lopsided pile
of gold coins. They were alone in Anne's outer chamber, with several of
the queen's ladies waiting in the chamber next door.

Anne tapped a card and then said, "Do you know them?"

"Know who?" asked George.

"The Seymours."

George shrugged, drew the cards together, and shuffled them. "I may
have met Edward, the eldest son. He's a cold fish. I don't know about the
others. Why? Are you afraid of them?"

"Father thinks they may be supporters of Mary."

"Ah, Mary." George put the cards down. "It's a pity she's not keeping
company with her mother."

"They tell me she's ill again. That for her comfort the king has given
permission for her removal from Elizabeth's household."

George waved his hand. "It's an act of kindness. No more than that."

"No. He's still fond of her. He always was, and still is, though to my
face he pretends otherwise."

George looked at his sister. "How ill *is* she?"

"Very, so I'm told. With a fever and constant vomiting."

George picked the cards up again and dealt. "Then, with God's grace,
we may not have to meddle with her after all."

"The king has offered to serve you?"

"Yes, Father."

John Seymour looked about their apartment and then back at his son,
Edward, and his daughter, Jane, with a great smile on his face. "I'm not
surprised. And it means he does not seek an easy conquest!"

Edward, standing beside the fireplace, nodded thoughtfully. "He has
formed an affection. What's important is that it should be carefully, as-
siduously nurtured. I urge you, Jane, not to submit yourself or yield your
virginity to the king, however forceful his persuasions."

Seymour held up his hand. "Jane does not need to be lectured on the need for modesty or virtue, Edward, when she possesses them in her nature."

"Still," said Edward. "Imagine what it would mean for us as a family if he *did* grow to love her."

Seymour nodded and turned to Jane. "I am certainly aware that there are some at court who should like the queen replaced."

Jane caught her breath. "Wait! Are you saying that I might be queen instead of her?"

Edward stepped close to his sister and placed his hands on her shoulders. "Would you like to be?"

Jane did not need to answer.

King Henry considered Sir Henry Norris as he stood in the middle of his chamber, hands on his hips. He wore a new purple doublet with fashionably slashed sleeves and ruffs of silk. The gold chain around his neck bore emeralds the size of a wren's eggs and his boots were newly fashioned by the royal cobbler from the softest calves' leather. The new clothing was an outward sign of the new joy in his life, and he relished their feel upon his body.

"Tell me, Sir Henry," the king said at last, a small smile on his lips, "are you engaged yet to Lady Margaret?"

The older man, dressed in light gray velvet detailed with blue and red stitching, shook his head. "Not yet, your Majesty. I—I have not so far asked for her hand."

Henry laughed a single laugh. "For God's sake, why not? She's young. She's—she will give you more children, I know."

"I know it," said Norris. He looked uncomfortable with the topic. "But, I was married before and, I confess, I rather like the liberty of not being married again."

"Ah!" Henry slapped the man on the back. "That I can understand!" Henry strode to the window and watched a falcon riding the air above the gardens. "You know what? You're courting a young lady and I'm—"

He stopped, turned back, his brows up. "We should joust together again, as we used to. You always did grace the tiltyard. We ran many courses against each other and broke many lances."

Norris smiled and nodded.

"Let's do so again, and you can organize it," said Henry. "Soon."

Norris bowed. "Majesty."

The pope's audience room was vast, filled with the pageantry of red-robed cardinals, indigo-clothed bishops, and glittering Swiss guards swarming around the white-tiled floors. Banners waved and trumpeters sounded, announcing the arrival of the king of France. Upon his dais, Pope Paul III watched for the monarch to enter and then took a silent breath when he saw a bareheaded, bearded man in a simple shift emerge through the throng.

It was Francis, the French king.

The pope stepped down from his dais to embrace the king. "Majesty. You have come to us as a pilgrim and a penitent. You surely deserve Heaven's graces."

Francis dropped to his knees and kissed the pope's feet. "Holy Father," he said. There was an audible murmur of approval throughout the crowd, followed by wholehearted applause.

The pope led him to a seat beside his own on the dais. He raised a ring-covered hand and said, "We welcome you to Rome, to the Mother of our Church, of which you are a most obedient child. When others fall by the wayside, you remain loyal to us and to the truth of Christ."

Francis postured himself on the seat, speaking so all could hear. "As a child to a father, I say to all here that I would gladly lay down my life in order to serve you, Holy Father, in whatever way you choose."

The pope smiled, savoring the devotion. Then he said, "I have decided to carry out the Bull of Excommunication against King Henry of England. A father must seek for ways to forgive his children, but Henry's crimes against us and against the Church are too profound to forgive. Moreover, he shows no repentance, no contrition."

"The king of England has always been the hardest friend to bear in the world," said Francis. "He is continuously capricious. In some ways, Holy Father, I would describe him as the strangest man in the world."

The pope nodded, then drew Francis close with a request the king could not refuse. He lowered his voice. "In which case, I am sure I can rely upon you to execute the bull."

Francis's brow creased. "Holiness . . . ?"

"My son," said the pope, still smiling. "Surely you understand. If I excommunicate a fellow prince, then that prince is not only separated from God, but also from the communion of the faithful. His rule becomes invalid. And it is a religious imperative to overthrow him."

The French king's performance faltered, but he continued to sit straight, listening.

"You are a great Catholic prince. You have ships and guns. So I ask you, in all humility, as your Holy Father, will you invade England? Will you remove and kill the apostate and return that poor country to our common faith?"

Francis did not answer but the pope did not care. It would be done. He drew the king close and hugged him. The gathering of the holy men applauded once more.

The pounding of hooves against the ground and the snap of flags in the breeze drove a thrill through the crowds seated in the brightly decorated pavilions along the lists and standing by the railings. Nobles and ladies, dressed in their finest spring clothing, gazed with wide eyes as knights upon caparisoned horses raced toward each other, armor catching the sun, lances aimed. Knight after knight took a spill, driven from his saddle with a well-aimed blow. The winner of the joust stood in his stirrups to receive the cheers from the onlookers.

In the center of the main dais, beneath the shield bearing the initials *H & A*, sat those closest to the king and queen—Thomas and George Boleyn; Brandon's wife Catherine, the Duchess of Suffolk; George's wife,

Lady Rochford; and numerous other nobles of favor. However, the royal thrones remained empty.

Catherine touched the golden chain about her neck and leaned over to Lady Rochford. "Is Her Majesty not attending the tournament today?"

Lady Rochford kept her eyes on the far end of the list, watching for the next competitors to appear. "No," she said. "Apparently she's worried that the excitement of the tournament might harm her unborn son." She cast a quick glance at Catherine. "Or so she supposes it to be. Personally, I hope she did not visit the same astrologer as before."

Catherine opened her mouth to reply, intrigued by the biting sarcasm in Lady Rochford's tone. But she said nothing.

Henry would love the shirt. It was made from the finest brocade, stitched through with silver and trimmed with black fur. Anne sat by the window where she could hear the distant noises of the tournament, and pushed the needle in and out, in and out. Then she stopped, looked at the wall, and sighed.

Mark Smeaton, who had been playing a soft tune for the queen on his violin, also stopped. He placed the instrument aside and moved close to Anne.

"Why does the king joust," he asked gently, "and put himself in harm's way?"

Anne fingered the needle, pressing it to her thumb though not hard enough to prick. "I suppose he feels the need to prove his virility."

Smeaton smiled and looked at Anne's bulging belly. "Has he not already proved it?"

Henry's mount was ready, snorting and tossing its head in anticipation of the joust. One of Henry's pages held the horse's cheek strap with both hands, keeping the anxious animal in check. Henry strode toward the horse, dressed in half armor, his visor up, followed by another page carrying the lance and shield. A line of courtiers watched the king's preparations, bowing and curtsying as he approached. Among the crowd was Jane Seymour.

"Lady Jane," said Henry, stepping close to the lady.

Jane held her curtsy, her eyes downcast. "Majesty."

"I am going to fight. Would you do me the privilege of allowing me to wear your favors?"

Jane stood and looked up. In that moment Henry felt his pulse quicken. Such tender and gentle beauty there, such a perfect blush!

Without a word, Jane removed a strip of green ribbon from her sleeve and handed it to the king. She curtsied again.

Henry kissed the ribbon and tied it upon his wrist. Then, walking to his horse, he gathered the reins, swung into the saddle, and collected his shield and lance. He urged his mount into a trot toward the list.

Trumpets sounded, high and shrill, announcing a fresh contest. The herald called out, "His Majesty the King has just entered the list and will now joust, *à la plaisance,* with Sir Henry Norris."

The audience in the lines and those in the pavilions cheered as the two men entered the list on opposite sides. Henry and Sir Norris spurred their horses into a frothy, frenzied gallop toward each other. The lances held steady but at the last moment, both missed their targets, and the men rode to the end of the list, spun their horses about, and prepared to charge again.

On the dais, Boleyn squinted and frowned. He leaned to his son. "The king's shield," he said. "An odd device. It bears a flaming heart. What are the words above it?"

George turned in his seat so he could best see. "*'Declare je nos.'*"

Boleyn bristled. "Declare I not! Above the sign of a heart on fire. He is—in *love*!"

God forbid it! Bolyen thought in a panic, his blood gone cold in his veins. *This could be the beginning of my family's downfall!*

With a howl of triumph, Henry leveled his lance and drove his heels against his horse's sides. Sir Norris did the same. Both horses took off like cannon fire. The crowd shouted; wind-battered banners clapped.

The horses pounded down the list, closer, closer, and then Norris's lance struck Henry in the chest with a thud. The lance shattered, the two pieces spinning into the air. Henry swayed in his saddle, throwing his horse off balance. They crashed to the ground. The horse rolled over Henry, then struggled to its feet.

The crowd screamed and then went suddenly silent as Henry lay motionless and bleeding in the dust. Grooms and physicians raced forward to the king. Brandon and George Boleyn forced their way through the confusion and into the list.

"Is he dead?" George shouted hysterically. "Is he dead?" He tried to get closer but Brandon held him back.

"Let others help him," said Brandon. "You can't."

A physician kneeling by the king called to the men near him. "Take him with all care into that pavilion, so I may serve him better."

George clenched his fists nervously.

"And pray for him," the physician added.

CHAPTER FOURTEEN

The door flew open and Madge burst into the queen's chamber, her face contorted with terror. Anne stood, her sewing falling from her fingers.

"What is it? What's happened?"

Madge curtsied shakily. "The king has fallen from his horse and been crushed. They—they say he is likely to die."

Anne felt the floor shift beneath her. She groaned, clutched her stomach, and swayed. "Oh, Mark—"

Smeaton rushed to her and caught her.

"Say it is not so," Anne moaned. "Say it is not so!"

Madge stared as Smeaton held and comforted the distraught queen.

The king lay on a camp bed inside a canvas-walled pavilion beside the jousting yards. Outside, frantic courtiers were held back by guards at the door. Inside, frantic nobles, grooms, and servants hovered about the bed, unable to do anything, watching the physician with anxious eyes. Brandon, George, and Boleyn stood closest, though allowing the physician room to perform his duties. Near the head of the bed, Lee, the king's chaplain, made the sign of the cross and prayed.

The physician, his hands streaked with the king's blood, held a nosegay of smelling salts to Henry's nose. Henry, pale-skinned and cold, did not stir.

"Will you bleed him?" asked Brandon.

The physician shook his head. "I don't think so. I do not see it would help him. His Majesty is now in God's hands."

Boleyn urgently motioned to George to join him, and they left the tent for their horses.

"Where are we going?" George inquired.

"Back to Whitehall," said Boleyn as he gathered the reins and swung into his saddle. "Don't you understand anything? In such a crisis, all could disintegrate. So the center has to hold. And we must hold it. Or perish!"

Secretary Cromwell's office door stayed open with the arrival of messenger after messenger, bringing news of the king's condition. Cromwell paced across his floor, hand to his chin, considering the implications the death of the monarch would have on the country.

A new messenger hurried into the office and bowed.

"What news?" asked Cromwell.

"There is no news. The king still shows no signs of life."

"How long since the accident?"

"Almost an hour, Your Honor."

Cromwell nodded and glanced at the clock. It read 11:40. He could feel the anxiety in the palace, could sense the prayers raised for the king's recovery. But if the Lord did not see fit to let the king live, Cromwell had much to do.

On his way out, the messenger was nearly knocked over by George and Thomas Boleyn. Boleyn hissed at the man, then turned his attention to Cromwell, who had moved to stand by the window.

"Mr. Secretary," Boleyn demanded. "What's to be done?"

"I am making arrangements," said Cromwell, "in case of the king's death, for the coronation of the Princess Elizabeth, with your lordship's approval. She would be in a minority, but under the wardship of her mother and yourself as Lord Protector."

"And have you posted a guard on the Lady Mary? And closed the ports?"

Cromwell nodded. "All that is in hand, my lord. As are preparations for an emergency recall of Parliament."

Boleyn shook his head. "Bah! The king had no need of Parliament in the old days!"

Cromwell shook his head. "These are not the old days, my lord."

Upon the cold ground beside the king's cot, Sir Henry Norris knelt in silence, his hands folded, his grief-swollen face turned up toward Heaven. The knight's eyes were filled with hot tears of regret and despair. He prayed God to save the king, to bring back his friend and his lord.

Near Sir Norris, Brandon, John Seymour, and other courtiers had gathered to pray. Norris could feel their urgency, their fear and desperation. He hoped God would hear them and favor them.

Almighty Father, return our king to us . . .

It had been nearly two hours since the king's fall. George and Boleyn sat in a private chamber off the main corridor, waiting for news. Boleyn's hands were clasped, though he did not pray. George's head was bowed, but neither did he pray.

After a long moment, George looked up and whispered, "You know, I cannot think whether it would be a bad thing or a good thing if he died. For, as Lord Protector, you would, ipso facto, be king of England."

Boleyn looked at his son and though his lips remained tight, there was a renewed gleam in his eyes.

Thomas Cromwell sweated in the cool of his office, signing warrants and orders that would go into effect were the king to die. There was much to handle, much to consider. Every decision Cromwell made opened up even more to be made. Servants and assistants rushed in and out bringing new papers, taking new orders. All had to be in place.

In case the worst was to happen.

Suddenly, Cromwell slammed his quill down and pushed the papers aside. He stood, jaw clenched, and hurried out, leaving servants and warrants to stare after him.

The Chapel Royal was silent, except for the soft rustling of a gown, the staggered breaths of one in agony. Cromwell walked up the aisle to find Queen Anne kneeling before the altar, trembling hands clasped in supplication. She heard his footfalls and glanced around, but then turned back to her prayer.

Cromwell, overwhelmed for the first time in years, sank to his knees and began to pray for the life of his king.

There was a soft groan.

"Your Majesty?" said the physician. "Your Majesty!"

Brandon opened his eyes and looked up from his prayer. The physician kneeled beside the wounded king, his face drawn up in wonder. Henry had not shifted on the bed, but his eyes had flickered open.

Can it be . . . ?

Courtiers around Brandon stood, awestruck, silently waiting for the next miracle.

Henry licked his dried lips and whispered, "Charles."

Brandon jumped to his feet. "Oh, thank God!" he said. "Thank God!"

Henry's hand clawed weakly at the sheet that covered him as if struggling with an enemy, and found the ends of the ribbon that was tied around his wrist. He clasped it in his fist and sighed.

Anne was exhausted from her hours at prayer and the terror that had prompted her to pray. She sat in her outer chamber, hands folded atop her abdomen, searching for the peace in her heart that should have come with the good news, but coming up with only more worries. Her father stood beside her, his arms crossed.

"We must be grateful that His Majesty took no hurt in his fall."

"Yes, thank God."

"But—" Boleyn pursed his lips. "It means that the safe production of a son from your womb is more than ever imperative. So I beg you to be always careful. Take no exertions or excitements. Shut yourself away as much as you can from the world."

Anne looked from her father to a small dusty spider, dangling from the ceiling. "I wish I could remove Mistress Seymour from among my ladies, but I dare not. I think it would anger the king."

Boleyn threw out his arms. "This is what I mean! If you fret about little matters then you may poison the child inside you!"

Anne looked back. "It's not a little matter to me."

"It is for now. Afterward, when you've given the king his great desire, you will have all the power to deal with her as you like."

Anne sighed and looked at the floor. Her father stepped to her and gently cupped her face in his hand. "Think that I am the angel come down to tell you that you carry the Christ child in your belly."

Anne turned her eyes sharply toward her father.

Henry's entire body burned and ached, but he was alive. He'd been returned to his bedchamber to be attended by his physician, and lay abed as his body was examined. He sucked air silently through his teeth as the physician gently probed the king's leg, then stood and shook his head.

"What is it?" asked Henry, propping up on his elbow.

"Because of the fall this old wound on your leg has reopened. An ulcer has formed."

Henry frowned and looked at the dark gash. "Can you heal it?"

The physician nodded. "Most certainly, Your Majesty. But you must wear a dressing and have the leg bound up."

The physician turned to reach for the dressing on the bedside table, then turned back. "If—Your Majesty will forgive me offering advice?"

Henry nodded.

"Though Your Majesty is still a young man, you are not as young as you used to be. In those days you could joust a whole day and not feel the effect. But now . . ."

Henry's eyes narrowed. "Are you advising me not to joust?"

The physician blinked, hesitated.

"I am asking if that is your advice," Henry pressed.

"That is my professional advice," the physician said after a moment. "And since I have a great care for Your Majesty, it is my personal advice, too."

Henry did not reply, but inclined his head for the physician to go about his business. As the physician's back was turned, Henry opened his hand to look at the colorful ribbon, Jane Seymour's favor.

It was a joy for the Seymour family to have their daughter, Jane, visit with them at Wulfhall, but it was agony for Henry. He had bid Brandon to carry a message to the ancient, distant manor house, and Brandon had mounted up immediately in spite of the cold and pouring rain.

When he reached Wulfhall, soaked and tired, he was greeted warmly by Sir John Seymour and his son Edward in their great hall.

"Your Grace," said Seymour. "How good to see you again."

"I bring a message from the king, for your daughter."

Brandon could see the obvious pleasure this information brought to Seymour as he quickly sent Edward to fetch her.

The hall was decorated with all manner of instruments of war—battleaxes, sharp-tipped pikes, swords, and shields. Brandon gazed at the weapons and smiled. "It was pleasurable to remember those great days in France, when we fought together with the king."

Seymour folded his hands behind his back and nodded. "Indeed. When men have fought in battle together they form a bond that is very special, and often indissoluble. They know their friends." Seymour's smile faded. "And their enemies." Seymour held Brandon's gaze for a long moment, and he smiled again.

Edward entered the hall, followed by Jane, dressed in a dark green kirtle and pale green gown, her hair braided and crowned with a velvet coif. Jane curtsied to Brandon, then her brother and father left them alone.

"Your Grace," said Jane softly.

"Lady Jane," said Brandon, taking a folded paper from his coat and holding it out. "His Majesty is pleased to send you this letter."

Jane took the letter without a word.

"And this purse." Brandon untied a leather pouch from his waist. "He commends you to accept these gifts in the spirit in which they are offered."

Slowly, Jane reached for the purse and peered inside. It was full of gold coins. Her expression was difficult for Brandon to decipher. He waited for her to speak.

Jane kissed the letter and then handed it back. She fell to her knees, one hand to her heart, the other still clutching the purse. "Your Grace. I must ask you to beg the king, on my behalf, to remember that I am a gentlewoman of fair and honorable lineage without reproach, who has no greater treasure in this world than her honor, which for a thousand deaths she would not wound."

Brandon made to protest but held his tongue.

"I must also return the purse," said Jane. "If the king deigns to make me a present of money, I pray that it might be when I have made an honorable marriage."

Brandon looked at the purse as she held it out, and after a moment, took it back. "I will tell His Majesty exactly what you have told me," he said. Then he bowed to the lady, turned on his heel, and left the hall.

Several nights later, the royal couple dined not in their private chambers but in the larger public hall, Henry moving easily to prove that he was recovered, Anne all smiles. The nobles who served them and the courtiers who watched on appeared calm and grateful that life at court appeared to be normal again.

Mark Smeaton drifted around the room, playing lively music that he claimed enabled good digestion and good humor. The table was spread with pork and lamb, goose and duck.

Taking Henry's hand, Anne whispered, "I am so happy to see you well. I was so alarmed and afraid."

"So was I," Henry replied, "when I thought that through my own foolishness you might lose the child."

Anne's brows drew together. "*Your* foolishness?"

"It was a mistake for me to believe I could behave as I used to. In any case, those carefree days are gone."

Anne appeared relieved. "When our daughter was brought to court everyone admired her. I think she will be a great beauty."

"Of course she will. Look at her mother."

Anne smiled and linked her arm through Henry's. "Will you not ask King Francis to reconsider his refusal?"

Henry's smile fell away. He pulled away from Anne, picked up his knife, and sawed a duck wing from its roasted body. He did not want to hear any more of this!

Anne pressed, "If we delay much further to find a good marriage for Elizabeth, people will talk, even more than they do now."

Henry spoke quietly, coldly. "Why do you talk of Elizabeth, when even Mary is not betrothed yet?"

Anne's eyes widened. "Surely you have more of a care for your legitimate child?"

Henry said nothing but continued to stare at Anne, until he saw Brandon enter the room from the far door. Stabbing his knife into the table, Henry left the table, the pain in his leg flaring again and the limp returning.

"What did she say?" Henry asked urgently when he reached his friend.

Brandon bowed and said, "She returned the letter unopened, and the purse both. She said that she has no greater treasure than her honor, and that if you wanted to give her money, she prayed it might be when she made an honorable marriage."

Henry rubbed his chin and looked about the hall, his gaze only touching briefly on Anne. Then he smiled and put his hand on Brandon's shoulder. "Then," he said cheerfully, "she has behaved herself in this matter very modestly."

Thomas Wyatt was among the courtiers watching the royal couple dine. He stood among them but apart, listening to their conversations and observations, but not responding beyond a nod.

He watched Anne sadly, noting that although she held her head high and retained a smile, she was uneasy, vulnerable. Oh, that he could go to her, to comfort her, to hold her.

But, of course, he could not. She was the queen, and her feelings and her fate were well out of his hands.

The night had grown long and cold. Candles on Cromwell's desk burned low, and the fire on the hearth was in need of a stoking. Cromwell sat with folded hands, looking at Ambassador Chapuys, waiting for the question he knew was coming.

"I wondered if you had put the emperor's proposal to the king?"

"Not . . . exactly," said Cromwell. "And not yet. I reiterate to you, here in private, that I favor and support, for the sake of this kingdom's security, an alliance with the emperor. It is quite impossible to trust the French."

"I'm glad to hear you say that, since the emperor will soon declare war on them once more, to recover Milan."

Cromwell nodded, taking it in. "I wish with all my heart that we could reach a speedy accommodation. However, I must tell you that in the question of legitimizing the Lady Mary, there remains one great obstacle."

"You mean the queen?" Chapuys smiled coolly. "I know she hates the emperor as Katherine's nephew. They say that when she was told of his victory over the Turks she looked like a dog being thrown out of a window."

Cromwell's lips hitched, forming a near smile himself.

"But," said Chapuys. "What can we do?"

Cromwell stood and lifted the poker by the fireplace, and stoked the coals himself. "If there is an obstacle in our path, Excellency," he said, "we must find a way around it."

He heard the door open, and savored the image of what he would see when he glanced up from the papers on his desk. The door closed, and he could hear her gentle breaths. His heart swelled, and he looked.

"Lady Jane."

Jane Seymour wore a most beguiling satin gown and coral necklace. Her hair flowed free about her delicate shoulders.

Henry tried to stand, but a dagger of pain cut through his leg. He motioned to the lady. "I pray you come closer."

Jane approached without a word.

"Closer still."

Jane came around the desk to stand beside the king.

"Here now, sit on my knee. Don't be afraid."

Jane uttered a soft gasp at the request, causing Henry's heart to swell. *Such a dear and perfect lady!* But she obeyed, lowering herself upon his lap, trembling slightly.

Henry spoke softly, touching Jane on her arm. "I respect your honor, believe me. In the future I will only see you when other members of your family are present. I just had to see you now."

Jane glanced at the desk, the papers, and then directly at Henry. "Yes, Your Majesty."

"Your favor saved my life."

"No . . ."

"Yes. When I lay there, your image came to mind, and I woke to its promise."

Jane looked away again, her long lashes momentarily obscuring her eyes. "What should I say?"

"Will you let me kiss you, Jane?"

Without looking up, Jane nodded. Henry took her face in both his hands, as if holding a precious bird, and kissed her lips tenderly, respectfully. Her scent, her warmth, her tenuous innocence burned into him, and he kissed her again, more passionately. Jane responded in kind, her mouth drawing against his.

The door opened. "Oh, my God!"

It was Anne. Her face was twisted with a mixture of horror and dismay. Jane quickly stood from Henry's lap.

"What *is* this?" Anne cried. "Just when my belly is doing its business, I find you wenching with Mistress Seymour!"

Henry stood with effort. "Hush, sweetheart."

"No, no, no! Why are you doing this? Why did you have to do this?"

Henry gestured to Jane, who skirted Anne and left quickly. Anne did not take her eyes from the king. She put her hands to her face and began to sob uncontrollably. Henry made his way to her. "Sweetheart . . ."

Anne's hands went to her abdomen and she took a sharp breath.

"Peace, sweetheart." Henry reached her. "All will go well with you. Peace now."

He put his arms around her and after a moment she relented, burying her face on his shoulder, her sobs still coming hot and seemingly bottomless.

Nan and Madge entertained themselves with rounds of cards in Queen Anne's outer chamber. The queen had retired to bed early to sleep, looking more worn than Nan had seen her in a long time.

As Nan picked up the deck of cards to shuffle them, a piercing scream erupted from the queen's bedchamber. Nan and Madge leapt to their feet, knocking over the table and throwing open the door between the two rooms.

Madge put her hand over her mouth as Nan's cries joined those of the queen. A large pool of scarlet blood was spreading from beneath the queen, staining her white nightdress and the white linens. As Anne moaned, writhed, and clutched at her belly, her tiny, blue, unborn child was miscarried.

* * * *

The court was silent and almost deserted, as if those in the palace knew it best to stay away, to let the terrible matter run its course without comment. Henry walked with two of his grooms to Anne's private chambers. On his entry, Nan and Madge curtsied, their faces furrowed with angst. Even from the outer chamber, Henry could hear Anne weeping. Drawing a breath through his teeth, he pushed open the bedchamber door and strode in.

He did not go to his wife, but stood in the middle of the room, staring at her. Anne tried to stop her tears, though her body continued to shudder.

"You have lost my boy. I cannot speak of it, the loss is too great," said Henry coldly. "But I see now that God will not give me any male children. When you are up, I will speak to you."

He turned to leave, but Anne called out, "It is not all my fault!"

Henry looked back at her.

"You've no one to blame but yourself," said Anne, her breath hitching but her words pointed. "I was distressed to see you and that wench Jane Seymour. Because the love I bear you is so great, my heart broke when I saw you loved others."

Henry's fists drew up and his teeth clenched. "I said I will speak to you when you are well." With that, he stalked from the room, leaving Anne folded up on her bed, crying bitter tears once again. She had wounded and betrayed him. And betraying a king was a dangerous thing to do.

Cromwell and Chapuys stood outside the king's private chambers as Henry returned. Cromwell took a quick study of his master's face as he approached. The secretary and ambassador bowed silently as Henry passed them and entered his outer chamber.

"Now," Chapuys whispered to Cromwell, "he has lost his savior!"

Cromwell did not reply, and followed the king inside.

The king stood by the window, his forehead pressed to the glass, gazing out. Cromwell did not speak, but waited for Henry to say what he would say.

At long last, the king spoke, though it seemed more to himself than to his secretary. "It's true what they have whispered. I shut my ears to them but now I know it to be true. I made this marriage seduced by witchcraft. And for that reason consider it to be null and void. And the evidence is that God will not permit us to have male issue." He drew a breath and let it out. It steamed the glass, then began to fade. "So I believe now, with all my heart, that I might take another wife."

Cromwell nodded, but the king did not see. He continued to look out at the gardens, the city beyond, and the pale blue of England's sky.

Chapter Fifteen

The royal physician placed the fetus back into the large bowl where it drifted silently, lifelessly in the water. Henry did not look at it, but instead nodded at the physician to give the final word. Jagged energy pounded his temples and seared his blood, but he held it in check.

"The child had the appearance of a male, about four months old," said the physician. Then he hesitated. "However, the fetus, there were signs of deformity, of abnormality. Perhaps, after all, the queen's miscarriage was a blessing in disguise."

Henry said nothing, but nodded, then dismissed the physician with his hand. The physician bowed and said, "Majesty." He lifted the bowl and took it with him, leaving Henry alone with his thoughts.

"Ah, Master Seymour."

Edward Seymour entered Thomas Cromwell's office, his face revealing a mixture of hesitation and hope. He bowed deeply. "Mr. Secretary."

Cromwell rubbed his chin with his thumb. "We don't know each other very well, but we shall. I have every confidence."

Edward nodded, his brows raised.

"It is His Majesty's pleasure," said Cromwell, "to appoint you a gentleman of the Privy Chamber. In that capacity, you will attend His Majesty daily, and as he sees fit to use you. It is, as you will well understand, a most privileged and special position."

"I do understand," said Edward, clearly pleased. "And I am deeply honored, Mr. Secretary."

"There is one other matter," said Cromwell. He leaned back in his chair. "His Majesty has indicated to me that he would like to pay court to your sister from time to time, although to avoid any scandal attaching itself to your sister's name, only in the presence of a member, or members, of your family. In which case, I am more than happy to surrender to you and your family my personal rooms in the palace. As it happens, they are adjacent to the king's private chambers, with a connecting gallery for greater privacy."

Edward said nothing for a moment, as if taking it in and turning it over. Then he inclined his head and smiled. "You are most generous, Mr. Secretary. I am sure my father will want to repay your kindness."

Without another word, Cromwell returned the smile.

It was evening at Whitehall Palace. The Great Hall was free of its commotion, with many of the courtiers having retired for the night, leaving silent guards, flickering torchlight, and echoes. Anne waited on the spiral stairs, gazing down at the French ambassador as he moved through the Hall and into an adjoining corridor. She hurried down the stairs and called to him urgently, quietly.

"Monsieur Ambassadeur!"

The ambassador turned toward her, and seeing it was the queen, bowed deeply. *"Madame."*

Anne approached him, her hands shaking. It was all she could do to keep from reaching out and grabbing him in desperation. *"Monsieur Ambassadeur,* I beg you. King Francis must be persuaded to accept the marriage of his son to our daughter Elizabeth, so that I may not be ruined or lost."

The ambassador retained his calm, though Anne knew he was most likely taken aback by her urgent, emotional request. It did not matter. All that mattered was the retention of her throne and the assurance that her daughter would have what was rightfully hers.

King Takes Queen 255

"I see myself very near that," Anne said, "and in more grief and trouble than I ever was before my marriage!"

Suddenly footsteps echoed up the hall, and voices. Forms could be seen in the torchlight, coming her way.

"I cannot speak to you more fully now," said Anne, "nor can I dare express my fears in writing. But please, as you love me, do the best you can for me, for God's sake!"

Then she turned and moved away.

Henry stood beside the document-strewn table in his outer chamber, staring at Cromwell. Cromwell could feel the anxiety in His Majesty's demeanor, and wanted to say nothing to tilt it any further.

"You gave the Seymours your room?" asked the king.

Cromwell nodded. "Yes, Your Majesty."

The king leaned his knuckles against the table and looked at some of the papers. "We have just given royal assent to the act stripping the bishopric of Norwich of the town of Lynn. The new beneficiary is to be Thomas Boleyn, Earl of Wiltshire. I also intend giving him two of the dissolved abbeys." Henry looked up, his gaze piercing. "You must inform him of his good fortune."

"Yes, Your Majesty."

Henry pushed from the table and strode to his chair, then back. "I am almost decided to make a treaty with the emperor." He stopped, glanced at the ceiling and down again. "There are many things, Mr. Cromwell, that will soon have to be decided."

Yes, Your Majesty.

Her hair was combed carefully and braided through with beads and ribbons of lace. Jane stood quietly and obediently, watching herself in the mirror as her mother crowned her with the finishing touch—a circlet of gold set with tiny scallop shells.

"Come here. Let me look at you."

Jane turned from the mirror to face her father. He stood beside Edward, arms crossed, nodding appreciatively. The family was in their new quarters, the rooms given them by Thomas Cromwell. They were austere rooms, with black and white tiled floors, dark draperies, bare walls, and marble busts and statues of Greek origin. Jane walked to her father and curtsied.

"How very beautiful," he said.

"You remember what we told you about the rumor?" asked Edward.

"Yes."

Seymour held out his arm to his daughter. "Shall we go through?" Jane took his arm and he guided her through a rear door into the private passage that led to the king's chambers. Edward followed. At the king's door, however, Seymour did not enter, but gave Edward the charge of escorting Jane.

Jane's heart picked up a quick rhythm as she and Edward stepped into the king's bedchamber. The room was awash with the light from countless candles, and the walls were covered in colorful tapestries. The large bed stood in the center, its tall posts of delicately carved dark wood, its bed curtains drawn back revealing snow white linens and pillows.

Henry turned from Brereton, his groom, to face Jane. His smile was tender, his eyes wide and hopeful.

"Jane," he said.

Jane curtsied. "Your Majesty."

The king drew Jane up gently and gazed at her longingly. Jane felt her heart stir with his attention, his affection.

"I have something for you," said Henry. He gestured to Brereton, who stepped forward with a velvet cushion bearing a small silver locket and chain. "Take it, I beg you."

Jane lifted the locket and opened it. Inside was a miniature portrait of the king. Jane took a breath, amazed at his apparent love. "Thank you. I will treasure this all my life. And if they ever open my grave, they will find it again, close to my heart."

Jane put the locket to her heart, but then she suddenly glanced down at the floor, her eyes pinched at the corners.

"What is it?" Henry asked.

"I heard something from His Grace the Duke of Suffolk," Jane said slowly, "and my father both, which upset me."

Henry's voice tightened. "They upset you?"

Jane looked up and nodded. "I am sure I should not repeat it to Your Majesty, but they told me there is some little doubt about the—about the legitimacy of Your Majesty's marriage. This I cannot believe, especially as the queen has delivered you of a sweet daughter."

Henry stared at her. "They *both* said this?"

Edward spoke up hastily. "Majesty, forgive me, but they are not alone. So many people are now openly saying it, even at the risk of Mr. Cromwell's censure, or worse."

Jane trembled as Henry glanced between Edward and herself, his face clouding. "Oh, God forbid that my beloved father, or His Grace, should be punished for my stupid ignorance!" Jane pleaded, putting her hands to her mouth.

But Henry shook his head slowly. "No," he said reassuringly. "They will not be punished."

The door to Cromwell's palace chambers opened, and a servant ushered Ambassador Chapuys into the room. John Seymour stood, hands clasped behind his back, amid streaks of hearth light and evening shadow.

"Excellency," said Seymour with a nod.

"Sir John," said Chapuys.

"Please, be seated," said Seymour. He gestured toward a chair. "We have a great deal to discuss."

The new clothes Queen Anne had requested had arrived. Beautiful gowns, capes, cloaks, and furs were presented with a flurry to Anne's approval and placed carefully into new trunks built and carved for that purpose. Anne's servants were busy with their daily chores of changing the linens in the bedchamber, chasing out the dust, changing the candles, and trimming the wicks as her ladies-in-waiting sewed and chatted with one another, waiting to be called upon.

Anne took a book to a chair in her outer chamber and settled down to read. Though the business in the room continued, it grew quiet. Servants spoke in whispered tones and walked softly so as not to disturb the queen. In one corner of room, Sir Henry Norris sat with Madge Sheldon, chatting quietly. Anne noticed Sir Norris glancing in her direction on occasion, but dismissed it as his general nervousness. Several minutes later, Sir Norris stood and bowed to Madge, then turned and bowed more deeply to Anne. His face bore an intense and almost pained look of devotion.

Anne leaned over to Nan, who sat beside her embroidering a linen kirtle with scarlet thread. "I wonder why, after all this time, he still will not marry Madge?" she whispered.

Nan replied, "I think Norris comes into your chamber more for Your Majesty than he does for Madge."

Anne blinked. "For *me*?"

Nan giggled softly and nodded.

Anne turned back to read, but then noticed Jane Seymour through the open door to Anne's bedchamber. Jane was seated on a trunk, sewing a loose bit of trim from one of the queen's new gowns, but she kept touching a silver locket that hung from her neck.

Nan saw Anne looking at Jane and said, "The Seymours have taken over Cromwell's rooms here at the palace."

"Cromwell's rooms?" Anne was stunned. *Why have that wench and her family moved into Cromwell's rooms? There is a private passage from those rooms to the private chambers of the king!*

Anne noticed Jane pause in her sewing to touch the locket again. She opened it and gazed inside. This was too much for Anne. She put down her book and walked quickly into the bedchamber.

Anne stopped in front of Jane and pointed at the locket. "What is that?"

Jane blanched. "A locket, Your Majesty."

"Let me see it!"

Anne reached for the locket and flicked it open. Upon seeing the image of Henry, she drew a sharp breath of rage, then yanked the chain around Jane's neck. Jane winced and cried out as the chain broke free in Anne's hand. Clutching her neck, Jane dashed from the room. Anne stared down at the chain and the deep cut it had sliced into the flesh of her finger. Hot, red blood poured from the wound and spattered onto the tile floor at her feet.

"Mr. Secretary!" cried Cromwell's scribe, jumping to his feet and dropping the quill with which he was writing. Cromwell looked up from his office desk to see Queen Anne standing in the doorway, gazing at him menacingly.

"Mr. Secretary," she said coldly.

Cromwell smiled, stood, and bowed. "Your Majesty."

The queen said nothing more, and the look in her eyes caused Cromwell to motion his scribe to leave, quickly.

The scribe bowed nervously, then scurried around the queen and out the door. Anne's eyes never left Cromwell.

Cromwell wasn't going to let this unnerve him. He smiled even more broadly. "I have good news for Your Majesty," he said. "The bill to dissolve the large monasteries has just been passed by Parliament. Our reformation is gathering even more pace."

Anne did not move. She did not even blink for a long moment. Then she said, "I have been told privately, Mr. Secretary, that the king has already sold Sawley Abbey in Yorkshire to one of his courtiers, even before the bill has reached the Statute Book, and plainly on your advice." Her head tilted back slightly. "Our reformation was never meant to be about personal gain. Religious houses should not be sold off but converted to better uses."

Cromwell's jaw tightened but he retained his smile. "Madam, the confiscated assets will be used to the pleasure of Almighty God and to the profit of this realm, which is but a pygmy, but will one day be greater than even Spain!"

Anne was trembling now, slightly, but obviously. She worked to contain herself, though her voice bristled with rage. "Is it true you have given your private rooms here to the Seymours?"

Cromwell wasn't expecting this. His mind scrambled, searching for the best answer.

Anne stepped closer. "I am the queen of England. You will answer me. Is it true?"

"Yes. It's true."

The queen stared at him for a moment. "Mr. Cromwell, you have overreached yourself. Believe me, you have placed yourself in very great danger." She paused. "Do you believe me? Or do you suppose I no longer possess the power to crush you?"

Cromwell said nothing as Anne gave him one last look. After she had turned and left his office, he bowed to empty air.

Dinner at Cromwell's house was over, and servants quietly cleared the plates from the table. A low fire crackled on the hearth and a cat was curled up before the dancing flames, its whiskers twitching. As Cromwell moved to the sideboard to pour himself another goblet of wine, another servant appeared at the door. "His Excellency, the Imperial Ambassador."

Chapuys entered, wiping raindrops from his cloak.

"Ah, Eustace," said Cromwell. "How very good of you to come all this way to Shoreditch." He poured a second glass of wine for his guest.

"Believe me, Mr. Secretary," said Chapuys as he took the wine, "I would travel a great deal further for the pleasure of talking to you." He raised his goblet and Cromwell did the same. They both took a drink.

Then Chapuys continued. "May I be blunt? Is it true that you have fallen out with Queen Anne?"

"Yes. I believe that she hates me and wants to have me executed."

Chapuys frowned. "Are you not afraid?"

Cromwell flicked his hand. "No. I trust so much in my master I fancy she can't do me any harm."

"Nevertheless," said Chapuys. "I cannot but wish you a more gracious mistress. One more grateful for the inestimable service you've done the king."

Cromwell turned to the window, seeing his reflection against the glass and the damp night. "For the sake of argument," he said. "What if the king *was* considering taking another wife?"

There was a long pause before Chapuys spoke. "It would certainly be to his advantage, if true. For here is a king who has so far been disappointed of male issue, and who knows that his present marriage will *never* be held as lawful."

Cromwell looked from the window to his guest. "His Majesty wants to receive you at court. I am sure he means to confirm a new alliance with the emperor. What else he means to say to you, I cannot guess."

Raising his glass, Chapuys smiled. "Then I look forward to finding out, Mr. Secretary."

Thomas Boleyn had to devise a new way of remaining in the king's good graces. Anne had foolishly lost her son, and the Seymours had become a threat to his family's security. He came to Anne's chambers and, once they were alone, explained that they needed to give up the idea of a French alliance. Clearly, Henry would have none of it. Instead, he seemed to favor a new alliance with the emperor.

"It seems that most of the country is also in favor of an Imperial alliance," said Boleyn, "so it would serve us nothing to swim against the tide."

Anne seemed annoyingly disinterested, staring off out the window as he spoke. "No," she said.

Boleyn took her hands. "The Imperial ambassador is to be received at court. You will make a great fuss of him. In the first place by inviting him to kiss your cheek. Then you and the king will dine with him. You will say some harsh things against the French in the presence of the other ambassadors, saying how they have betrayed your trust, are hypocrites, and false friends. Whatever you can think of."

Anne nodded but still would not meet her father's gaze. It was then Boleyn felt the rough spot on Anne's hand, and looked more closely to find a long red gash, just newly healing. A sewing accident? An errant splinter? Anne tried to pull her hand away, but Boleyn held tightly.

"Anne, we have come so far!" he said. "No one is going to be allowed to destroy us. No one! Do you understand?"

Anne looked at him at last, though her face looked more defeated than determined. It was all Boleyn could do to shake her, to make her angry at herself and their most precarious circumstances.

"Yes, Father," she said finally.

The court was well prepared to welcome Chapuys, the Imperial ambassador, with all manner of foods, music, and attention. Mark Smeaton was among the courtiers at the doorway as the chamberlain made his proclamation. "His Excellency, the Imperial Ambassador."

George Boleyn stepped forward, the first to greet Chapuys as he came through the arched front doors. "Excellency, you are most welcome to court!"

Chapuys nodded respectfully but coolly. "My lord."

"His Majesty is very anxious to talk to you, and you are to be royally entertained," said George.

Cromwell moved through the lines and bowed. "Excellency."

"Mr. Secretary."

Smeaton marveled yet again at the impassive demeanor of powerful men who played at civility and respect, when it all seemed, at times, to turn on the whim of the wind.

Cromwell folded his hands and lifted his chin. "Her Majesty invites you to visit her privy chambers where you may kiss her cheek."

Chapuys held Cromwell's gaze for a long moment. His expression did not change. "I am honored by Her Majesty's invitation," he replied. "But since the emperor has not agreed to the protocol, I must with the great-est regret decline it."

Cromwell bowed.

George retained his cheerfulness. "Never mind. The king invites you to join him in celebrating Mass. Perhaps Your Excellency would wait here?" He gestured toward a comfortable, sunny alcove off the corridor. Chapuys nodded and stepped over.

Thomas Wyatt pushed through the crowd to join Smeaton. Immedi-ately, Smeaton noticed his drawn face and dark-ringed eyes.

"What's wrong?" Smeaton asked.

Wyatt shrugged, the side of his mouth hitching. "I lost some money today. A small fortune."

Smeaton shook his head. "You shouldn't gamble."

"No, you're right. I gambled with my heart once, thinking I had a good hand. And I lost."

Smeaton studied his friend's face. "Then you still love her. You still love . . ."

"Their Gracious Majesties," called the chamberlain, pounding his staff on the floor and bringing all conversation to a halt.

The royal couple appeared side by side, moving with solemn dignity as the courtiers to either side bowed and curtsied deeply. As they passed Chapuys, Anne paused and looked at him directly. Chapuys responded with a cold and formal bow. Boleyn walked close behind the royal cou-ple. He smiled and bowed at the ambassador. Smeaton and Wyatt both noted that Chapuys returned neither the smile nor the bow.

As the couple reached the far end of court and prepared to pass through the doorway into the chapel, Anne whispered to Henry, "After Mass, Mr. Chapuys is sure to dine with us?"

Henry said nothing.

Anne glanced over her shoulder to see if Chapuys had joined the pro-cession. He was nowhere to be seen.

Anne was stunned. "But he's gone!"

"It is not without good reason," he replied, not looking at his wife as they moved through the doorway, their fur-trimmed robes gently brushing the jambs.

Smeaton and Wyatt looked at each other. They had witnessed the frosty reception and watched the ambassador exit court without a word, leaving a chilly, troubling vacancy.

"Something is happening, Mark," said Wyatt. "I just don't know what it is."

Chapuys dined alone with Thomas Boleyn in the king's presence chamber. Boleyn maintained his pleasant countenance, though his cheeks ached with the effort. As the boiled stew and pastries were served, he spoke with calm control.

"Eminence, I know that in the past there have been misunderstandings between my family and you. Some intemperate words. Certain things that should not have been said and are now regretted. But we both live in a real world. We must take our friends as we find them." He paused as a servant placed a tray of beautifully arranged fruits on the table. "I know the emperor is keen to protect his lucrative trade links with England. And obviously my family is in a position to help and assist him, which is what we are determined to do."

Another servant stepped forward with a silver flagon and filled the men's goblets with a rich red wine.

"So," said Boleyn, raising his glass. "I think we should drink a toast to new beginnings, new friendships, and a mutually beneficial future."

Slowly, Chapuys raised his own glass.

"Salut," said Boleyn.

"Salut," said Chapuys.

The king and queen entertained dinner guests in Queen Anne's private outer chamber. The large table was covered in a colorful tapestry and silver candlesticks, and laid with brawn, rabbit, sides of stag, and boiled tongue. Nobles elected for the occasion moved constantly, silently amid the diners, bringing in new foods and refilling silver chalices with wine.

The guests were the ambassadors of the empire, with the exception of Chapuys, who was not present. Henry claimed the head of the table with the queen to his right. Anne tried her best to be charming and regal, remembering the conversation she'd had with her father.

"To your health, Excellency," she said, lifting her glass and turning to the guest on her right, an old man with drooping lids and a spastic tic in his cheek. "Where are you from?"

The old man cleared his throat. "I am proud to be the ambassador from Milan, Madam."

"Ah, Milan," said Anne. "Were you not occupied by the French?"

The ambassador nodded. "Alas, we are still occupied by French troops."

"Then you agree with me that the French are deceitful in everything?" The ambassador blinked at her with his rheumy eyes. Anne turned to address the others at the table. "In fact," she said, raising her voice, "can anyone here tell me that the French are anything but liars and hypocrites? Do they ever tell the truth? How many treaties do they honor, how many promises do they keep?"

The ambassadors stared at her, and then at Henry, who did not reply.

Edward Seymour pressed through the milling crowd outside the king's presence chamber. There was a tension in the air that could not be ignored, with messengers moving to and from, whispering to their masters, and courtiers watching the open doorway, faces tight with expectation. Edward waited at a distance as the solicitor general, Richard Rich, spoke quietly to Cromwell and moved away. Then Edward approached the secretary.

"What is happening?" he asked.

Cromwell spoke quietly. "His Majesty will soon have an audience with the ambassador. That's what we're waiting for."

Edward said nothing, but nodded and moved away.

* * * *

The king strode through a side door into the presence chamber, and walked straight to the table where Chapuys and Boleyn sat, their meal done, waiting for their audience. Both rose and bowed.

"Excellency," said the king, nodding to the ambassador.

With a toss of his hand, Henry dismissed Boleyn, who frowned but withdrew from the room. Then he led Chapuys to the privacy of a window embrasure.

"So," Henry said. "Your master is anxious for an alliance?"

"He is, Your Majesty."

"On what terms?"

"On such terms as Mr. Cromwell has outlined to us. The restoration of some relation between England and Rome, the inclusion of the Lady Mary in the line of succession, and support for the emperor in his war with France over Milan."

Henry and Chapuys noticed movement in the room. They looked over to see that Cromwell had entered quietly.

Chapuys turned back to the king and continued, quietly. "As far as the Lady Mary is concerned, it may be that God has not thought to send Your Majesty a male issue because He has ordained that England should have a female succession."

Henry shouted, loud enough for Cromwell to hear, as well as those pressed against the other side of the now-closed doors, "What are you alleging, Excellency? Am I not a man like other men? Am I not? Am I not? You do not know *all* my secrets!"

Chapuys's face fell and his eyes widened. He quickly stepped back and away from the king. As he did, Cromwell quickly crossed the floor to Henry and the two began to argue quietly but passionately.

Boleyn reentered the chamber with Edward Seymour, and they stood with Chapuys as the disagreement between king and secretary escalated. After a moment, Cromwell bowed abruptly and turned from the king, his face taut. He brushed past Boleyn, Chapuys, and Edward as he moved for the door.

"Forgive me," he said in passing. "I need some water."

Henry stood alone, hands on hips, staring after Cromwell. He approached the three other men, who bowed and said nothing.

Henry waited for Chapuys to look up. Then he said, "I need everything in writing. The emperor's offer. Everything."

Chapuys fumbled, "That is not possible, Your Majesty."

Henry's face contorted with angry sarcasm. "Do you think I am a child, to be first whipped and then petted? If the emperor wants to deal with me, he must first apologize for all his past ill treatment of me. He must accept Queen Anne. I don't have anything else to say to him."

Henry pushed past Chapuys and left the chamber. As he rounded the corner he spied Cromwell on a marble bench, sipping a cup of water. He said nothing to the secretary, but he paused. Their eyes locked for a brief moment. Then Henry stormed off as courtiers all around him dropped in quick and humble obeisance.

Cromwell returned to the presence chamber, still looking quite shaken over his encounter with the king. He nodded to Boleyn, Edward, and Chapuys. "Princes are different from us," he said, "and are not to be easily understood. I have decided to leave court for a while. Gentlemen."

He nodded again, even more somberly, and walked away. Boleyn noticed that Edward looked crestfallen, his brow furrowed, his eyes pinched. On the other hand, Boleyn looked victorious. Exultant.

Henry took broad strides back to his private chambers, staring straight ahead, wishing someone would step in his way so he could knock them over. Brandon appeared beside him, bowed quickly, and matched his pace with the king's.

"Your Grace," said Henry, giving Brandon a quick glance.

"Majesty," said Brandon. "As your old friend as well as your most loyal subject, I feel it's my duty, however painful, to report some truths to you."

Henry stopped in his tracks and spoke under his breath. " 'Truth?' said jesting Pilate. 'What is truth?' "

"There are rumors about the queen's behavior. It seems she entertains men in her rooms, flirts and behaves intimately with them."

Henry looked at Brandon and said nothing.

Followed by her ladies, Anne passed through her private outer chamber. It was crowded with courtiers who brought with them some business or other that needed her attention. She caught sight of Sir Henry Norris, looking wistful, and then Mark Smeaton, beside the window, appearing particularly dejected.

"Mark," she said, pausing to speak to him. "Why are you so sad?"

Smeaton shrugged. "It doesn't matter," he said.

Anne felt a sting of embarrassment that he would speak to her so casually in front of her ladies. "As an inferior person, Master Smeaton," she snapped, "don't expect me to talk to you as if you were a nobleman."

Smeaton's voice and expression didn't change. "I don't," he said. "Just a look is enough for me. You know that."

"Madam?" It was Nan, who curtsied deeply before the queen. "Lady Rochford is here."

Anne gestured for George's wife, Jane, to come forward. "Lady Rochford, what can I do for you?"

Anne's sister-in-law curtsied, but her face revealed great displeasure. "You could ask your brother to be kind to me. He is cruel in every way."

Anne was dumbfounded. "I don't believe you."

Lady Rochford directed a furious glance at Mark Smeaton. "There are others he has preferred to me."

Anne trembled with rage. "Hush!"

"You don't understand," said Lady Rochford. "He does not treat me as his proper wife, as the king treats you."

At that moment, Anne noticed Jane Seymour nearby in a window seat, sewing a petticoat. Anne spoke loudly enough for Jane to hear her.

"Let me tell you something, Lady Rochford. The king cannot satisfy a woman. He has neither the skill nor the virility."

Jane looked up. The expression of shock on her face matched that on the face of Lady Rochford. Satisfied, Anne laughed and walked away.

The gathering in the king's presence chamber was formal, the atmosphere heavy. Henry had gathered before him Brandon, Thomas Boleyn, Sir Henry Norris, Cromwell, and the solicitor general, Richard Rich.

"Sir Henry," said the king from his throne, nodding at the older man. "I trust the preparations are in place for the May Day hunt?"

Norris bowed. "They are, Your Majesty. Lord Rochford is made Master of the Hounds for the day."

"And then afterward," said Henry, "I have decided to undertake another visit to Calais, with the queen. Your Grace will make the arrangements."

"Yes, Your Majesty," said Brandon.

Henry stroked his trim beard, considering those before him. "It has come to my notice that some acts of treason, and other offenses, have been committed nearby in Middlesex and Kent. Mr. Rich, as solicitor general, I appoint you and Mr. Cromwell to head a commission of oyer and terminer to investigate whether these offenses be true."

Cromwell and Rich nodded as the others looked on, silently, unknowing, unmoved. Henry savored their ignorance. He relished with dark joy what was to come.

Chapter Sixteen

Nan had only seen the Tower from a distance, never from within. Yet here she stood in the cold, ominous guardroom before Cromwell, Richard Rich, and a dour-faced clerk at a scarred wooden desk. She shivered both from the cold and from fear. She had sworn to tell the truth, and had been warned not to repeat what transpired during the interview. Now, Rich was standing before her, his unblinking gaze cutting into her heart.

"I must warn you, my lady," he said, "that all who conceal the truth from those commissioned by the king to discover it are themselves guilty of treason and are very likely to be hanged."

Nan trembled uncontrollably and began to speak.

The following morning, Lady Rochford was called into Cromwell's palace office. She was uncertain of the reason behind the summons, but it did not take long for her to discover it.

As she sat on the edge of one of the carved wooden chairs, Cromwell leaned over his desk and said, "I hope you do not mind me asking you some questions—regarding your husband, Lord Rochford. And—his sister."

Lady Rochford didn't answer. Cromwell leaned even closer, his hands folded, his nails clean and reflecting little bits of light from the window. "Tell me," he said, "what is your opinion of your husband?"

* * * *

The next interview to be conducted in the guardroom of the Tower was with Anne's lady, Madge Sheldon. She stood as straight as she could even as her legs beneath her threatened to give way. Cromwell was questioning her as Rich observed calmly and a clerk scribbled at the desk.

"Lady Sheldon," said Cromwell. "You are on oath, and I warn you not to repeat to anyone what passes between us."

Madge nodded.

"You live in close attendance upon Her Grace the Queen. I must ask you if she has ever entertained men in her chambers in what you would consider an inappropriate way?"

Madge looked at the narrow window behind the desk and saw a falcon circling on a distant breeze. She shook her head.

Cromwell drew a breath and began to walk around the lady, asking her again to think. To recall. To share anything she might have witnessed that was unseemly. Madge felt trapped, jailed by his insistence, his maddeningly calm demeanor and dreadful suggestions.

At last, she offered, "It's true that some men would come into the queen's chambers at undue hours."

Cromwell stopped in front of her and smiled encouragingly.

"And sometimes she flirted with them, but . . ."

"What are their names?"

Madge licked her lips but they remained dry. She took a pained breath, then another. She could feel her heartbeat in her throat. "Lord Rochford, of course. And Sir Henry Norris, and . . ."

"And?"

"The king's groom, Brereton, and Mark Smeaton, the musician. And . . ."

"And?" said Rich, stepping up now to stand beside Cromwell.

"Well," she said, "I saw her kissing and hugging her brother, but thought nothing of it."

Cromwell and Rich nodded and looked back at the scribe, to make sure he'd written it all down.

* * * *

The evening was warm, and Henry was on edge with expectation and hope. His lady was coming to his chamber momentarily. To see her face again, to take in her scent, her essence was all his heart's desire at that very moment.

The door from the secret passageway opened, and John Seymour escorted his daughter into the bedchamber. Henry caught his breath; she was more beautiful this night than ever before. Was God giving him a sign, then, that she was the true queen he had searched for?

"Jane," he said softly.

Jane curtsied. "Majesty." She kissed his hand and looked up into his eyes.

"For very good reasons I want you to leave Whitehall for a while," said Henry, "and go back home with your father."

Jane's brow creased slightly. She did not want to be away from him, and it touched his soul. Yet, obediently and without hesitation she said, "I will do anything Your Majesty commands me to do."

Henry could not help himself. He reached out and touched her soft cheek with the tip of his finger. "I want to tell you that in this slippery world, you represent for me everything that is innocent, everything that is good, unsullied, uncorrupted."

Jane lowered her eyes, and Henry smiled.

"It won't be for long, believe me," he continued. "And after that— after that we shall have all our desires."

His beautiful lady gazed up at him fully, her eyes brimming with love.

Mark Smeaton had been summoned to Secretary Cromwell's house in Stepney, and he came with dispatch, wondering what the secretary's request might be. Did the king desire a performance, a new melody? It could be no more than that, surely, for Smeaton was only a musician, only a commoner, as Queen Anne had so clearly pointed out.

Cromwell stood in the shadows of the front hall as a servant introduced Smeaton and quickly withdrew into another room. There was a sudden movement, and two large burly men appeared beside Cromwell, their faces cold and ugly, their hands meaty and chapped.

Smeaton's heart kicked, and he turned for the door, but before he could escape the two thugs grabbed him and forced him into a chair. They held him down as he struggled.

"Mr. Cromwell! Mr. Cromwell, what is this?" Smeaton pleaded, but Cromwell did not answer.

One of the men stood before Smeaton and leaned heavily into his wrists so he could not move while the other slipped behind him and pulled a rough, knotted loop of rope across his eyes. The rope was tied to a cudgel at the back, creating a garrote. Unable to see, Smeaton called again, more desperately, "Cromwell, please, what is this?"

Suddenly the man with the cudgel turned it, tightening the rope over Smeaton's eyes, driving knots into them. Smeaton inhaled sharply with the pain.

Cromwell spoke evenly. "I want to know when you slept with the queen. And how many times you slept with her."

"I never slept with the queen, Mr. Cromwell. Who is saying this? I don't understand."

There was a pause, and then the garrote was tightened again. This pain was even sharper, brighter, and Smeaton groaned.

"You have to tell me the truth," said Cromwell. "Or God help me it will go badly with you. You are only a poor musician, and yet recently you spent a great deal of money on horses and liveries for your servants. Where did you get the money? It must have been for services rendered."

Smeaton's heart pounded beneath his ribs; panic stole his breath. He gasped and tried to swallow. "Your Honor, I swear by God Almighty— that I never ever slept with Her Majesty nor even imagined it! Please don't hurt me anymore!"

There was another pause, and the garrote tightened again, more, more, until with an explosion of white-hot agony, his right eye burst. Smeaton shrieked and kicked as blood dribbled down his cheek.

Amid the gaiety in her outer chamber, Anne felt a storm brewing. When George entered the room, the smile she'd forced upon herself faded. George looked pale and nervous.

He met her in the center of the room as the ladies-in-waiting laughed and several musicians played a cheerful melody on drum and lute. Leaning in, he whispered, "Mark Smeaton is arrested."

Anne recoiled. "Mark? For what?"

"We don't know yet," said George. "And there is something else. Your visit to France with the king has been postponed for a week."

Anne stared at her brother, then slowly nodded. She looked around and noticed that everyone in the room was staring at her.

He knew it was nighttime by the calls of the owls and chirring of the night insects. But Mark Smeaton could see very little, for one eye was destroyed and the other bruised. He'd been taken to the Tower by the burly men, and made to wait upon a cold floor, bound at the wrists, until new guards traded off and dragged him into the bowels of that most hideous place.

Down the winding staircases and narrow corridors he was taken, until they came to a room with an open door. Through the opening, Mark's blurry vision revealed what he was to endure next—the rack.

Dear Holy God!

Horrified, Mark struggled to flee, but the guards held him tightly and dragged him toward the formidable instrument of iron and wood.

There were fewer visitors in her outer chamber that evening, but Anne paced back and forth, ignoring most of them, unwilling to engage in mindless banter. She noticed Sir Henry Norris near the fireplace, chatting with Madge yet watching the queen. His long-suffering and pining drove a thorn into her side, and she stormed over to where he stood.

"Sir Henry," she said. "You are here again! Yet you never seem to have the courage to marry the lady!"

Norris bowed, and kept his calm. "Madam, marriage is not something to hurry into."

"No. I know the truth!" said Anne. "You look for dead men's shoes."

Norris frowned, confused. "Madam?"

"I mean you suppose that if anything bad came to the king, you would think to have me."

The words clearly stung the man. "Madam," he said, "if I ever thought such a thing, then I wish my head was cut off."

Anne's eyes narrowed and she scoffed, "Oh, that could be arranged."

Norris turned from Madge without a word and retreated hastily. Anne spun from the lady, seeking out Nan.

"Nan," she called. Her lady hurried over from the other side of the room. Anne lowered her voice. "Nan, get them to fetch Elizabeth to me tomorrow. I want to see my daughter."

Nan nodded. "Yes, Madam."

"And Nan." Anne's voice lowered even more, causing the lady to lean in to hear her. "If anything happens to me, will you promise to care for her?"

Nan hesitated, then nodded slowly, silently.

Mark Smeaton had been stripped of all but his braes and forced onto the platform of the rack. His ankles were tied by ropes to a roller at the base; his arms were stretched over his head with his wrists secured to a roller at the top. Time had no meaning to the musician now, only the pain and the terror. He had been put to the question until his wrists and ankles were bloodied and swollen and his muscles and tendons were ready to tear. Sweat cut his face, and the taut skin of his abdomen felt as though the devil's knives were flaying it.

Cromwell sniffed and came close to the rack. He looked down and shook his head. "Sooner or later, Mr. Smeaton," he said calmly, "you *will* tell me the truth."

Smeaton opened his mouth and tried to speak but he could only gasp and babble. Cromwell gave the signal to the torturers, who turned the levers at each end of the platform. The rollers turned and the ropes tightened. Smeaton screamed as his limbs were stretched more and yet more, until, with a gruesome popping sound, his arm and leg bones were dislodged from their sockets.

The May Day hunting party paused in the wide field to give their horses a rest. The hunters dismounted and stood about, waving gnats from their faces and chatting as the dogs sniffed the ground. Henry stood apart from the others, his cloak swept back, staring at them all with a dark and thunderous expression.

Thomas Boleyn was nervous, and drew his son close to speak to him.

"The king has called an emergency meeting of the council," he said.

George glanced from his father to the king across the grass. "Why wasn't I told?"

Boleyn snarled. "Because I wasn't told, either! For God's sake, make sure you keep the king always in sight!"

There was movement on the far side of the field. It was Cromwell, riding to join the party.

Father and son exchanged tense glances.

Henry strode over to meet Cromwell. Cromwell dismounted and bowed. "Smeaton has confessed," he said quietly.

Henry held the secretary's gaze, then turned abruptly and walked to his horse. "Sir Henry, with me!" he called.

As the rest of the hunting party looked at one another in confusion, Henry and Norris mounted, and Henry spun his horse about and heeled it into a gallop toward the woods. Sir Henry and the yeomen of the guard fell in behind.

After a few minutes, Henry slowed his horse to a walk, and waved his hand for Norris to ride beside him. Norris reined his horse to fall in with the king's.

Henry savored the moment and dreaded it at once. He turned to Norris and spoke as evenly as he could. "Did you know the queen was pregnant again?"

Norris's eyes widened. "No, Your Majesty! How should I?"

"Because you may be the child's father, since you love her so well, as many have testified."

Norris was silent for a moment, the shock of the accusation draining the color from his face. "Your Majesty is being ridiculous!" he said.

Henry drew his horse up to a halt. "Then I'm a figure of ridicule to you?" Before Norris could protest, Henry called, "Guards!" The guards rode in close behind. "This man is arrested. Take him to the Tower!"

Without giving Norris another look, Henry spurred his horse onward.

In the week that followed the hunt, there was a flurry of arrests throughout court. Brereton was taken by the guards as he prayed in the chapel. Thomas Boleyn was confronted and seized as he approached the king's private chambers.

George Boleyn planned on seeing the king, to plead with him, to reason with him, when he was stopped by Thomas Wyatt in a side corridor leading to the king's rooms.

"Where are you going, my lord?" asked Wyatt, his face contorted with brutal sarcasm.

"I have to see the king!"

But Wyatt only shook his head. "It's too late, George. Much too late."

At that moment, four guards blocked the corridor with their swords and pikes. One moved toward the two men and announced, "My lord. Master Wyatt. You are both arrested for High Treason, and having carnal knowledge of Her Majesty the Queen."

*   *   *   *

"Your Majesty."

Henry turned to see Anne amid the blooming roses, holding little Elizabeth in her arms. He had come to the private gardens alone to think and to plan. The last thing he wanted was to look the whore in the face.

"Henry," said Anne.

Henry glowered at her as she held the child out toward him.

"For the love you bear our child, for the love of Elizabeth, please have mercy!"

But Henry shook his head. "You lied to me. You have *always* lied to me."

"No!"

"You were not a virgin when you married me. You were not what you seemed. Your father and your brother arranged everything."

"I loved you. And I love you still."

Her words enraged Henry even more. He strode off as she called after him, "Give me a chance! For all we were and have been to each other. Please, Your Grace, Your Majesty, I beseech you!"

George could not sit still. His face was swollen and red from weeping, and his arms trembled with terror.

"You know why you have been arrested," said Cromwell as the Tower clerk learned over the desk and scribbled his words. "It is not enough for you to commit vile incest with your sister, the queen, having been procured to violate her, alluring her with your tongue in her mouth and hers in yours, against the commands of God Almighty. But you must also plot regicide against the king, so that Anne could marry one of her lovers and rule as regent for her bastard child."

"No, sir!" George stammered. "You—baffle me. My enemies have poisoned the very air with their horrid lies! Whatever my sister has done—it is not with me, or mine. I am innocent, Mr. Cromwell. I swear to you on the blood of Christ! I am innocent!"

He broke down again, leaning over, sobbing.

* * *· *

"Tell me this, Mr. Brereton," said Cromwell as the groom sat on the chair in the guardroom of the Tower. "Did you ever have carnal knowledge of the Queen's Majesty?"

Brereton opened his mouth to speak the truth, but then realized what would befall him if he denied the accusation. Better to face the swifter consequences of a lie.

"Yes," he said quietly. "Yes, I did."

Thomas Boleyn stood in the guardroom of the Tower. His face was impassioned, his eyes unblinking.

"I condemn them utterly," he said, speaking the words he had planned out while awaiting his interrogation. "All those men, whatever their rank or station, who deceived the king and slipped between the sheets with his lawful wife. For such awful adultery, there should only be one punishment."

So many arrests! So many terrible, unfounded lies made and sworn about her!

Anne sat at her dining table, looking at the foods prepared for her, but she could not eat. Her ladies stood about, trying to behave as if all was well, but it was clear they were as fearful as the queen.

Anne picked up a pastry but put it down again. Even the texture of the bread was unpleasant to the touch.

The doors flew open. Anne looked up, startled but not surprised. Brandon and Solicitor General Rich entered, cold faced, and bowed.

"My lords," Anne managed. "Why have you come?"

Brandon presented the queen with a scroll. "This is the warrant for your arrest."

The ladies gasped and looked at one another.

Brandon continued. "You are charged with committing adultery with Mark Smeaton, Sir Henry Norris, and William Brereton. Both Smeaton and Brereton have already confessed their guilt."

"We have come at the king's command to conduct you to the Tower," said Rich, "there to abide during His Majesty's pleasure."

Anne pushed back from the table with as much grace as she could manage. "If it be His Majesty's pleasure, I am ready to obey." She turned toward Madge, but Brandon held up his hand.

"There is no time for you to change your clothes or pack anything. Money will be provided for your needs—at the Tower."

The lower Tower was as dreadful as she had imagined, a claustrophobic and terrifying place of dark corridors, dark noises, damp walls, and cruel-looking guards. Brandon and Rich forced Anne down stone steps and through narrow passageways, where they were met by Sir William Kingston, constable of the Tower. The guard, a huge and hulking man, bore a flickering torch in his hand. On seeing him, Anne sank to her knees. Her ladies, who had come as well, stood back and watched aghast.

"I pray God will help me," she said, "for I am not guilty of these accusations." She looked back at Rich and Brandon. "I beg you, before you go, to beseech the King's Grace to be good to me."

They said nothing, turned away, and retreated into the gloom.

Kingston helped the queen to her feet. Anne could hear the distant calls of despair and hopelessness from deep within the Tower. Spiders, their shadows stretched long upon the wet walls, seemed to watch her with cold curiosity.

"Mr. Kingston," she asked, her voice quivering. "Do I go to the dungeon?"

"No, Madam. There are lodgings made ready for you."

"It is too good for me. Jesus have mercy on me!" The tears she had been holding back rushed out. "I am the king's true wedded wife! My God, bear witness there is no truth in these charges. I am as clear from the company of man as from sin!"

"Madam, this way," said Kingston, inclining his head in the direction of a side corridor.

Anne nodded and followed, her body shivering uncontrollably.

"May I have the Holy Sacrament placed in my room, so I may pray for mercy?"

Kingston did not answer.

Archbishop Cranmer burst into Cromwell's office. Cromwell knew what he would say before he did. Yet he asked anyway.

"What is it, Your Grace?"

Cranmer stood before Cromwell's desk, hands clasped, his face tight with anxiety. "I've just heard of the queen's arrest. My mind is clean amazed. I cannot believe she is guilty of such abominable crimes."

Cromwell put down his quill and said nothing, waiting.

Cranmer hesitated. "Yet I cannot think the king would have proceeded so far unless she was culpable."

"It has caused both the king and myself great pain to discover her deceit," said Cromwell, placing his hands upon his desk. "The depth of her depravity!"

Cranmer shook his head. "The fact is, I loved her not a little for the love which I judged her to bear toward God and the Gospel. Next to His Grace the King, and yourself, I was most bound to her of all creatures living."

"Then you must learn to live without her."

"But without her is not our reformation in danger? Was she not our great supporter and advocate?"

Cromwell touched his chin. "Who would likely have become our greatest liability. Sometimes, Your Grace, in order to defeat evil, one must consort with the devil. Now, the king is waiting for Your Grace to discover a reason why his marriage to Anne Boleyn should be considered null and void. He expects your verdict presently."

"What of the others?" Henry asked. He sat in his private chamber, candles around the room burning away at the night. His face was wet with tears but he did not move to wipe them away. Brandon understood. He always had.

"Smeaton, Brereton, Norris, and George Boleyn are all found guilty," said Brandon, standing before the king. "They are to be executed tomorrow."

Henry rose and walked closer to Brandon. "But you know what Cromwell told me? The bitch had had to do with over a hundred men! She slept with over a hundred fucking men, Charles!"

Brandon nodded, his face tight.

"And you weren't even one of them!" said Henry. He put his arm around Brandon's neck and began to weep aloud. "You know what? My daughter Mary owes God a great debt for having escaped the hands of that cursed and poisoning whore! It's true! She planned to poison her, just like she poisoned Katherine. We have proof. And the baby, her baby, was *deformed*! Did you know that? So it couldn't have been mine. Perhaps Elizabeth isn't even mine! That fucking bitch! She humiliated me, and I *hate* her, Charles, I *hate* her!"

Wyatt could see his reflection in the bowl of water that had been brought to his cell. He was ashen faced and unshaven, with red-rimmed eyes and a pinched mouth. How quickly to fall into this state, so easily at the hands of others.

"The queen was tried yesterday at Westminster Hall," Cromwell said. He stood near the door, head tilted slightly. "She pleaded not guilty to all the charges against her, but the evidence being overwhelming, she was sentenced to death, either by burning or by decapitation, according to the king's pleasure."

Wyatt pushed the bowl aside. "And her coaccused, Mr. Cromwell? What of us?"

Cromwell crossed his arms. "Smeaton, Brereton, Norris, and George Boleyn are found guilty as charged."

A pause. "What of me?" asked Wyatt, almost afraid to hear the answer. "Am I to be tried, too, Mr. Cromwell?"

The secretary looked at the poet for a considerable time, then at the narrow window that overlooked the Thames. "No," he said at last. "We found no evidence against you. You are to be released. Eventually." He retreated and the door closed behind him.

Wyatt looked back at the bowl of water and his broken reflection. "And yet," he said, "of all those poor men, I am the only one who is guilty."

A steady, grit-filled breeze cut up from the river to Tower Hill, which stood just outside the confines of the Tower itself. The scaffold, built years earlier for the dispatching of noble traitors and aristocratic criminals, had been fortified and scattered with fresh straw. A crowd of citizens had gathered, the curious, the enthusiastic, the old, and the young.

George Boleyn was the first to ascend to the platform to face the headman's blow. The guards who escorted him turned him to address the crowd. His face was softened and resigned.

"I say to you, trust in God," he said clearly, speaking the words he'd planned out in his cell over the past days, "and not in the vanities of this world, for if I had done so, I think I would still be alive as you are now."

Then without hesitation he knelt before the block, lowered his head, and the executioner lifted the ax. With a swift and perfect move, he swung it up, around, and down. George's head was cleaved cleanly in a single blow.

The crowd gasped quietly as the head and body were tossed into a cart beside the scaffold.

Anne, forced to watch from her Tower window, drew her hands to her heart and began to weep. Her brother, her dearest brother, was condemned and now dead.

Next was Sir Henry Norris, who appeared an old man now, ravaged but not destroyed by the Tower and the scourge upon his name. He addressed the sea of witnesses, lifting back his head a bit as if addressing God as well.

"I thought little I would come to this. And in my conscience, I think the queen innocent of the things laid to her charge, and would die a thousand deaths rather than ruin an innocent person."

Ah, my poor Sir Henry! Anne thought.

He knelt, whispered a silent prayer, and the blood-streaked ax fell.

Brereton climbed the scaffold steps in a fit of religious euphoria, his face twisted in a smile that made him appear to have already crossed to eternity. He stared at the heavens and prayed, "Have mercy upon me, O God, according to Thy loving kindness!"

He dropped before the block. The ax came down with a bone-severing thwack and the blood ran hot and red. His head and body were thrown into the cart.

Mark Smeaton was next. He could not walk well from his time on the rack. He had to be helped up the steps, and even then his legs and arms wobbled like those of a newborn colt. His head bobbed back and forth, and for a moment Anne caught a glimpse of his destroyed face, and recalled the charming, teasing gleam in his eye when they had first met.

She could watch no more. She tore herself from the guards who held her at the window, and threw herself onto her bed.

Mark Smeaton only wanted to die. His body was nothing but agony, beyond his control, burning and torturing him of its own volition, constantly and without relief. He stepped onto the blood-soaked scaffold and tried to fall before the headsman to beg, *Kill me now, please, do your duty for the love of God!* But the guards to either side held him up and around to face the crowd, so he would give a final word.

He opened his mouth and whispered, "Masters—I pray you—I pray you all pray for me. For I have—I have deserved the death."

That was enough. The guards let go of him and he fell upon the platform. Smeaton tried to stretch out his arms to make room for a clean blow, but could not do it alone. The guards stood to either side and moved them for him.

And then, mercifully, the ax fell.

The day was done. The crowds, having had their fill of death, had retired to their homes, their meals, their beds. The sky relinquished its hold on the sun, and the golden orb rolled away without sound in the west, leaving the land awash in the red glow of sunset.

In his cell, attended by a single candle and a pair of rats, Wyatt dipped his quill into his inkwell and wrote upon the paper he'd been allowed.

> *These bloody days have broken my heart,*
> *My lust, my youth did then depart,*
> *And the blind desire of ambitious souls.*
> *Who sought to climb seeks to revert,*
> *And about the throne the thunder rolls.*

Chapter Seventeen

Dawn, pale and tentative, rose from the east, reaching through the thick forests and orchards along London Road, urging the lone rider away from the brine-dampened town of Dover toward the king's great city. The rider was a man of large build and gentle eyes, dressed in dark cape and trousers, and bearing a specially forged weapon wrapped in velvet across his shoulders.

It was made of steel, larger and heavier than an ordinary sword, its blade honed to exquisite sharpness and decorated with an intricate, scrolling pattern. The sword had been created for one purpose only, the execution of Queen Anne.

Onward the rider traveled, his horse keeping a fast and steady pace, the gray mists of morning scattering in their passing.

Anne's ladies stood quietly in the darkness as their queen knelt on the hard stone floor of her Tower room, her hands folded in impassioned prayer before the crucifix upon the table.

"I will give glory to Thee, O Lord, for You have saved me from injustice and from slanderous tongues and an unjust king. My soul shall praise Thee even to my death, because Thou, O Lord, delivers those that wait for Thee, and savest them out of the hands of the nation."

As she prayed, the golden rays of morning found the windows of her cell, and silently made their entrance.

* * * *

King Henry lay in his bed in the darkness, his eyes hooded and haunted. He had not been able to sleep during the night, his mind and body tossing about in anger and angst. At last he threw back his covers, dressed quickly with the help of his silent grooms, and made his way to the Chapel Royal.

The music from the girls' choir was ethereal and poignant, a song of loss and love, endurance and tribulation. Henry knelt in his private pew, watching the choir, listening, trying to free his thoughts of their tangled torments, but the music only drove them deeper and more painfully into his soul.

At last he stood and shouted to them, "Enough!" and strode from the chapel. The music died on the choir's lips and faded away.

As morning continued its rise across England, William Kingston, constable of the Tower, entered Anne's room to the somber curtsies of her ladies. Anne, seated at her table, folded her hands and nodded at the constable.

"Master Kingston."

"My lady," said Kingston with a bow. Then he inclined his head to draw the queen aside to the window.

"My lady," he said quietly. "I can now tell you that the king has decreed you will not be burned, but suffer a quicker death by decapitation. In his mercy, the king has also acceded to your plea to use the services of the Executioner of Calais, who is even now on his way here from Dover."

"When am I to die?"

"At nine o'clock."

Anne kept her head high. "I am content. Will you please send for Archbishop Cranmer, so he may hear my last confession and administer Holy Communion?"

Kingston bowed. "Madam." He left the room, and the guards in the hall bolted it from the outside once more.

*   *   *   *

"Make way for the Lady Princess Elizabeth," said the chamberlain. "Make way for Her Grace."

Two-year-old Elizabeth, laced up in the most formal and restrictive of gowns, walked along the corridor in the proscribed manner, the chamberlain and guard leading the way, her chaplain, ladies, and governess following. She was helped into a tall chair at the table, where she was served tiny portions of pastries and meat pies. A bright flicker of morning sunlight played upon the table before her. She looked at it but did not make to reach for it as other young children might do. In a moment, the light danced away.

Henry stood before the glassy waters of a pond in the royal gardens. He was transfixed by the movements of two white swans, arching their necks, sliding along the surface, pure, untouched by human foibles, human jealousies. They considered him for a moment with their black eyes, then shook their feathered heads and gracefully swam on.

"How is the lady?" Archbishop Cranmer asked Kingston as he was escorted through the Tower toward the queen's quarters.

Kingston made a soft tsking sound. "Truthfully? In the first days of her captivity she spoke rather wildly. For example, that it would not rain until she was released. But now, according to her almoner, preparations for her death have increasingly occupied her thoughts, so I believe she is reconciled to it."

"I'm glad," said Cranmer. "Although it grieves me that I must cause her further pain."

They reached Anne's room and the guard unlocked the door. Cranmer entered reluctantly.

Anne looked up from her reading and smiled.

"My lady," he said with a bow. Then he hesitated.

Anne's smile faded, and her eyes narrowed.

Cranmer forced the words out. "I am obliged to tell you that your marriage to the king has been declared null and void."

"On what grounds?"

"On the grounds of your close and—and forbidden degree of affinity to—to another woman known carnally by the king."

If Ann was surprised she did not show it. "My sister?"

Cranmer nodded.

"Then my daughter is—?"

"Yes. Elizabeth is to be declared a bastard."

With this, the hurt was visible. Anne's lips trembled.

"Madam," Cranmer offered, "I swear to you that I will do everything in my power to protect and support her, and keep her always in the king's good graces."

Anne's mouth tightened. Her control was back. "Thank you. And now, since my time approaches, I beg Your Grace to hear my confession. Also, I should like the constable to be present when I receive the good Lord."

Kingston was let into the room. Anne put her book down and knelt before the table.

Cranmer made the sign of the cross. "My child, do you have a confession?"

Anne nodded. "I confess my innocence before God. I swear, on the damnation of my soul, that I have never been unfaithful to my lord and husband, nor ever offended with my body against him." She drew a breath. "I do not say I have always borne toward him the humility which I owed him, considering his kindness and the great honor he showed me and respect he paid me. I admit, too, that often I have taken it into my head to be jealous of him. But God knows, and is my witness, that I've not sinned against him in any other way. Think not I say this in hope to prolong my life. God has taught me how to die and He will strengthen my faith. As for my brother, and those others who were unjustly condemned, I would willingly have suffered many deaths to deliver them. But since it pleases the king, I will willingly accompany them in death.

With this assurance—that I shall lead an endless life with them in peace." Then she lowered her head.

"Master Kingston," said Cranmer, "please go and make sure to report my lady's true and last confession so the world will know it."

Kingston bowed and withdrew. As Cranmer laid the sacraments upon a white linen towel, Anne moved closer to him on her knees and whispered, "Mr. Cranmer, I do not suppose that, even at this last hour, the evangelical bishops we put in place might intervene for me?"

Cranmer was taken aback. He scrambled for his voice. "I—ah, Your Majesty, please."

Anne drew back and shook her head as tears welled in her eyes. "No, no," she said. "I understand. How could they? Forgive me."

Sweat catching the rim of his cap even in the chill of the Tower, Cranmer said nothing more, but turned to prepare the host.

Henry could not sit still, and paced about his outer chamber as Cromwell sat at the desk, taking a dictated letter.

"To the emperor," said Henry. "Nephew, this day will bring you, I think, news of great satisfaction. Let us now put all quarrels behind us and—" Henry put his hand atop the globe on the desk and gave it an idle spin. It rattled softly on its axis. "—and work for an accommodation which will increase the trade and prosperity between us." Henry stopped the globe with his finger on the map of France. "And unite us against that bastard the king of France!"

Satisfied, Henry moved to the window to gaze out at the gardens and the pond and the swans on the water.

"Above all," he said, "I love the prospect of change."

Brandon felt a certain smug joy at seeing Thomas Boleyn in such a humbled state, standing in the middle of a dismal Tower cell, his eyes rimmed red with fear. But Brandon's joy was tempered by the fact that Boleyn would not face the same fate as his son.

"Am I to be tried?" Boleyn asked, his voice flat, trying his best to retain his dignity.

"No," said Brandon. "You are to be released."

Boleyn took a breath, and the tight line of his mouth shifted into a small, cold smile, one that made Brandon think of a badger preparing to escape a trap.

"But," Brandon added, "His Majesty commands that, since you no longer enjoy his trust or affection, you are to be stripped forthwith of all your official titles and posts. You will no longer serve on the Privy Council, you will relinquish the role of Lord Privy Seal and all its privileges."

Boleyn watched Brandon, unblinking, his smile holding.

"His Majesty also desires you leave court," Brandon said, "and never show yourself in his presence again on pain of death."

"So I am to keep my earldom?"

Brandon looked at Boleyn with disgust and nodded. Then Brandon moved to the window and peered down at Tower Green, where Anne's scaffold had been built. The platform was draped in black cloth and the straw had been scattered. "Did you watch your son die?" he asked. "What about your daughter? Will you watch her suffer? Will you watch her die?"

Boleyn did not answer. Brandon looked back at him. "Tell me this, Boleyn. Was it all worth it?"

The morning was long and fretful, and Henry eased his mind by thinking of his beautiful Jane. He stayed abed, his hands moving across his crotch, imagining they were her hands, soft, insistent, probing. He envisioned her unlacing his codpiece and removing it, then opening his braes with feather-light movements. Then, her virginal lips pressing themselves to his hard, deliciously aching flesh.

He could stand it no longer. He stood abruptly and went to the groom at the door.

"Tell them to have the horses ready," he said quietly. "But tell no one else of our destination."

The groom nodded and slipped away.

She was prepared for her death. Her ladies had dressed Anne in a gown of dark gray damask trimmed in black fur over a crimson kirtle. The shining dark hair that had once been caressed and kissed by the king was now brushed and gathered up from her neck into a white linen coif.

The queen's almoner, a young clergyman with pudgy fingers and innocent eyes, read from the Bible as the final touches were made on Anne's appearance. Anne stared at the almoner though could not focus on his face. It was as though he had no clear features, it was as though he were part of a foggy dream. Even his words sounded distant, far away.

"To everything there is a season, and a time to every purpose under Heaven. A time to be born and a time to die. A time to plant and a time to pluck up that which is planted . . ."

Anne brushed her hands slowly along the sides of the gown, the last one she would ever wear. An odd numbness had settled over her mind, her soul, and in that was a peace.

"A time to get and a time to lose, a time to keep and a time to cast away, a time to rend and a time to sew. A time to keep silence and a time to speak. I said in my heart, God shall judge the righteous and the wicked, for there is a time for every purpose under the sun."

In her bedchamber at Wulfhall, Jane Seymour's ladies prepared her for her own date with destiny. They combed her tresses and wove them through with satin ribbons, sprayed her blue gown with the essence of lilac, and adorned her with earrings and a necklace of pearls and rubies.

She considered herself in the mirror, then turned to her ladies and smiled. She was ready.

* * * *

The door to Anne's Tower room was unlocked with a clank and squeal. Anne was startled to see Kingston enter and bow. It wasn't quite time yet, was it?

"Am I to go now?" Anne asked. "I thought—"

"My lady, forgive me," said Kingston. "The executioner has been delayed on the road from Dover and your execution is now postponed until twelve o'clock. I—I wanted to tell you, in good time, in case—" He stopped, clearly not knowing what to say next.

Anne looked at her ladies, down at her dress, and felt the peace in her soul and mind begin to break apart and fade away like morning fog before a harsh sun. "Master Kingston," she said, "I hear you say I will not die before noon, and I am very sorry for it, for I thought to be dead by then, and past my pain."

"Madam," said Kingston softly. "There will be no pain. The blow will be subtle."

"Yes," said Anne, "I heard the executioner was very good. And in any case, I have only a little neck." Then she put her hands around her neck, felt the warm flesh there, and burst out laughing.

Lady Mary stood from her prayers in the chapel, thrilled to see Ambassador Chapuys at the rear just inside the doors. She crossed herself and smiled as Chapuys walked up the aisle, bowed, and kissed her hand.

"Is it done?" Mary asked, barely able to contain her excitement. "Is the harlot dead?"

"I don't know," said Chapuys gently. "But certainly, she will be dead before very long."

Mary crossed herself again. "The Lord is good." She took Chapuys's arm and walked with him toward the doors. "Tell me," she said in a whisper. "Why is she really to die?"

"They say that her child, Elizabeth, was not conceived with the king at all, but with one of her countless lovers."

Mary stopped. "How many lovers was she supposed to have?"

"According to Mr. Cromwell, over a hundred men, including her brother, Rochford."

This was shocking news to Mary, yet it all the more proved the need for Anne's disposal.

"But," Chapuys continued, "I'm told she also blames me for what has befallen her, and holds me accountable for her doom. Naturally, I'm flattered by the compliment, since she would have thrown me to the dogs if she could."

Praise God for His holy and perfect judgment!

Mary began walking again, still holding the ambassador's arm. "Tell me about this other lady, this Jane Seymour?"

"I have been told in confidence that she is of our faith, and that the king loves her and means to marry her, and that she means to restore Your Grace to the succession."

"And Elizabeth will be a bastard now, as I have been a bastard?"

Chapuys smiled and nodded. "Yes, Princess, yes. The brat is now officially a bastard."

There was a crash and the raspy sound of cloth tearing, and Brandon looked up from his reading to see his young son holding a wooden sword and looking sheepish. In his play fighting, he had knocked over a small statue and put a slash in the parlor draperies.

"Edward!"

Edward's brows drew up, but then he grinned, cried, "Huzzah!" and dashed toward his father with his wooden sword pointed at him. He jabbed Brandon several times in the chest with only enough effort to sting a bit. Brandon ruffled the boy's hair and laughed. "Edward," he said, "this is not a toy."

Edward put the sword down and looked at his father in all seriousness. "Yes, sir," he replied. Then he tilted his head and put his hands on his hips. "So, have you ever killed someone?"

Brandon rubbed his chin. "Yes, in battle."

"What did it feel like?"

"He was my enemy. I didn't care."

Edward nodded as if he understood. "I would really like to see some-one die." He balanced his wooden sword, then looked back at his father. "Can I go to the execution with you?"

Cromwell looked up from his desk to the clerk, seated at a nearby table. "How much did they charge for the scaffold?"

The clerk flipped through a stack of papers. "Twenty-three pounds, six shillings, and eight pence, Mr. Secretary."

Cromwell grimaced and wrote the figure on his list. "Daylight rob-bery," he said. "And what is the headsman to be paid, *if* he ever ar-rives?"

"Fifteeen pounds."

"*Fifteen* pounds? For one stroke?" Cromwell sighed noisily and wrote the figure down. "My God," he muttered. "He makes a damn good liv-ing."

The day had grown long and hot along the winding London Road. Rom-baud, the headsman, had dismounted to inspect his horse's front hoof. The fleshy frog at the bottom of the foot was cut deep from a sharp stone, leaving the animal lame and unable to carry a rider. He looked about, seeing no one on the stretch of road who could come to his assistance. And so he adjusted the wrapped sword on his back, collected the reins, and began to walk. The next town was miles ahead.

"Well," demanded Henry as Cromwell entered his private outer chamber. "Is it done?" The clock had slowly, slowly been creeping toward noon, and Henry had been watching the agonizing pace of its hands upon its face. Surely, praise God, Anne was dead by now!

Cromwell cleared his throat. "No, Your Majesty. Unfortunately we must postpone the execution again."

Henry's teeth set against each other. "What?"

"The executioner is delayed. His horse became lame."

Henry's breaths came heavy and hard, as if forced by a blacksmith's bellows. He stepped close to Cromwell and snarled, "Then get someone else to do it! Do you hear me? Fetch the axman who did the others! He was good enough, wasn't he? He didn't botch the thing!"

"Your Majesty," said Cromwell, "you made a promise. I—"

Henry grabbed Cromwell's coat. "Damn you, Cromwell! What do I care about my promises to that whore?"

Cromwell's face did not change. He waited until the king let go of him and said, "Your Majesty's promise is public knowledge. That is all I meant."

Henry's hand raised, shaking, ready to strike the man, but then he drew his fist back. "I still don't care! I commanded you to get someone else. I want her dead. I want it over with. Finished! Go and do it or by God's blood you will join her."

Cromwell bowed and quickly left. As the door closed, Henry looked at the clock, at the window, and realized he'd made a mistake.

Curses!

Henry raced to the door and tore it open, shouting out into the court for all to hear. "I said—postpone it!"

Cromwell, down the corridor a distance, turned and bowed. "Majesty," he said.

Turning back to the groom inside his chamber, Henry said, "Let's go!"

Anne's throat was dry and her hands clammy. She stood in the center of the room, her thoughts on God and His Christ, on their mercy and on Heaven. Over her dark damask gown her ladies had secured an ermine mantle with a gable hood. Anne's eyes, though not closed, did not focus on anything earthly.

The door rattled open and Kingston entered. Anne blinked, and said, "Master Kingston. I am ready."

Kingston's voice was hesitant, quiet. "Madam, you must forgive me once again. But the executioner is still not arrived."

Anne's thoughts flew back from the Lord and onto the uniformed constable. She suddenly felt the cold of the room, the damp of the walls. "What—do you say?"

"Madam, your execution is put off until nine o'clock tomorrow morning."

"No!" Anne looked from Kingston to her ladies, who could do nothing more than mirror her anguish. "It cannot be! It's not—that I desire death, but I thought myself prepared to die. And now I fear, I fear another delay may—may weaken my resolve. Is it not possible that—?"

Kingston shook his head. "No, Madam. It is the king's express command." He bowed, and turned to leave.

"Wait!" Anne moved to Kingston and took his arm. "Wait." She looked at his face, studying it as a child might study the clouds in search of something charming, something lovely. "Perhaps I am not to die. These postponements are meant for something. The King His Grace is doing it to test me, and then—then I will be sent to a nunnery!"

But she saw in Kingston's face that he did not believe it. It could not be true. She let go of his arm and stared at the floor as the constable was let out of the room.

Finches and meadow pipits flew up and away as the king and his mounted retinue of grooms, servants, and musicians thundered across the field of tall grasses toward Wulfhall. Henry leaned forward in his saddle, his eyes straining for the first glimpse of Jane Seymour's home. The farther from court, the better his mood. He was already free of the cold, damnable specters of the clock and of Anne's impending execution. Ahead of him lay warmth and sweetness, desire and life.

Henry was off his horse before the horse had stopped. He let the reins fall to the dirt; a servant would care for the animal.

"Gentlemen! Ladies!" Henry bellowed cheerfully as he strode into the house, followed by most of the entourage who hastened to keep up. John Seymour, his son Edward, John's wife, and Edward's fiancée were in the hall to receive His Majesty. They bowed deeply, and Henry laughed. "A good day to you!"

"And to Your Majesty," said Seymour.

Ebullient with joy, Henry embraced Seymour tightly. "My comrade-in-arms!"

Seymour bowed again, clearly pleased with the affection. Henry turned to Edward and his face grew severe. "Edward!" said Henry.

Edward flinched. "Majesty?"

"I have something to say to you. Kneel!"

Edward dropped to his knees and bowed his head. Henry smiled again, and gestured to the musicians, who began to play a regal tune upon their lutes and drums.

"Bow!" called Henry. A servant passed a hunting bow to the king, who touched it to Edward's shoulders, one at a time. Then Henry grinned at the Seymour family and said, "Arise, Sir Edward Seymour."

Edward stood, his face wide with surprise and happiness. Henry embraced him and patted his shoulder. Then, "Where is Lady Jane?"

A voice from behind Seymour said, "Here, Your Majesty." The family parted and let Jane through. She curtsied before the king and for a moment, Henry felt his voice stolen away by her beauty.

"Come closer, Lady Jane," he said at last. "I have a gift for you." A groom stepped forward and handed Jane a small package wrapped in velvet.

"May I?" asked the lady.

"Of course," said Henry.

Jane unwrapped the package and drew a sharp little breath when she saw what was inside. The gift was a diamond ring, the stone the size of an acorn, the large jewel surrounded by tiny emeralds.

"It's too beautiful," said Jane in a whisper.

"Not for you. Put it on."

Jane slipped the ring onto her finger.

"Let me see," said Henry. Jane stepped closer, lifting her hand to show the king. Henry took her hand gently and kissed it. "My lady," he said.

The tender hope and gentle surrender in Jane's eyes moved his heart and he held her hand another moment. Then he let go and said, "I've brought you something else."

Jane laughed. "What have you brought?"

Henry nodded at the musicians, who had been joined by two singers. "Happiness," Henry said. And the musicians began a lively tune.

The midafternoon feast was lavish, with chargers and platters and tureens offering up the most succulent meats and delicious stews and breads Henry had ever tasted. As the musicians played on, the Seymours and their royal guest ate, discussed days gone by, and laughed. Jane sat directly across the table from Henry, and his heart picked up its rhythm each time he caught her smiling at him.

"Sir John," said Henry. "I'm sure you will be aware that my marriage has been declared null and void."

Seymour nodded. "I've been made aware of the circumstances, Your Majesty. And, like everyone else, I have been shocked and utterly amazed at what I've heard. I have also been angry on Your Majesty's behalf."

"I am grateful," said Henry. "These have been very difficult days. But I must tell you that the Privy Council, despite all these recent hurts, have pleaded with me to venture once more into matrimony, in the hope that my bride will produce a legitimate heir."

Seymour raised his wine glass. "Why not? Your Majesty is still young and lusty. Alas, I am past my prime, but you have reached a ripe age, and in this life ripeness is everything."

"I think you know my choice has fallen upon your daughter." Henry was pleased and moved to see Jane blush and lower her eyes.

"I do," said Seymour. "And I am prouder than I can say that I will give my beloved daughter away to the king of England."

Henry leaned over and embraced Jane's father. Then he looked around the table. "Tomorrow you will all travel by barge to Hampton Court, where our betrothal will be announced. Until then, you mustn't appear in public." He grinned. "Perhaps you could spend the time choosing your wedding clothes."

Everyone at the table smiled and laughed. A pretty young serving girl approached Henry with a pitcher, and silently refilled his goblet with wine. When done she turned away, but Henry called her back.

"No, wait. Tell me your name," he said. "I want to reward your service."

The girl looked stunned and confused.

"Come on, girl, don't be afraid. Tell me your name."

The girl glanced at Seymour, then at the floor. She stammered, "Anne . . . Your Majesty."

There was a sudden chilling silence in the room. Even the musicians faltered at their instruments. Henry's smile vanished. But then he forced the smile back, dismissed the girl, and said, "I swear to you, Sir John, that from tomorrow *everything* will change. We will be merry again as we used to be!"

"No, no, no! I don't want to go! I don't want to!"

Elizabeth stomped her foot and struggled as two ladies attempted to dress her in her traveling clothes. The little girl was being removed from Hatfield as quickly as possible, and the entire household was in an upheaval as furniture, crates, and cases were hauled outside.

"Lady Elizabeth!" shouted Lady Bryan as she entered Elizabeth's bedchamber. "You must do as you are told. Now hush! Or I will hit you!"

Elizabeth's mouth fell open. She had never been scolded before. Stunned, the child ceased her wriggling as the last of her buttons were done up.

A lady-in-waiting, who had been folding clothes into a trunk, glanced at Lady Bryan with surprise at the sharp words. But Lady Bryan would have none of it.

"Don't look like that! We are ordered to remove the child so she can be kept out of sight of the king."

The lady-in-waiting put her hand to her mouth. "Poor Princess Elizabeth."

Lady Bryan shook her head. "She is no longer a princess. She is a bastard. And Master Cromwell has asked for her accounts to be settled, also in respect of necessities provided for her mother in the Tower."

"You mean," asked the lady, "the child must pay for her mother's imprisonment?"

"Yes. Out of the money the king pays for her household." Lady Bryan pursed her lips. "The world is a slippery place, my lady. If you would take my advice, find a rich man to marry who is so stupid that he knows nothing about politics. Then, perhaps, unless you die in childbirth, which is likely, or from the plague, which is almost inevitable, then you will be happy."

Without another comment Lady Bryan gestured, and the former princess of England was led out of the room and out of the house. The little girl's ladies watched after, heartbroken.

The sun held low between the trees, sending tendrils of gold across the fields behind Wulfhall. Henry and Jane walked together, close but not touching, with Seymour and Edward keeping a respectful distance.

"What would you like to talk about, sweetheart?" Henry said.

Jane glanced west in the direction of the sunset. The light bathed her face, making her seem as a saint, an angel. "If Your Majesty would allow," she said, "I should like to talk about your daughter, Mary. When I am queen I would hope to see her reinstated as heir apparent."

This was not what Henry expected or wanted to hear. He stopped abruptly and glared at Jane. "You are a fool to hope so. You ought to solicit the advancement of the children we're going to have together and not any others."

Jane looked immediately chastised and embarrassed. "Majesty," she said, lowering her head. "I thought I was asking not so much for the good of others as for the good, the repose, and tranquillity of yourself, as well as the children we may have ourselves, and for the tranquillity of Your Majesty's kingdom."

Henry took a breath, his irritation melting away. "Forgive me," he said.

But Jane remained mortified. She put her hands to her face.

Taking his lady gently by the arms, Henry said, "I so much want this to be a new beginning. A renaissance. Sometimes it is hard to be reminded of things. Do you understand? You are so pure. I don't want you to be affected by anything that's gone before."

Jane lowered her hands and Henry stared into her eyes. "May I kiss you, Jane?"

The corners of Jane's mouth tugged slightly as if she would laugh. "Aren't you the king of England?" she teased.

Henry pressed his mouth to his lady's lips, deeper then, and harder, inhaling and tasting her sweetness, savoring the promise of passion that held just beyond his reach, knowing that soon it would be his to explore, to probe, and to own.

My Jane!

Seymour and Edward, standing beside the hedgerow, watched the king kiss Jane.

"It's true that everything will change for her," Seymour whispered. "That kiss is her destiny and her fortune."

Edward nodded. "And ours."

The late afternoon air was sour with a scent of sickly sweet decay. Thomas Boleyn drew a deep breath, his first since stepping out of the Tower, and covered his nose with a cloth. For a chilling moment he wondered if the stench was that of the blood of the men who had died the day before on Tower Hill. Brereton. Smeaton. Norris. His own son, George. Their putrefying blood crying out, demanding vengeance. But then he recognized the smell of dead fish and waste. It was only the river, not ghosts.

He crossed Tower Green, led by Constable Kingston. They passed a tall wooden structure on the grass, and Boleyn paused to look at it. It was a scaffold, built within the Tower walls because its intended victim was royalty and the public would not be allowed to witness. Boleyn glanced up at the windows behind him and saw Anne, his daughter now just a small, fragile figure, watching him from her room. Quickly and guiltily, Boleyn turned away and did not look back.

The men passed through a stone doorway and into a smaller court-yard. In the shadows on a bench sat Archbishop Cranmer, his hands folded, weeping.

Boleyn paused before the man, surprised and offended by such a display of weakness. "Why do you weep?"

Cranmer stared at Boleyn. "You know why! Because she who has been queen of England will tomorrow become a queen in Heaven."

Boleyn scowled and walked on, toward the gates, toward freedom.

Anne sat upon a chair with her ladies gathered about her. The day was nearly done, and evening—the bringer of nightmares and claustropho-bia—was on its way. Yet Anne's thoughts had flown from the room, from the Tower, and back to another time and place.

"You know," she said wistfully, "when I was a girl, I served at the court of Margaret of Austria. It was a wonderful time. There were pag-eants and dances, so many dances. At one I appeared as queen of the Amazons, a naked sword in my hand and a crimson headdress topped by a great plume!" She smiled, seeing no one but those in her memories. "But Margaret was wise, too. She said to us, 'Trust in those who offer you service, and in the end, my maidens, you will find yourself in the ranks of those who have been deceived.'"

The ladies did not respond. There was nothing to say. One lit a can-dle while another picked up the Bible and, with a nod from the queen, began to read aloud.

The blue of the sky had faded to the pewter gray of twilight. Henry led his retinue away from Wulfhall, across the far reaches of the estate, heading toward London. They came upon a manmade pond in which a marble statue of a woman stood at center. The surface of the water was covered in leaves and petals that had blown in on the wind.

"Do you see this?" Henry asked, reining in his horse. "Do you know what this is?"

The servants, grooms, and musicians stopped their horses behind the king, and waited.

"It's the Fountain of Youth!" Henry declared. "And I was meant to find it!" Henry dismounted and waded into the pond, staring at the statue as if it had something to say to him. Then he suddenly submerged himself, held his breath, and let the water flow around him, clean him, renew him. After a long moment he rose up, held out his hands, and cried, "Look! I am reborn!"

"This way, Monsieur," said Kingston. "I greatly regret that you were delayed."

The constable led Rombaud into the main room of the Tower Armory. The headsman was weary but relieved at last to have reached his destination, though the hour was very late.

"May I see it?" asked Kingston.

Rombaud placed the bundle atop the table in the center of the room and carefully removed the velvet cloth.

"It's beautiful, *non*?"

Kingston studied the sword for a long moment, clearly impressed with the size, design, and craftsmanship. "Yes," he said softly.

Rombaud wrapped the cloth about the sword once more.

"The execution is ordered for nine o'clock," said Kingston. "You will be awakened two hours before in order for you to have breakfast. So, if that is all—"

The headsman held up his hand and spoke carefully in labored English. "No, I must say some words. The lady must not be restrained in any way. So, it is very important she does not—like this." Rombaud looked about over his shoulder. "Look back, for fear of the sword. To avoid that, first, I hide the sword. She doesn't see it. That is good, but still, she try to look around to see when I strike with the sword. Is very natural. I see it hundred times. You want to know where your death come from, *non*?"

Kingston nodded.

"When she is finished her prayers and is happy to go, I say to a boy in front of her, 'Fetch my sword!' So, she looks of course at that boy. And this is just the perfect angle for me. When she looks at the boy, then I strike. You understand?"

"I think so, yes."

"Is very quick. She feels no pain." The headsman held out his hand. *"Le money."*

Kingston counted out the coins on the table and Rombaud scooped them up. *"Merci, Monsieur,"* he said. "You will not be disappointed."

"I'm sure," replied the Constable.

Her ladies were unable to keep the late-night vigil and had fallen asleep in the corner of Anne's room. Anne knelt alone in her prayers before her crucifix.

"O Father, O Creator, Thou art the Way, the Life, the Truth. Thou knowest whether I deserve this death. Not my will, O God, but Thine be done. I will give glory to Thy name, for Thou art my help and my protection. Thou hast protected me and preserved my body from destruction, from the snare of . . ."

The prayer faded from her lips as a vision unfolded before her eyes. It was Hever Castle, its gardens blooming with roses and cornflowers, asters and bleeding hearts. Two children—a boy and a girl—were in the garden, racing about, laughing, playing hide-and-seek.

"George!" called the little girl.

The boy skipped around the hedge. The girl ran after him but when she turned the corner she did not see her brother. Instead, her father was there, smiling joyfully. The girl rushed to her father, and he gathered her up and hugged her tightly.

"Anne," he said tenderly. "Anne."

The girl was comforted.

On her knees before the table, Anne wrapped her arms about herself and closed her eyes, comforted and warmed.

* * * *

Dawn had come yet again. The nineteenth day of May had arrived, as had the headsman from Calais. Henry got up from his bed, moved to the window, and parted the draperies. A distant falcon circled, held, and soared away. But Henry's attention was drawn to the gardens, the largest pond, where two white swans glided. They seemed part of the morning mist, lovely and perfect. Henry watched them for a long time, imagining the warmth and softness of their feathers, the power of their wings, the fragile grace of their necks as they probed beneath the surface for their food.

The Chapel Royal was empty at the break of day. Thomas Cromwell walked silently into the church, past a cleaning woman scrubbing the tiles on her knees. He reached the altar and knelt on the velvet cushion. He clasped his hands together tightly, hungry for the peace of the Lord.

He tried to pray but the words eluded him. He could not even recall the simplest of child's prayers, taught him by his mother so long ago. Agonized tears welled in his eyes and he shook them away.

God, hear me! Do not turn from me!

But the Almighty had no pity for him. There was no healing hand upon his heart.

Cromwell knew at that moment that he had lost God.

Anne's door opened and Kingston appeared in the doorway.

"Madam, the hour approaches, you must make ready."

Anne stood from her chair and nodded. Once again, she was dressed for her death, once again her ladies gathered about her for their final stroll.

"Acquit yourself of your charge," Anne said. "For I have been long prepared."

Kingston nodded and stepped forward with a leather pouch. "The king asks you to take this purse. It has twenty pounds in it, to pay the headsman for his service and distribute alms to the poor."

Anne took the pouch. "Thank you."

"Will you and your ladies follow me?"

Anne collected her purse and her prayer book. They left the room and took the corridor and stairs downward and to a heavy door that, when opened, let in such a flash of sunlight that Anne blinked and shaded her eyes. But as she stepped out onto the Tower Green she put her hand down. The sun was kind and warm. She would savor its gift.

The scaffold was large, and the crowd to witness her death was small. She recognized Thomas Cromwell, Archbishop Cranmer, Charles Brandon, and his young son. Then she focused ahead to the scaffold, and measured her steps evenly, regally.

She mounted the steps with composure, her ladies and Kingston joining her atop the platform. Anne gazed for a moment at the headsman, his assistant, and the priest. Then she looked over at Kingston.

"I pray you, Master Kingston, not to give the signal for my death until I have spoken what I have a mind to speak."

Kingston inclined his head.

Anne smiled at the crowd below. "Good Christian people, I have come here to die, according to law, and thus yield myself to the will of the king, my lord. And if, in my life, I ever did offend the King's Grace, surely with my death I do now atone."

She could hear her ladies weeping and saw that some in the crowd were also moved to tears. She drew a breath. "I pray and beseech you all, good friends, to pray for the life of the king, my sovereign lord and yours, who is one of the best princes on the face of the earth, who has always treated me so well, wherefore I submit to death with a good will, humbly asking pardon of all the world. If anyone should take up my case, I ask them only to judge me kindly."

A murmur of sympathy rumbled softly through the crowd.

Anne beckoned for her ladies to come forward. One took the Bible; another unfastened and removed the cloak. A third waited for Anne to remove her earrings and necklace and, with a sad curtsy, collected them and stepped back. The queen's neck was bare and ready.

The headsman knelt before Anne and said, "Madam, forgive me for what I must do."

"Gladly," said Anne. "And here is your purse." The headsman stood and Anne turned once more to the crowd.

"Thus I take my leave of the world and of you, and I heartily desire all of you to pray for me."

Steadily, Anne knelt before the block, not bending over as those who were put to the ax did, but holding straight for the blow of the sword. She began to pray.

"Jesus, receive my soul! O Lord God, have pity on my soul!"

She caught sight of Brandon, holding his son, who struggled to look away. Brandon forced the child to watch. Then Anne glanced back toward the headsman to see if he was ready to strike.

"To Christ I commend my soul—"

She looked back again, seeing only the headsman standing still, arms to his side.

"Jesus, receive my soul, O Lord God, have pity on my soul!" She glanced back yet again, unable to stop herself.

Then the headsman pointed to a boy standing at the top of the stairs and said loudly, "Boy! Fetch the sword!"

Anne turned her head quickly to see the boy, to see him bring the dreadful sword. But as her gaze met his young and innocent eyes, she heard an airy whistle behind her, arching down and around.

And the world flew apart.

CHAPTER EIGHTEEN

"Make way for the king's breakfast!" called the chamberlain. "Make way for the breakfast of His Gracious Majesty!"

Henry sat at his dining table, dressed in white, nodding and smiling. Servants and nobles brought in great silver platters and a large gilt tureen. The tureen was placed before the king as the whole of the company bowed.

A priest standing near the head of the table made the sign of the cross and said, "May the Lord Jesus be drink and food."

The lid of the tureen was lifted, and there was a collective gasp and then spontaneous applause. Within the large dish were two roasted swans. Yet the birds had been decorated with their feathered wings upon their backs and their heads posed beautifully down their sides as if they were still swimming in a lake.

Henry, quite pleased with the feat of culinary artistry, turned about in his chair, encouraging his attendants to continue clapping. As they did, he lifted his knife and began the feast.

About the Author

Elizabeth Massie is an award-winning author of horror/suspense novels and historical novels. Her mother's family moved from Scotland to the "New World" of Virginia in 1747, and many of their descendants, including Elizabeth, still live there.

Elizabeth grew up in a small town in the Shenandoah Valley. Her father, William Spilman, was the president of the town newspaper. Her mother, Patricia Spilman, is a well-respected watercolorist and teacher. Elizabeth's immediate family nurtured creativity in many forms—music, painting, drawing, writing, and acting. Long times in the car on family vacations were never boring—the family created wild and goofy round-robin stories, drew on the bottoms of one another's feet to "guess the picture," and made up songs about anything they might spot along the way. Elizabeth and her sister, Barbara Spilman Lawson, a popular actress and storyteller, remain best friends.

Historical fiction helped young Elizabeth develop a love of history. She says it was realizing people of earlier times loved, worried, ate, slept, feared, grieved, and celebrated much as we do today that helped her connect to them as people, not just names. This deep and lasting impression plays a major part in Elizabeth's writings—the commonality of the human experience, the human condition.

Elizabeth began writing stories as a child and never stopped. She received her degree from James Madison University and taught in grades 4–7 for nineteen years, but continued to write during this time. In 1994 she stopped teaching to write full time. She lives three miles from the town where she was born, now sharing life and abode with illustrator Cortney Skinner. Her sister, Barbara, lives next door, and her grown children, Erin and Brian, and their families, are all within "shouting distance." They all continue to have wild and fun times creating.

Visit her website at www.elizabethmassie.com.